Passing
by
Samaria

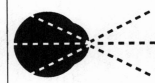

Passing
by
Samaria

Sharon Ewell Foster

Thorndike Press • Waterville, Maine

Published in 2003 by arrangement with Multnomah Publishers, Inc.

Thorndike Press® Large Print Christian Fiction Series.

The tree indicium is a trademark of Thorndike Press.

The text of this Large Print edition is unabridged. Other aspects of the book may vary from the original edition.

Set in 16 pt. Plantin.

Printed in the United States on permanent paper.

Library of Congress Cataloging-in-Publication Data

Foster, Sharon Ewell.
    Passing by Samaria / Sharon Ewell Foster.
      p. cm.
    ISBN 0-7862-5572-2 (lg. print : hc : alk. paper)
    1. African American women — Fiction.
2. African Americans — Fiction. 3. Chicago (Ill.) — Fiction. 4. Mississippi — Fiction. 5. Large type books.
I. Title.
PS3556.O7724P37 2003
  813′.54—dc21   2003050952

First, I lift this book up to God. I release it into Your hands. May it be everything You want it to be. May it be medicine, food, sweets to Your people, to those who are isolated. May Your Spirit be alive in each word.

Second, this book is dedicated to my children, Lanea and Chase, who were my first editors, as well as my friends. May God bless you to love and be loved in Jerusalem, in Judea, in Samaria, and in the world.

Finally, this book is for those who have not been invited. For the weak ones, the broken ones, those wrapped in shame. For the least, for the rejected, for the spotted, for the stained. For those unloved. The Spirit of the Lord says, "Come."

As the Founder/CEO of NAVH, the only national health agency solely devoted to those who, although not totally blind, have an eye disease which could lead to serious visual impairment, I am pleased to recognize Thorndike Press★ as one of the leading publishers in the large print field.

Founded in 1954 in San Francisco to prepare large print textbooks for partially seeing children, NAVH became the pioneer and standard setting agency in the preparation of large type.

Today, those publishers who meet our standards carry the prestigious "Seal of Approval" indicating high quality large print. We are delighted that Thorndike Press is one of the publishers whose titles meet these standards. We are also pleased to recognize the significant contribution Thorndike Press is making in this important and growing field.

Lorraine H. Marchi, L.H.D.
Founder/CEO
NAVH

★ Thorndike Press encompasses the following imprints: Thorndike, Wheeler, Walker and Large Print Press.

Thank you to the following people. (Hold your hat, I have lots of people to thank.)

Love to Chester, who knew the rhythm of my heart.

Love to my mother, father, and my brothers, who bore the burden of a child who read Kahlil Gibran and who believed so passionately about such strange things. Thank you for opening the door.

Thank you to my friend Patricia Mallette, who gave me a journal and some stars so that I could write.

Thank you to my friends Lena "wanna-play-Racko" Edley Dye, Debbie Reed, Angela Bledsoe, and Stephanie Warr for vivid memories.

Love to East St. Louis, Illinois, where I learned of splendor in the midst of ruin. Keep your heads up, children! I love you, Ms. Allen.

Thanks to Bob, Brian, Debbie, Marla, Fabienne, and Jill, all knights in shining armor.

Thanks to Kent and Vonzaa Humpherys, for your generosity.

Hugs to all the Alabaster women who took me in, especially Francine.

Blessings to Stephanie, who didn't know me, but gave me a computer because the Lord said so.

Thank you to the Women's Executive Leadership program and all my classmates and teachers who nourished me when I was weak, so that I could close my eyes and leap!

Thanks to my agent, Sara Fortenberry, who helps me feel safe, even when I whine.

Thanks to my editor, Karen Ball, who held my hand, even when I whined.

Praise to Ida B. Wells, W. E. B. Dubois, Robert S. Abbott, and other heroes of the black press, "Soldiers without Swords." Special thanks to Thomas Fleming who generously shared his recollections of living, breathing history with me.

Thanks to all the good souls at the Defense Information School.

Thanks to Lisa and Carol, who were brave under fire.

Thanks to Doretha Brown, my praying California mama. If you get this message, call me.

Thank you and blessings to all the preachers that preached me into and through this: Rev. Reid; Rev. Priscilla Hawkins; Joyce Meyer; Rev. G. E. Patterson; Evangelist Jackie McCullough; and Rev. Dr. Walter Scott Thomas, Pastor of New Psalmist Baptist Church.

Thanks to my bestest buddy, Portia Starks Maynor, and her family (remember, I do have papers).

Finally, thank you to Bishop Howard Oby, at whose knee, studying, I began to fully understand the beauty of the truth set before us. Love you and Miss Portia.

A new heart also will I give you, and
a new spirit will I put within you; and
I will take away the stony heart out of your
flesh, and
I will give you an heart of flesh.

EZEKIEL 36:26

". . . And ye shall be witnesses unto me both
in Jerusalem, and in all Judaea, and in
Samaria, and unto the uttermost
part of the earth."

ACTS 1:8

One

In the spring in Mississippi there were perfect days. They were storybook days.

Gentle breezes stirred the magnolia blossoms. Their sweet fragrance hung in the air almost palatable, almost tangible. The same sweetened breezes tickled the undersides of cotton plant leaves and found their way to the collard green leaves on the girl's father's small farm.

The soil was fertile and the grass so green it looked painted, like someone's memory, someone's image of grass. Plants grew ripe and lush as the land Alena's father owned. Her daddy's farm sustained her family. Alena was never hungry. What he grew was fruitful, green, and tidy.

The fruits of her father's labor — sweet potatoes, onions, tomatoes, watermelons, greens, okra, squash, green beans, field peas — fed Alena; her father, Amos; her mother, Evelyn; and many others that lived near them.

They were good people living in the

midst of good land. Alena was nourished and was grown strong on the farm in the shelter of her parents' love. Her skin glowed with love and happiness.

"We are blessed," Alena's mother told her all her young life. "God has given us much, and He expects much from us. We got to strive to do our part."

Sitting on the porch, just home from school, Alena remembered many young days walking proudly beside her mother, entrusted with carrying bright yellow summer squash to old Mrs. Johnson or someone like her. Alena also remembered being just as happy to eat pear preserves, supplied by some neighbor, off a spoon extended by her mother's warm brown hand.

Now, at eighteen, Alena dangled her long, brown legs over the porch, running her toes through grass soft as carpet, carpet that met the weathered wood of her porch. Alena's black, button-up shoes sat beside her. Many of her friends didn't have everyday shoes to wear. She was grateful for them, but she was happy to take them off and feel the cool grass on her feet.

While Alena sat studying, daydreaming, studying, her eyes looked out over the field to see her father driving his mule through the fertile rows. Her father was a good man, full of wisdom and courage.

Alena looked at the spot next to her where J.C. normally would have been. Where was her friend by now?

"You visit my mama," J.C. had made her promise over a year ago. "She's gonna be lonely for me. She might try to act like she all right, but she gonna be lonely."

Alena had promised her friend that she would visit. "Don't put it off, Alena," he had pressed her further. They had ended the conversation laughing and tussling, just like when they were kids. But J.C. was the first to notice they weren't kids anymore. He had gone north to join the war effort.

"This'll be the war to end all wars. Once we able to prove ourselves, prove the colored man, the Race, is willing to fight and die for our country, I know things gone change." Then things would be wide open with opportunities for a man like him, he had said, echoing the words of men from other generations.

Alena's mind moved back to a time when she and J.C. were six, maybe seven or eight, out by the pond looking for tadpoles. She could still remember J.C.'s feet covered with mud, his second toe on each foot longer than the big toes.

"I got one, J.C. I got one!" She could remember the smell of new spring in the air. "It's a baby frog." So little it was. So hard to believe a frog could be so small — fully formed, but so tiny. "I'm gone take him home, J.C. I'm gonna put him in a jar and keep him."

"Girl, that frog'll be dead before you know it. You can't keep nothing that small, can't keep it from its home and 'spect it to live."

She looked at J.C. He always had a look in his eye like an old man, like he knew better than all the other kids, even when he was playing. "I don't care what you say, J.C.," she defied him.

"Okay, Alena, but he gone die. That's for sure. How you feel if somebody take you from your mama and daddy while you little? 'Fore you can take care of yourself?" He even seemed to think like an old man.

Alena could feel her lip trembling. Cool wind blew over mossy water and tugged at the ribbons on her plaits. She hated when she looked like a baby in front of J.C., but she hated the idea of being away from home, from her mother and father, even more. She rubbed one stubby, nail-bitten finger gently over the frog's back. She wanted it, hurt to give it up . . . but she knew J.C. was right, like always.

"You doin' the right thing, Lena," he said, calling her by the nickname he only used when they were by themselves. J.C. consoled her as she gently lay the bitty creature on a stick floating near the place where she'd plucked it from the water. She knew J.C. was right, but for the moment it would have felt real good to punch, or at least pinch, her best friend.

Still she missed him. They had started school together, been baptized together, sat next to each other every Sunday in church. The old people said they would marry someday.

Where is he now, she thought. Alena's hand rubbed the spot on the rough wood where her friend regularly sat.

Alena stood to stretch. She was taller than all the girls at her school, taller than most of the boys. As she stood, her skirt fell to just above her ankles. Alena smoothed her hands down her body to straighten her blouse and skirt. She was sturdy and well built, but her movements were grace, dignity, and femininity.

"You hear any word from J.C.?" Alena's mother called to her, as if she had read the girl's mind. Her mother's words, and the smells that came through the front porch screen door, pulled Alena from her thoughts.

"No, Mama. No word. I went by to see his mama though. She sure does miss him."

"Well, I just got some newspaper clips from your aunt talking about our boys coming home from the front. Coming home from France with medals and everything. Can you believe it? Just make me so proud. It just made me think about J.C. and how brave he was, volunteering and all. Seem like he ought to be coming home soon, too. I sure do miss that boy."

"Would you miss me if I was gone, Mama? If I wasn't here to go with you on your missionary visits? Would you, Mama?"

"*Miss* you?" her mama teased. "Why things might go a little faster. For sure I would come home with more preserves or cake, whatever the people give me. That's for sure."

"Aw, Mama."

"You know I'm just playing, baby. You know Mama would be heartbroken without her chocolate baby."

Alena smiled at her mother. Love mixed with pride. Today, Tuesday, was the day her mama always went to help the older widows in the community. Her mother had already cooked two dinners and cleaned three different homes while out doing her church service.

Mama turned her back and continued to hum, sometimes singing, while she cooked for the three of them. The smell of candied yams made Alena's mouth water and her stomach rumble.

She smiled at her mother and stood in the confidence of her parents' love. She was their pride and joy. When other children her age were working in the field to help support their families, her mama and daddy sacrificed — Alena was spared, still in school.

Alena loved her family, the farm, her life. *Let nothing ever take me from here,* she prayed silently to God.

"We want you to have more than we had," her mother told her as they sat down to supper. One could almost touch the love Alena's mother smiled at her.

She could feel her mother watching as she pushed back the hair that always fought to fall into her face. Her mama smiled at her. It was the same hair; they had the same hair. Deep brown-black with sunlit cherry highlights. Hair that could not decide if it was kinky or curly. Cotton candy hair. Alena could imagine what her mother was thinking. She knew the smiles; they had talked about it over and over again.

Alena's annoyance with her hair always made her mother smile in just the way she was smiling now. Their hair wouldn't lay flat like hair that had been pressed into submission with a hot-iron straightening comb. It was not tame like hair that had had the curl chemically relaxed by one of Madame C. J. Walker's potions.

Alena's hair did not respond as fashion dictated, but her hair was beautiful. It was beautiful, it was bountiful.

"Um-um-um, that chile got a head of hair!" Alena had often heard people comment. Men and women found themselves compelled to acknowledge that, even beyond fashion's rules, Alena's hair was beautiful.

Now she watched her mama touch her own hair, smiling. *In time,* Alena knew her mother was thinking. She had heard her mother say often enough, *In time you'll be grateful for its glory.* Beautiful, bountiful.

"I can feed you all," her father, unaware, interrupted the silent hair fight. "I can feed other people. But you, you got a gift, baby. You can read and write in a way that can make people whole. Me and your mama, we make do, but you can find the truth where other people can't. You can write. You can write about the truth. You got a duty to tell and write about the truth, and you know what I always tell you —"

"The truth will make you free!" Alena forgot about her hair, and she and her mother joined in laughing across the table.

Alena saw her father look across the table at the wife of his youth, then her gaze met with her father's. The girl had heard him, late in the night, telling her mama how his daughter's laughter, still like a child's, wrapped around, enfolded, renewed his heart. How, when he was plowing the last row and tiredness would bid him stop, the memory of Alena's laughter moved him to push beyond his arm's strength.

"My baby's laughter and my baby's eyes," she had overheard him say. Said she was in so many ways beautiful like her mother — nutmeg brown skin, glorious hair — but her eyes were his mother's eyes, she had heard him whisper to her mother. The same almond shape and peculiar color brown. She had heard the words just before there was a muffled silence.

In her father's eyes Alena saw gentle

pride — love at who she had become. *Certain, strong, intelligent,* his eyes seemed to say. "We got another letter from your Aunt Patrice." Alena turned toward her mother. "She want to know when you going to visit. Patrice say Chicago is a sight to see. And she went on again about that young man, James. He must be something special, being a colored military officer and all. Those articles from the *Chicago Defender* got his picture all over the front page. I tell you, those are some brave children."

"Mama, they're not children."

"I know, baby. You know what I mean, facing bullets, mustard gas, and who knows what else. A lot of them ain't made it back. The paper got pictures of this one unit from Illinois, the Fighting Eighth, they call them. Uniforms, medals, and everything. Colored doughboys.

"James is one of them. Right there in the newspaper on the front page. Let me read it to you." Her mother picked up the February twenty-second edition of the newspaper, an edition that had been passed from hand to hand before it ever reached hers, from a stand near the table.

"The 370th Infantry, the old Eighth Regiment, now known as 'The Fighting

Devils,' are back home. Monday they carried their colors down Michigan Avenue, bearing flags that 'never touched the ground.' These 'boys' covered themselves with glory and in their ranks marched 26 who wore Service Crosses and 68 Croix de Guerre. This is a magnificent record, one that Illinois and America might feel proud of, a regiment that was 'on the firing line' and 'went over the top.' A halo of glory and honor covers every mother's son of them. No regiment of all the allies ever fought braver, without complaint, than these noble sons of Chicago and Illinois. For their heroism, their noble record and daring on the battlefields, all Chicago honored them Monday."

She lay the newspaper on her lap. "Ain't that something? James is a *major*. I can't hardly believe it. And good looking, too. Seem like they doing all right for theyselves in Chicago." Her mother smiled. "Maybe some place where you could do all right, too."

"*Mama*." Alena glanced sideways at her father. "I am not leaving here. I'm not leaving you all. I'm staying right here in Mississippi. I can make a home here. I can do good here. I can write here. There's truth for me to tell right here." Alena could feel the cool breeze blow round her heart. It felt like the same breeze from the pond where she and J.C. knelt with the frog.

She shuddered.

Sitting to one side of her, her mama took her hand. "Such a pretty girl."

"Oh, Mama." Alena looked back with love to her mother across the dinner table. In between them, on the table, her plate was full: yams, biscuits, chicken, and greens. Alena loved to eat. The only item she refused was okra. She always eyed it with something between disgust and suspicion. How could something so slimy taste good?

Even worse, she knew the icky, gooey pot the okra was boiled in would be waiting for her when she washed dishes after dinner. The family always began dinner with grace and finished with Alena washing dishes in water heated on their woodstove.

If only the dishes and pots would disappear. But that thought was not enough to ruin the sweet taste of the yams or the buttery softness of the biscuits as they passed over Alena's tongue.

"Mama, we're going to save what's left for Cottonball, right?"

"Girl, you and that dog. That dog is just

wild. I don't know what he would be eatin' if it wasn't for you."

"I 'spect he thinks he's her dog," Alena's daddy teased her. "Dog so wild you can't even hardly tell he used to be white."

"All right, Alena," Mama answered. "Why should this day be different than any other day." More like a statement than a question. "Just make sure you don't starve yourself trying to make sure Cottonball gets enough to eat."

"Cottonball, *hmph*," her daddy went on. "Don't look like no cottonball *I* ever seen."

After dinner, Alena washed dishes. In the background, her parents read and shared sports news reported in the weekly newspaper.

"This basketball is good enough, but ain't nothing like baseball. No, sir. Lincoln Giants, Philadelphia Hilldale Club, Tate's Stars. I love that baseball. We gone have to write to Patrice and tell her to clip the *Tribune* so we can follow the White Sox, too."

Life was good. God provided all of their needs. "God, let me never leave," Alena whispered again in almost silent prayer. "I will never leave," she vowed to herself.

Finding the body changed everything.

Two

Happy. That was Alena in every way. Happy in her father's house. Happy in Mississippi. Happy the school year was ending. Happy to be graduating. Happy to be moving toward adulthood.

Part of that movement was her parents' agreement that she was now old enough to have gentlemen callers.

When other girls much younger were already married and even having children, Alena's parents kept telling her, "Not yet, baby." They reasoned she had to be mature enough and clear enough in who she was to make a wise decision about something that would impact her for the rest of her life.

To Alena, her daddy and mama's approval seemed long in coming. So she jumped and shouted when *the word* came. Her parents' decision almost coincided with the church social that celebrated the end of winter, spring's song, and the children's dismissal from school just in time for the planting.

The picnic was a painting in pastels. Women and girls wore white or pale, pale colors. Even sackcloth dresses seemed light, air bound.

In the sun, they forgot to worry if they were beautiful, and so they were. Normally bowed necks arched toward the sun, reaching, almost quivering, too delicate to bear the splendor. Brown, cream, ebony. Hands waved. Flashes of God's pearls in faces that had let worry go. Shame had no place. They were splendid. Lilies in the field.

Alena moved among her friends and neighbors cloaked in her new permission. The boys and men she had always walked among now seemed different.

"When you look at a man, look down the road. Not just at what you see right in front of you," Alena's mother had counseled her. "When you look at a man, imagine him in the future, down the road." The words played with her while she moved by and among those graced with more muscle than she.

Some were tall, some short; some handsome, some not so handsome. Some were well dressed, some not so well. Some had deep voices, some not so deep. Some were dark, some not so dark. Some quiet, some not quiet at all. Alena was pleasantly over-whelmed by what her senses took in.

Mama's words still played around Alena's ears. She tried to look at Marcus, with his missing teeth, down the road. What Alena saw was an old, bent-over Marcus with even fewer teeth.

When she looked at squarely handsome Archie, who always won every race, down the road; she saw an older, gray-haired, handsome gentleman who, though unable to win at running anymore, still brought grace and style to each horseshoe tournament.

Alena had grown up with these two young men, among others. It seemed perfectly clear to her that what they looked like now was pretty close to what whoever married them was going to have to look at later.

She thanked her mother's voice for its counsel and promised she would be careful in her choices. Alena did not want to live a life of quiet dissatisfaction, a life of swallowed screams. "If I make a bad choice now," she warned herself, "that choice will only get worse with time." Armed with her mother's wisdom, she smiled as she walked, comforted that she had the secret to choosing the right man.

Alena wandered among her church family, watching, observing. She did take time, of course, to sample the ribs, chicken, and sausages; the apple pie, the custard pie, and the chess pie; the baked beans, potato salad, and cole slaw. While the smell of barbecued, sweetened, charred meat dominated, the apples, peaches, and watermelon provided cool, light accompaniment. Alena did her very best to help the cooks by taking away a respectable portion of food. She believed in doing her part. Nonetheless, she spent most of her time absorbing the sights and sounds of the day.

It was beautiful. The sky was a clear, deep blue with wisps of angel-hair clouds. The grass and tree leaves enclosed, provided a living frame for the clearing. Human butterflies, vanilla cream to bold coffee-black, moved between activities.

There were men calling, laughing, joshing each other. Pulling their suspenders during horseshoe matches. Other men and boys played baseball, while clusters of women and children looked on cheering. "I know you can hit better than that. You too busy thinking 'bout them ribs."

A guitarist strummed chords while music lovers — men, women, and children — sang camp songs and rhythmized hymns that painted colors in the air.

Blessed quietness, holy quietness
What assurance in my soul!
On the stormy sea He speaks to me
How the billows cease to roll.

Others walked in twos, threes, and quartets in and around the edge of the colored picnic clearing.

A group of girls, small and large, claimed one spot bare of grass to take turns jumping and turning thick, once-white ropes for their double Dutch game. Alena's feet and hands remembered the routines, but now she watched. Girls' feet stirred the dust while their mouths sang:

A sailor went to sea, sea, sea,
To see what he could see, see, see,
But all that he could see, see, see,
Was the bottom of the deep blue
sea, sea, sea.

Alena turned to walk along the edge of the site, smiling, nodding, stopping for moments to join in — still mostly observing. Alena paused to look at the wild-flowers growing along the edge of the clearing. She looked into the trees beyond. A dull, shadowed glow of yellow and emerald light filtered through dense leaves that canopied the woods.

With just a second's pause, Alena stepped into the strange green world. Entranced, she walked farther in amongst the trees. She did not look back. The sounds of her friends and family, of those she loved, who loved her, grew fainter . . . and fainter still. Alena's heartbeat quickened. She was excited by being alone in this new world. A world that was at once tranquil and threatening. Sounds and smells she had not experienced pulled Alena farther in with thoughts only of going even farther — until she saw him. She beheld him.

Her brain slowed and refused, resisted comprehending what she saw. Then, just as suddenly, knowledge and panic flooded in on her.

She knew him. Not this way, but she knew him. Charred pieces of a uniform. Shirt, pants, shoes. Holes on the chest as if medals had been torn away. There was still enough familiar about him that she knew him. Something about the feet, not blackened with mud this time, blackened by something else, something more permanent.

Alena grasped her throat. Her hands ripped at the starched white collar, buttons, and ruffles, grasping for air. She fell backward over something and hit the ground hard. Still grabbing at her collar, then clawing at the ground, she could not take her eyes off him. She continued stumbling, wrestling something invisible . . . trying to fight her way back into the world she knew.

A world where boys played baseball, not where they hung from trees. A world where boys did cartwheels, not where their arms hung like lifeless extensions from a body on a rope.

Alena heard a voice screaming. *Maybe they know,* she thought. *Maybe the others see it, too.* She wanted to add her own voice to the voice that screamed. The hand that grasped her collar moved to her mouth, and Alena realized the horrified voice was her own.

The world went black.

Alena awoke in her room, in her bed. She felt her own sheets and blankets wrapped around her. There were the walls she and her mother had painted the faintest rosebud pink. There was her window with God's sunlight having begun its glow in the distance.

It was a dream, a nightmare, she comforted herself.

Everyone knew J.C. left just days after he graduated, wearing his favorite shirt. He left with high hopes and spirit bound for glory, for the city where big dreams were possible, for the army where he could fight for a chance. J.C. was smart and good. Somebody's son; she knew his mother, knew her only son. J.C. kept himself from evil, so she knew it was a dream.

Alena smelled her mother's coffee. And bacon and eggs and biscuits. It had been a dream. And if she slept a little longer, she would lose all memory of the nightmare.

The girl turned on her side in her bed, pulled her covers up near her eyes, and snuggled up warm in the home of her mother and her father. She quickly buried herself in sweet, healing sleep.

When Alena awoke a few minutes later, her mother and father sat on the edge of her bed. Lamplight filled her room.

"Mama's sweet baby," Mama comforted.

"Is breakfast ready?"

"Oh, baby, it's way past breakfast. I set you aside a dinner plate. It's way later than you think. I'm so sorry, baby." Her voice was wet with tears, as was her face.

Alena's daddy laid a hand of comfort and reassurance on her mother's arm and said, "Me and your mama always tried to keep you from anything like this. We never wanted you to see or know the world was this kind of place or that men could be so mean." His voice broke.

"What are you talking about, Daddy?" She felt a thought of the dream trying to fight back to the surface of her mind. *It was real, it happened. . . .*

"It couldn't happen! He's not even here. Nobody would do that. It's not real. Why are you all crying?"

Alena knew the answer.

The small family fell into each other's arms. Wrapping arms around each other, closing out the pain, horror, and unfairness of their lives.

"Why, Jesus, why?" her mother shouted toward the sky.

"Oh, God in heaven," her father pleaded toward the stars, "only You know and see all. We see as through a glass darkly, and, Lord, we wrestling with this our burden. That men would look at us, who You have made in Your image, and see us as less than them." A shudder passed from father to wife to daughter. "That they would look on what You created and so easy, with such hard hearts, take the life of Your child. God, only You know what would make men, who can't make nothin', look on us and forget Your Word which says, 'Whatever you do to the least of mine, that you do also to me.'"

Alena fought to keep her eyes closed, to keep her mind on the prayer. To keep her thoughts from wandering to hopeless images of J.C. hanging.

"God, You see these men who do these things. God, You know who they are. They hide their faces and sneak about in darkness, but You know who they are. Lord, convict their hearts. Help them to see the truth, that it is grievous to You that any man should behave falsely and with hate against any that are Yours. God, circumcise their hearts."

Alena could feel her mother and father's hands squeezing her own. Could feel their shoulder hunkered over her own, like human shelter, like a breach between her and a hateful reality.

"And, Lord, while You work on them, give us the courage to move through another day. Help us not to stand still, or hide, or keep our lives and gifts hidden because of fear. Help us not to pick up anger and to sin like the ones who have sinned against us. Help us not to pick up their weapons."

Alena shook her head as tears squeezed from the corners of her eyes, while her lips opened and closed though no words would come out. How could she be asked to listen to a prayer for murderers? For people who had torn safety, stability from her world? For people who offered no prayer for her friend?

"Help us to remember, oh Lord," her father continued, "that we fight not against flesh and blood, but against principalities and powers."

Alena felt the breeze again, this time colder around her heart. This thing. This was what she had heard her parents whisper about. Heard the old people tell the children about. About terror in the night.

The terror that burst through doors, that burned away dreams. The horror that kept men from standing up, from speaking out, from being men, from protecting their families and the virtue of their wives and daughters. The horror that kept little boys and little girls from playing outside safely under the moon's glow. This was that beast now come alive. And yet she heard her father still pray.

"Help us to keep our hands in Your hand," he said sounding as though his teeth were clenched. "Help us to tell the truth so we can shine light into the darkness. God help all our souls."

Alena and her parents sat that way until almost morning, comforting, crying, questioning, and cleaving to each other until finally she fell asleep.

When Alena awakened late that morning, she was in her bed, in her room, and it was God's sunlight shining through her window, but she also knew the truth. J.C. was dead.

She got up and moved silently through her morning routine. She slow walked into the kitchen, into her father's and mother's arms. They hugged each other, grateful for another day, but she saw in their eyes uncertainty about tomorrow.

"What are we going to do about it? What is anybody going to do about it? Is the sheriff going to find out who did it?" The words fell out of her mouth into the silence, the vacuum around their breakfast table. Fell out like she was one of the ones who could demand justice. Who could expect, take for granted that justice would be done.

Her mother would not meet Alena's eyes. "There's nothing we can do. Nobody's gone do anything but keep watching and praying."

Alena watched her mother pick at the tablecloth like there was something important she had to get off of it.

"Alena," her father said, "we got some idea who did this. But they some of the same people we should be going to for help. We know it. And it ain't enough of a problem for the other good white folks to get involved in. They don't want no trouble either. They praying, they doing what they can do. They might donate the coffin, some might even send flowers to his mama. . . ." His voice faded. He looked out the window toward his fields.

"Not enough to get involved?" Alena looked back and forth between her mother and father, not believing. Not from the people who told her to stand up when it was right. "Somebody killed J.C. and left him that way! For no reason! He never hurt anybody. He loved everybody. He was always talking, laughing, encouraging. When something like this happens, somebody, *everybody*, the law has to do something. *We* got to do something. Tell somebody. Write *somebody*."

"Oh, Alena. We . . ." Alena's mother laid her hand on top of her daughter's, looked briefly into her eyes seemingly searching for words. Finally she looked at her husband. "You tell her, Amos."

Her father's face was grim, set. "Alena, the truth is white people don't consider us the same. I never wanted to have to tell you that. Tried to pretend like we could get around it. I hoped you wouldn't have to see it, and I sure didn't want it to be me that told you." Men's tears hung, just barely, on the rims of eyes.

"But you of a age and this trouble knocking right at our front door." He looked to his wife for confirmation. "We love J.C. They know him; they might think it's wrong, but they don't want the riders bothering them over some dead colored boy.

"They don't want no trouble. They didn't do it, so they don't want no responsibility. They wash they hands of it. I guess they feel like, what can they do." He rubbed his hands together like he was knocking off invisible crumbs.

"Sometimes, the good folks is the wives

37

of the ones that did it. Sometimes they the brother of the ones that did it. Sometimes they the preacher or the deacon of the ones that did it. Sometimes they know the ones who did it. Know the sheriff or the deacon or the grocery man. Sometimes the ones that did it is good to them, and they have trouble working out in they minds how somebody good to them could be bad to somebody else. They rather make the victim be wrong than face that they loved one did wrong." Her daddy cleared his throat, looked at his wife, then briefly back out to his fields, his land, like he needed to see something permanent.

"If they face up to the wrong, the good ones know they can't just go along, and they don't want to separate from the ones they know is wrong. Sometimes they think the ones that done wrong is all they got." He turned back and looked at her, and Alena thought she saw something old, something sagging, something defeated hanging in the corner of his eyes. It shocked her.

"They willing to do little things, give you apple for free, offer you the opportunity to wash they clothes for a nickel, but they ain't willing to sacrifice they friendship or position or family relationships for some black-skinned boy. 'He don't know how much we got to lose,' I guess they say when somebody like J.C. come knockin' on they conscience. I guess they tell theyself he musta brought it on hisself. 'Cause I guess they would feel guilty; they would have to do something if they believed the young man was innocent. They don't even think they should have to feel guilty about something like this. They get angry if a guilty feeling knocking at they heart."

Alena kept looking. Kept trying to figure out the thing she saw around her father's eyes. It looked a little like fear, something she had never seen there. She listened to his voice but concentrated more on his eyes.

"We know that boy ain't never done nothing to nobody —" indignation rose in his voice — "but we ain't got no power. We ain't in control, and we got to live here. I built this here," he waved at the house and the land, "so we could live, and I could keep you away from this ugly, mean world.

"If we try to point at the ones we know did it, then they relatives, they friends, and even ones that done like them is gonna stand up with them. The good folks will act like we did something wrong for bringing it up. I don't understand it, but it's like we wrong for speaking up against the act of the bad ones, even if what they did is ungodly."

Alena thought she heard an apology in her father's voice, and she was not sure if she liked it. And God. Where was God? When J.C. cried out, where was He? She wondered if J.C. had cried, called out for his mother? A man calling out for his mother. She had never heard her friend cry before.

"We know it's hard for you to understand, baby." Her mother's voice sounded like she was trying to comfort her, reassure her. "I guess it's how the devil make us choose between, on one hand, our earthly relationships, our positions, our power, and on the other hand, what's righteous and God."

Her father continued on, and Alena fought to keep off her face what she felt inside, at least until she was more sure what she really did feel. What about all the things they had told her all her life? What about truth, about speaking out?

"You don't like it," her father said. "Your mama don't like it. And I sure don't like it, but we got to live here. More of us dead won't help that boy."

"But, Daddy, what about the truth?" The words seemed to pop from her mouth before she could control them.

He looked away. "I know, baby, but I ain't willing to give you up. You got to keep quiet. You ain't gone talk about it. And you ain't gone write about it. We got to keep on living." Her father looked at her, then toward the fields, then back at her. What she saw in his eyes did not look like courage. It looked like weakness, uncertainty, maybe even fear, and she did not like it.

Softly, but looking directly into her father's eyes, Alena said, "I don't think I can do that, Daddy."

For the next two days, until the funeral, the family discussed J.C. and what was right, or they discussed nothing.

Funerals in Alena's community were often times of celebration. Spirit bulged through slats between wood boards, under the doors, through window cracks. Jubilation that at the end of a full, God-fearing, Holy Ghost-filled life, the servant was going home to be with Jesus. There were few songs of sadness. Most were songs of joy and homegoing.

My heart has no desire to stay

Where doubts arise and dreams dismay.
Though some may dwell where these
   abound,
My prayer, my aim, is higher ground.
Lord lift me up and let me stand
By faith on Heaven's table land.
No higher plane than I have found,
My prayer, my aim, is higher ground.

or

I'll fly away, Oh Glory.
I'll fly away.
In the morning when I die,
Hallelujah, by and by,
I'll fly away!

and

I'll go sweeping through the city.
Yes, I'll go sweeping through the city.
And I'm going to sit on the banks of
   the Jordan River and
I won't be back, I won't be back,
   I won't be back,
No more, no more, no more!

Somehow, though, at J.C.'s funeral the
spirit would not rise. The truth and injustice of his young death hung heavy in the

air. It hovered like a threat to all the mothers' daughters and to all the fathers' sons. It hung as a threat to hope. It hung as a voice struggling to be heard. And that voice threatened to wail from anyone who would speak or sing or read.

So few mouths opened, afraid that accusing pain, anguish, righteous indignation might compel someone, that a witness might rise from any one of their mouths against the evil that was done to the young man. At the gravesite all the fathers, mothers, sons, and daughters were still.

During the burial ceremony, the sheriff arrived, hat in hand. He did not often attend black burials. Particularly since the burial place for blacks was separate from the burial ground for whites. Separate and far from the main roads. Alena watched, knowing Sheriff Bates was not there by accident, neither did he indicate sympathy for the bereaved family and community. He stood opposite the group, some fifty yards away, quiet, expressionless. His feet on grass, on ground the people opposite him considered holy. A simple wood box in six feet of opened ground separated them. The smell of the new earth, of coming rain surrounded them.

As if by order, the few people who cried

softly toward heaven, dropped their eyes and bowed their heads. Trained to respond without thought, all heads bowed in the sheriff's presence, and the group grew quieter still.

Except for Alena. She watched the sheriff. She looked at the group of good people who surrounded her.

"It's not right," she whispered to herself. "It's not right," she said, this time loud enough that a few heads turned. "You know who did it. We know who did it. It's not right!"

The truth would not be still. She could not stop herself. "Why don't we say something?" She whispered the question defiantly in the background of the minister's words at the grave.

The small shifting in the group must have caught the sheriff's eyes, for he moved to a more alert posture. His mouth became a thin, mean, straight line.

"Oh, Lord, help us," a woman moaned softly.

"Hold your peace, Alena!" her father whispered urgently. "You gonna get everyone killed."

Bates scanned the group to gain sight and sound of what the disturbance was.

The best way to stop trouble from spreading was to end it quickly. He stayed on alert for signs of trouble or disorder. When he found them, he ended them. It was his job. He knew his job. He knew where trouble often was. He knew what it smelled like, what it looked like. He did his job well. He protected and served.

Bates was dedicated, so he did not wait for trouble to come to his people. Today, he did what he often did: He went looking for what he thought might be the embryo of trouble and aborted it. Like this boy, big talk, going north, joining the army, fighting in the war, going to France. Thinking to come back home and spread big thoughts, bring disorder.

Not anymore. Not anymore. The right side of his mouth twitched.

"It's not righ—"

"Jesus gettin' us ready for that great day," Alena's mother sang loudly, covering her words. As if they knew the plan, the group joined in, "Jesus gettin' us ready for that great day. Jesus gettin' us ready for that great day, who shall be able to stand."

While they sang, Alena's father grabbed her and covered her mouth. Another man took hold of her legs, so she could not kick. She writhed in their arms, trying to break free. Other men surrounded the three and walked with them shouting, "Thank You, Lord!" while the rest of the crowd continued singing, "Jesus gettin' us ready for that great day."

Across the grounds, Bates smiled and came off alert. This he also understood — religious carrying-on. He saw the boys carrying the writhing girl away. Religious frenzy. No trouble here. His way was safe — his wife, his family, his way.

He left the site satisfied.

That evening, Amos and Evelyn called their daughter into the kitchen. They sat at the table where they always broke bread, at the table that held memories of prayers and conversations.

They held hands. Amos attempted to speak, then looked to his wife.

"Maybe we should begin with prayer," she supported.

"Father, I stretch my hands to Thee," her daddy began. "No other help I know. If Thou withdraw Thyself from me, whither shall I go.

"God, grant us wisdom. God, show us the way. Clean our hearts and minds that we might hear from You. Move us out of the way that we might be the tools of Your handiwork. Comfort, guide us, and lead us. In Jesus' name we pray. Amen."

Alena saw her father squeeze his wife's hand. "Thank you, dear." Then he turned to Alena. "You know your Aunt Patrice has always loved you like you were her own."

At the mention of her aunt's name, Alena smiled. Years ago, Aunt Patrice had left Ellisville and moved to Chicago. It had been years since Alena had seen her aunt, but the love Patrice planted still grew strong in her niece's heart. Aunt Patrice was beautiful and warm. Alena remembered spreading her arms wide to hug her aunt. She remembered Patrice's smell and the sound of her aunt's voice when she snuggled on her ample lap and laid her head on her aunt's chest while she talked. Love and patience surrounded Aunt Patrice like a cloud.

And she made the best biscuits in Alena's whole extended family. Patrice was well known in Ellisville for the soft, light, golden brown delights. Alena associated not only the smell of the biscuits with her aunt, but also the warmth, the pleasure, the filling, and even the color of the biscuits. Patrice was the same color as the golden brown biscuit tops — golden brown with a mass of soft wavy hair — hair she sometimes sat on — and warm compassionate eyes. Alena deeply loved and trusted her aunt.

For just a moment, Alena drifted in memories of her aunt. For just a moment, J.C. didn't exist.

Her father's voice called her back. "Alena, each one of us is who we are. I been preaching truth to you so long, it's just in you. I don't believe you got any choice, long as you here, but to tell."

The girl leaned forward and squeezed her parents' hands, happy to hear that they now supported her speaking out on J.C.'s murder. "I've been thinking about a story I could write to send to —"

"But, baby, I also am who I am. You know I believe in the truth, but I can't see my child sacrificed to the truth. If you speak out on this, Bates will kill you. He'll kill us, too, 'cause he'll have to. Then other people in Ellisville will have to suffer 'cause Bates and his riders will have to make sure they have scared and hurt enough people to keep things quiet. And they'a do it, too. Whole towns been wiped out before.

"Now, I'm not worried about me." His

voice was defiant. "But, I can't let them do to you what they did to that boy. They don't think nothing about it; it don't mean nothing to them. No, sir," her father said. He pressed down on his knees like he was holding himself in place. "You my child, and I'm not gone let them tear you up and throw you away like you wasn't nothing. You our child; you God's child, and I, me and your mama, we got a charge to protect you and see that you got a chance."

Her father's voice rose, as if he were in a pulpit. "You smart, Alena. You good hearted, you just coming into your womanhood, and I'm not gone let them just ruin you. They hard-hearted, evil men, Alena. And if you open your mouth, they gone kill you, and I can't let that happen —" he choked through tears. Alena stared across the table, stunned.

"Me and your daddy been talkin' and prayin'." Her mother's tone was soothing. "We know the right thing to do. You just can't tell this here, and your nature is not gone allow you to be quiet."

Alena's face was warm, then hot. She could hear the breath blowing in and out of her nostrils. She could feel water suddenly in her eyes. A cinder block sat on her chest and constricted her air. What were these words? Not from her strong, upright, do-the-right-thing parents.

Outrage, anger, betrayal filled her heart and sat on the tip of her tongue, but they stayed there. In Alena's world, one did not talk back to parents with anger or disrespect. Her lungs heaved and her body shook with the effort it took to control her tongue.

"I know you upset," Alena's mother said, still holding her hand.

Alena looked at her hand in her mother's, then to her other hand engulfed in her father's hand. Her gaze traveled up his arm and into his eyes. Her young body shook and a moan escaped her lips. How could this be happening?

Her father cleared his throat, the signal that there would be no argument. "I know you upset. But we been talking. Your Aunt Patrice always be talking about Chicago in her letters. It sound so wonderful. It sound like you could have a chance there. Patrice say that they got colored writers there. They even got they own newspapers and magazines. She been telling me for a long time that you could go there and write. And she say they got some fine young men. They respectable and they going places."

Young men? Young men? How could she

talk about young men when J.C.'s image, his essence still hung in that tree? *They must be crazy.* She tried to pull her hands away.

Her mother held fast to her hand, spoke as if she didn't notice Alena trying to pull away. "She always talk about this one in particular. That major. Patrice say he so fine and upstanding. He starting his own newspaper, and Patrice say he is God-fearing and Spirit filled. You know, I read to you about him before, about James."

Alena stared at her mother, sure that the woman was not clothed in her right mind. What was she thinking? Where was she? Had she left Ellisville?

So this was the solution. Ship her off to Chicago so everyone else could live safe and undisturbed. That was the solution: ruin her life, make her pay for the sins of others. She would be the scapegoat. *Hypocrites. Years of nothing but lies.*

They didn't ask her what she wanted; they just shook her and moved her around like they were playing baby dolls. *Oh, and make it sound good by spreading the promise of handsome men. A colored Prince Charming walking on the earth that now covered J.C. Mississippi to Chicago.*

"If you're afraid, the solution is ship

your daughter to Chicago!" she wanted to yell at them.

Her mother's words interrupted Alena's thoughts. "And Patrice say he is so handsome. . . ." Her mother tried a new direction, "You and your Aunt Patrice love each other. You'll be happy; it will be the best thing for you. . . ."

Alena's father looked across the table at his wife. "We know it's best. So tomorrow morning we gonna take you to the train." His eyes came back to her. "I know you upset, but we know best. It's better for you to be upset now and live for a greater day than to stay here and let all our labor and love go for nothing."

It was all about you! About your desires, your fears, your dreams. Where was the holy truth in all this? Hypocrites. Her thoughts boiled behind cast down eyes.

They sat in silence, Alena raging in her mind until, finally, her father spoke. "You better go to bed, baby. Your mama got to get you packed, and we be starting out early in the morning."

Weaklings! she screamed to herself as she sat slumped, tears rolling down nutmeg plains.

Three

The wagon ride from Ellisville was hot — hot, humid, strained. The Mississippi sun was in full glory. Alena's father waved away flies as he drove, and with them, most likely, any thoughts of spring planting days he was losing.

For two days, Alena and her family arose at the first light of dawn so that most of their travel was before noon, when the sun's heat took full control of the day. The family now avoided the same sun they normally prayed for during this season.

There were few if any places safe for a black family to stop along the way for water or shelter. Night was a dangerous time. White faces roamed through darkness, threatening. Better to stick to the day.

No appetite, Alena limited herself to biscuits and syrup when they stopped. The biscuits were dry and cold. *It's what they should be eating,* she thought, watching her parents. How could they think of food, of enjoying food? Each choking bite was penance for breathing air that J.C. could no longer breathe.

"We gonna get through this," her mother would say sometimes, out of nowhere, as if she were convincing herself. Her eyes looked toward the treetops, toward the sky. "Folks been through worse times than this. Ain't the first time. Won't be the last. Least we still alive, we still got hope. Yes, sir, we still got hope." Shoulders braced, she would pat her husband's knee, look away, and then lapse back into silence. A silence like they had packed the funeral with them, like death was following the dried wooden wagon.

Every hour or so, Alena's mother would talk — to herself as much as to her daughter and husband — about good times past, good times to come. Each time she spoke, Alena grew more and more angry, so much so that she was barely breathing. She wasn't sure why. Maybe it was the sound of her mother's voice, trying to be happy, trying to cover up despair.

Alena had seen her mother's determined encouragement at work during their missionary visits. The girl was just as determined, however, to resist any attempt to disguise her routing from Mississippi as anything other than punishment. She was being punished for believing and attempting to act on what they had taught her. *"Hypocrites!"* she screamed inwardly. This from the people who had preached truth and courage to her. . . .

She would not be tricked into false happiness over their cowardly behavior, not even by Aunt Patrice. While the wagon wheels turned and layers of dust beaten from hardened clay coated the family, Alena nursed thoughts of return, of fixing their happy plans.

She kept her conversation with her parents to a minimum. She avoided calling them *Mama* or *Daddy,* or even looking into their eyes. If they wanted to send her away, she would not go willingly. She almost could not bear to look at them — to watch her mother trying to smile, to watch her father sitting straight, trying to look brave. Each attempt felt like a lie, made her more and more angry.

Her father flicked the horses' reins and clucked his tongue. "This not where we seen ourselves, but, Lord, Your will be done. Keep us bound by love." Her father's prayers, which had always comforted her and made her feel safe now irritated her. *Shut up,* she thought while she stared at the large sweat stain that ran from between her father's shoulder blades down his back. That's as far as it got though, a thought. She was angry, not crazy. Not yet anyway. Not crazy enough to speak out loud to her parents in that way.

Her father looked toward her mother. "Could have been worse. Least they didn't make no show of it. Lots of times, they make a show of it." Alena sat behind them but thought she could still see fear playing around the corner of his eyes when he turned toward his wife, like he was seeking reassurance.

"Mama, you know about it. How they put up posters so folks can come from all over to watch. To make picnics, play music, and give speeches while they do the lynching. Men, women, children watching, enjoying it, learning hate right up close. Not just ruffians, but supposed-to-be good people coming to see and participate. Taking body parts home for keepsakes. Least his mama don't have to live with that. They beat him bad and all, but at least they . . ." Her father stopped talking, flicked the reins again. The consolation was no consolation.

I don't know these people. Alena was sure she didn't know them. *Is this supposed to be comfort? Why not just ride in silence?* Maybe

Chicago was not far enough.

Alena did not feel like talking. Did not feel like praying. What was there to pray for now? It was over. J.C. was dead. She felt dead. Maybe if she prayed, God would finish it. He would take her. Right out of the wagon. Right off the road out of Mississippi. Maybe He would finish it.

He would take His big hands and roll her into a ball, drop her down the well of pain she felt. Maybe He'd let her trade places with J.C. Let J.C. ride along while she hung. Let him try to figure out what kind of world this was. Let him try to smile, try to figure out how to feel while she rested. Let him look at Bates walking around. Let J.C. be angry, even feel hate toward his parents for being weak, for being scared. Let him live with the shame of knowing his parents were afraid. Let his life be over while he lived.

If they wanted to send her away, she would not go willingly, she told herself while she rubbed knots in her stomach and chest that she could not reach. The knots were spiritual pain. She did not acknowledge it. Instead, she told herself, *No one will hurt me. I will be strong; they won't hurt me. They want to punish me, but I'll hurt them first. I'll give them what they want. They want to get rid of me, separate me? I won't wait for Chicago. We'll separate now.*

In the seven feet of wagon space, she held herself aloof from her parents all along the hot, bumpy ride. And all the anger she felt, all the confusion — at God, at the lynchers, at her parents, at the world — just kept spinning, kept twisting, made her face tight and drawn.

When they bedded down near the open-topped wagon, she held herself miles and miles away from them.

Evelyn rubbed her husband's back. "You got to sleep, Amos. You ain't had a wink since we left," she whispered.

"How am I supposed to sleep? That boy was like my son, and look what they doing to my daughter. Look what they doing to us. How we going to go on from here? How I'm supposed to take this and be a man? How I'm supposed to go back and walk around like I'm a man, like ain't nothing happened?" He turned slightly away, but she saw that his face mirrored his anguish. "Maybe she right. Maybe I'm thinking too much. Maybe I shoulda just killed —"

Evelyn leaned her face nearer to her husband. "Amos, you know better. She a child. She ain't been through this like we have. You know wouldn't be no end to what you talking about. They would kill you, then us." Evelyn's hand reached and turned her husband back toward her.

"Amos, I married you 'cause you was a man. I seen you do things. Like the time you hit that crazy horse upside the head with your bare hand. Brought that horse to his knees." A sad smile played at the corner of her lips while she looked in her husband's eyes. "I ain't never seen nothing like that. Ain't no telling how many people woulda been hurt that day if you hadn't stopped that horse. He was just gone crazy. All the other men was running for guns, and you just stepped right out and grabbed that horse 'fore he could run somebody down or stomp them."

Her finger traced the shape of his lips. "When I saw that, I knew you was a man. That came straight up out of your belly, straight up out of your heart. I said to myself right then you was the one I was gone marry. I ain't never liked no weak man. You wasn't no coward then, and you ain't one now." Amos closed his eyes as though trying to close out the recent past, or maybe like he was trying to keep back tears. He lay one hand over his wife's hand.

She reached to intertwine her fingers with his. "What you are is wise, Amos. And that's why I trust you with my life and our daughter's life. I didn't want no fool either. If I was gone marry and obey, I knew it had to be somebody I respect, somebody with good sense." She moved to take his hand fully in hers, then kneeling, traced the shape of his eyes with her other hand.

He squeezed his eyes tighter. "I just can't stand to see her this way. She hurting. I just can't stand it."

"Yes, you can." Evelyn gave him a quick, short peck on the lips that held more correction than affection. "That's what you always telling me. Yes, you can. This one, we have to put in the Lord's hands." He opened his eyes. "You always telling me that. When we weak, He show Himself strong. You all the time telling me that. We ain't children in the Lord, Amos. We done growed up, and we know sometimes it get hard, and you just have to hold on and trust. Alena heard us saying it, but she got to learn it for herself. She got to learn to lean in hard times. Ain't no way to learn that but to go through it."

Amos raised up on his elbows so that his face was near his wife's, their noses almost touching. His eyes looking deeply into hers. "Just seems like I should be able to do something. I'm her daddy. She look up to me. It just seem like I'm failing. Look at her over there." He turned his gaze toward his daughter.

"Baby, she hurt. You hurt. We all hurt." Evelyn laid one hand softly on her husband's chest. "But ain't no way to learn but to go through it. She can't go around it, and she can't pass by. She gone be all right. She gone come through." Her hand patted the spot just over his heart. "What you decided was best. It's hard on all of us, but it's the right thing." Crickets chirped; the moon hid behind nighttime clouds.

Evelyn rubbed the spot she had just patted. "You being a man. You ain't running, you ain't hiding." Gently, her hand touched his shoulder and encouraged him to turn over to his side. "She gone see. 'Sides that, we got to learn we ain't God. We ain't Jesus. We got to learn we can't do everything; we got to let her lean on Him." She massaged the knotted muscles in his shoulders. "And ain't no way to learn, but to go through. It's gone be better days. We seen worse." Evelyn leaned to kiss the back of her husband's neck, then the place behind his ear. Her right hand rubbed his stomach and chest.

He caught her hand and pressed it against the warmth of his stomach. "Ain't nothing left to say, is it?" He pulled her head down until their lips met in renewal.

When they resumed travel, Alena continued quiet. *No more. No more pain. No more hurt.* She built a strong wall between herself and her parents. She was tired of thinking about it, trying to figure it out. How she felt, how she should feel. She only knew she hurt, and she wanted it to stop. If she could separate from them, from the pain, the anger, the disappointment *they* caused, others would be easy. *They want to put me away, punish me. Want me to be scared with them, play along in the lie. To send me away.* But she would withdraw first.

It was twenty more miles to the Jackson station. The wagon ride was long and painful. All hearts yearned toward something else.

Four

Rebellion had already joined Alena by the time she boarded the train. Her father and mother hugged her and cried openly over her leaving. She responded with indifference. She kissed them without passion and willed that her eyes would show that her love for her parents had died. It hurt, but she did it anyway.

No control over her circumstances, wronged and betrayed, she would use what small weapons were available to her. Her own parents had sent her, *delivered* her from Ellisville, Mississippi, to a train in Jackson that would take her to Chicago. She was sure their smiles masked the hollow aches in their chests as she boarded the *City of New Orleans*. Alena wrapped thorns around her heart so it would not betray her and speak love back to them. Instead, she carefully painted her face with rejection, with indifference, and with the loss of her respect for them.

It was hard this first time to withhold her

love, but she had to protect herself from hurt. The briars she wrapped around her heart would keep others away. *They started it, they did it,* Alena told herself. They had hurt her this once, but they would not be able to hurt her again. The thorns wrapped tighter and pressed inward.

Her heart ached, but it was worth it to protect herself. They didn't love her. They'd betrayed her, and she would not trust them. They made this choice.

The briars wrapped tighter. It hurt to protect herself this time. She was sure though, it would get easier. Maybe someday she would not even feel the pain. But pain or not, Alena was sure it would get easier to hide her tenderness and to put on an older, harder, sharper, wiser face.

The train was hot, sweaty, and cramped. There were babies, a few old men, mothers, and fathers. Alena did not see any other people her own age on the train. But all of the passengers had one thing in common: They were black.

At the Jackson station where she had boarded the train, it was clear from the signs and the separate boarding lines that colored people were not allowed the privilege of riding with white people. Colored people, for the same or higher fare, sat packed together in the cars closest to the engine where it was loudest and dirtiest. Every whistle blew through them.

Porters and redcap service were for the white cars toward the rear of the train and for the Pullman cars that lay beyond. Sleeping service, food service were for the cars at the end of the train. At the front, there was just an occasional pass by of a Pullman porter who brought something to some well-dressed ebony someone. Someone who had paid in advance for limited food items, no trays, no dining cars.

Alena heard that there were a few invisible ones. Ones whose green money bought them separated passage on Pullman cars. She heard of such black men, but did not see them.

She stared out the window. *No one's going to take care of me but me,* she reasoned to herself, justified by her pain and anger. She felt alone, like somebody — some-*bodies* — had died. Somebody more than J.C.

People are going to do what they want to do, look out for what they want. So you better start looking out for yourself. Pain and Anger were already speaking to Alena in familiar tones, like they had been conversing for a while when she became aware of them.

They whispered to her that she had been foolish and childish all her years, being so goody-goody. They mocked her for her trust and innocence. They asked Alena what she had to show for years of goodness, long-suffering, patience, and meekness. They quickly and firmly supplied the answer they wanted her to hear: *"Nothing!"*

Bitterness joined the three, and they shamed the girl the entire train ride. They brought to Alena's mind memories of individuals who didn't play by the rules and magnified their successes before her. As their presentation gained power, Rebellion, Pain, Anger, and Bitterness brought to her mind the image of J.C.'s lifeless, defeated body hanging from the tree. And so Fear joined her sisters to ride and counsel.

She spoke quietly, clearly, and insistently to Alena, as if she really cared for the girl, as if Fear wanted to protect her. Fear told Alena that she could and would meet J.C.'s end if she did not put herself first. The five sisters warned Alena to take up arms. It was the reasonable thing to do.

Alena's traveling companions held her hand and whispered deep into her ears. *"You have been letting people walk on you,"*

66

they told her. *"Look out for yourself."* They stoked discontent just beneath the surface of consciousness. *"Put yourself first — everyone else does it. Try it out, see if it doesn't work,"* they said to Alena after hours of coaching.

An old man sat sleeping beside Alena. He snored. His head dropped onto Alena's shoulder. A small, still voice warmed her, told her the old man was tired and probably more uncomfortable on the train benches than she was. The small voice — a familiar voice, a familiar knowing — urged her to share the homemade quilt draped over her lap.

The five sirens mocked her, dared her to try out what they said. Yelled that she might listen. *"Go ahead. Watch and see, it will work. Don't be a fool. Don't be a child. Don't be used."*

The thorns tightened and pricked her heart. Alena inhaled and gave herself permission. In a small, quick movement she reached out her hand, pushed the old man's head away and turned from the voice she knew . . . the still small voice that pleaded with her.

"Oh, I'm sorry, Miss!" The old man's hands reached to smooth his wiry gray hair and to check his face. "Let me move over and give you a little more room. I guess I just fell asleep. . . ." His voice disappeared into the cold look on Alena's face.

She felt pleasure in a new place. His embarrassed reaction was her victory. Emboldened, she set her face like flint in response to the old man's words.

"I-I'm so sorry."

Alena drew her body away from him and pretended to look out the window.

His face said he had gotten the message; he was old and a nuisance. He continued to apologize until others in the train car noticed.

Alena continued looking out the window until finally she focused a hard, sharp look on the old man. He sputtered and stopped speaking.

"See, we told you," the five harped. *"It works. This is only the beginning. . . ."* The sirens tutored the girl all along the journey, between each stop and along every mile. Alena stared out the train window into darkness.

"Hey, little girl."

Alena heard a man's voice speak to her. She was no longer a little girl, but she was sure the voice was speaking to her. It was strong, smooth, teasing.

She turned from the window, prepared to set her face. He was dressed in white. He was handsome, even pretty. "I know you probably not supposed to talk to strangers, are you, little girl? What you doing so far from the path?"

His eyes seemed to take in everything about Alena.

" 'Scuse me, Pop. Find you another seat," the man in white directed the old gentleman seated next to Alena.

"Maybe I got you wrong," he squinted his eyes, like he was focusing to get a closer look at her. "Maybe you ain't wandered off the path; maybe it's Little Bo Peep that's looking for you." He threw his head back and laughed, showed off a mouth full of pearly teeth.

Alena didn't know what to say.

"I'm Pearl. That's what my friends call me." His smile flashed.

"Excuse me, Porter," a woman carrying a child interrupted him. "Sir, do you know where I can get some cool water for my baby?"

"I'm busy. I ain't on duty now. You got to talk to someone on duty." Pearl barely turned his head to acknowledge the woman. He rubbed his hands across the pomaded waves in his hair, then pulled and snapped at the front of his jacket so his uniform sat squarely on his shoulders. He used his tongue to wet his lips. "You might be able to find someone in the car behind this one, but I'm busy. You know I don't work in this car, no way." He stared down at the woman, then turned his brown eyes and smooth-skinned face back to Alena.

"Can't she see I got things to do?" He smiled at Alena; the woman with child no longer existed. Without a word, the woman carrying the baby moved quickly away.

"What's your name? I mean, you know my name. Say my name. Come on, say *Pearl*. But, oh, I forgot — maybe your mama told you not to talk to men, especially men like me." He winked and continued, "Maybe a young boy wet behind the ears, maybe a church boy, but no man." He straightened his shoulders and pulled himself up to his full height. "No man like me," he continued taunting Alena. "You probably scared. You don't know nothing about no high life."

Other train passengers continued up and down the aisle. They were careful not to disturb the porter or brush up against his uniform.

"I'll go tell Bo Peep you looking for her."

Pearl turned as if to walk away.

"I'm not looking for anybody." Alena was not sure what made her respond.

"Oh! Oh! A country girl." He threw back his head and laughed out loud. "I thought you might be. You look a little green. Cute, but green."

Alena drew her body closer to the window and wall of the train.

"Where you trying to scoot to?"

She turned her head to stare out the window.

"Oh, so you mad at Pearl now? You not gone talk. Well, if you don't show me some respect — and your ticket — guess what? You gone have to get off the train. Don't you know who I am? No, I guess you don't," he answered his own question. "I'm a porter, baby, and ain't nobody got more power on this train than me, except maybe the conductor. I'm a Pullman porter, little girl. You'll learn more about that now that you're off the farm. So, if I was you —" Pearl raised an eyebrow, an eyebrow that looked as if it might have been arched — "I would let me see your ticket."

Annoyed, unsettled, Alena reached into her bag and retrieved her ticket.

"Like I thought, Mississippi to Chicago. Girl, you green as new grass. Now I know you ain't supposed to talk to nobody like me. Too bad. Fun don't start 'til I arrive, but you a little girl, and you don't know nothing about that." He grinned. "How old are you, little lost sheep?"

"I'm not lost. I ain't no little child. I'm eighteen, and I'm going to Chicago to make my own life, my own story, my own way."

"Seem like you got a little chip on your shoulder. You don't like home; did you run away?"

Pearl's questions touched the bruised, sore place in Alena's heart. She looked quickly out the window. She willed herself not to cry.

"Come with me, Miss. I got something to show you that will take that lost look off your face." Pearl's expression was briefly sympathetic and sincere.

Alena paused unsure, worried that she did look like a lost lamb.

"Come on, Miss Mississippi," Pearl chided, "get up now."

Still unsure, still confused, she stood.

"Don't worry about your things. Leave them there," Pearl said to Alena. "You watch 'em for her, Pops," he directed the old man that Alena had sat beside.

She saw concern cover the old man's

face. He cleared his throat, as if he were about to caution Alena, but he spoke no words. She stepped across the old man into the aisle, looked back with grown-up disdain at him, and passed by.

"I'm going to take care of you, Miss Mississippi." Pearl smiled. He seemed pleased at the new nickname he had given Alena. She felt uncertain, but he continued. "As a matter of fact, I'm gone call you Miss Miss. It will be our secret. Nobody else has to know how green you are, from Mississippi and everything. But I'm going to take care of you." He looked deeply into her eyes. "Don't you even worry. Don't think about it. Just trust me."

Alena had never had a man look into her eyes that way. It was intoxicating, comforting, and frightening. Neither had a man ever spoken to her in the way this man spoke. His eyes, his words said she was an adult, said she was worth having. She was wrapped, enveloped, and she felt herself falling into something dark and comfortable.

As she moved down the aisle with the porter, he kept one of his hands just above the small of her back, directing her toward the rear of the car.

They moved through the door, and Alena noticed that people moved out of the aisles to let them pass. The train sometimes swayed and lurched, but the passengers, after seeing the porter, moved quickly, sometimes stumbling to stay out of his way. Pearl walked as if he owned the train. He took backseat to no one.

Being with him, his hand on her back, conferred that same status on her. Alena and Pearl passed through three Jim Crow cars — segregated cars full of black faces. And faces that had not noticed her before now paid attention. Who was she that she was with him, Alena read in their expressions.

Was this how Cinderella felt?

Pearl's hand directed Alena through the cars packed with people. At the door of each car, he reached around Alena with his free arm and expertly pushed the doors open, his other hand still on her back.

Alena liked the pressure. Liked the feeling. It was exhilarating. She did not resist the control Pearl exerted over her. Something about his self-assurance and the hand on her back made her feel protected, made her feel he was not afraid of anything.

Something about his hand made her feel

small and fragile, petite, safe, rescued. It filled a place she had not known was empty.

She had always been the tallest one, the one who did not need protection. It was as though people assumed that her size, her height, correlated with her frailty, her neediness, or even her gentleness.

Alena had seen men and boys rush to open doors, carry packages, fight battles for more petite girls. *But never for me,* she often thought. She had seen men offer comfort, a shoulder, an arm, protection to women of smaller stature. *Why not for me?* Alena had asked herself.

She loved her height but hated that it kept her from being allowed to feel small, fragile. She had been teased since she was twelve about being a giant, an Amazon. Alena had wondered if protecting an Amazon was too much of a challenge for any man.

But now, here was this man, Pearl, who made her feel weak and uncertain. Who teased her, chided her, threw her off balance. He made her feel defenseless, yet the hand on her back directed her, controlled her, and offered protection. One single hand on her back. The firmness, the strangeness made her feel vulnerable, feminine, lovable. Alena surrendered to the feeling.

As they approached the third door, an aroma let her know she was hungry. Her stomach growled and rolled.

Pearl led her from the Jim Crow cars to the porters' car, which separated the all-black cars from the dining car, the more comfortable all-white riding and sleeping cars.

The porters' car was full of black men dressed in white. White in constant movement. A few men shined their shoes, a few looked in mirrors and brushed their hair. Four men sat off in a corner playing some sort of card game. The men moved quickly and spoke boldly, as if they were free.

"Miss Alena, these are the porters. Brothers, this is Miss Alena. Miss Miss," Pearl announced.

"You look like a nice young lady to me. What you doing with that scalawag?" one of the brown-skinned men called out to Alena in that way that men send a warning wrapped in a joke. "He ain't never meant no lady no good," he said over the background of stomps, hoots, and thigh slaps from the other men.

"Behave now, Pops," Pearl chided the gray-haired porter. "She's a lady, and she ain't used to a lot of hooligans like you all. Miss Miss is on her way to Chicago."

One of the card-playing porters laughed. "Her and how many other people? Man, Negroes is running from lynchings, running to money, running to Chicago like ain't no tomorrow. We had to add extra cars on just about every run. This train packed with 'em. They think gold in the streets. Just wait —" he held out his hand, and another card-playing porter slapped hands with him in agreement — "Just wait 'til they see how it really is."

"Miss Alena," another porter spoke a veiled warning, "you look like a nice church girl to me. What you doing with this snake? He don't mean you no good. He got women up and down this line. Pearl ain't no good for you. Now *me*, on the other hand —"

The other porters laughed over the rest of his speech.

An older man nodded toward the still-laughing porter. "Oh, Smitty, leave the young lady alone. Come on in, Miss. Have a seat. Make yourself to home. Men, act like there's a lady present."

"Thank you, Deac," Pearl said to the older porter. "I don't know why they giving me such a hard time. Do you,

Deac?" He settled Alena on a seat next to him.

"Don't try to get me to lyin' with you," the older porter countered. "I wouldn't let you nowhere near a daughter of mine. I'm just trying to look out for the young lady." The other porters continued laughing in the background. "Are you hungry, Miss?"

Alena's home training told her to decline the invitation, but her stomach growled again. The smell of fried chicken made her mouth water.

"The food car is the next car back, and we —" Deac nodded his head toward the other porters — "get to eat for free. There's roast beef with gravy and mashed potatoes, baked fish almondine, or my favorite, fried chicken with baked potato and green beans." Alena hoped the men couldn't hear the noise her stomach made.

"This some of the finest dining in the country. Yeast rolls melt in your mouth. Ain't nobody on this train goes hungry. We keep 'em full and satisfied." He spoke with pride until he saw the puzzled look on Alena's face.

"Aw, Miss Miss," Pearl explained, "he mean don't none of the white passengers go hungry. Everybody know we don't serve no colored people. We porters get to dine as fine as anybody, but we don't serve in the Jim Crow cars. Might take some sandwiches or something back. That's about it. Everybody know that. Shoot, if they want food, they know they better bring it or make some arrangements beforehand." Alena looked between the two porters. Looked around the room at the other men.

"Oh, but we'll serve you, Miss Alena," Deac entreated. "Tell me what you want and it's yours."

"You ain't never served me. What's going on here, Deac?" Pearl joked with the older man.

Deac smiled but looked directly into Pearl's eyes. "This here is a nice young lady. I can see she is well raised and the light of Christ yet shines around her. That light will keep shining if she stays away from rapscallions like you." The two men stared at each other while Alena continued to look between them, continued to try to make sense of it. The two stared and then laughed.

Turning to Alena, Deac asked again, "So what will it be, Miss? I'm ready to serve."

Alena thought of what her mother and father would have said. She was sure they would not accept the food. They would not even have come here with Pearl in the first place. And they would not have approved of his hand on her back.

Pearl raised one eyebrow. "What's it gone be, Miss Miss?"

Alena knew what he was implying by invoking the nickname, that she was country, green, unable to care for herself. The new spirit growing within her, encouraged by Bitterness, Pain, Anger, Fear, and Rebellion, rose up defiantly at Pearl's teasing.

"I'll have the fried chicken dinner and . . . some coffee," quickly settling on the most grown-up drink she could name.

Deac's face showed concern. "It's kind of late, Miss. Do your parents drink coffee at a late hour such as this?"

"I don't have any parents. I am on my own, and I drink what I feel like." Alena lifted her chin.

Pearl laughed out loud.

"I'm sorry, Miss. I didn't mean to offend you. You just appear to be well raised and cared for. You don't have that hard edge, like you been fending for yourself. Of course, Miss, you can decide to drink whatever you want. I was just concerned, that's all."

Deac's gentle reply pressed against one of the thorns wrapped around Alena's heart. She was pricked and, at that moment, sorry for how she had spoken to the elderly gentleman.

"I'm sorry, sir. I don't usually speak that way. I'm just tired, I guess. And you're probably right; I shouldn't have coffee so late at night. Maybe lemonade would be a better choice."

Deac nodded. "Don't you worry about a thing, Miss. It's coming right up. Deac's got on his serving clothes now. Yes, ma'am. I know how to do my job."

Alena smiled again as she watched the older porter walk away.

"So what's with you, Miss Miss? Just like I thought — a goody two-shoes. A church girl." Pearl spoke just loud enough for Alena to hear. "Deac's a fool, always preaching that do-right stuff. You go on if you want to, Miss Nicety-Nice. But let me tell you, you won't last a minute in Chicago. It ain't Mississippi. They'll eat you up alive. You really are green. I don't need nobody green with me.

"I should have left you back there with the other Negroes in the Jim Crow cars. Shuffling, taking low, letting people walk on 'em. Not me, baby. Not Pearl. And not anybody that I want to be with." Pearl looked at Alena as if to say, *you know what I mean.*

"Yeah, that stuff might be all right on Sunday, but I ain't taking backseat to nobody. I'm looking out for number one. I ain't taking backseat to nobody — not those Negroes in Jim Crow, not even these white men that think they so high and mighty." Pearl jerked his thumb toward the *whites only* cars.

"You better get it straight, Miss Mississippi. If you want to survive, if you want to live the good life like me, you better look out for yourself. Stop bowing and scraping."

Alena leaned in to listen to Pearl, her eyes wide. She had never heard anyone speak this way. Control. He was in control. He was speaking his mind. He didn't keep it bottled up inside, worrying about other people's feelings. And no one disrespected him. People moved out of Pearl's way. They moved out of her way when she was with him.

He was beautiful. His skin and wavy hair were groomed and pampered. His hands were manicured. He was a handsome man, an exciting man. Alena felt her heart pounding, losing rhythm, changing rhythm. Suddenly, her mother's words came to her again: "Look down the road."

Alena squinted her eyes, just barely, so

that she could look at Pearl with long-term vision. What she saw was a wealthy, powerful, dapper, gray-haired man. While she thought on Pearl's beauty, Deac returned with a tray covered with silver lids.

"Come on over here, Miss, and let me serve you." Deac stopped by a table along one wall of the porters' car. The table was more like a booth; seat and table were connected to the wall. The table was covered with a white damask tablecloth. A single rose in a cream-colored vase sat on top.

"Come on, Miss, so you can eat this good food while it's hot." Deac balanced the tray while unfolding a cloth napkin for Alena. He lifted a lid. "Um-um-um. Look at the steam. Smell that bird. Ain't nobody nowhere can make better fried chicken."

Deac removed the lid from each plate with a flourish and set the plates before Alena. "There's mashed potatoes with gravy and green beans. The mashed looked too good to pass up. I thought you might like them better. And here's a slice of cherry pie to give you a sweet memory to think on when the meal is over." He set the lemonade glass in its proper place and bowed, ready to take his leave. "You enjoy it now."

Alena could feel her face flush. "Thank

you, Mr. Deac. I've never had anyone serve me like that. Where did you learn all this?" Alena looked down at the feast, not sure where to begin.

Deac smiled. "Just dig in, honey."

"Yeah, you better go ahead and eat, Miss Miss. Chicago gone be up in no time. And anyway, I'm gonna be gettin' off in East St. Louis this run. If you want to be with me, you better go ahead and eat that mess. Ain't nothin' special. Pay no mind to Deac clowning like a fool."

This must be jealousy. Pearl is jealous that I'm paying attention to Deac. It made her feel special that someone would fight for her attention. *He could have anyone he wants, but he wants me.* Her face flushed. Pearl's jealousy pleased her. "Oh, Pearl . . ."

"You go ahead and eat up, Miss," Deac said.

Alena took a few bites then pushed the food away. "Thank you, Mr. Deac. I'm just not hungry anymore." Her eyes were on Pearl.

He picked up a rag to shine his shoes, his expression sullen.

"I'm finished." She didn't wait for Deac to unseat her. Instead, she moved to sit at Pearl's side, eager to give the attention she was sure would return his good nature. Silently, Deac began to clear the table.

"My stop is coming up soon, but I know Deac will look out for you; he's so holy," Pearl jabbed just above a whisper.

"Don't be that way. He was trying to be nice."

"Don't worry about it." Pearl got up to leave. "Look, you're grown. You know where you're going."

Alena looked around the car to see who might have overheard. The other porters seemed engrossed in their own stories and activities. Deac continued cleaning.

"Please, Pearl," she whispered. "Don't be upset."

"Yeah, but my stop is coming up. I probably won't never see you again. Why should I fall for you and let you break my heart two hours from now? I'm getting off in East Saint. No point in getting caught up in something that will end as soon as it starts. Besides, you worried about yourself. You ain't thinking about me. You thinking about who you gone see in Chicago. You'a be done forgot about me before your feet touch the ground."

"Oh, Pearl. I would never do that. You come to Chicago, don't you? We can see each other then."

"I don't know if you want to see me."

Alena's head and heart pounded. She felt like she was spinning. "Pearl, I . . . no one ever talked to me like you do. No one ever treated me like an adult. In just this short time you've taught me so much about taking care of myself. You've been taking care of me. You told me you would take care of me."

Pearl flopped into the seat next to Alena. He wore a small closed smile on his face.

Quickly she looked around the room to see who was watching, who was taking in their conversation. She saw only Deac watching. His lips seemed to be barely moving, his eyes fixed in a far place as though he were talking to himself.

Pearl smoothed his waves of hair with his hands. "Okay, Miss Miss. Don't look so sad. I can't stand no sad woman." He looked across the room at his image in the mirror. "That's why I can't find the right woman to marry."

He looked into Alena's eyes. "I need a woman who will support me. A woman that will encourage me and lift me up."

The room spun in another direction, and Alena's heart changed rhythm. *He is saying something to me. He wants to make me a promise.* The voices of her traveling companions were silent. They offered no advice, no warning. They did not caution her. Alena vowed within herself to make Pearl trust, believe, and ultimately confess the love she was sure she saw in his eyes.

Alena spent the next two hours of the trip with her heart unto Pearl. She focused on him, on saving him from the sadness she thought she saw just beneath the surface. She listened, leaning toward him until the train reached East St. Louis, Illinois.

At Pearl's destination, he prepared to disembark from the train. He'd led Alena back to her seat in the first Jim Crow car, seeing that she was settled. Once at her seat though, he hastily brushed her hand with a kiss. He seemed distracted and quickly left the train.

The East St. Louis train station was small, twice as large as the Tupelo station, but still small. Hoping to catch a glimpse of Pearl, Alena looked through the grime on the train windows at the people on the platform and those moving in and out of the station building. There were men, women, children — black and white — selling wares, greeting family members.

Alena's heart quickened when Pearl

came into sight on the platform. He no longer wore the porter's uniform, though the pride and confidence remained. Now he was dressed stylishly. High buttoned collar, charcoal gray suit with vest and watch fob, side-buttoned leather shoes, flat topped straw hat. He carried an expensive-looking leather suitcase.

Looking out the window, Alena saw Pearl stop, then throw back his head. Even through her window, Alena could hear his laugh. Two women approached him. *Fancy women.* The words popped into Alena's mind. She had never seen any, but inwardly she knew what they were. Their faces were made up — even from this distance they looked painted. Their clothes were too short, too far above their ankles, too tight. Their bearing caught the eye of men passing by them. As the two women attached themselves to Pearl, another word came to Alena. *Familiar.*

Her young heart jumped and jerked. Revelation and understanding beyond her place filled her mind. Both of the women kissed Pearl, one on the mouth, the other on his cheek. One arm went about his waist, another arm and hand wrapped around his shoulder and neck.

Alena was afraid and confused. Her face

was warm and flushed. How could this be happening? One minute he kissed her hand, and now . . .

The train began to move. Jerk. Stop. Jerk. Whistle. Steam discharge. Alena's eyes followed the three figures still entwined on the platform. Her stomach knotted. Alena's jaws tightened in the back, saliva and a metallic taste flooded her mouth. Nausea pressed its way upward.

Her brain attempted to reconcile the image from the platform with her memories and images from the dining car, from the walk with Pearl's hand on her back. Over and over her mind replayed the recent image against the brief history as she had interpreted it and stored it, attempting to establish a bridge, a thread of logic that would make what she had just seen acceptable and possible. But each time she played it, her brain could not leap the chasm between what she had just seen and what she had believed was true about Pearl during their train ride.

After failing at attempts to reconcile the information as it was, Alena's mind began to reprocess what she had stored. Perhaps he wasn't such a gentleman. Perhaps the other porters were warning her. *Perhaps he feigned interest in me. Perhaps he was taking advantage of my being green; perhaps he mocked me, he did not care for —*

A new voice interrupted her. *"What did you really see? Are you sure you saw what you thought you saw? You are tired, you know,"* Self-deception said to Alena as her five sisters hummed in agreement.

"Besides," Deception continued, *"they grabbed him. He's a handsome man, lonely and looking for love. You can save him."* And so the voice continued until Alena arrived in Chicago.

Along the way, when the train passed through Springfield, she tried to silence the thoughts. She tried to remember everything she had heard about Abraham Lincoln. He had been a young lawyer from Springfield. He worked, she believed, for Illinois Central, the train line she was riding right now. He was the sixteenth president. . . .

None of it worked. The voices continued, miles of preparation, of yelling, rehearsing, convincing.

By the time the train pulled in to the station, Alena was determined she would be the first person out the door and off the train. She didn't know where she was rushing to, but she was determined that she would not wait for or help anybody. If she got out quickly, she would not have to risk anyone asking her for assistance — no mothers with babies, no old people, no one.

The still, quiet voice was quieter still.

In the porters' car, Deac sat in silence, praying for Alena's protection. He had seen it before. Usually the women were a little older, a little more evenly matched with the pursuer. He shook his head against the image of Pearl with the girl.

The young man seemed to be getting worse, not better. This one was not much more than a child. His stomach knotted; he worried for both of them. The girl did look like a lost lamb. Didn't know nothing about who she was or where she was. And Pearl, he just kept pressing further and further.

Deac had been praying for a long time that Pearl's heart would be changed. Nobody else seemed bothered about him, but there was something about the young man . . . maybe something that reminded him of himself years ago. "Come on, Jesus. Come on, Holy Ghost. Move quickly," he whispered.

Five

The smell of newly scraped metal was in the air. Its metallic taste was in Alena's mouth, and steam billowed all around her.

Alena saw Patrice waiting, eyes searching, before her aunt saw her. In seconds she was down the steps and in the comfort of familiar arms.

"Oh, baby. Oh, baby, I'm so happy to see you. So happy you're here. Mm-mm-mm. Look at you. No little girl anymore. Just so precious." The woman held on to Alena, who bent to lay her head on her aunt's shoulder. She was comforted. "Well," Alena's aunt smiled the smile she remembered, "I guess it ain't no need in spending the rest of our lives at this train station. I can take you home and hug you, can't I?" Alena smiled, not speaking, just breathing in her aunt's presence.

"Oh, baby, it's a great day!" Patrice turned her head and nodded in the direction of Alena's luggage. "James, will you grab her bags for me, darlin'?"

Only then did Alena notice the young man standing behind her aunt. He had deep brown eyes and his face was open and kind, not weak. His short-cut hair was well groomed, center parted, and brushed back in the style of the day.

"Of course," James replied to Aunt Patrice's question. His voice, his manner was kind and attentive. Confident.

Alena raised her head and watched as he stepped around the two women to grab her luggage. James did not appear muscle-bound, yet he grabbed the bags as if they were nothing.

"If you two ladies will be all right —"

Alena watched James curiously as he spoke.

"— I'll take these bags on ahead." He smiled at her and Aunt Patrice.

There was no hiding in James's smile, and Alena found herself smiling back at the young man. She figured him to be in his early to mid-twenties — he looked young, but his manner was steady, mature. Alena's eyes lingered. She felt her heartbeat speeding and a warmth she had not experienced before moved up through her and pressed at her face. Without thinking, she raised one of her hands to feel her face. Was she blushing?

"Child, what am I thinking about? I'm just so excited to see you —" Alena's aunt squeezed her — "that I didn't even introduce you two. Alena, this very fine young man is my friend James." Patrice smiled and said the word *fine* like she was biting into butter on one of her biscuits. "James, this is my favorite and only niece, Alena." Aunt Patrice beamed.

"My pleasure." James nodded at Alena. "I'm sorry, my hands are a little full right now." He laughed about the suitcases he held — one large one in each hand and two smaller ones under each arm. Something about him said *order*.

"I can help you," Alena offered.

"No, I have them." He smiled. "I'm just going to take them on outside. I'll meet you ladies out there," he acknowledged, nodding.

His smile is real, Alena thought to herself as he moved quickly down the platform ahead of her and her aunt. There was something about him, something that held her attention. . . .

Aunt Patrice's words interrupted Alena's thoughts. "I have missed you so. I am just so happy you are here! We are gone have us a wonderful time." She pressed a kiss on Alena's forehead.

She hugged her aunt and smiled into her eyes. Without thinking, Alena's eyes sought ahead for the now tiny figure and found him just before he disappeared into the Chicago train station.

"We got so much to do, so much to see!" Patrice squeezed Alena's hand as they moved toward the station. Through the steam and the sounds of whistles and brakes, Alena saw more people than she had ever seen before. Her recent memories of her home in Mississippi contrasted with this scene of men, women, and children of all races moving by and around each other. She looked — even stared — at men and women talking, laughing, and moving at a city pace. But her eyes continued to be drawn to the wrought iron fence that separated the station from the street. She looked, hoping to catch a glimpse of the man she had just met.

"He is a special man," her aunt interrupted her thoughts. "Hard working and good looking, too. Don't you think?" Her aunt smiled. Alena smiled, looked down, and then away.

Maybe Chicago would not be so bad after all.

Aunt Patrice reached to squeeze Alena's hand. "James is special though. There are plenty women making eyes and throwing theyselves at him, but he lives what he say he believes. He always says he's not going to jump the fence; he's going in by the gate. He's not going to try to steal nothing he didn't ask God if he could have. A good man, got a good head on his shoulders. He been to the war and back — he was just one of only a few colored officers. He been to college. A good man. When won't nobody else help me, James is there helping me at the mission, even though he got his own work to do.

"Right up the street from the mission, he done started his own newspaper. Nobody work there but him and Jonathan. You will meet Jonathan and his sister when we get to the mission," Patrice turned her head to explain to her niece. "There's another big paper in town for us; it's a good paper. But James and Jonathan say they ain't gone compromise; they got to tell it. They telling the truth the way it is — even if folks don't like it. Just the two of them."

They made their way slowly through the crowd, through the cloud of different languages and tongues that swirled about them. Aunt Patrice nodded. "Yeah, that James, he a good man. I told your mama all about him."

Alena felt an invisible hand slap her face. She watched Patrice's mouth moving but heard no sound. Not from her aunt, not from the people around her. Not even from the screech of the brakes or the scream of metal on metal as the giant trains moved in and out of the station.

That was it, of course. She had almost fallen for it, fallen right into the plan. The plan that yanked her right from Mississippi, from her life and the place where she wanted to live, love, and write. The plan that would make them all feel better about being hypocrites, about taking her from the home she'd never wanted to leave, the plan that left Bates walking free, J.C. dead, and her in Chicago. The plan to pacify her with a prince charming and a job at some pretend newspaper. Their plan to kill her dream with their own.

Her aunt's voice moved to her slowly as though the words were fighting their way through some strange, thick, clear jelly. "I wrote her all about him and about the newspaper. Evelyn told me she told you, angel."

"I don't remember." Alena looked at her aunt. *How will I ever figure out how to love someone I don't trust?* Fear told her to gather her skirts and run, but the girl knew she needed someone.

In that moment, with crowds of people around her and her favorite aunt by her side, Alena felt alone and lost. She remembered feeling that way one other time, when she was lost from her mother in town in a store. The shelves had seemed so high, the aisles so long, and everything was something she hadn't seen before. Tears had come, but just before she screamed, her mother's arms had lifted her and held her.

Now she watched mothers and fathers of all colors and languages walk by as she and her aunt made their way to the station. She wondered about her parents and wished for their arms to comfort her like that time when she was afraid.

Bitterness, however, quickly reminded her that there had been another time, a time when she was afraid — a time after J.C. — and her parents had not held her, kept her then. They had not comforted her, but instead sent her here, to Chicago.

She vowed in her heart never to forget what had been done to J.C., and never to forget or forgive what had been done to her. She would not soothe their consciences by accepting the man her family dangled before her.

"I'm sure Evelyn told you. He gives time working with me, but he works at all kinds of things trying to keep that paper running. With just he and Jonathan, it ain't enough hands to do everything, trying to investigate it, write it, print it, and deliver it. But it's needed, you know. They telling the whole truth, the good and the bad, about how people being treated in Chicago. Poor people come here looking for one thing and finding another. James and Jonathan doing something needs to be done. Some people don't like it, but they ain't stopping."

Aunt Patrice's eyes looked ahead like she saw something coming, something in the future. "Jonathan and his sister, Dinah, they both work at the mission, too. They don't have to do that; you know people talk, but they just keep right on working. And what Jonathan do with the paper, well he just always tell me, 'Right is right, Miss Patrice.' Yes, I'm just blessed. The Lord surrounded me with good children, and now I got you, too, baby! I know you gone do good things. You gone make a difference at the mission, and I know James is gone love your writing. I'm gone have to fight him for time, he's gone want you down at that newspaper office writing day and night."

Alena stopped short just before she and her aunt entered the station. She looked into her aunt's eyes and lied. "I'm not interested in writing anymore. Not here, not anywhere.

"I love you, Aunt Patrice, and I'm happy to see you. But I did not want to be here. I'm sure you know about everything, about J.C. and everything. I wanted to tell it, to write the truth —" Alena's words said what her home training would not let her show on her face, showed anger she could not exhibit to her aunt in tone or expression — "and that's how I got here. I learned something. It's not my duty to tell the truth. Nobody else has to tell it. So I'm going to be just like everybody else."

Alena stepped through the station door. "I love you, but I'm not going to get a job writing or marry some man so they won't have to face the truth of what they did to me.

"I'm not going along with it. Why? So they can make themselves feel better? So they can tell themselves they did it for me? I loved my home, and all I wanted to do was what they told me to, to tell the truth. . . ."

The two passed through the station, gilt

and marble, mirrors and chandeliers. Even in her frustration, Alena could not help being fascinated by the city. While her widened eyes scanned the station, her ears listened for the sounds of Chicago. Sometimes she heard accents similar to her own: slow, soft, wrapping around, dragging through the words. Other times she heard strange vocal rhythms moving foreign words. Finally, though, her ears began to make out a voice that was Chicago. Clipped, no frills, tell it like it is, *R*s that seemed to stop short of crashes with air walls. A jaunty "my way or no way" kind of sound. So different . . . but not different enough to make her forget who she was and why she was here.

"Alena, you know anything your parents did, they did out of love. They only want the best for you."

Alena stiffened and looked away as her aunt spoke.

"You may not want to hear it now. But you cannot run from that truth. In time you'll understand. You can't shut out your family, baby. You'll just be cutting off a piece of yourself." Her aunt put a plump arm around her shoulders. "Anyway, baby, I am happy you're here. It's going to be a good time!"

Alena did not resist her aunt's affection. There was something irresistible about the love Aunt Patrice exuded. *I'm not going to give in though.*

Passing by food counters, magazine stands, small shops, and shoe shine stands, the two women exited the station. James was parked in front of the building. He opened the car doors for the two ladies, then made sure the doors were firmly shut. Alena rode in back while her aunt rode in the passenger seat next to James.

Storefronts, office buildings, beeping cars, horse-drawn wagons, and what looked like millions and millions of people — downtown Chicago was a riot of activity. Alena was lost in image after image that flashed by her. Chicago looked in charge.

"How was your trip?" James asked as they headed down Michigan Avenue, moving toward the South Side.

He sounded innocent and well meaning . . . , *but,* Alena reminded herself, *he's part of the plan.* Instead of answering, she turned her head and looked out the window as though she had not heard him.

From the corner of her eye she saw James look at Aunt Patrice, then shrug his shoulders.

He tried again. "I know you must be tired. All that way on a train. How long did you travel?"

Alena opened her mouth to tell him to stop trying; the plan wasn't going to work. He must think she was one of those women who was panting for a man's attention, who was giddy when any handsome man spoke to her. He would know her better soon. Instead, she turned away, still silent. She remembered Pearl's advice: *Look out for yourself.*

"Oh, yes, baby!" Alena's aunt spoke into the silence. "I have your room all ready for you. Nice clean sheets with a little rose water sprinkled on them. I scrubbed and washed to get ready for your coming. Everything is just right."

Alena couldn't resist smiling at the enthusiasm in her aunt's voice.

"And food, oh, I put my foot in it if I do say so myself!" Her aunt looked at both of the young people, wrapping them together in her conversation. "I got the macaroni and cheese ready. Just the way you like it, lots of cheese. I wasn't sure what else you would have a taste for, so —" Patrice's eyes twinkled — "I made all your favorites. And whatever we don't eat, my people at the mission know what to do with it!" The woman smiled.

"Yes, ma'am, they know what to do with it! And so do most of the people on our street. Myself —" James cleared his throat — "included." He smiled at Alena in the rearview mirror and turned a puzzled look to Patrice when Alena looked away.

Patrice patted his arm and pressed on, turning in her seat so she could see both Alena and James. "I cooked baked beans and fried some cabbage. The market had some nice collards, so I made a big pot of the greens with some ham hocks and made some candied yams. I can't make them like Evelyn. Your mama always could cook. But I came pretty close. I fried plenty of chicken. All I got to do is throw the biscuits in the oven, and we'll be in business!

"Normally, when I cook, I cook everything in the mission downstairs 'cause we always end up eating with the people. Ain't no point in cooking twice. But since you were coming, baby —" Patrice stopped short. "I know I don't seem excited *at all*."

Alena couldn't help laughing while her aunt mocked herself, patting her own plump, dimpled cheeks.

"But since you were coming, I thought it would be nice to have dinner upstairs, just us. You'll see everything. The Lord blessed me with the building. I live upstairs, and the mission is downstairs, which is where we are all the time. So much work to do, so many people needing help." Alena saw her aunt's face change as she talked about the mission. For a moment, her mind seemed to go some other place, but quickly she was back.

"Anyway, that's enough about that; you'll see it all soon. I got your room all cleaned up and ready. I just keep thinking about all that food though. I can't wait. I probably cooked too much."

James's laugh sounded like it erupted in his stomach and rumbled through his chest. "Yes, Miss Patrice, but everybody loves it when you *probably* cook too much. The people at the mission count on you *probably* cooking too much. Nobody leaves your aunt's mission hungry," James said to Alena's image in the rearview mirror.

Alena was almost caught up in the conversation but quickly gained control of herself. Without blinking, she spoke into the mirror. "I know just how good my aunt can cook. I look forward to the meal." Simple words, but her delivery was ice cold and chilled any further attempts by James to make conversation. Alena saw him give her aunt another puzzled look. Patrice patted him on the arm, reassuring him; Alena turned again to stare out the window. She tried to look as though she were not bothered, not moved, while inside she boiled.

There were people everywhere. Like ants, and they seemed to move and talk at the same pace. People everywhere, busy. All kinds of people, moving in, out, around each other. And buildings. Tall buildings that extended beyond where Alena's neck could turn her head to see as she rode in the car. Each road they turned down had more buildings, buildings that looked like they weren't going anywhere. Granite, brick, marble, concrete, all reaching up to the sky. Packed close together, like everybody wanted buildings so they had to be built almost on top of each other.

Alena wondered if Chicago grew buildings instead of cotton, instead of squash.

People in a hurry moved in and out of the buildings — buildings with closed fronts and revolving doors. Some people disappeared in while others appeared out of buildings that had mannequins behind plate glass windows. There were more people on the street, bumping each other, sidestepping each other — a complicated dance in and around more carts. And there were vendors hawking food, jewelry, clothes. They hollered, right out in public, not calling livestock but people to buy hot dogs, peanuts, cloth, salves, and creams. Still her ear was drawn to the voices, the many languages.

"They new here, like you. They immigrants," Aunt Patrice spoke, reading Alena's thoughts. "Some from Italy, some from Germany, from Poland and Ireland. Some are Hebrew; some are Catholic; some Protestant, but they all here in this big city, just like you. They looking for the same thing, a new start, freedom to be who they are. And opportunity."

Perhaps they are like me. Alena studied the scene before her. *But they weren't forced to come here against their will for something they haven't done. Without a doubt, most of them don't look like me.*

Up from Chicago's soil burst rows of concrete and cobblestones that bore great buildings of granite, of glass, and of steel. Men and boys drove horses that pulled wagons, *clip-clop, clip-clop,* while other men sped by in motorcars. Cars with flat roofs and open windows puttered by at dizzying speeds — fifteen, even twenty miles an hour.

People, like bees, buzzed from structure to structure, moving up and down the rows, the streets of the "city of broad shoulders." People brash and afraid, overjoyed and anxious, moving to a rhythm, winding, tightening. Occasionally, for Alena, there was a familiar smell when they passed a horse or a vegetable wagon.

For the most part she saw few black-skinned people in the street scenes before her. Alena wondered where they were, if they lived in another section, just like in Mississippi. Maybe some things stayed the same no matter where you went. Were there back entrances to these skyscrapers? Back entrances where people of color entered to buy what they needed or where they entered to take out trash, to mop floors?

Just as suddenly, when they turned, traveling south on State Street, everything changed. The people moving in and out of the buildings were black. Sepia-toned, caramel-colored, cream-colored, biscuit brown, and almost blue. Their hair was kinky, wavy, curly, processed, straight, and almost straight.

The buildings were not so tall here, but still grander than anything Alena had ever seen. She still heard some foreign tongues, and sometimes that Chicago melody, but all in a different cadence and different rhyme, but one she understood. Colored Chicago. Bronzeville. The South Side.

There were men, women, and children. Some that looked like preachers, some like doctors; some like lawyers, some like merchants; some like cooks, factory workers, musicians; and some that looked like maids heading back uptown. There were churches, dance halls, restaurants, liquor stores, cleaners, soul food, and Chinese restaurants all on the same block. Women like deaconesses passed by women like nighttime. Finger-popping men bumped shoulders with men wearing neckties. She saw more colored people doing more things, wearing more possibilities, than she had ever seen.

Alena could not make out their words, not exactly. Just sounds from the man selling vegetables from a cart, the shoe shiner, the Watkins man selling salves and ointments right next to the spices and vanilla extract — but what she heard on the wind, what she smelled in the air, though unfamiliar, was familiar. People at home on their land. What she smelled was the same food of her consolation. Instinctively, without thinking, she sat back in her seat, relaxed. This was their place. She smiled.

Unconsciously, it was a pattern she understood. At home in Mississippi, town and its outskirts north, west, and east of town were inhabited by white folks. Her people were only allowed in for certain things: to serve, to clean, to buy supplies. They returned quickly to their place. If their place was not comfortable, at least it was safe. If they were hungry in their place, at least they were safe, safe from being unwelcome . . . *unless the riders came. Unless someone came with a gun or a rope.*

A deep sigh escaped Alena, and she retreated deeper in thought.

Aunt Patrice turned in her seat, and her movement caught Alena's attention. "It won't be long now, baby," her aunt said softly. "We're almost home. Some people call Chicago the Promised Land. They leaving the South coming here for jobs and new life. I guess in some ways they right. There's jobs and opportunities here we never had in Mississippi. There's more freedom here, in some ways. But just like in God's Promised Land, there's also lots of temptation and still a lot of battles to fight. Some people come expecting gold streets, but find out life is real hard. But we ain't never without hope."

Aunt Patrice smiled through her clouded expression. "Welcome to Chicago."

Six

The car slowed and stopped in front of a brick building.

"We're here, baby! Come on, we're home." Aunt Patrice slid from the car and walked through the doorway under the sign that read, "Bread of Life Mission."

Down the street, a mongrel snapped and snarled at anything near and at anyone that passed it by. It looked as if it might have been broad and handsome once. Now its fur was patchy, rough in places, bare in others. It sat, snapping, biting at the air, its haunches twisted off to the side.

Alena stopped to stare. The animal turned, its eyes fixed on hers and began to walk toward her. It moved past the other people, not noticing them, eyes locked on Alena's eyes. She did not think to be afraid but watched the mangy dog coming toward her. Something about it reminded her of home. Of Cottonball.

The dog continued, still focused. The distance closed. Eight feet from Alena, the animal hesitated as if suddenly afraid. Its shoulders hunkered slightly; it looked right then left. Head down, eyes softened, the dog looked at Alena. It remained still, poised no more than five feet from her, head cocked as if it were deciding.

With no warning, the animal turned, walked at an angle to the other side of the street, and resumed snapping and snarling, not looking back.

For a moment, Alena stared after the beast. "Chicago," she said to herself.

James grabbed the bags and moved toward the building. "You're going to be all right," he said softly, privately, as he passed by Alena.

How would he know? What would make him think he could tell her anything about her life? Why was it any of his business?

Alena stared at everything. At nothing. Her past was too far away to be seen; her present was too unknown for her to imagine a future. She could not even release herself to a sigh.

One foot in front of another, she followed him under the sign into the building, turned left and followed her aunt, then James through another doorway and up stairs that led to a hallway. Past bright colored wallpaper, mahogany wood, and the smell of biscuits, fried chicken, and ham. She focused her eyes on James's back so that she would not cry.

Alena watched how he moved and carried the bags. She was certain that she hated him, just as much as she would hate her new life.

Once directed further upstairs to her room, Alena stepped inside and closed the heavy wooden door. Tears blurred the images around her: the same wallpaper, more dark wood, iron radiators that would produce steam heat in the winter.

She turned her head toward one of two windows, both of which faced the street. Lace curtains framed concrete streets. So far away from home . . . Alena wondered if she would live.

She rubbed her hands across the smooth, almost white paint on her window sill as she remembered the wagon ride, then the train ride that brought her to Chicago. She would not think about her parents. And what about Pearl on the train, on the platform, in the dining car? Would she see him? Could he get her home?

Alone, Alena wept.

Seven

"Come on, baby, before the biscuits get cold."

Her aunt's voice awakened her stomach. Alena was hungry. She must have stood staring out the window longer than she thought. Now she became aware of smells, smells like Mississippi, bidding her to the kitchen.

"This seat is for you," James said to her as she walked into the kitchen, indicating the chair he held for her. "I know you have to be hungry, and your aunt has cooked up just the remedy for what ails you!"

Alena glared. James smiled.

He thinks he'll hold a chair for me, and I'll swoon. Like I would believe he cares. Like he knows me. He just met me. Like he's so handsome, so wonderful I should just fall over and say, I do. I'm so ready to give up my life and live yours. I hate him.

Not even hate and anger, however, could keep her desire away from the food her aunt had prepared.

"James, will you say grace, please."

Alena did not close her eyes but stared at James as he prayed. How different he was from Pearl. Much different. She smiled to herself. Here James sat pretending to be good, to be perfect. *"I do what I want. I take care of myself. I ain't bowing to nobody,"* she could hear Pearl saying as her memories of the women on the platform faded in importance. *"Take care of yourself. Get what you want."* Her smile pulling into more of a smirk, she closed her eyes and bowed her head just before James finished praying. "Amen," they all said together.

"Why don't you two run ahead while I finish up these dishes." Patrice's arms were almost up to the elbows in suds. Her cream-colored apron matched the cabinets and the enamel that covered the sink. "There's still some daylight, and I want you to see the mission, Alena. If you leave now, you'll have time enough to see the newspaper office, too."

Alena opened her mouth to protest, but her aunt cut her off.

"No, I don't want to hear it. You heard what I said. I still know how to get a switch if I have to. You about to be grown, but you ain't grown yet. And really, you ain't gone never be too grown for me to help you remember I'm your aunt." Patrice winked and swatted at Alena with a dish towel. "Go on now, you two. I'll meet you back at the mission."

James showed Alena quickly through the mission. "It's usually not this quiet," he said as he showed her around the kitchen area, the dining area, and meeting/resting areas, all in one great room. "You'll see more tomorrow. But come on, let's go." He held the screen door open for Alena. "Your aunt wants you to see the newspaper."

He blamed it on her aunt, but Alena could see that the excitement was really his.

"It's not very much, not very big. I'm most of the staff," he continued as they walked past other buildings, restaurants, barber shops, a doctor's office, all side by side, some on floors above, some on floors below.

"The printing press doesn't always work. I got it *really* used, but I wanted to be able to print my own, control my own work. Sometimes things get a little tight, but I know I'm doing the right thing. People need this paper. I mean *our* people need this paper. I just feel like I'm supposed to tell the whole, the uncompromised truth, whether people like it or not. It's not always easy, but so far, thank God, I've — *we've* been able to keep it open."

For a moment, Alena forgot. She opened her mouth to join his passion, to tell him how and what she wanted to tell. For a moment she forgot they were in Chicago and that she was supposed to hate James. She looked into the earnestness in his eyes, felt the passion in her chest moving toward him. But the thorns around her heart, the wall of ice around her, stopped the words, froze the feelings before they betrayed her, before she forgot who she was, where she was, and how she got there. Quickly, she looked away.

"It's just a little storefront," James said as he turned the key. "Not much furniture, not much to look at. But it's a start." Excitement flashed on his face as he moved about the room straightening chairs, adjusting levers on the iron printing press. "Want to see how it works?"

"Not really —" she paused — "I'm not interested. I don't know what my aunt told you or what you have planned, but I'm not interested. Not in *anything*," she said pointedly. "You are wasting your time. I'm not interested." She looked without blinking into his eyes.

"Is this a temporary ailment?" James braced his shoulders. His face and voice were calm, a practiced calm.

Alena stared, confused. "What do you mean?"

"I mean, is it temporary? Are you always like this, or is it temporary? Your aunt described this kind, lovely, intelligent, sensitive young woman to me, and I'm still looking for her. If you're who she was talking about, she's been pretty wrong about most of it. I just wanted to know." He took a step toward her.

"I know this has been hard on you, leaving your home and family. Coming here. But you're not the first person to go through it." James paused and took a deep breath. "You're going to be okay."

They stood in silence, Alena searching for words. Outside, an occasional car honked, children laughed, and hurried footsteps moved up and down the street.

"We better get back now." James reached for her elbow.

"Don't *touch* me! Don't you touch me!" Alena jerked her arm away, away from any hand that might try to comfort her, and stumbled backward, almost falling on the press.

Quickly James reached his arms about

her to catch her, then held her for a moment. "You're going to be okay." He breathed reassurance into her hair. "You're going to be okay."

Alena lay her head against his chest and smelled the starch from his shirt. With her eyes closed, his steady heartbeat reassured her. She felt his hand brushing the curls that had escaped her hairpins away from her face. She nuzzled his comforting hand and brushed it with her lips.

Until she remembered.

"I don't need anybody!" She pushed herself away from James. "I can make it by myself. I can take care of myself." Her hands pushed at the tears that tried to fall from her eyes. "Just stay away from me!" She turned to run out the door and almost charged into a young blond-haired man that stood in her path, filling the doorway.

Eight

Alena felt her knees begin to buckle.

Bates.

Same hair. Same eyes.

No, this man was younger, smiling in a way Bates would never smile. But still. He reached his hand toward her. Flustered, Alena ran down the street and through the front door of the mission.

Aunt Patrice turned at the sound of the slamming door. "What's the matter, baby?"

"Nothing, I'm fine."

Her aunt wiped her hands on her apron and started toward Alena. "You don't sound so fine. What's the matter with you, girl?"

Alena opened her mouth to tell her aunt about James, about how rude he was, about how pompous he was, about how holier-than-thou he was, about the white man in the door who looked like he could be Bates's son . . . when suddenly she saw what was before her.

A small blond woman with light-colored

eyes sat not more than ten feet away in a rocking chair, holding a little black child. She kissed his cheek. He wrapped his arms around her neck and laid his head on her shoulder. She continued to kiss him as she carried him — she appeared to be Alena's age, though she was not much bigger than the child she carried — to the back of the room where there was a jar filled with cookies.

"Who is she?" Alena breathed mistrust and disbelief.

"That's Dinah." Patrice smiled in the woman's direction. "She and her brother Jonathan, they are always here, helping out. Whatever they can do." Patrice turned her smile back to Alena. "The Lord sent them here. He spoke, they listened."

"I'm surprised you didn't see Jonathan. He walked down to the office to see if he could catch you two there." Her eyes moved back toward Dinah, and she watched while the girl shared a cookie with the young child. "She's a godsend."

For what seemed like the one hundredth time that day, Alena felt her pulse quicken, her breathing shallow. She froze and stared at the tiny blond girl and the dark-skinned baby.

"There are so many people in need

here." Aunt Patrice looked around at the men, women, children sitting in groups throughout the room. "People that sold everything or never had anything, scraped together whatever they had to come to Chicago. Now lots of them worse off. No jobs, no food, no place to live. It ain't but a few jobs a colored man or woman allowed to get, and it's too many people got to fight over them." She walked back to the sink, back to her work. "They don't want us in they neighborhoods, and they sure ain't building no housing for the colored. So people just here with nothing. They ain't got enough to go back home." Patrice reached her hands into hot, soapy dishwater, squeezed out the rag, and wiped the countertop.

"And I tell you, I don't understand it." She shook her head. "People see it and know it and don't do nothing about it, and then go sit in church on Sunday after they done turned their back on somebody. Shut the door in they face. Saying, *Amen* like that's okay with God. I don't understand it."

Alena had never seen her aunt so indignant. And she'd said it all right in front of Dinah, right out loud. Alena could feel her heart pounding.

"Aunt Patrice!" Alena whispered the warning, nodding toward Dinah.

"Oh, Dinah knows how I feel. I ain't soft-spoken about this. God won't let me be. It ain't got nothing to do with a color, about being white or black. It's about being wrong. I say it out plain." Aunt Patrice nodded her head toward the young woman and child. "Dinah, as quiet as she is, will tell you out loud, too. How you gonna hate, misuse, mistrust, not care about any of God's people? God loves them. If people would come down off their high horse, they would see."

Aunt Patrice reached for a large wooden bowl on the counter, then into a drawer for an equally large wooden spoon. "It ain't about white; it's about wrong, and believe me, wrong don't just belong to white people. While you here in Chicago you gone see white people doing other white people wrong at the same time they doing colored people wrong. You gone see colored people doing other colored people wrong, Chinese people doing other Chinese people wrong, Spanish people doing other Spanish people wrong, Jewish people doing other Jewish people wrong. God don't like none of it." She reached into the cabinets above her for a large can. She removed the lid with a yank, reached inside, and scooped out several measures of flour before she shoved the can back on the shelf.

Alena tried to whisper, outrage in her tone. "But you can't compare what colored people might do to what *they* did to J.C."

"I know it might not seem that way in our eyes, but God hates every little speck of it. He hated it when the Egyptians did it to the children of Israel. And He hated it when the children of Israel did it to Moses' colored wife. You know you heard it all your life: It's not the people He hates, it's the sin." Aunt Patrice bent and reached in a lower cabinet for another large can, this one containing lard.

"It's just right here and now white people got more opportunity to be in control, to say who can and who can't, to hold on to power. But I'm telling you, God is gone get tired of it. People just gonna keep on until He say, 'That's it!' " Her aunt used the spoon to scoop out an ample amount of the fat. She threw each scoop in the bowl as though she were also *tired of it.*

Alena's mouth hung open. She did not know her aunt this way . . . had never known that she felt this way, had never known that she and her aunt shared similar feelings about injustice.

Patrice sighed. "But it ain't everybody doing wrong. God's got His people. Some people listening."

Alena watched her aunt look back at the blond-haired girl, then focus her attention between her niece and the bowl in front of her. "Everybody ain't passing by Samaria."

"Passing by Samaria?"

"In the Bible the Lord gave a charge to His disciples. He told them to spread the good news. First to Jerusalem — to they own people, they families — then to Judea, to people like *them,* not they neighbors people that come from where they come from and think like them." Using a fork, Aunt Patrice began to cut the lard into the flour, mashing and mashing until the mixture in the bowl resembled elongated, beaded crumbs.

A small child tugged on Alena's skirt, asking for water. Alena fetched the water and helped the child drink it. She rubbed the little boy's head and sent him back to play with the other children. As she walked back toward her aunt, the woman continued as though they had not missed a beat.

"Then come the hard part. Next, God told His children to go to Samaria, to people they hate, people they don't understand. They live right with them, but they don't get along. They think they too good for the Samaritans. Then, after that, they could spread the good news to the world. But you know, it just seem like to me people want to jump right over that Samaria part. They don't want to spread no good news, no blessings to people that is they Samaritans."

Alena watched her aunt clap her hands together.

"Um-um-um. Trying to do too much at one time. Talking too much, mashing too hard." Aunt Patrice shook her head. "I forgot the baking powder. Mercy."

Aunt Patrice pulled the canister of baking powder from a cupboard and sprinkled it on the mixture, then tried to cut it in with the fork. "Everybody ain't passing by though," she said as she mixed and mumbled something to herself about hoping the biscuits would come out right. "Jonathan and Dinah are faithful," she continued. They just like James. They come here and work from their hearts. Dinah comes here and does what other people would think is beneath her. She counts it a privilege to help those that needs help. I guess other people just don't understand."

Alena looked at the girl across the room with distrust. What was her aunt thinking?

"Jonathan is always right there with James." Aunt Patrice picked up some of the mixture with a fork, tested the consistency. "Running hisself ragged trying to help with that paper. And don't you think people ain't mad at him. Lotsa colored people don't trust him and wonder what he's up to. And white people hate him cause he telling the truth. Say he betraying his race when he tell the truth. White folks can't deny it when he say it. He know the truth. He *been there* and he can get in places to hear what's going on where we can't go. He and Dinah, they was born with silver spoons in they mouths — had everything. They family is mad, but they just keep on doing what is right." Aunt Patrice poked at the biscuit mixture. "But, you'll see. You'll figure it out for yourself." Alena's aunt frowned down at the bowl. "I sure hope this works."

"So, you made it back safely?"

Alena started at James's voice behind her. Listening to her aunt, she had forgotten about him and the man — the one who could be Bates's son — in the doorway.

"You left before you could meet Jonathan."

Alena turned to glare at James. He stood with his arms about Jonathan's shoulders. In that moment, Alena was not sure which of the two she despised more. Bates had followed her to Chicago, it seemed. For the millionth time, she wished she had a way back home.

Nine

"You got anything to spare?"

Pearl glared at the man standing in front of him. "Man, you better leave me alone! Don't even look at me. This *my* money." He took several bills from his pocket and shook them at the beggar. "This my money. I made it. Don't none of it belong to you. Get you a job!" He cursed the man.

"I-I been looking." The man cowered. His eyes shifted left and right as if he were looking for help. He focused on Pearl for a brief moment, then looked down. "Ain't nothing out here. You know how it is."

"No, I don't. You shiftless, lowlife, beggin', sack of . . ." Pearl watched as the man crumpled inward. "You trifling, ignorant, country Negroes running to the big city, to the promised land. You too lazy and too ignorant to work, so now you want to beg me for mine. I don't think so, buddy. You gone have to wait for some other fool to mooch on. I made mine."

Pearl took a step closer to the man.

"Can you spell that, you ignorant fool? M-I-N-E. *Mine*. I worked for it. Now I'm gone spend it!" Pearl could feel his victory smile settling in as the man started to stumble backward.

"Get away from me, man. You stink. Here!" Pearl threw a quarter on the ground. He turned his back, smiled, walked eight more paces, paused, and turned into the doorway of his favorite bar.

He closed his eyes and breathed deeply, pleased. He could smell summer on the way. Pearl turned his head to look back where the beggar had stood. He laughed out loud one time and stepped into the bar.

Leaning against the smoothly polished mahogany bar, Pearl watched himself down a whiskey, straight. He smoothed his hair and set his shoulders. Everything was in place.

He liked the burn as the whiskey went down, and he liked the way he looked.

He rubbed his hand over his chest, then his taut stomach. He sighed at the feel of the silk against his fingertips. Pearl felt good in Chicago. He liked being on the train, but he liked Chicago nightlife even more.

Deac was probably still on the train or at

a prayer meeting somewhere. Old fool. Fussing over that girl, Alena. Miss Mississippi. Pearl laughed to himself as he continued watching his image in the mirror. The old fool had kept going on about her. Well, what was so special about her? All women were the same.

"Leave her alone, Pearl."

That's what Deac had said. Pearl smiled. He would leave her alone, all right. He would make sure he found her, and he would dry that wetness behind her ears. It would be easy. He could tell from watching her on the train.

She couldn't read him. Miss Miss was seeing what she wanted to see. He could tell. She hadn't even recognized the smile. His victory smile. She hadn't known it was a game. A game he liked to win, a game that was almost too easy. He had done it before with other women, and it had worked with Miss Miss, too. He thought about the train ride. It had been the same routine: Look interested, look like he was listening, and Miss Mississippi couldn't tell that his mind had moved on to bigger, tougher game. She would be easy. He smiled again at his image in the mirror.

Soon . . .

Right now, he had other business.

With no movement of his head, he watched the mirror and observed what was going on at both ends of the bar. It was dark. The music was soft, accented by soft-spiked laughter, male and female. Perfume hung in the air. He looked ahead into the mirror and rubbed his sideburns. In the reflection he saw that several women were admiring him, including one at each end of the bar. Yeah, Miss Mississippi would have to wait, little church girl. He didn't have time to teach anybody now. He had other business.

He chose the one on the right, whose hair was dyed almost-blond. He mouthed hi to her reflection in the mirror, smiled, then turned and moved toward her end of the bar. It was going to be a good night.

Ten

"You are fine," she told him.

Pearl laughed, pleased. It was what he expected. They exchanged glances and conversation, happy for the mutual admiration. Pearl felt her eyes acknowledge the beauty of his hair, his smile, his movements.

In the low light, he sat on the side of the woman's bed facing the mirror on the wall. His hands smoothed his chest muscles. He checked his triceps, then checked his face for signs of early stubble. In between, he watched the woman. He could not remember her name.

She gazed up at him, eyes wide with appreciation. "You originally from Chicago?"

Pearl smiled. "Aw, baby, you know ain't nobody originally from Chicago. We all here looking for the same thing, a piece of the pie. I'm like you, baby, don't give me none of that pie in the sky stuff. Put my piece on my plate now." He looked at her for a moment, then his eyes went back to his image in the mirror.

"I ain't originally from Chicago either, but I been here a long time. Since before the war. I know my way 'round." She laughed.

"Oh, I'm sure you do," Pearl laughed as her hands began to journey up his arms. "I'm sure you know a whole lot." Their breathing deepened. Their pupils dilated.

"You know anything about a mission?" Pearl asked as they began to entangle. "Run by some woman named Patsy or something like that. Or Teresa, or something," Pearl watched her hand rub his shoulder.

"You must mean Miss Patrice." The woman gazed up at him, hunger in her eyes. "Oh yeah. Everybody knows her —"

Pearl's eyes flickered. *Bingo! Information about Miss Miss. This was really too easy, just too easy.*

"More holy, holy and pie in the sky, and you know that ain't my thing! But she all right," the woman continued, lost in her hunger. "She do a lot of good. She help a lot of people. But, you know, what she talkin ain't what I want to hear." She rubbed his shoulders. "You like that?"

"Yeah, baby, that's fine." He looked at

his reflection in the mirror and watched her hands on his arms. "You know where the mission is?"

"What's on your mind, daddy?" She pulled her head back to look into Pearl's face. "You planning on getting saved?" The woman laughed, looked like she was searching his eyes. "Just let me know. You a choirboy on the side? You sure don't look like no choirboy."

"I got to explain everything to you? You confused about something? Just let me know now. I can get on up out of here." He jerked his shoulders out of her hands, turned his eyes away. "Lotsa women don't ask no questions. That's what I want. If you ain't that, let me know. And don't call me no daddy. I ain't your daddy. I ain't nobody's daddy, and I didn't care too much for the one I had."

"I'm sorry, baby. You know I didn't mean nothing. I just like to play sometime is all. Don't be mad."

Pearl relaxed his shoulders back under her fingertips. "Don't worry about it. I just want to make sure you know where we stand . . . Miss Chicago." His eyes focused on hers, and he pulled the woman closer to him. "So now where you say the mission is?"

"On State Street. It ain't far from here." She closed her eyes and sighed in between sentences as his fingertips traced a line up her arm. "It's a big old brick building. The sign out front say something like 'Bread of Life.' "

"Um-mm. You sure got a lot of information for such a sassy girl. You sure you ain't been there? You sure you ain't been trying to get saved?" He laughed and took one more look just before he turned out the light.

Pearl woke early and slipped into his clothes and out the door. After asking directions, he walked the six blocks to State Street. This early in the morning, it was still kind of hot outside. Not many months ago, he would have seen his breath puffing and curling in early morning air. Now, instead, the water came up like fog from the cobblestones beneath his feet. The mist circled around his legs and disappeared, it seemed, up his pant legs. It was the last moments of dark and everything, just about, was still quiet.

There was something about this time he liked. Nothing around but some cats fighting somewhere. His shoes clicked lightly on the dewy bricks beneath his feet.

He stopped for a second in front of what seemed to be a small newspaper office and, cupping his hands around his eyes, attempted to look inside.

The street lamps made the darkened windows mirrors. Without thinking, he lifted his black fedora and smoothed his hair. A smell distracted him. It came from farther down the street, so he started walking again until he stood outside the mission.

Light from the windows reached out into the surrounding darkness. He stood just beyond it. Biscuits, that was the smell. He watched a woman far back in the large room wielding a rolling pin. *That must be her aunt. . . .*

Pearl watched others moving back and forth, wiping tables, stacking dishes, stirring pots. Then Alena came into view.

He watched her move slowly, eyeing the others. While they moved quickly, it seemed to take forever for her to place a stack of bowls. One young man spoke to Alena. Her facial expression, and his in response, said that her reply was less than friendly. Pearl smiled. The man looked to be a square: white rolled-up sleeves, suspenders. Miss Mississippi was still green, but obviously a little something had rubbed off on her.

Pearl thought of the things he would have said to her if she had disrespected him, but the square seemed to mostly ignore Alena. Pearl could see her standing, staring after the guy.

Pearl smiled in the darkness. Miss Miss still had that little lost sheep look. It would be easy, almost too easy.

Alena moved to the window and looked outside into the early morning darkness. The smell of biscuits made her think about her mother. She wondered about her father, if he were harvesting fall crops. Looking to the edge of the light, she wished for Mississippi and her parents' arms. Her hands went to her cheeks as she thought about J.C., then Bates. Turning, she stared at Jonathan, his blond hair, his blue eyes. He smiled and nodded to her.

Alena hated who Jonathan represented. Every time she looked at him, she saw Bates. Everyone knew Bates had murdered J.C. or had something to do with J.C.'s murder. Alena looked coldly at Jonathan and turned away.

And now here she was. Mississippi was so far away. All she still had of her home was the pain. The memories stirred that pain, but she held on, letting the hurt press deeper, deeper.

I am alone.

Out of the corner of her eye, she watched James work, organizing tables. So much in control, so confident . . . so like and yet unlike Pearl. Pearl's image came to mind. Where was he?

Pearl leaned against the lamppost and smiled, pleased. A lonely, unhappy woman was easy prey. Almost too easy. But just almost. He laughed. Miss Miss was pretty. Of course, he had seen much prettier women, but the church girl thing, the good girl, the innocence, the keep-your-hands-off-of-it all made her exciting. Always a dare, messing with the good, like could he get *it* or would *it* get him. She was ripe. He would just have to figure out the right time to steal over the fence and get her.

Pearl watched for a few more minutes, then walked away quickly before daylight reached the spot where he stood.

Eleven

Dearest Evelyn and Amos,

I pray that this letter find you safe and blessed.

Alena is doing fine. Most times the home-sickness on her is so thick you could spread it between two pieces of bread. But I don't bother her. Not just yet, anyway. I'm trying to give her a little time to find her way.

There so much hurt for her, for any young person to have to deal with, and she's just trying to cover it with anger. I'm being patient because, good Lord knows, we've all had our hard times.

I think it's good for her to be around the other young people. They are such sweet-spirited, hard-working people. And every once in a while, I catch her looking at James. He is a fine young man, and he has been very patient with her. He's not pushy with her, but he's not a pushover either.

She still tries to act like she doesn't like him, but I think she's acting just a little too much.

Well, I'm fixing to go to bed. You all know I still love my sleep. Sorry, I didn't get to include any sports clips, Amos. But I will make up for it. Somebody just brought me an Afro-American, *and when I get through reading it, I will send you the clips from that paper, too.*

You two pray for me, and I'll pray for you. Write back soon.

Love,
Patrice

Evelyn refolded her sister's letter. "We did the right thing, I know we did the right thing, Amos." They sat at the dinner table. Evelyn took turns with her husband looking toward their daughter's room. They'd repeated this ritual every meal since Alena's departure. The room they sat in was gray. The food on their plates did not taste the same, did not smell the same.

Amos looked at his wife, then looked away, as though he didn't want the woman he loved to see bitterness when she looked into his eyes. "I know, but how come right don't always feel good? How come if we right, we don't have our baby here with us? How come we poor and sad and lonely, and the ones to blame riding high and mighty? How come we sitting here crying,

142

and the sheriff is riding around like he in the right? He ain't had to send away the children he love. I see him walking around like he the king of the world. It's *my* baby gone. It's that boy J.C. is gone. Ain't nothin happen to Bates, and you know he had something to do with it."

"Amos, this don't do no good." Evelyn reached for her husband's hand. "You know we got to trust God. He been takin' care of us all our lives, and He is still takin' care of us. We can't do nothin' to bring J.C. back, but our daughter is alive. And it ain't over, Amos. You know that. It ain't over till God says it's over. I don't know when. It may not be in our lifetime, but God says what's done in the darkness is gone come to the light."

Amos filled his chest with air, then breathed it out, less like a sigh than a cleansing. "I know, Evelyn. I know."

She squeezed his hand. "Our baby is safe, ain't nothing can hurt her where she is."

"Where you off to, Mr. Hyde?" Deac asked the young porter.

Pearl smiled and admired himself in the mirror. A good-looking man if he had to say so himself.

"It's a lotta places to go in Chicago." Pearl watched himself touch his face. "A lot of women that need me to talk to 'em. They lonely, unloved. And you know *I'm* the *one,* old man. Your fire might be gone out, that old wick sputtering —" he laughed — "but I still got a whole lot of heat left. Mm-mm-mm, I love Chicago."

"You just watch you don't burn yourself up." The old man laughed. "Hey —" his voice changed — "you ain't planning on bothering that little girl, are you?"

Pearl stopped preening and looked at Deac, frowning. "I hate when you do that, like you inside my mind like some kind of who-do man. What's it to you, anyway? She wanna see me — told me she wanted to see me and told me everything she knew about where she was gone be. She want Pearl, just like all the rest." He turned back to the mirror. "And it ain't none of your business, old man. Just cause you old and stale don't mean I got to be. You just go on to church and mind your own business. You have your fun — church on a Saturday night — and I'm gone have mine!"

Deac's response was soft. "Time gone run out for you, young man. I hope it ain't before you get a chance to get things right."

Pearl turned to laugh, but no sound came out. *Old fool! Old fool!* Always talkin' like he knew him. All that prayin', like that was going to stop him. Deac always actin' like he was his daddy, like he could stop him from doing what he wanted to do. Well, not Deac or his prayin' had stopped him last time; wouldn't stop him this night, either.

Pearl grabbed his hat and walked.

Twelve

James and Jonathan walked quietly together. No words. Focused on their mission. At Twenty-first Street, the edge of the colored community, James shortened his stride. Jonathan lengthened his. Still no words. The routine was practiced, precise, just as they had done it many times before.

Jonathan dressed in the uniform of trust: suit, high-starched collar, tie, vest with watch fob. James, in the workingman's uniform: dungarees bearing the ghosts of past machine oil stains, frayed collars and cuffs. He slumped his shoulders and bowed his head to finish the costume.

The two walked, separated by fifty paces. Within twenty minutes, they reached J. Riggings Steelworks. Jonathan stood knocking.

The door creaked open.

"Any work?" Jonathan made his voice solid, firm. "I'm checking for two of my men."

"Uh, what kind of work you looking for,

sir?" The man wiped his mouth with his plaid shirtsleeve, straightened his pants, and tucked in his shirt.

"Just something a man can live on, a decent wage to support a family. Professional type work, say, for an engineer or architect."

"Well, we always got room for able-bodied, ambitious men, sir." The man turned and nodded to his friends inside the gray, weathered shack. They in turn rose to their feet, preening, trying to look busy.

"When you want 'em to start? We got all kinds of places we can use somebody like that. You want to come inside and talk some?"

"No, thank you." Jonathan drew up in a manner appropriate to his supposed status. "I'll just give my men your name." He reached into his inside pocket and extracted a small notepad and fountain pen. "Let me see. J. Riggings, that's the name of your company." Jonathan's mannerisms mimicked that of the men who had raised him. "And what is your name?"

He wrote the name and shook the hand the man extended to him. "Very well," he said with the same practiced lack of enthusiasm. "Good day."

What was it that caused the difference?

Jonathan turned his back and walked away, disappointment coming over him in waves. He'd hoped that at the end of the day his friend would have met with the same responses, with friendly greetings and accommodating handshakes. But experience told him not so.

All along the dock there were men working. Working to feed their families. To build dreams. Most working just to survive day to day.

The smell of the waterfront rose up to meet him. Chicago was a growing town. Steel skeletons were being erected all along the city skylight. The El entwined itself further in and around the city. Each day more and more trains moved in and out of the city carrying the products of commerce and men with dreams.

While he walked, Jonathan watched the men's faces — the reactions, the changes when they noticed him. Men looked down or stepped to the side to give him more room.

Was it his clothes? his haircut? the way he walked? the ring on his finger? What caused the men to tip their hats? To move quickly to their feet, to straighten their clothes as if he, who had no power, had influence over them.

It was not respect, for just beneath the surface lay a grain of contempt. Small, subtle looks told him, insolently, that he was not better than they. He might be richer, but he was not stronger, not tougher. Yet, they still almost bowed to him. Was it his hair color? His eyes? Did his blue blood show?

Maybe it was not him. Maybe it was something they wanted, something they thought he might be able to do for them. Maybe it was fear. Or maybe it was greed.

What if his clothes were different? What if he wore work boots and dungarees? What if he knocked on their doors standing beside the friend that now walked behind him? How would they receive him then? What if his skin was just a little darker? Jonathan thought of one of the sons of his father's cook. The boy was fair, just a little darker than he. What if that were his color?

Why was he chosen for this life, for this color? Jonathan fought back shame, guilt over his privilege and thought of his friend. How must James feel? Was it worth this? Worth the way he felt? Was the story worth it? Would he and his friend someday push the boundary too far?

The questions pecked away at dark hidden places in his mind, places tender to truth's touch. Places guarded, even in the mind of truth seekers, by fear and dread. As if to stop the pricking, the pecking, Jonathan shook his head to clear his thoughts, to preserve himself, and pressed on to the next door.

Not far behind his friend, James tapped quietly at the side door of the shack that housed J. Riggings Steelworks. "Any work, mister?"

"No, uncle. We ain't got no work here for you. Where you from anyway, boy?"

"I've just come up here trying to take care of my family, sir. I have a degree and experience in engineering. Don't you have any work I can do, sir?"

The man's eyes sparked. "Now, boy, you don't want me to take food out of some man's mouth to give you work, do you, uncle? And you have some mighty uppity thoughts. Engineer. Boy, I know you ain't qualified for nothing like that. You need to quit making up stories if you're really trying to get a job. When did a boy like you have time to go to college? You thinkin' mighty big of yourself. Engineer."

The man smirked. "That would put you in charge of somebody like me. Have a white man like me calling you *boss*. You are dreamin' or crazy."

The man leaning out of the doorway spit out the side of his mouth onto the ground. "Maybe some sweepin', some dish washin' somewhere, boy. But ain't no construction jobs for you, especially not engineering —"

James listened for the man's inflections, tried to figure out what side of Chicago the man came from. His mind searched for distractions, something to block the man's words.

"Not here. Not nowhere near here, I believe. Maybe you be better off just shufflin' on back home. Ain't that right, boys?" The man turned back, speaking into the shack, laughing with his friends.

As the man turned, James noticed a tender spot on the underside of his jaw. A sweet spot. A spot that might remove the sting of the offense he'd just experienced. His fist on that spot might make it all better. His right hand twitched.

Instead, he turned and walked away, the men's laughter pelting his back. It could have been worse, he consoled himself. Sometimes they threw things.

James walked, measuring each step.

Fighting against humiliation and anger. Reminding himself he was playing a role, doing research. Research for a newspaper story. This wasn't who he was. Wasn't his real life. But sometimes . . .

Sometimes it was hard to tell the difference. The wounds didn't feel any less painful.

Thirty minutes ago, he and his friend walked together, shared hopes and dreams, were equal. Now they walked apart, separated by the sinfulness of men's natures. Why was one man worthy because of color and another man not.

Who were these men who thought themselves superior simply based on the color of their skin? Men who had less education than he but thought themselves superior based on an accident of birth. Men who thought their welfare and the welfare of their families mattered more than his welfare and that of his kin.

He listened to his feet on the pavement and the beating of his heart. Both rhythms had increased in pace, while his breathing, turned shallow, provided accents on the beats. Sighing, he slowed his pace.

This is an exercise, nothing more. Fact-finding. It was not about him. It was not personal. They did not see him, didn't know who he was. They were not offending him, only the character he portrayed.

Sometimes his forced self-encouragement helped. At other times, like now, it rang shallow. Or it did not come soon enough to defend his heart. Sometimes the stinging, the insults, came too quickly even for him to pretend that the words, the actions, the pain did not injure his manhood. His image of himself as a man. Too quick to stop his wondering why.

Why has God chosen me? Singled me out. Why? He seldom had days when it was not an issue. *Why am I crazy enough to keep putting myself through this.* Was it worth it? Did the men who behaved this way have families? Wives? Children? Did they go to church? Did they hope? Did they fear? Did they love? Did they wonder about him? Had he fought near them in the war? Had their blood mingled on the battlefield? Had one of his bullets spared their lives? Why, now, no jobs, no shelter for him? What changed since the world war?

Bitterness and Anger danced about him. "God is good," James whispered and the two fled. "Worth it," he said when the questions and doubts filled his head and sought to take his breath. "Worth it," he said.

Has it been too long? Have the receivers and the givers been bound so long they cannot recognize their bondage? He shook his head. *It may take some time.* Surely though, in twenty years — no more than fifty — this would be behind them all.

"Who will go for us?" pain-filled voices whispered, both from his past and from a future he could not see.

"Here am I, Lord, send me . . ."

James whispered the words, squeezing his insides together, and walked on. *It will be a good story. A good front-page story for the first edition. Someone's mind will be delivered.*

The thought was enough. For now.

Jonathan walked on, only minutes from the next site, hoping the next foreman would not be a respecter of persons. His stomach tightened, however, braced for the next disappointment.

He looked up and back, briefly, in his friend's direction. He would have to remind him again. Sometime soon, maybe next month, they needed to target the beach area.

Alena and Dinah walked south along State Street, past stores and beauty shops — beauty shops with iron hot combs used for pressing hair straight instead of perms used to give hair curl. Past churches where choirs practiced and pianists played stanzas and hymns driven by rhythms of memory. The two young women had already delivered ten dinners. Only one left to go.

And in a place where there was no music, should have been no music, children fought for it. Made rhymes, jumped cadences with their feet accented by ropes slapping the pavement, by hands clapping, slapping in time.

From windows, mothers and grandmothers sang "Precious Lord" and "Amazing Grace" up through tenement floors to God's ear bowed low. Victrolas played from wealthier homes and from dance halls, loud enough to bless those passing by. Out of windows, out of doors, Noble Sissle sang,

See him marchin' along
Oh, hear him hummin' a song
Watch that baby throw out his chest —
    whoa, boy!
See them medals pinn'd on his breast
Lord love him!
I'm so happy and proud
I just feel like shoutin' out loud:

My honey — come, come to your mammy
My choc'late soldier Sammy boy.

And the ropes kept turning, kept turning, kept turning even while hope fought for breath.

Dinah was leading. Alena did not like the idea that she did not know where she was going. Her displeasure showed in the line knit between her eyebrows, and occasionally in the way one eyebrow would lift in annoyance while the other one lowered. The two only talked when necessary.

Focusing on how much she disliked the other girl — the way she walked, the color of her hair, the way she spoke — Alena didn't notice the change in scenery until it was over. She chided herself for not paying more attention to street names, to direction in case Dinah should leave her. Now here she was, more street lights, broader concrete sidewalks, bigger houses, broader lawns, obviously closer to the invisible line that separated white and black Chicago. "Where are we anyway?"

Dinah looked at Alena, then turned her head away without responding.

Alena could feel her jaw muscles tighten. "What are you so angry about?"

"*What* did you just ask me?" Dinah

stopped, still. "You didn't just ask me what I'm angry about? Not you that walks around like the world owes you something? Not you?"

"Listen, Dinah —"

"No, *you* listen. You walk around here like everyone owes you something. Owes you an apology. Like we all lynched your friend. Well, I don't owe you anything. And I'm not going to apologize. I won't do it."

Alena's eyes narrowed; she could feel her shoulders tensing. "Don't you even bring up J.C.! Don't let his name come from your mouth. He was a good person. He didn't hurt anybody."

Dinah, chin up, took a short step closer. "You expect me to apologize for something, to be sorry for something that I didn't even do. I didn't even know about. What have I got to do with J.C.?"

"Don't you say his name. Don't you say his name. You say it like he was nobody. Like he didn't matter. Like he was nobody's son. Well, he was somebody's son. I know his mama. And he was my friend. *Mine*. Not just nobody. And somebody ought to care. Somebody ought to know about it. It shouldn't pass. He shouldn't pass like nothing, like nobody."

Alena beat her chest as she raged. "He

was *mine*. All my life. I knew him all my life. Somebody ought to know. Somebody. Not just pass away like nothing. Like it doesn't matter because his skin was black. He was *mine!*"

Dinah stared back. Paused. "That may very well be, but I didn't hurt him. I didn't do it. I didn't even know him. I'm not responsible." The two girls stood glaring at each other.

"Somebody is."

"Well, *I'm* not." The words seemed to squeeze from Dinah's pores. "I'm doing all I can. I do more than you. I do more than most of you. And I'm not going to take the blame for all of this. I didn't start it. And I'm trying. Why don't you point at the ones who did it instead of pointing at me? How much do you expect me to pay?"

"I don't know." Alena paused and looked at the girl in front of her. "I don't know. But just because you come down here and work at the mission, that doesn't make it all better. It doesn't make it go away."

Dinah's face was bright red. "Why not?"

"I don't know why not." Frustrated, Alena looked around herself for the answer. "I just feel like you come here to do your part, to do good among the *coloreds*, to take away the guilt."

158

Dinah sucked in her breath. "I —"

"No! Let me finish. You come here to put a bandage on the wound, like on one of the kids. Only this is not like one of the kids. We didn't get hurt just because we fell down or didn't look where we were going. Something happened to us. Something keeps happening to us. Somebody is wounding us. And you know who they are."

Alena looked around, still searching. "Maybe if you tried, you could make them stop or make them . . . or talk to them. But you won't because you keep telling yourself that you are not responsible. It's not your fault. You keep pointing the finger at us like, 'Why do you keep falling down?' Like you are mad because we keep falling down when you see with your own eyes that somebody pushed us."

Dinah closed her eyes, shook her head. "This is ridiculous. You just want somebody to feel sorry for you. You want somebody else to make it all better. Well, who makes it better for me? Why is your life any different than mine? I work as hard as you do. I have disappointment, too. Why is your life any different?"

"Because it is! You come down here every day by choice. I see what you are doing. I see you with the children. And I see on your face what you think about how I work."

Dinah raised her hand to interrupt, and Alena quickly cut her off. "Don't stop me!" And even as she spoke, a part of her mind acknowledged that this could not have happened in her home in Mississippi. Not in her town where some men drank from fountains while other men could not. Not in her former world where old men bowed their heads, said "yes, sir" and "mister" to boys less than half their age.

Never would she dare to argue with a white woman. Never. Certainly not as equals on the sidewalk in broad daylight. Some man would have inserted himself to stop her insolence. To snatch her up and teach her a lesson.

Even in other parts of Chicago some heads would have turned, would have put an end to this. If they were not in her part of town, if Dinah were not known in the community.

Alena continued. "You don't work as hard as me — most times, you work harder. But for all your work, I don't see you doing anything I couldn't do. I don't see you stopping the oil man from charging my Aunt Patrice more for her oil than what he charges white women where you live."

People passed by, giving them wide berth, staring ahead, looking away, as if the two young women of contrasting hues did not exist.

"I don't see you making the bread man be more fair to my Aunt Patrice. He comes to the mission to do her a favor, all right. Bringing that old bread, some of it molded. Then he wants her to pay him something! Money for something he would throw away. He don't care that she's trying to stretch nothing to feed all those people. What does he care? They're just colored people. He wants him some money. And you know he wouldn't think of selling that old bread to a white woman. Would he take it to your mama's house? And he sure wouldn't try to make her pay for what he considers garbage. But he don't care about Aunt Patrice. She just another colored woman."

Dinah's face contorted somewhere between pleading and anger. "What am I supposed to do? I didn't make the rules. I can't change the world. I'm not that man."

"But you won't even say anything to him. You won't even let him know you see him. You won't even try. You know he

161

won't listen to me, but he might listen to you. You won't even try though. And I ask myself, 'Why is that?' "

Alena's hand moved to smooth her hair. The Chicago breeze, the last of the spring breezes, blew between the two young women. The current lifted her hair, curled it, tangled it, kinked it from the loose braid and ribbon she had hoped would keep it in place. Funny how at moments like this when she needed everything focused, funny how hair, a coat button, a shoe-string, food on her teeth, something would betray her, distract her.

Dinah's hair betrayed her, too. Curls lifting blond in the wind, some strands almost white. She swatted at the pieces, irritated. Her eyes — blue irises sur-rounded by watery pink betrayed her, too. "Why do you hate me?"

Traffic continued moving by.

"I don't hate you!" Alena forced her voice to lower. "I don't hate you, but you can go home. You can take off your apron and go home. And when you get there, all your friends and family are safe inside, safe in bed." She spread her hands. "My friends are not safe. My family is not safe. You ain't lost nobody. You don't know how it feels. You ain't even got to worry about it.

162

I've lost everything, and I can't even go home."

"But that is not my fault. I didn't make the world. What do you want me to do?"

More air blew between them. Blew their hair, blew their skirts not far above their ankles. After what seemed eternity, Alena, all the air gone out of her, answered.

"I don't know."

Worn by their conflict, the two moved silently to deliver the last meal before dark overtook them.

Thirteen

"Alena, I got something else for you." Aunt Patrice smiled and then motioned for Alena to come to her. "The print shop could use a good scrubbing. You take the bucket and mop and get the scrub brush and some rags and go on down there and work for a while."

Aunt Patrice fanned her hands in the general direction of the print shop. "James and Jonathan away working on stories and making deliveries so won't be nobody there to bother you. Go on now while it's plenty daylight."

Alena thought of other things she would rather do. She looked at her aunt, nodded, and gathered the items. She wanted to do lots of things, but being disobedient to Aunt Patrice wasn't one of them.

Once outside the mission, she walked quickly down the concrete sidewalk. When she reached the print shop door, she turned the key Aunt Patrice had given her in the lock, which needed oil, and stepped into the small silent office. There wasn't much in the room. Nothing unnecessary. But what was there seemed too big for the space, seemed to crowd it.

There were two big desks, second or thirdhand like everything else. How had they gotten them through the door? Even beyond that, how had they gotten the presses inside? Big hunks of oiled metal. Maybe they brought them inside in parts. Or maybe they set the desks and all into the shell of the building and then added the front wall.

Alena was grateful for the time alone. Time without guards. In between sweeping and halfhearted mopping, she explored. Buttons, cranks, papers in boxes . . . Conveniently, she mopped and scrubbed herself, but not to the doorway. She scrubbed, surrounded by the eye-opening, clean smell of ammonia, until the only dry place for her was sitting at James's desk.

Without thinking, she placed a sheet of paper on the desk in front of her. She touched the pens lying on the desk as if they were gold, as if she were sneaking to touch precious instruments. She opened the ink bottle and dipped in a pen. She breathed deeply the sickening sweet smell of the blue-black ink, looked at the liquid on the tip of the pen. Alena could never quite remember which flower the ink smelled like.

She wiped the excess ink on the side of the bottle and began to write. First, her name, the date . . . then words began to flow. Words about Mississippi, about J.C., about Sheriff Bates. Alena forgot time and place.

"Well, my, my, my. If it ain't Miss Mississippi."

Alena gasped and then froze when the man stepped into the room.

"What's the matter, Miss Miss? You act like you seein' a ghost. It ain't no ghost, baby. It's me, Pearl."

He moved into the room like he knew it, like it was his. Something was wrong with how he just walked in, how he invaded the space — but that feeling was overwhelmed by larger feelings Alena had. It was anxiety. It was threat. It was danger. It was excitement. It was intimidation. Her synapses delayed, and though she jumped to her feet, she felt like she was rising, pushing through molasses.

"You still look good, Mississippi, for a green country girl."

Her hands flew to her hair, sure it had frizzed, snapped out of place.

Pearl continued into the room, closing the space between them. "It wasn't easy finding you, Miss Miss. I thought sure you would give Pearl a hug."

Alena's hands moved to straighten something invisible on the desk. Instead, she knocked the ink bottle to the floor.

The intruder laughed out loud. "You are happy to see me, ain't you, baby?" Like a tiger stalking, toying with his prey, he moved closer while Alena, flustered, quickly tried to clear the ink before it stained.

"You know, Deac been telling me I ought to stay away from you, leave you alone. He been praying against me. But, you see, I don't think that old fool got enough juice to keep me away from you. And you don't want me to stay away. You wanted me to find you, didn't you? Seems like I can hear you, 'specially at night, calling me. You missed me, didn't you, Miss Miss?"

Pearl bent over Alena where she worked on all fours. She could smell his aftershave, smell his breath . . . feel his warmth and his hand on her back in the same place as when they were on the train.

"Say my name, Miss Miss."

It's almost too easy, old man. Pearl let a

smile tip his lips. *Almost too easy — and that old fool was supposed to be praying.*

"Didn't you miss me, baby?" Pearl moved his hands to Alena's wrists to lift her from scrubbing to a kneeling position. "Didn't you miss me?" He wooed Alena to confess.

"Yes."

A small quiet word, the first she had uttered since he stepped through the door.

Almost too easy. "I didn't think to find you in this place. So much for 'they can't make me write; I won't ever write,' " he mocked her.

"I, uh, my aunt told me to clean . . . I mean, she . . . I mean I-I wasn't . . . I'm not writing!" Alena jerked her hands from Pearl's. The ink that remained continued soaking into the floor.

"Oh, don't get mad, Miss Miss. I ain't trying to stop nothing. I can't make you do nothing. I ain't got no papers on you." Pearl laughed, then abruptly switched tones. His tone became more seductive, more supplicating. "I just been thinking about you. I can't get you off my mind."

He toyed with her. "Why don't you have anything to say? Your aunt tell you not to talk to men like me? You can't talk? Too young? A little girl?" Pearl watched her eyes, saw her fear, her uncertainty, but spoke the opposite. "No, you are a woman. I know you are. A strong woman. I been everywhere looking for you. Why can't you talk?" As Pearl spoke, Alena backed away from him, confusion in her eyes.

"I been looking for you. You just took off on the train and didn't leave me nothing, no way to find you. But you knew I wasn't gone let you go that easy." The words slid around his tongue. "I found you. I seen you the other night in your aunt's mission." Pearl laughed. "I just thought of something funny. Maybe her and Deac need to meet." He slapped his knee. "That ought to be a couple."

He held his stomach, laughing. He stopped though, just as he thought he saw irritation begin to flicker in her eyes. He would have to remember not to mention her aunt. "Anyway, though, I was standing outside in the dark, in the cold, just wishing I was with you. You was looking outside." Miss Miss seemed to be calming. He went on, turned up the wistful charm. "Staring straight out, like you was looking right at me. Like you was looking for me."

"Well, why didn't you come in?" Alena squeezed the question out in a little girl voice.

"Oh no, baby, not me. Pearl don't do that auntie stuff. No mamas and daddies. I ain't trying to meet no relatives, no kinfolk. I just got my eye on you."

Closer again, Pearl reached out his hand to touch Alena's face. *Almost there, old man.*

"Alena!"

The girl turned her head quickly to see Dinah standing in the open doorway. "Your aunt sent me to tell you to come home." Dinah paused as she looked from Alena to Pearl. "She said to tell you that you had done enough *work* already." Disapproval was wrapped around each of the girl's words. The last traces of the sun outlined her figure and played on the gold in her hair. Dinah looked at the two people before her again, then to the ink stain on the floor between them.

The three stood in silence, staring at each other. Alena wondered what to say. What did Dinah think? What would her aunt say?

Pearl just stood there.

Finally, Alena spoke. "Dinah, this is Pearl." Her tone was almost pleading. "We met on the train —"

"Ain't none of her business!" Pearl cut

in, furious. "Ain't none of her business." He emphasized each word and began to move away from Alena. "She don't need to know who I am. She ain't none of my keeper." His eyes flared at Dinah. "I told you —" he watched Dinah as he spoke to Alena, "I don't do that family thing, no friends."

He moved toward the door where Dinah stood still, firm. "No, ma'am, I ain't got to answer to nobody. No matter who they think they are." Still looking at Dinah, he added, "I ain't got no masters." He stopped just in front of Dinah, then turned back to Alena. "I'll see you later, Miss Miss, when ain't so many of your keepers around." With that, he nudged his way past Dinah out into the streets.

Dinah looked several times from Alena to the dried pool of ink at her feet. "Your aunt wants you home," she said dryly.

"I know . . . I know what it . . . I mean, I came down here. I was cleaning and the ink . . . I . . ."

"You don't owe *me* any explanations." Dinah turned abruptly and stepped into the air.

Alena grabbed for her cleaning supplies, locked the door, and ran to catch up with

Dinah. What if the other girl told Aunt Patrice about the ink? About Pearl?

Alena grew angry that she should have to worry what Dinah, of all people, should have to say to *her* aunt.

"I guess you can't wait to run back and tell my aunt. Can't wait to tell." Alena gasped the words, struggling to catch up, struggling with fear and anger.

"It's none of my business —" Dinah stopped and turned to confront Alena — "how you want to live your life. If you want to play games, that's up to you. If you don't care about your reputation, that is up to you. But for somebody that is always watching and judging other people . . . just don't you ever look at me or my brother again!"

"Go ahead, then, tell it."

"Listen, Alena, it makes no difference to me. Why should I care what you do? You walk around with this big attitude, this big chip on your shoulder, like you can treat anybody any way you feel because something bad happened to you. Well, I didn't do it. And I don't care what everybody else does, they can cater to you and pet on you, but I'm not going to do it."

Dinah threw her hair while she marched up the street. "You don't like me? Fine. I don't like you. I'm here to work, to help your aunt, not you. I love the kids; I want to help the people, but that has nothing to do with me and you. So let's keep it like it's been. I'll stay out of your way. You stay out of mine. And as for your little meeting, your little *visit,* that's between you and your conscience." Dinah walked in the door of the mission and let the screen door of the mission slam hard behind her.

At the sound, Patrice looked up to see her niece standing at the door, still on the outside, looking anxious and frustrated. Handing out cups of water, the woman sighed and wondered how much longer it would be before things came to a head.

Across the room, Dinah tied herself into her serving apron. Patrice watched until she caught Dinah's eye, then she smiled and mouthed, "thank you" across the room. Dinah nodded and quickly turned her head away.

Patrice's attention turned back to the people she served. Old, young, more young since last year's flu epidemic had left many orphans, disabled, unemployed, newly migrated. The numbers seemed to be growing daily. And soon summer would be here. She looked into eyes that did not, could not, really see her. *Not long.* She watched Alena walk quickly by. *No, not long at all.*

On a pew in the back of St. Stephen's A.M.E. Church at Austin Avenue and Robey Street, Deac continued to pray. He thanked God for the changes in his life and sent up petitions for similar changes in Pearl's life. He remembered the anger that had made his life heavy and miserable, that had made him want to hurt other people.

"Don't let him be lost."

Other people's prayers had helped save Deac. He was sure of it. Church people that would not give up on him, no matter how rough he had acted. They had seen something inside of him, something like he saw in Pearl.

Funny . . . Now he knew the pain, the worry those church people must have felt. The pain of praying for someone who sure looked like he was determined to go the wrong way.

"Don't let him be lost," he prayed again, turning Pearl over to the only One who could help him.

Fourteen

Alena slumped to the floor. Hiding in the dark hallway behind the pantry, she didn't worry about etiquette — she let her back slide down the wall and she sighed. In her mind, surrounded by the darkness, she saw images of her father in the Mississippi fields, her mother carrying meals to neighbors, and she sighed again.

"Oh, God . . ." She spoke into the darkness and sat, her arms wrapped around her legs, staring into nothing. Losing track of time.

"Hard day?"

Alena started at the other voice, but before she panicked, she recognized him, his breathing, his smell.

James.

"Me, too. Your aunt told me you were in here. I thought I could do with some quiet time, too."

Even in the darkness she could feel James's calm, his reassurance.

"You've been working really hard lately.

More cleaning, taking more time with the people. I don't know. It's something. The people, caring for them, they seem to grow on you."

"Yes, they do." Alena's soft words flickered in the dark, quiet room. "There's so much that needs to be done. The families and the little children . . ."

She turned her head toward his voice in the blackness. "I miss my home so much. Sometimes I think I smell it. Sometimes at night I think I hear my mama or my daddy calling me. Sometimes I feel like I'm gonna bust wide open. I want to scream and start running and just keep running. And I don't know whether I want to run to home or away from home. I don't know if my heart aches because I love my folks so or because I hate them. I just feel — I'm scared I'm just starting my life, and it's already over." She sighed more deeply.

Silence surrounded them again.

"It's going to be all right."

Just one small statement into the blackness. Almost as if he could see her, James reached and squeezed Alena's hand. They sat breathing, side by side, shoulders touching. First they breathed in separate rhythms, then suddenly, without trying, they were in unison. Deep cleansing, encouraging breaths.

Alena wasn't sure how much time passed before James spoke again.

"I'm going to go now, but you come when you're ready. Give yourself some time." His words parted the darkness, but not the peace. He let go of her hand, and Alena could feel his presence leave.

A good man, she thought, tired of fighting it. A good man.

Fifteen

Pass me not, O gentle Savior,
  Hear my humble cry,
While on others Thou art calling,
Do not pass me by.
Savior, Savior,
Hear my humble cry;
While on others Thou art calling,
Do not pass me by.

The soloist sat as the pastor found his way to the pulpit. "As we all know, we have a long, hot summer ahead of us. Housing is scarce. What we can find, we are often overcharged for. Some of our people who have tried to move into other areas have had their houses bombed and destroyed. Hot weather flames the fires as we remember how our men and women were beaten mercilessly in Washington Park, while three other men were killed in separate incidents."

Alena looked over the sea of hats — white waves, blue waves, pink, red, yellow, green, broad brims, ribbons, flat crowns. Some dipped over eyes, tipping forward, back, rippling with the minister's intonations. In between the hats were the bobbing heads of children, slicked and pressed, and the pomaded heads of men, hair brushed to submission, necks ringed with white, starched, sometimes detachable collars. And over the sea, purple velvet banners on the polished wooden walls that announced the Sunday school attendance and offering totals at Olivet-Woodlawn Baptist Church.

"Help us, Lord." Several voices from the congregation encouraged Reverend Boynton Williams.

"Our boys have returned to find, after their sacrifices for freedom abroad, that they are still treated like enemies at home." The reverend looked out over his congregation. "Returning soldiers have been beaten and killed after coming home, just for wearing the uniforms they so valiantly served in. Though they served in segregated units, they were shot with the same bullets, inhaled the same mustard gas, their lives were in the same danger as their white brothers. They were given the same rewards, allowed to eat in the same restaurants, were treated as the same heroes on foreign soil. Yet in their homeland they find themselves treated with dishonor and disrespect. They find that the 'war to end all wars' did not end the war of discrimination and hatred that still awaits them on American soil. Lynchings are still far too common. In one state, in fact, the governor made open statements supporting such brutal actions, while the perpetrators of the vile deeds go unpunished."

The sea of hats rippled as women shook their heads and wept openly. The men stirred in their seats and looked as though they were trying to keep lids on something that wanted to boil over.

"This is not news to us. It should not be news to others. Just this week, I was reading a series of articles in the *Chicago Daily News* written by a young man, Carl Sandburg. The words he penned to paper were powerful and full of truth, and I expect we're going to hear more from that young man. I just hope that someone reads, someone hears, someone does something before it's too late."

Alena looked over the sea to the pastor in the pulpit, then around the sanctuary. *Ten churches the size of my family's little church could fit inside this one.* Her eyes moved along the vaulted ceilings and came to rest on her aunt, who fanned steadily to distance the Chicago heat that overpowered the room. The cardboard fan was stapled to a wooden stick just larger than a tongue depressor. On one side of the fan were printed the words, "Benders Funeral Home, 3535 State Street, Chicago, Illinois." Just above the words was a picture of the Bender family.

Maybe her eyes wandered so that they would not fix on J.C.

"With all of this considered," Reverend Williams exhorted his flock, "still I ask that you behave as reasonable people."

Alena watched the fans all around the sanctuary, white butterflies on a tranquil sea.

"And even more, I ask that you act as godly people. No matter what our fairer-skinned brothers and sisters might do, I am asking that you remember that you and they are the sons and daughters of God, siblings of the firstborn, Jesus Christ."

"Wonderful Jesus!" one of the deacons called out.

Has he lost anyone? Has he seen anyone hanging lifeless? Has he had his life cut off?

"There is no passion of the human heart more diabolical than a mere race prejudice. To hate a fellow human being

181

because he is of another race is to prove that we are survivals of savagery, and that evil spirits still dominate our hearts and minds. It does not matter who the hater is. Whether he be of African descent, Anglo-Saxon, Spanish, French, Korean, Japanese, Russian, or Cherokee, such hatred is the antithesis of God."

Just bow our heads then. Stoop our shoulders. Shuffling along. "Yassuh, boss." Just accept J.C.'s death? Is that the solution?

Almost as if he heard Alena's thought, Revered Williams continued, "This reliance on God does not make us timid weaklings. If we follow the biblical examples, we see Moses, we see Joshua, we see David. We see that Jesus was himself a confronter of men and the wrongs they do, a confronter of injustice, of inhumane systems. But the stand, the resistance of the ever-living Christ, was based on a commitment to peace for all people, was based on His love for His Father and His Father's love for Him — everlasting love that gave Him courage even in the face of death."

Alena looked away from the pulpit, back over the sea, her gaze resting on faces, old and young, uplifted. *Never. Never.*

"And just so you aren't tempted by self-righteousness, just so you don't get too high-minded, just so you don't spend too much time asking yourselves 'how could those people behave that way?', consider that the hate of race prejudice is no different from the hate that causes you, causes us, to poke fun at our Chinese brethren that walk among us. It is the same hate that causes us to make fun of our brothers and sisters who have less, who don't dress as stylishly. The same hate that causes you not to speak to your cousin, your brother, or your mother. It is the same hate that causes you to bear grudges, even though you know you shouldn't. To nurse grudges, to hold on to them, even though you know you shouldn't. It is the same hate between family and friends that keeps us counting offenses, real and imagined. That hate that keeps us bound to bitterness and unfor- giveness, while we ignore the good that men do. It is the same hate."

The pastor's voice rose, seemed to shake the room. "It is *all* hate, and it is all born of the same source. All of us have sinned, and the time is long past when we can point fingers in judgment."

Reverend Williams paused, left silence where there had been thunder. Then he spoke again. "And just to make sure you don't get caught up in pride, remember that all sin is sin when God looks upon it. One man's hatred is no different than another man's thievery. That man's thievery is no worse than a woman's gossip —"

"Ouch! Hallelujah!" came from beneath one of the hats.

"I see I must have stepped on somebody's toes. Well, that's all right, sister. Confession is good for the soul." The laughter in the edifice dispelled some of the heaviness. "I want you to know that I'm not saying these things to burden you. I am saying them because I love you, and I want to see you set free."

"Amen," several of the deacons agreed.

Alena turned her head and willed that the tears in her heart would not overflow her eyes. For a moment she felt her mother's hand on her hair, heard her father's laugh, smelled the Mississippi soil.

"The only permanent cure for social disorder and even for our own individual weaknesses is in the fear and love of God. He alone can cleanse the human heart, cool the fires of passion, and make men of all races dwell together in unity. We must know that He is greater. His words are greater. His thoughts are greater. And that we are bound together only by His love.

"We must know and we must spread the news that there is hope for us. There is hope for the aching and fear in men's breasts that cause them to sin against one another. There is hope for our sinful conditions. There is a prescription, a remedy. There is hope in God's love for us. There is hope in the One who came to reconcile us. If He can reconcile hopeless sinners to His Father, then he can surely reconcile us one to another. There is hope in acknowledging our sin and asking God for forgiveness."

Alena's heart swelled and pressed against the briars.

"King Solomon prayed a prayer for all of God's people, for the people of Israel and also for the strangers that dwelt among them, that God would hear the prayers of all the people that prayed to Him. He prayed that God would hear their prayers acknowledging their sin and begging for His forgiveness. That God would dwell in the midst of them.

"And God said, 'If my people, which are called by my name, shall humble themselves, and pray, and seek my face, and turn from their wicked ways; then will I hear from heaven, and will forgive their sin, and will heal their land."

Outside the church, Alena breathed in summer Chicago, grateful that it was Sunday, that the packing houses' smell was not in the air. The sea of hats flowed around her. Aunt Patrice walked beside her. The girl was grateful that her aunt left her to her thoughts.

The two strolled in silence down State Street. "I Will Overcome" drifted from the windows of a church and encouraged memories of Mississippi. Alena wondered if the congregation at home was singing the hymn.

This world is one great battlefield
With forces all arrayed,
If in my heart I do not yield
I'll overcome some day.
I'll overcome some day,
I'll overcome some day,
If in my heart I do not yield,
I'll overcome some day.

Both seen and unseen powers join
To drive my soul astray,
But with His Word a sword of mine,
I'll overcome some day.
I'll overcome some day,

I'll overcome some day,
But with His Word a sword of mine,
I'll overcome some day.

A thousand snares are set for me,
And mountains in my way,
If Jesus will my leader be,
I'll overcome some day.
I'll overcome some day,
I'll overcome some day,
If Jesus will my leader be,
I'll overcome some day.

Though many a time no signs appear,
Of answer when I pray;
My Jesus says I need not fear,
He'll make it plain some day.
I'll be like Him some day,
I'll be like Him some day;
My Jesus says I need not fear,
He'll make it plain some day.

Women passed by in broad-brimmed
hats, in the drapy, fluid styles of the day.
Alena looked at her reflection in the
window of the dry goods store they passed.
Her eyes lingered on pale blue fabric displayed in the window. As she and her aunt
walked, they moved in and out of clouds of
hymns.

Nothing between my soul and my Savior,
Naught of this world's delusive dream;
I have renounced all sinful pleasure;
Jesus is mine, there's nothing between.

Nothing between, like pride or station;
Self or friends shall not intervene;
Though it may cost me much
    tribulation,
I am resolved, there's nothing between.

Nothing between, even many hard trials,
Though the whole world against me
    convene;
Watching with prayer and much
    self-denial,
I'll triumph at last, there's nothing
    between.

Further down the street, they passed several barbershops, then Bert's shoe store.
Wagons, cars, limousines passed by. Alena
stopped again and admired a pair of button-up shoes. Colored policemen strolled
the block, tipped their hats, and called
respectful greetings to Miss Patrice. Further up the street there were restaurants,
the office of the *Chicago Defender*, Mac's
Furniture Store, Pullman Sister's Restaurant, and the Big Grand Theater located

right next door to the Phoenix Theater, also known as the Little Grand.

She looked at her reflection in the window of one of the many barber shops; her hair was always trying to escape the hat. She turned her head quickly, thought she saw his reflection in the window. Pearl's reflection. It was only Aunt Patrice and her.

On one street corner, Reverend W. C. Thompson, pastor of the Pentecostal Church of Christ encouraged his members, "New things is coming altogether diverse from what they has been." Then he joined his church members as they encouraged one another and those passing by, singing:

O Jesus is a Rock
in a weary land,
a weary land,
a weary land;
O Jesus is a Rock
in a weary land,
A shelter in the time of storm.

Alena and her aunt continued to the mission door, while a church down the street played:

We are tossed and driven on the

restless sea of time;
Somber skies and howling tempests
    oft succeed a
bright sunshine;
In that land of perfect day, when the
    mists have
rolled away,
We will understand it better by and by.

By and by, when the morning comes,
When the saints of God are gathered
    home,
We'll tell the story how we've overcome,
For we'll understand it better by and by.

Alena wondered if she would ever understand.

Sixteen

Alena smiled and moved among the children, setting their places for them, preparing for the games. With them she forgot that Chicago was strange, that she did not want to be there.

The cars, the noise of the city was far away. When she jumped rope with the children, surprisingly, they knew her songs:

Miss Mary Mac,
Mac, Mac,
All dress in black,
Black, Black . . .

With them she felt light. She felt herself. It was like before J.C.'s murder.

Alone in the room with them — no parents or grandmothers or uncles — they talked of China and buried treasure. Sometimes, like magic, she took a little girl's hair and made ten braids into two. They did cookie dances, swaying, singing, jiggling, wiggling, while homemade sugar cookies pirouetted on their tongues.

K-K-K-Katy, K-K-K-Katy,
You're the only g-g-g-girl that I adore.
When the m-m-m-moon shines,
Over the cowshed,
I'll be waiting at the k-k-k-kitchen door.

They sang and dissolved in laughter.

Alena and the children *glug-glugged* down huge glasses of water from jars — jelly jars that looked like crystal goblets. They pretended the water was ginger ale. The ginger ale had bubbles. They wrinkled their noses against the imaginary effervescence.

Sometimes the water was tea for tea parties, all the dainty girl fingers crooked in the air. During tea parties, they spoke in hoity-toity voices, while the boys retreated to imaginary barricades and bunkers on the other side of the room. Sometimes the girls played dress up, singing "A pretty girl is like a melody" and humming the rest of the words they did not know.

From the children, Alena received all the affection she'd missed since her parents . . . since the betrayal. Little fingers, tiny kisses on her face like droplets, like rain, like waterfalls.

In their playroom, her friends renewed her. Behind the door, in secret, they laughed and squealed and stomped and rolled away from all the disappointment, confusion, the pain that had prematurely disrupted their lives.

It was comfort for all of them, but for Alena, behind the door, she took off the mask she had worn to Chicago. Removed its smothering heaviness and breathed.

Now they were playing make-believe. All lying on their backs pretending to count clouds.

"Miss Alena, Miss Alena, you see that cloud? That one, over there? It look like a sheep to me."

"Uh-huh! I see it, Matthew." All eyes saw the sheep.

"What about this one, Miss Alena —"

"It's not your turn. It's *my* turn."

"No, it ain't. Nuh-*uh*. It's my turn."

"Everybody will get a chance. Candy, why don't you let C.J. finish?"

"C.J. always get to go first. He don't never let me go first."

"Candy."

"Gone then, C.J. But hurry up before my cloud blow away."

"Like I was sayin' —"

"C.J."

"Sorry, Miss Alena. My cloud, it's over there. See it? It's shaped like a Wrigley Field."

"A wiggly field? What does a wiggly field look like?"

"Not a wiggly field, Miss Alena. A *Wrigley* Field. Like a place you play baseball. I ain't never seen it, but I know that's what it look like."

"How you know then?"

"Candy."

"All right, Miss Alena. But what about my turn? My turn right? There my cloud. It look like a pony."

"Every time, Candy, your cloud look like a pony."

"Well, that's what I see, *Cee-Jay*. A pony and a ballet dancer."

Alena stifled a laugh and then pointed. "See that cloud? It looks like a little white dog, at least he was little once, a little dog I knew at home in Mississippi. Cottonball."

"Cottonball?" They all laughed together. Alena could feel and hear the sound in her chest and stomach. "And over there, that's a Magnolia, the state flower. And that one's like meringue, like my mama makes for lemon pie." Tongues rubbed lips and eyes rolled.

"Well, I still see Wrigley Field."

"Me, too, buddy." Alena started. That voice! She shot upright. He lay spread on the floor. How did he get in? How did he come in without her knowing? What was he doing here?

"Maybe some day we can get to a game. If not at Wrigley Field, somewhere else good."

"For real, Mr. James? All of us? Even the girls?"

James laughed. His voice seemed deeper lying down. "Yep, C.J. Everybody."

How had he sneaked in? Alena resented his intrusion — and in the same moment became self-conscious about being on the floor.

"How-what-why are you in here?" The children began to pop up like dried corn at the tone of Alena's voice.

Wasn't there *any* place she could have to herself? How long had he been listening. What did he hear? Rearranging her skirt and blouse, Alena quickly covered her ankles and her vulnerability.

She stared at him. "You need to knock next time. Besides that, we have everything working just fine. We're fine," Alena repeated.

James's face darkened. Slapped by her words, he looked around, as though he were embarrassed in front of the children. His eyes looked like fifty different replies passed through them. Instead he held his peace.

"I am very sorry." Each word precise, clipped. James paused as if to say more, then quickly left the room.

Seventeen

James stood outside near the huge receptacle where they burned trash. Frustrated.
His hands gripped the large, heavy garbage
can he held over his head. Gripped so hard,
so tightly, his hands and arms strained with
effort. Every muscle in his face was taut,
stretched, frowning.

He was sick of her. He had his own life.
His own frustrations. He didn't need this.
He could get over it — this attraction he
felt. How could he even think he liked her?
Love was out of the question.

He was poised to throw the entire can he
held, not just its contents, into the larger
receptacle in which refuse burned before
him. At the same time, his muscles
strained not to throw the vessel. His eyes,
his countenance, were focused on the fire
and not the irony of his desires.

The heat, or maybe the strain, brought
perspiration to his face and forearms. His
face muscles twitched. He felt on edge, as
he warred internally over whether the

motion of his arms, the same set of muscles, would end in an act of destruction or construction. He held the can poised. The clammy Chicago evening heat, such a contrast to the winter, added to his sweating.

"You don't want to throw it, baby."

He had not heard Aunt Patrice open the back door of the mission and step out into the alley.

"I know she frustrates you sometimes."

James sighed and looked at Patrice as he lowered his arms, embarrassed that she had caught him out of control.

"But I can see it in your eyes that you care for her. And you doing the right thing, being patient. She's changing. You can see she's warming up," she said almost like a question. "But sometimes, you know we people are funny. We don't change or get it right all at one time."

James took a deep breath and shook the refuse from his can into the fire. He worked hard to keep his face emotionless, not to let a muscle twitch.

"You know I see you working with these men in the mission. You not their commanding officer, not a major anymore, but you just right with them. They keep falling, you keep picking them up.

"I see you do the same thing, working

for hours on them old printing press machines. Look like to me you need to give them to the junk man, but you just keep on greasing and twisting and poking."

James stared into the fire. Afraid, if he looked at her, she would see the pain in his eyes.

"I see you working to get stories —" she paused to wipe her brow with a small cotton rag she kept tucked in her waistband — "People tell you, 'no, you can't see so-and-so,' or 'no, you can't go there,' and that don't stop you. You just keep on pushing 'til the truth be told. No matter whose nerves you have to get on."

James tilted his head, breathed, relaxed a little, and gave Aunt Patrice a small smile.

"That's better, that's what I like. You a determined man. A young man, but you got a mind. Look what you been through. So many things that could throw a young man off his track. Losing your mother and father at the same time, the war and all, but you still got a mind." She moved closer to pat his back. He tilted his head down, staring at the ground beneath his feet, tried not to let his back untense, to show her how much he needed to be comforted.

"God know what He doing. That child been hurt, too."

James turned to Patrice ready to speak, but she plunged on.

"I know she ain't doing nothing to make it no better, but you know most of us act ugly when things don't go our way. 'Til we learn. You a good man, feet planted, strong back, good sense, good home training, battle hardened, and a mind to serve the Lord. So, I know you not going to let some little girl make you lose your peace!"

James raised his head, started to defend. "But, she —"

"I know, baby." Patrice alternately patted and rubbed his shoulder. "I know she is trying your patience, but you just gonna have to dig way down deep. She mad at the whole world right now. That include herself. She know she being ugly. And she stand upside you and you shining, and she can see just how ugly she is in your bright, shiny reflection."

"Are you saying I need to start acting, acting like, like a bad guy . . . ? That seems to be what women want. I could act like a fool, too. Right with her." James shook his head, perplexed, frustrated.

"No, I ain't saying no such a thing. I don't know what it is about you men. You spend hours on them old machines and things. They don't do right, you just keep on working. But, oh, let it be a woman you got to work on, and you just about to have a breakdown."

"Machines don't go out of their way to be nasty." James could feel his facial muscles tightening and willed them to relax. "They don't change from minute to minute. They don't try to hurt you."

"I know. I hear what you saying, but I think you all just get afraid. Men get afraid. Afraid of getting what you really want and need. You know sometimes I'm just sure it's the mean ole devil. I think he just hate love so much when he smell it coming, he make it his business to put a good dollop of fear on you men. And just spread it all around 'til you get stuck, 'til you can't move."

James made a noise that meant he doubted Patrice's theory but laughed, just a little, at her words. Affection washed over him for the older woman.

"I'm serious," she continued, laughing now herself. "Why I've seen men in love get so scared they run away from the woman they love and end up married to and unhappy with somebody they don't hardly love. They so scared. Don't you do that, James."

Their laughter stopped. James looked

back into the fire for a moment, then at Patrice.

"You know, James, you don't never let her see how you feel. You don't need nobody; that's how you make it look. Always strong. Taking care of everybody, don't need nobody to take care of you. Somebody got to sneak up on you in the alley just to see you being human."

James smiled a small, self-conscious smile, his profile to her, head lowered, one dimple exposed.

"Yes, women want a big strong man. But sometimes, just sometimes, they want that big strong man to need them. To get a thorn in his paw so she can feel needed. So she can help pull that thing out." The muscles in James's jaw flexed slightly. He shifted in discomfort.

"She don't want no big old baby crying in front of everybody. But just sometimes, alone with her, a big old strong man got to let his guard down. Let her know he need her and that he soft to her, just her."

He turned toward Patrice. "This is way too complicated. I'm not trying to be someone else. I'm just plain and simple. I —" Frustration seemed to be overtaking control.

"I know you think I don't know what

I'm talking about. But, baby, that's all right. I ain't got gray hair for nothing. This frustration you feeling right now, she don't know nothing about it. You trying your best not to let her see it, but she *need* to see it. Not in a crazy way, but she just need to know she moving you." Patrice shook her head. "You know, that's part of what the draw is with bad boys."

James stopped, alert. "What do you mean?"

"Bad boys, they walk around tough and hard all the time. Acting like they don't care about nobody. What women see underneath all that tough acting is a glimpse of pain. We trying to see where is the thorn in his paw that's making him act that way.

"Bad boy, see, he figure this out about women and use it to his advantage. So when it suit him, he shows the girl a little bit of his pain. Just a peek. Girl fall for it. Can't help herself. She don't know he fooling her. Don't *want* to know he fooling her. Seeing what she want to see. Bad boy know it. He know the girl gone love it."

James turned to fully face Aunt Patrice, his eyebrows knit together. "Love it? *Love* it? Why?"

" 'Cause she feel like don't nobody know

that little piece of him but her. She feel like he won't show that paw to nobody but her. She feel like she rescued him. You know, women all the time saying they want a man to rescue them. Most of us can't get rescued 'cause we too busy rescuing some man our own self." Aunt Patrice wiped her hands on her apron, looked toward the fire.

"Yes, that girl feel like that paw is hers and hers alone. What the girl don't know is he showing this same little ol' worn-out paw to three other women. Maybe ten women. Maybe it get real good to him, and maybe he showing it to more than he can count," Aunt Patrice's laugh was sardonic.

"A man can keep a woman hooked this way all her life. 'Cause, see, she wanna fix that paw. She believe if she fix it, he turn from the beast she see most of the time to the prince she been waiting for. The boy want her to believe, but then hate her 'cause he think she so stupid. And all the time, old slew foot just laughing." Patrice shook her head and fanned her apron in the direction of the flames.

James stood silent. Silent, frustrated control was better than the risk of exposing himself in an outburst. He watched Patrice's face lit by the fire.

"See, old slew foot is a mean old man. He know sure enough the bad boy been hurt, and he just using it against him. Slew foot know men's and women's ways. Been watching a long time. Know all the tricks.

"Old slew foot watch them bad boys out there looking for love. When the bad boy's heart find somebody it think can help him, old slew foot come up and whisper in that lost boy's ear, 'Ain't no such thing as love. She just trying to use you.' "

James looked into the fire as if there were sad memories there.

"Bad boy ain't gone let nobody use him, so he use her first. And it just keep on going: heart searching, devil whispering, boy using. 'Til it's a wound-up dirty mess, and the boy don't believe no one can help him. Ain't no love to save him. And he right. Can't no woman's love save him 'cause old slew foot got a permanent ride on that boy's back and is messing up everything that boy touch."

The fire crackled and sparks danced above the flames.

"Now, them girls that boy touch, they got a piece of his emotional disease. They been hurt by the boy and start to feel like they can't trust nobody. Them girls start to feel like they soft heart got them in trouble, so they just harden up they hearts with slew foot steady there encouraging them to do it." James closed his eyes briefly against the image.

"The girls keep on being attracted though to these beasts with thorns in they paws, wanting to help them. The beasts hurt the girls. The girls' hearts get more hard, and pretty soon the good girls stop thinking they so good. Start thinking they ain't fit for nothing but bad.

"If a good man do come in they life, they so emotionally diseased up, they heart so hard, they good man give up and go away, feeling rejected. Good man go away all hurt and bruised on the inside. Them girls don't even know they hurt the good man. They just know he gone away and they feeling rejected. So what they do?"

"Harden their hearts even more?"

Patrice turned toward James and nodded. She looked sad, as if she had seen the scene too many times. "That's right. And old slew foot all the while laughing 'cause that disease done spread to somebody else. He know women want to heal and love the man. He know the man want to be loved but need to be strong. Old slew foot sit back and laugh at men and women trying to love. Good, bad, he try to use them all."

Patrice held her hands toward the fire. James looked at the woman and thought of his own mother. He could hardly remember her face anymore, but something about Aunt Patrice reminded him of her.

"He try to get them caught up in a spiral," Patrice continued. "Plenty a woman caught up in the spiral. They think it's they hearts keeping them there. It ain't they hearts. Hearts all busted up, broken up, battered and torn. It's old slew foot come against her mind. Mind, that's all she got left, and he try to take that. Heart all full of pain, then old slew foot try to scare her. Say, 'Look at you. Who else want you?' Then he tell her, 'You know that man love you. What you do to him? You know it's your fault. It's gone be the same with any other man.' He just keep her confused. Slew foot steady laughing while her heart steady breaking." There seemed to be a glow of wisdom around Aunt Patrice.

"Woman steady trying to fix it. Pull out that thorn. 'You can make him better. Don't give up,' old slew foot say. But how someone broken gone fix somebody else? Can't do it. Slew foot know can't nobody fix it but God. And old slew foot steady laughing. He gets some of his greatest pleasure ruinin' men and women's relationships."

James turned his attention back to the flames. The situation seemed almost hopeless. The sparks rose higher and higher in the air that felt almost like summer.

"Slew foot scared of men and women in love. 'Cause he know love make us grateful. Love soften our hearts." James glanced at Patrice and saw that the corners of her mouth had turned up just slightly.

"We learn a lot about love from our mamas and daddies. But, see, we know they ain't got much choice about loving us. A man or woman though that love us, they making a choice. They loving us 'cause they want to. It make us feel special, like we worth something. Like we can do anything. Devil don't like that." The woman smoothed her hair into place and nodded at no one in particular.

"When somebody love you, you can be worried and afraid, and you get in that person's arms and that fear just disappear. When you in love, you start looking at the stars, at the moon, the flowers, the one you love, and ask yourself, 'How this come to be?' That one you love touch you and you come alive — it make you start thanking

God, getting grateful. Old slew foot know he done for then. When a man and woman stand naked before each other in the power of God's love, it's a mighty thing. Darkness and demons flee from that light."

Something about her face, her voice, told James that she had been to that place. She had known love.

"See, what's flowing between that man and that woman is God's love. God get all wrapped up in them two people. His love make them whole and strong. They love alone can't do it. Got to be God's love. It's a wonderful thing. It's His love that heal our souls."

Patrice's eyes seemed to stare back through time.

"See a good girl can't heal what's hurt on a bad boy. It ain't his paw, it's his soul. And that girl can't heal his soul. Only God's love can. That girl be trying to heal him herself with slew foot coaching, and she end up getting sick herself. But if she just wait on the Lord, let God do the healing, God can use that girl's lovely ways to show that boy to the One that can fix him." She smiled, as though at some pleasant memory.

"I know I'm just running off at the mouth." Patrice looked now at James, seemingly back from the place her spirit had taken her. "Let Alena see you need her. Let her know you got a place that she bring balm to. Just give her a little peek at your sore spot and melt away some of that hardness around her heart."

James felt uncertain and worried that it reflected on his face.

"Don't you talk yourself, and don't let fear talk you out of what you feel, what you want, what you need. Alena is a good girl. She got a good heart. She don't know nothing, really, but good. She from good people. She been through a bad time, and right now she mad at the world. But that ain't gone be always. She growing up. When she get through this trouble, she gone be something worth having."

Patrice reached out and gripped each of James's shoulders with motherly affection. He held back, afraid that he would surrender to her comfort.

"God is taking that sweet little girl's heart she got. He giving her wisdom and understanding, and He gone put it in a fine woman's body. She trying to be something, trying to be hard, trying to be something she don't even know nothing about. But she gone come forth good as gold. So you hold on, baby."

Patrice slid her hands down and squeezed James's forearms. "Just keep on. It's gone be all right. Just do like you do with them machines. Keep working at it. It's gone be all right." She smiled up at him. Reassurance.

Patrice wrapped her arms around James as if he were her son, and they stood alone in the dark, thick heat, lighted by the fire in the mission alley in early summer Chicago.

Eighteen

Pearl watched from across the street, standing in the spot where he had stood for several days, casing, learning the routine. As soon as he saw Alena, he moved quietly and stealthily to her.

"Hey, Miss Mississippi," he whispered. "Girl, where you been?"

Alena crossed her arms over her chest, rounded her shoulders, seemed to be guarding her heart. Her eyes were closed tight.

"I been thinking about you, you know that? At night, I can almost smell you so good I can taste you. Your eyes, your smile, your clothes. You don't belong no place like this. A girl pretty as you ain't got no business living like this. This a way for a ugly woman. Can't get no man. If *they* call, ain't nobody gone answer them."

Alena turned her head away, seemed to enfold on herself even more.

"But, mercy, not you, baby. So fine —" Pearl moved closer as he talked. He reached out, lifted her chin, his eyes on her eyes — "You don't want to be here. Where you want to go, baby? Where you want to go, girl?"

Alena began to cry softly. "Home. I want to go home. Can you take me home?"

"Home? Baby, you out of Mississippi. Come on with me, girl. You will be sitting on top of the world."

Alena stopped crying abruptly and stood entranced.

"Come on, girl. You ain't got much time. Pretty soon, you gone be one of them. Look at you. They got you carrying slop like some old field hand. 'Sides, baby. You know Pearl ain't gone wait but so long." He circled the girl, bold and insistent. Just seconds from the back door that led into the mission, he walked around her, his circumference tighter and tighter. Alena's eyes remained fixed on the spot he had come from across the street.

"You know you want to be with Pearl. Look what you can have, baby." Pearl dangled a delicate gold chain with a small embossed locket. "This ain't nothing, baby. Nothing 'cept to let you know you meant for better things."

His breath, his words, his presence wound themselves around the girl.

"This necklace, it ain't nothing, just the beginning. Jewelry, pretty clothes, get your hair straightened, waved, and curled. I'll have to fight the Negroes off of you." His fingers twisted in the hair that had made its way loose. "Come on, girl. Come away."

Sudden footsteps near the door knocked at the spell.

"Here, baby girl —" Pearl pressed the necklace into Alena's free hand as he backed toward the street — "I'll be back. I'm gone collect what's mine." He nodded toward her, then moved quickly, seeming to vanish in the night.

"What's the matter, Alena? You look like you've seen a ghost."

Alena dumped the waste in the can, careful not to drop her necklace. "I'm fine." She brushed past Jonathan, the locket squeezed into her hand, and stalked into the mission.

Nineteen

"Breeze, you can't keep on the way you're going."

Alena watched quietly while James stood talking to one man amongst the group. She liked listening to them, watching, hoping they would not notice her. There was something about the way James was with the men, *his* men, that made it difficult for her not to like him.

His smile, he always wore it. A smile just a little too loving for a black man in a weary world. A face just a little too open — but eyes, black eyes that said, "You don't know me. Can't see me, into me." His face looked like a handsome portrait. What someone would expect a colored major to look like. Well groomed, just a few war grays.

"Yeah, Major, I hear you. You know it ain't no jobs. How a man supposed to take care of hisself? I got to have me somethin'. I don't always want to be takin' handouts. That may be okay for the rest of you all, but I got some pride." The older man craned his neck around to take in the rest of the group.

"Young fools become old fools!" one of the men said while the others laughed.

Breeze shook his head. "Laugh if you want to, but I'm gone be a man. You hear about them blowing up people's property, blowing up colored people's homes just 'cause they don't want them living in they area. Where a man supposed to live? They know it's too crowded. Man, things gone blow up, just like East St. Louis. Just like in Washington, D.C. They had to bring in troops from Camp Meade in Maryland, yesterday, just to quiet things down."

James and Jonathan were quiet for a moment, exchanging looks. "Breeze, you're just trying to justify what you know is wrong. I bet you were stealing before you fell on hard times."

"Oh, now, Major, don't talk so hard to an old man." Breeze gave James a look that begged for sympathy.

"You sure got him pegged." The men laughed and looked to James, waiting for his comment. He had been one of only a few colored officers that served during the world war. They listened to his words and admired him like a young son, a nephew

216

that had gone away and returned a man, a success.

"I'm not trying to be hard, Breeze. I just don't want to see you locked up some-where. You're too old to be doing stupid time. You ever try for a job with the trains, porter or redcap?"

"Now, no disrespect intended, Major, but I tell you, old Cool Breeze don't want to work nowhere somebody calling him *George*. That's what they do, you know. Call all the colored mens *George*. You got to be willing to take a lot of stuff, and right now, I ain't willing. Take a special kind of man can put up with all that. All mens ain't got that kind of patience. Besides that, my mama didn't name me no George."

"What *did* your mama name you?" A voice out of the group. "For sure, she didn't name you Cool Breeze."

"You leave my mama out of this, Negro. Don't you get yourself all worked up wor-ried about my mama. You start talkin' about my mama, I guarantee you'a be writing a check you ain't able to cash. No, sir! You just need to know I ain't gone be called George, Uncle, Sambo, or nothing else. That ain't nothing for one man to call another man, is it, Mr. Jonathan?"

Alena eavesdropped, setting the tables, as the old man questioned the younger man.

"You're right, it's not." Jonathan sat as one among them. Accepted. Something he had not said. Some look he had not given. Something in his eye, perhaps not in his eye. Some time when he leaned in when they would have expected him to lean out. Some time when he turned his head. When his eye twitched. Some shrug, some laugh, some invisible thing that let them know he was safe, they were safe. Let them know he could be trusted to sit with. They could take their coats off with him. Tell jokes. Loosen tongues.

Rare.

So they let him in, didn't stop to pause. Let him witness the secret offenses covered by smooth, seamless faces. Something that told the men that he did not see them as less because they were black, and even more, he did not see himself as more because he was white.

Jonathan saw color. It just didn't matter.

Breeze reached out a hand, touched Jonathan's shoulder. "One man acting like he more than God. Don't the Good Book say one man ain't more than another one?"

"Yes, it does."

"Then a man would be crazy to think he know more than God. God say every man the same, but he say he know more than God, he better. Now, that's a crazy man. A man that would put hisself and his thoughts about a thing in line ahead of God and His thoughts, that's a man gone get a good talkin' to on the other side. Not Breeze. I'm gone be at the end, way back behind God. Let that other man get on up ahead. He gone get set out and set down, that's what I think. Course now, I ain't saved, ain't studied the Word, but that's what I think. That man setting hisself up to get set down."

Breeze pulled up on his pants, adjusted them to keep them from falling. "Course, it ain't my job to warn him. That's the job of you good people, you *saved* people so worried about that man. Breeze just worried about hisself. 'Sides, Breeze ain't about to leave Bronzeville, ain't about to leave the Black Belt. Chicago my home."

"Man, Breeze, what you talking about? You from Alabama."

"Don't you worry about me, big shot." Breeze hiked up his pants again. "Ain't nothing like a big-time Negro."

"Gentlemen!" Patrice yelled across the room, "this ain't your picnic table outside, and it sure ain't the barber shop. I don't want you getting rowdy in here."

Alena tried not to laugh out loud. Hoped that she could keep a telltale smile off her face.

"Sorry, Miss Patrice. Sorry. Keep it down fellas."

"Breeze, man, you crazy."

"Maybe Marc Garvey got the right idea. Maybe we should just pack up and leave here. Leave it to them. Go back to Africa."

"Africa? Man, what I know about Africa? This the place I done bled and sweated for. Anyway, I ain't leaving here. Man, you see them little ladies walking down State Street, nice ladies, skirts way above they ankles, getting shorter and shorter. I'm telling you, in a few years, skirts gone be above they knees."

"Breeze, you're crazy."

"That's all right, Mr. James, but you remember old Breeze told you. Things is changing. Why the other night I was at the Savoy Ballroom. Mens and womens in there dancing, some white mens, too. Ain't never heard tell of nothin' like that 'cept maybe in New York. Standing around like regular people talking about boxing. Whether Dempsey gone knock Williard out, whether Jack Johnson took a fall, talking 'bout the White Sox and the World Series, 'bout the end to the war.

"Man, the women and the music. They was playing James Reese Europe's *St. Louis Blues.* Ain't that something? Lieutenant James Reese Europe leading the 369th Infantry Band. Ain't that something, General Pershing's own headquarters band. Just makes you proud. And man, that Noble Sissle can sing."

Breeze hummed and then began to hoof, cutting a few short, bent-over steps that told a tale of a man once agile in his youth. Now so thin his body looked like it was going to cut its way out of his old raggedy clothes, clothes that stayed up only by a miracle. Hair going every which way.

"Come on up here, Mr. Jonathan. Let me show you a few steps. You can't sit here with us and can't dance. Chicago, ain't nothing like it, the Pekin Theatre-Cabaret, the Big Grand Theatre, the Vendome, the Owl. Nothing like it."

Jonathan got to his feet and began to awkwardly mimic Cool Breeze's steps while the old man hummed, then sang. "How you going to keep them down on the farm after they've seen Paree," the older man crooned. The younger man, pink faced, blond haired, blue eyed, broad shoulders wearing joy seldom seen on a white man, shadowing the skinny black man. Old suit coat, old suit pants touching nothing, dancing in another place.

Jonathan shuffled in time, his cherub-like face at odds with his hands, his shoulders, with the fire in his eyes.

"You watch out there now, Mr. Jon."

"Aw, look out there."

"You cuttin' the rug now!"

Aunt Patrice's voice was louder this time. "Gentlemen, I'm not gone to tell you again. Do I have to ask you outside? I'm trying to be nice because that sun is beating down out there. Don't let me have to remind you."

Alena turned her back so the men could not see the glee she took in their being scolded.

"Oh yes, ma'am. No offense meant. No disrespect." Breeze stopped and nodded in Aunt Patrice's direction.

"And you, James and Jonathan, I know you know better. I might have expected Mr. Breeze, but not you two."

James and Jonathan shrugged like little boys. Patrice turned her back before they could see her smile.

"I think that woman love ole Breeze," Alena heard the man whisper to the group conspiratorially. "I tell you, that's a real woman. Good-looking woman and plenty of her. Good, upstanding church woman, widow woman. One day, when Breeze get that good job, when I get saved, yes sir," Breeze jerked at the waist of his pants pulling them above his waist, "I'm gone come calling. She need a good man, need to be married."

"Breeze, man, you calling all right. Calling at the moon."

Alena watched James across the room with the men, most of them older. They came day after day, especially the soldiers, to talk with him. Like magic, they seemed to know when he was in and gravitated to him. They surrounded him. Telling him stories of woe, stories of hope, asking him for advice. They shared stories of war, of waiting, of rejection, and hope that the rejection would end. Hope that their lives would change, that they had fought the last war. Occasionally, their voices would lower while they whispered some joke not intended for women's ears. A joke that would end with loud laughter and "Aw, man, you crazy." James and Jonathan were friends with the men. Brothers.

She was careful to make sure he did not see her watching. Watching and listening to his conversation, his determined patience, his care. Alena cloaked her watching with other activities — serving, pretending to be interested in conversations with the mothers and grandmothers. Occasionally, though, it seemed when she was most in earnest, when her focus was on someone else, when her mind was not on the wrong done to her — he would look directly into her eyes.

Sometimes across the room, his look made her feel within his arm's reach.

It always had the same effect. First, some flushing, a yearning, then a desire toward him. Until her mind reminded her who he was, who she was and where she had come from, how love had betrayed her. Then she was infuriated.

His presence, his attitude, made her angry. His smile, the nod of his head, sometimes a wink as though they shared a private joke. He smiled at her expense. He was laughing at her, like he possessed her. Like he knew she wanted him. He was wrong.

Sometimes when he caught her, he tried to approach her or call to her. Alena always found an excuse to leave quickly. Sometimes the men laughed. She was much more careful now.

"Come on, James. Tell us how it was when you was in Des Moines training to be an officer."

"Wasn't many colored officers at all, was it?"

Alena hoped the men's questions would keep James's eyes off of her.

"No, there weren't very many. Of course, there wouldn't have been any if folks like you, like the people at the NAACP hadn't pushed for change. Last I heard, there were about six hundred of us graduated from the program in Iowa. Men serving as lieutenants, captains, majors, even colonels. I wasn't the only one. Major Spingarn — you know, the one that ran the NAACP — he was over there right in the thick of things."

"That may be so. But you the only one we know up close." Breeze mugged for the group. "Man, we was so proud when you boys came home. Parading down the street. Medals all over you. That was something."

"Some people thought Race men couldn't be officers, couldn't even serve as an enlisted man next to a white man, but we showed them. Units like the Old Eighth showed we could and would fight. Most of us were fighting for freedom over there, but we were also fighting hoping that things would change for us at home.

"You know how it was," James continued. "When I became part of the Old Eighth, it already had a history of distinguished service fighting in Cuba."

"Now, James, all that is real nice. But I'm ready to hear my favorite part. Tell us about it. Tell us about when you was in France, about the music, about the *comment allez vous.*" All the men laughed at Breeze as he wiggled his old man's body, one hand on his head, another on a tired, stiff hip.

"Breeze, man, you gone break that thing!"

"Oh, you old fools hush. James know how it is. How it is when spring comes and a young man's fancy turns to love."

"Breeze, I think you seen about fifty springs too many!" The men stomped their feet and hooted.

"I told you all. Don't let me have to holler again!" Patrice yelled across the room to the group of men.

"Yes, ma'am, Miss Patrice. You know I's always a gentleman, and I try to keep these other fools, I mean these other mens in line. But you know how it is, we got our hands full, ain't that right, Mr. Jonathan?

Hands is full, yes sir." He turned back to James. "Come on, man. Tell the story."

"Breeze, you got problems, man." James turned his head and laughed more quietly with the other men.

"Why you want to deny an old man? Just 'cause the honey for your tea ain't but a step away, ain't no reason to deny me. 'Sides that, you know the women love me. That's why they call me Cool Breeze."

"You cool, all right." One of the men fanned in front of his nose.

"Man, don't make me come over there. Don't make me have to teach you a lesson. I ain't gone suffer no disrespect, that's for sure." Breeze halfheartedly started to remove his jacket.

"Wait a minute, Breeze. We know you can take us all on; we're just asking for a little mercy." James chuckled at the old man. "Let me just tell you about the band. Most of the colored units had a band with them. One of the best known was Mr. Europe's band. Man, they played that music, ragtime, syncopation; the French people went crazy. Crowds would be shouting his name, 'Lieutenant James Reece, Jim Reece Europe!' It was truly something to see."

"I should have knowed you wasn't gone tell me nothin'. Why don't you never talk about the fight? Tell us how it was. How many was killed? How many was gassed? How many you killed?" The old man pantomimed pulling a rifle site to his eye, squeezing the trigger, his shoulder kicking with the recoil.

Alena felt more than saw the slightest twinge in James's jaw muscles. Saw something happen behind his eyes. For an almost imperceptible time, his smile froze and turned.

Cool Breeze continued with his act, now turning the rifle to butt a fallen opponent. Some of the men laughed. Others grew quiet, uncomfortable, angry, fearful, not quite dead.

"All right, since you don't want to talk about that. That's all well and good. But Breeze, Cool Breeze want to hear about the mademoiselles." The old man began to wiggle again. "Forget the band, tell me about the —"

"Come on, Breeze, ladies is present," one of the men chided.

"I know, but they ain't listening to men's conversations. You ain't listening, are you, miss?" Breeze teased Alena.

Crash! Alena dropped one of the bowls she was setting on the table. What was she thinking?

"Alena, are you all right?" James was up, had parted the group, and was almost to her in one swift movement.

She did not answer, but shook her head. "Here," Alena quickly handed the rest of the bowls to Dinah and stooped to pick up the pieces. She stood. "If you don't mind," she said to Dinah almost as if the girl had knocked the bowl from her hands, "I'll leave this to you." She nodded toward the table. "I'll take these pieces out with the pan of garbage from this morning."

Without waiting for an answer, Alena brushed past the girl and headed toward the door to the alley.

Disgust on her face, Dinah looked toward Patrice. Patrice, however, was quietly smiling and looking between James and the trail of heat Alena left behind her.

Outside in the alley, Alena caught her breath and silently talked her heart into slowing its rhythm. It was too much. Chicago was enough. Leaving Mississippi was enough, but James was more than she was able to put up with. Because everyone else hung on his every word —

To her right she heard a low growl, then saw a flash of white, dingy white. It was the dog, the dog from the first day.

"Come here. Come here, boy," Alena coaxed. The dog drew her from her thoughts of James. "Come here, boy. You hungry?" She reached into the pan and held out a large bone, a used soup bone. "Not much left on it, but come here. You can have it."

She stooped to eye level with the dog. He shifted paws, side to side, alternately whining and growling.

"Come on, boy. I won't hurt you. Come on."

The dog inched toward her, sadness in his eyes, even though his mouth sometimes snarled. He licked his lips, his eyes darting between her and the bone.

"Come on, boy." As the dog moved closer, she could see what seemed like an old piece of bone or wood sticking from one of the animal's paws. "Come on, boy. Let me help you. I bet that's why you act the way you do. Come on, boy."

The dog ducked its head, as if still unsure, but it was closer, almost at arm's reach. "Come on, boy."

"Miss Alena, Miss Alena!" Three of the little ones from the mission rounded the corner. "Miss Alena!"

The children startled the animal who began to bark and growl with fury. His attention turned from Alena to the children, back to Alena, then to the children. The dog hunkered down into his front legs, the dingy fur raised on the back of his neck, as he began to step toward them. The children cried out but froze where they stood.

"No, boy, come here. No, boy!" The beast turned and snapped at her. Alena fell backward and raised her arms to cover her face as the dog turned, focused for attack. She could feel the heat, smell the breath. Better her than the children.

The dog poised to leap. Then there was James. Mid-leap, one of his large hands closed over the dog's snout, holding it shut to weaken the animal by cutting off its air. James's other arm encircled the dog and held it, writhing in his arms. Alena lay on the ground confused and terrified. The children huddled together and stared, frightened. Other men came from the building along with Dinah and Patrice, watching the struggle. James held the dog until it no longer fought, then laid it limp on the ground.

"Come on, let's move inside quickly and leave him to wake on his own." James stretched his hand to help Alena to her feet. She turned away, not sure if it was in shame or anger.

He moved away and turned to the dog. Noticing the foreign object in its paw, James pulled it out quickly and tossed it into the large rusted metal can. "He'll be up soon and probably move on. Let's leave him alone. I don't think he'll be coming around here any time too soon." James turned and reached out his hand for Alena.

Twenty

"What you smiling for, you devil, you? Did you bother that little girl?" Deac stared.

"What you worried for, old man? She ain't your daughter, and you ain't my daddy," Pearl answered with the usual bravado.

" 'Cause I don't want to see a devil like you ruin that young girl's life, and I can see what you got planned."

Pearl seemed caught unawares by Deac's comments.

"Oh, old man! You see everything, don't you? You don't scare me, old man, all that mumbo jumbo. And like I said before, you ain't my daddy, so just lay off." Pearl continued grooming himself.

"I want you to know, I been praying for you all this time. Praying that the Lord would have mercy on you, asking Him to forgive you and to show you His way. No matter what anybody's said, I been on your side, caring for you like a son. I know under all that swagger, someplace deep on the inside, there's something there worth saving." Deac's face and eyes felt hot. He could hear his own heart pounding.

"But I got to tell you, I'm praying against you this time."

Pearl froze in his grooming ritual. "What you talking about, old man?" He turned and stared at the old man, something just short of fear on his face.

"Yeah, I'm praying against you. I got to. I see you using people, taking advantage of 'em, women, men. It ain't right, but they using you, or you using them, just the same. But this time, your whole purpose ain't nothing but to ruin that girl. Nothing more, nothing less." Deac shook his head, eyes still boring into Pearl's.

"I'm praying that the Lord stop you. You ain't controlling yourself. You don't even know why you trying to do it. I know that, but you still got a choice. Leave that girl alone. You trying to change her into something she not. Trying to change her into what you are and don't want to be. I don't believe the Lord gone let you do this."

Pearl looked frightened for a moment, then shook his head. "Old man, I don't even know why I talk to you. You always talking crazy. Talking about somebody got control of me. Man, you crazy. I do what I want." His usual smile looked forced.

"I know you think you do, son. Don't you know the devil got rule of this world. Man gave it to him. Adam had everything and gave it up for little or nothing. Now, the devil rule this world. He rule this world and everything in it including you, boy." Deac wondered if the younger man was understanding.

"Don't you see yourself doing crazy stuff? Saying you having a good time when you ain't. When was the last time you was happy? I don't mean it felt good on the outside for a few minutes. But I mean down on the inside happy. You don't even know nothing about joy on the inside, peace on the inside," Deac's voice pleaded, father to son.

"Leave me alone, old man." Pearl turned away, back toward the mirror.

"Boy, you know I'm right. You being used. The prince of this world own you, and he making *you* pay the price for his owning you. It's like sharecropping; you steady working, working, just so the man can keep on owning you. Old Satan tell you 'Do this, do that, ain't it fun?' so he can get you caught up in his junk. And then he own you. Then you just like Adam; you done gave everything away for nothing. You paying him to take control of you. Then somebody else got to pay him in order for you to be free. It's just a bunch of foolishness. You trying to run from it, or talk big about it won't help. It just won't do it."

Pearl clenched his fists. "Won't do what, old man? You making me sick. I'm about sick of you now. Won't do what?" Deac had moved so that he could see Pearl's angry reflection in the mirror.

"Won't save you from the one who you done just give your life to. You *working* to go there. Doing whatever you big enough to do, paying your own fare to hell." Deac pointed at the reflection.

"Oh, here it comes. Fire and brimstone. Man, you crazy, Deac. Get on away from me now." Pearl laughed and mocked.

"Boy, you done already bought your ticket. I can't love you and not tell you. I can't stand by and watch you trick yourself like you don't know better. The wages of sin is death. The only way to keep you from going where you headed is for Jesus to pay, to buy that ticket. He the only one worth enough to pay. And ain't that something. He pay the price for you, pay the cost. That's why God sent His son. But He can't do it for you unless you ask Him."

Deac stared at the reflection, looking for the slightest sign of goodness.

"Old man, you giving me the heebie-jeebies. I thought you was crazy. Now I know it for sure. All that church mess. All that Jesus stuff. Man, all that stuff is for at church. If I wanted it, I would be at church. Man, what all that stuff mean anyway." Pearl's face contorted with anger. "I done heard it all before. That's for Sunday, but come Monday and Tuesday, you got to take care of yourself. Do Jesus come to work for you? No, you got to work just like me. Where was Jesus when my mama died? Where was Jesus when I had to take care of myself? Just leave me alone, old man. I got to go." Pearl turned and stormed from the room.

Deac watched the young man leave and prayed.

"Why you crying, girl?" Pearl stepped out of the darkness again. "I told you come on. Come away with me. It's gone be too late soon. Time is running out.

"I'm about to get me one of them good runs. Folks traveling by train to New York, Miami. Rich folks tip good. Not like that old Illinois Central line. Yes, sir, Pearl gone be big time."

His eyes looked as if he were already there, accepting gratuities, flirting, fawning and being fawned over in return. Like he was dreaming not only pretty, but high yellow pretty. And women, rich women. Alena looked at him and remembered him wrapped in the arms of the women at the East St. Louis train station.

"Come on, girl. Sitting here crying. Pearl got something for you. Something better than that necklace I gave you. I bet you ain't even got that necklace. You got it still? You give it away?"

Without words, Alena reached inside her collar and exposed the locket.

"My baby," Pearl sounded excited. "I knew you wanted Pearl. Come on, girl. Come away now. Ain't much time."

She needed to be alone, to think. She covered her face with her hands.

"What you waiting on? It ain't that old church boy, is it? That fool. Probably a little sweet around the edges, ain't he? He ain't no man. He ain't got what Pearl's got."

Alena looked up, defiant. "Don't talk about him." The firmness in her own voice surprised Alena.

"What you mean don't talk about him? You sweet on him or something?" Pearl's leer faded.

"Just leave him out of it." She tilted her head up and looked straight into his eyes.

"Don't bristle up at me, Miss Mississippi. Pearl don't take —"

Footsteps from inside the mission neared the back door.

"Ain't much time if you want me, if you want to be somebody. What you gone be, some old church lady? Great Sister Miss Mississippi," he mocked the girl. "If you want to be somebody, you can come with me. Tonight."

Alena shook her head. Still confused. "Tomorrow then. Come away tomorrow." Pearl danced backward into the evening. "This time tomorrow. Down by the office where I saw you. Across from the newspaper office. Be there," he directed and was gone.

"Baby, what you doing sittin' out here by yourself?"

Alena turned her back on her aunt's question, hoping Aunt Patrice would not see the tearstains on her face, hoping she could mask her distress. Alena had not heard the door open or shut.

"Come on, baby. Somethin' on your mind?" Her aunt reached out her hand.

Alena turned to her. "Nothing, Auntie.

239

Nothing." Alena turned and kissed her aunt. "I love you. I love you, Aunt Peaches."

"*Aunt Peaches.* Alena, you ain't called me that since you was a little bitty girl." Aunt Patrice smiled.

Alena hugged her aunt and held her as if she would never see her again. "I love you, Aunt Peaches." She closed her eyes tightly, spoke into her aunt's ear, and then ran into the building.

Twenty-one

Alena heard the ruckus outside. She couldn't hear the words, but she heard the tone. Knew the cadence, knew the rhythms. She ran for the front door. By the time she reached it, it seemed five years had passed.

A small circle of people had gathered, watching. Others stepped off the sidewalk to avoid stepping into trouble. Cool Breeze stood cuffed by police officers, arms behind his back.

"Don't struggle, old man. Don't give us any reason."

Alena paused to make sense of what she was seeing, then moved to help Cool Breeze. To respond, to —

An arm scooped around her waist and almost threw her back through the mission door.

"No, Alena. You can't." Jonathan's body blocked the door.

"Get out of my way!" Alena spat the words.

"No, Alena. There's been enough

trouble around town lately. Bombings, shootings. You're going to make it worse. Cause him to get beaten or killed, or maybe someone else."

"What do you know about it? You don't care. He ain't yours." Two car doors shut outside. The engine started. Alena heard the car pulling away.

"Move, get out of my way!" She charged him, but he held her in place by her shoulders. "Get away from me. Let me go!"

Jonathan took his hands from her shoulders and just held one wrist.

"Alena, stop. It's dangerous. I know how you feel. Don't you understand? You can't just charge like that. It's dangerous times."

"How do you know? How do you know how dangerous it is? How do you know? Nobody's threatening you. Nobody's beating you, trying to kill you. You know what? I'm sick of you. Walking around here so sympathetic. Trying to fool people. Like you care. Like you're trying to do something for somebody. Exactly what is it that you're doing? What are you giving up? What are you risking, Mr. Silver Spoon? I hate you."

"Alena, I know you're angry. I know you're hurt —" Jonathan reached to comfort her — "I know —"

"No, you don't know! You don't know nothing. Did you know I hate you? I hate you. I've been wanting to tell you since I first saw you. Know why? Because you look just like the one that did it. That killed my friend. Same eyes, same hair. You're not fooling anybody. I hate you."

"Alena, what is all this yelling? What is all this noise? What is going on here?" Aunt Patrice walked in on her niece gesturing at Jonathan.

"Cool Breeze is gone. He —" she gestured toward Jonathan — "let the police take him. He didn't do anything. They were shoving and pushing. They had him cuffed. I know they're going to kill him."

"There was nothing I could do. They caught him. He had the goods in his pockets. I couldn't do anything."

"You didn't try. You didn't even try."

"Alena, be quiet."

"No! No! I know they're going to kill him."

"Alena, get hold of yourself. You don't know nothin'."

"Yes, I do. I know they're going to try to kill him —" she said to her aunt, and then turned to Jonathan — "and I know you didn't even try to do anything. Just stood by and watched. Just stood by."

"What was I going to do, Alena? What was I going to do?"

"Get out!" she yelled. "Get out. We don't want you here. We don't need you here. Get out. Go on with the rest. You aren't doing anything. Just watching. Just sitting around, standing around pretending to be involved. Just standing by watching. Get out."

"Alena, shut your mouth. Shut it now." Aunt Patrice looked angry, fed up.

Jonathan backed toward the door.

"Jonathan, don't you listen to her. She don't mean what she's saying, and she sure can't kick nobody out."

"Get out," Alena hissed.

"Jonathan, you go on down to the paper. James is down there. Go on down there until I can get her under control. Get her calmed down. This don't have nothin' to do with you, nothin' you've done. Just give me some time alone with her."

"Get out. Get out!"

Jonathan backed out of the cool darkness inside to the hot white heat outside. "Get out!" Alena continued to scream at him as he stared back into the mission. "Get *out!*"

"Alena, Alena, what is into you, baby? This is enough. You ain't writing. You ain't lovin'. Miserable and trying to make everybody else around you miserable. How long you gone be mad, girl? How much is enough? When you gonna leave this place?"

Alena gasped and her eyes burned. "You, too? You want me to go, too?"

"Alena, I'm not talkin' about leaving here, this house, this Chicago. I am talking about the place you are at in your mind and in your heart. When are you going to move from there? You gonna waste your life and try to ruin everybody else's life, too? Other people ain't responsible for your misery. You choosing to stay there, to wallow there."

"I didn't bring this on myself. I didn't kill J.C. I didn't make me leave Mississippi."

"No, Alena. No, you didn't. But none of us here did it either. And you are steady pushing us away and locking yourself in."

Alena turned her back on her aunt. Tears burned her face, and her breath would not come.

"How long you gone stand in this spot? People tiptoeing around, scared anything might make you mad, set you off. And you actin' like they owe you something. Like they ain't got no feelings."

"But you didn't see him. You didn't see Jonathan. He just stood there. Just stood there while they took Mr. Breeze away. He didn't do anything."

"Jonathan and Mr. Breeze, you think that's all I'm talkin' about? That ain't all. James, Dinah, and everybody else that comes within fifty feet of you."

Sobs, small screams, jerked from inside Alena. Sounds she could not control, birthed from someplace she did not know, did not understand.

"I know you hurt. You angry. But do you think you the only one ever lost somebody? The only one things didn't go they way? Keep on livin', you'll see. Just because I don't go around mad all the time, don't think I ain't been through nothin'. Don't think James, Jonathan, Dinah ain't been through nothin'.

"One thing for sure though, you keep on the way you are, you stick right where you are, you gone surely die one way or another."

Alena hung her head in hurt, anger, shame. "I wish I —"

"Don't you say it. Don't you say it. Every day you keep on this way, you are letting him — what's his name? Bates? — you are lettin' him win. You are lettin' him end your young life, kill your promise just like he killed J.C. You ain't livin', baby. You ain't livin' your promise.

"And I want you to know, you ain't foolin' nobody but yourself. God knows you mad at Him. Taking it out on everybody else because you don't want to take that anger to Him. But you know what the Word says, whatever you do to those other people, you are doing to Him. So you letting your anger, your hatred of Bates kill your relationship with God.

"You lettin' him kill your family. You love your mama and daddy, but you won't mend with them. Because of what? 'Cause nothing. Mad at what? Because they wouldn't let you stay and get yourself killed. Hard head, stiff neck, ice-cold heart.

"Okay, so you choose to be mad at God, mad at your family. Then what? How you treatin' people here? Treatin' them the same mean way. People ain't done nothin' to you, but you just full of bile like they did it, like they killed that boy. People you could be helpin', you makin' sure you step on them to make sure they won't never get a chance to step on you."

Alena slumped into a chair and covered her face with her hands.

"Now, I'm tellin' you, you got to choose. You got to decide. You gonna stay where you are, stay in the wrong place, keep worshiping that hatred you feel, or are you going to move on?"

"I'm not going to let them hurt me. I'm not going to let anyone hurt me."

"You trying to seal yourself off, build a wall around yourself, like can't nobody get through. You only goin' to live life if it can be on your terms. Don't you know you can't live that way? Can't live without love. Can't live without connection.

"Trying to pretend like it don't hurt you not to be whole with your mama and daddy, not to be whole with God. Who you foolin'? What is that? Pride? Won't let nobody see you need or hurt just like everybody else. You so mad at Bates, what makes what you doin' any better? You are steady killin' people with your mouth. Sin is sin. Foul, mean words, evil thoughts is murder. Ain't no different from Bates. How God gone judge Bates a murderer when you murderin', too?"

Alena was folding in over herself, crying out loud.

"Don't you know you are just liftin' up your anger? Your self-righteous anger is the place you goin' to worship every day.

You are just makin' an altar of your anger, making it a high place, a stronghold."

"What do you want from me? Haven't I been through enough?"

"I want you to fulfill the promise that God has put in you. That promise is a complete promise. This the best way I know to explain that promise. You have to go to Jerusalem, Judea, Samaria, and the world. Remember, I talked to you about Jonathan and Dinah going to Samaria. Well, it's not just for them, that whole promise, that commission is for all of us.

"I think about Jerusalem as the place where each one of us learns to love and reconcile with God, with ourselves, and with our family. We have to work to love and be at peace there, to tell the truth, to tell everybody there about the good news.

"Then I think of Judea as our neighborhood, our community. We got to love and reconcile, learn to live with people like us beyond our family and share with them what we know, be a blessing to them.

"Then, just like Dinah and Jonathan, each one of us got to go to Samaria. You know those people that live around us, the strangers among us that we don't like, don't want to know. The Lord said we got to love and reconcile with them, too. The ones we been enemies with forever, the ones we don't understand. We got to bring life and encouragement to everybody, even the ones who don't love us. We need to finish our work in Samaria first. It's when we are able to carry the testimony of our reconciliation to our enemies and walk as one with them that we will have a testimony that will convince the world."

"I just want to be left alone. I just want to find someplace to be left alone."

"I don't think you can do that, baby." Patrice sat next to her niece. "You have to live the promise in you. You got to let that promise come forth, or it will kill you trying to break out."

"What promise, Aunt Patrice? What promise? Promise that dies hanging on a tree? Promise that's too scared to fight back? Promise that lets everybody walk all over them? Promise that kills us before we even live? What promise? Promise that made me leave my home? Promise that made me leave and let Bates stay. Promise that won't give us jobs. Promise that won't give us shelter and bombs our homes? Promise that wants to kill me?"

Patrice circled her arm around her niece's shoulders. "Alena, baby, I don't know everything. I don't know all the answers. I don't know why we have to be grieved sometimes, why sometimes we have to be hurt, have to be broken. I don't know what would make a man kill a boy."

Patrice's eyes looked into another place. "I don't mean to preach, but, baby, you got a life full of promise. But first, you got to make a choice. The promise, the hope that you have, people need that gift. People at home, people here, your enemies, they need the water you bring. What hope are you bringing living your life like you're not connected, like you ain't got no responsibility to the people around you? You got to make a choice to run, to choose to walk through, or to keep passin' by."

She leaned and kissed her niece. The two women looked out the window. Same direction, same scenery, but their eyes saw different things.

Twenty-two

The light bouncing up from the sidewalk was blinding. Burnt his eyes. The heat was mean, the sun brutal. It was still early in the day.

What could I have done? Just as quickly, he forced the thought away. In what seemed like only seconds, he was standing in the doorway of the *Optimist.*

"James!" A one-word explosion in the peaceful setting.

"What's the matter?" James's back, like always, was ramrod straight.

"Nothing. Nothing —" Jonathan spoke in man's language — "Everything is fine."

"You sure?" James turned his head from the machine where he worked to his friend. "You don't look like what I'd call 'everything's fine.' "

"It's hot. It's the heat and it's still not noon. This kind of heat can kill you. Makes everybody crazy." He pulled off his jacket, rolled up his sleeves, and began to tinker at the machine with his friend.

"I was thinking —" Jonathan grabbed a rag to wipe grease away from the gear so that he could grab it more firmly — "today might be a good day to go to the beach. To check the houses by the beach, maybe by the stockyards."

"Jonathan —"

"No. No. I mean it. I'm sure of it. Today's the day. We've been putting it off. We need to get it done. Today's the day. The housing situation is past critical. Today. Besides, maybe we can stop and cool off when we're done."

"What? Me on my side? You on yours? Come on, man. We're friends in here, but you know the real world. Whose side are you going to sit on? I won't live long if I sit on your side. Besides —" James controlled his tone — "the beach will still be there tomorrow and the next day. I'm up to my elbows in this machine today. Besides, it's cool in here." James forced a smile. "Sometimes, the way we live . . ." He turned his attention back to the machine.

"Today's the day, James. I'm sure of it. I've got to do something. We've got to do something."

James looked up from the machine. "What's the matter? What's wrong with you, Jonathan? Why right now? Why right this minute?"

"We've been putting it off and putting it off. Waiting for when it's convenient for us. What about the people? What about what they need and want?" Jonathan jammed his hands further into the machine. "What about the people? What about what they need right now?"

"Jonathan, what is going on? Your face is red. You're yelling, and I think you're going to take apart what I'm trying to put together," James pointed at the machine, then wiped his forehead. "Did something happen?"

"Look, James, nothing happened. Why are you trying to pick me apart?"

"I'm not trying to —"

"Well, I think you are. We need to go. I want to go, to get something done. Are you with me or not? I can go alone if you're too busy, too tired, or afraid —"

"Afraid. What are you talking about? Something is going on. This morning we talked about working on things here in the shop. If this equipment isn't working, it doesn't matter how many investigations we do or what we uncover. You know that. Now you're in here ranting and raving. What is going on?"

"I don't need this. If you've got some

reason for not going to the beach area, let me know. I'll go alone. But don't put it off on me. And stop trying to play Sigmund Freud."

"Jonathan."

"Look, James, every day we wait, more and more people get hurt, get lost. Maybe if we go today, some of those people . . . maybe we can stop . . . maybe we can keep some people from being lost."

"We don't have a plan. We don't know where we're going, who to target."

"Today, James, today. They came and took Cool Breeze away just now. They caught him with the goods. There was nothing . . . we have to go today."

James stopped, quiet, staring into the machine. He wiped his ink- and oil-covered hands on the rag that hung from his belt, a rag that looked unable to absorb any more.

"If we go today, it's not going to fix it. It's not going to bring Cool Breeze back. If not Breeze, it's going to be somebody else." James argued, but his voice had lost its resolve. "We haven't planned. What if something goes wrong?"

"It's now, James. Today is the day. I feel it, something's happening. Something's changing. Now, James. Today."

James stared at his friend. He opened his mouth, then closed it. "Okay," he said instead. "Okay."

Jonathan pulled his handkerchief from his pocket and tried to stop the sweat from reaching his eyes. Some places the sweat was big round drops that seemed to pop from his skin. Along his brow, the drops had joined and formed a puddle. The puddle headed down his nose, some of it down his brow. He caught it with the cloth just before the salty water began to sting his eyes.

"We have tension everywhere. Where we work or can't work, where we live or can't live. I just don't know why it's got to be this area today."

"You know I like her."

The two men had left the car and now walked along the path of the South Side elevated train tracks. James and Jonathan stopped their conversation, waited for the El to pass by. "I think she's a good person," Jonathan continued. "She'll be good for you." Jonathan, washed out, faded, smiled at his friend.

"What are you talking about, Jonathan?" James stopped, his eyes searching his friend's face. "Man, what is it? Where are you today?"

"I'm fine. Come on, we need to get there while the most people are still around. I-I-I know what I'm doing. I was talking about Alena. I think I understand her. She needs someone like you."

"I tell you what, Mr. Independently Wealthy, if you're looking for a job, I don't think matchmaking is the one for you." Sarcasm sharpened James's voice. "What she shows me isn't what I'd call love."

"Alena's been through a lot."

"You know, all this time I've been saying that to myself. *Give her a chance.* But I think I finally got the message. Besides, what's got you acting as her ally?"

"Cool Breeze. What happened to Cool Breeze. She was there, and I saw it. I saw it in her eyes, how deep the hurt is. I saw it and I knew it was time."

"What does Alena have to do with us out here sweating?"

"I don't know, man. I just felt it on the inside. Today, now is the time."

The two walked on in silence out of the South Side, past the stockyards, toward the beach area, while the elevated trains continued to rumble by. The stockyards area was poor, some tenement buildings not much better than the ones on the South Side. Irish, Polish, Italian youth lingered

257

on corners. Disappointment, rejection, anger sizzled in their eyes. James saw what Jonathan did not see, slowed his pace, hunched his shoulders, and kept his eyes from his friend's face.

"I was at the YWCA for a charity event the other day. I saw a young woman, prettiest blue eyes."

"I shouldn't presume that you spoke to her, should I, my shy friend?" Peripherally, James kept his eyes on the men that looked, that watched them. Hot, sullen, frustrated youth.

"No. Well, no, I didn't speak to her yet. But next week, I believe I'll speak to one of the women in charge, maybe Mrs. O'Shea, and ask her to introduce us."

"Maybe it's *you* that Alena has been good for."

"Maybe she's good for all of us. You know, James, I just wanted you to know that you are my friend. You have been the very best friend I have had. Sometimes I have thought about you in the war and wondered if I would do it. I think I would. I would give my life for you."

"Jon, what is wrong with you today? Any more last statements. These sound like the confessions of a dying man," James jibed his friend. "You sound like Miss Blue Eyes must have your boat sailing a little off course."

The men walked on discussing their plans, almost to the Twenty-ninth Street beach. James looked in Jonathan's direction. "Basically, we should follow the same strategy as with the employment. We'll separately check the same realtors, the same landlords. Compare what they say about openings and about rates."

"What do you think about when we separate. When you get things thrown at you? What do you think?"

"Honestly? I think how confused, how ridiculous things are. How much I hate the situation. How much I hate the people that perpetuate the situation. How ridiculous it is that we were free in France but not free at home. I wonder if there is any point to what we're doing. If it will change anything. I get angry that people see us differently, that they feel justified in thinking less of me and more of you because of our skin colors. I get angry that I'm trained to be an engineer, but white people think I should be satisfied with being a janitor. I wonder if we are really friends with all the differences between us, with society's hateful interference, if we really are friends.

"Not for long though. I watch you trying to knock down walls you can't even see. Giving your resources, your time, committed, laying your heart out there, and I know you're my friend. And someday, someday, it won't be like this."

Alena was tired of arguing, tired of being on guard. For hours she had hidden away in the storeroom, wrestling with herself until she was tired. Tired of being angry at James, at Jonathan, at Dinah, at her parents. She sat on the floor and stared at nothing.

She was just tired. Alena unbuttoned her shoes and rubbed her bare feet over the cold, stone floor. It reminded her of her front porch, her grass. She missed her home, missed Mississippi, missed her parents.

She closed her eyes and tried to remember. In the still, in the cool darkness, Alena sat, arms wrapped around her knees. No light, no images, just coolness. No threat.

She breathed deeply, one of the few deep breaths since the woods. She breathed again and felt the cool from the room rush her nose, inside, down her throat to her lungs. She felt the cool inside her stomach move to her thighs, her toes. Alena exhaled and steeled her shoulders at panic that flitted around her, that tried to gain entrance. The last time, James was here. Despite what she showed, his presence was comfort, was strong, was whole, and was love. But why trust? Why give to what might not last, might be taken away? She remembered his comfort in the coolness.

Her aunt's words were like light bursts in the darkness. Magenta, blue, green. Pearl's invitation was a counterbeat, a strange tone in contrast to the colored lights, to the cool darkness.

Alena sighed and then laughed. Like good and evil pulling at her. Like the good angel and the bad angel whispering in separate ears, like in the funny papers. Deep breaths to push the pressure off her chest, the pain off the back of her neck. One hand brushed her hair back.

Mad at God? Mad at God? Tears came to her, burned even in the cool darkness. Could she talk to Him again? Could He make sense of this? Should she trust Him? Would He forgive her? Tears took her breath away.

"I don't know what to do," she choked into the darkness. "I don't know what to do. If You still love me, please don't let me go wrong." Her heart pressed against the wire, against the thorns. She closed her eyes and sat rocking in His arms.

James and Jonathan shook hands and prepared to separate until they noticed the sounds coming from the beach. Yelling, profanity, police whistles blowing. Black and white feet kicked up sand on the beach. Games of tag turned violent. Fist, feet, chains, clubs, knives out of nowhere. Gangs of white men against black. Gangs of black men against white. Screaming. The sound of fists on flesh. *Whap! Whap!*

The two men stood staring as other men crossed the demilitarized zone — the invisible racial divide — and could not comprehend.

The violence — the violation, anger, oppression, rebellion — moved along the sand toward them, like war without bombs, without uniforms — maybe skin-colored uniforms. Soon there were no smooth spots on the sand. A white fist hit James and brought him back from what had seemed like a dream. He fought back, used what he had learned, ducked, punched. A white fist struck the jaw of a white man who held a bat, ready to swing at his head.

James looked to see Jonathan swinging.

Wrong side, James's confused brain said. *Wrong side.*

A black hand from behind wrapped around Jonathan's throat and jerked backward. Jonathan's body seemed to drift away floating on a cloud of dark hands.

"No. Jonathan. No — !" James looked toward his friend, but a white fist cut off his words, and he realized he needed to move if he intended to live. Take position behind the bathhouse. He fought until he was able to free himself. Looked in the direction of the cloud that held Jonathan and saw nothing. He fought, dodged for what seemed like hours but couldn't have been more than minutes, making his way toward the street.

"Come on, man!" Black hands reached to him from a black Model T like his own.

"My friend! They've got him," he told the hands, turning back toward the beach.

"Come on, man. It's too late. They got him. If you don't come on, they gonna have you, too. Come on."

James struggled against the hands that pulled him to safety.

"What did you do to my brother?"

Alena squinted her eyes against the sudden light.

"How dare you yell at my brother!" Dinah confronted Alena, still holding the storeroom door. Alena blinked, her eyes adjusted to the afternoon light. "Is this how it's always going to be? You yelling at everybody? Maybe you should be the one to get out."

Alena stumbled to her feet, opened her mouth to speak. To explain. To tell Dinah what God had said to her in the darkness. To explain that something had changed, that in that instant she had changed, that . . .

Alena looked at Dinah's face, at the anger, the anger her actions these past few months had put there. She hadn't really heard God say anything, had she? If God had said it, if He were restoring her, wouldn't He have made the path clear? Maybe she was imagining it. Maybe it was easier for her to go than to try to work her way back through all the anger, all the confusion she had caused.

Dinah's blue eyes were surrounded by pink, her face red, flushed. "Don't say anything. Haven't you caused enough trouble? Haven't you hurt enough people? Why don't you leave?"

Alena looked into Dinah's angry eyes. It looked like more anger than she could cross. Maybe that was the solution. She turned her back and began to walk, then run, to her room. *God, don't let me go wrong. Don't let me go wrong.*

Deac pleaded with the young man in front of him. "Boy, please don't do this. I'm pleading with you, son. I can feel something coming. Something in the air. Death riding in for somebody."

"You know, Deac, you used to be all right. For some reason, I used to look up to you. I thought you was a straight old man. Now, you just . . . you just like some old woman, trying to scare me into the arms of Jesus. Man, you crazy!"

"I'm not crazy, son. I'm just trying to help you. Help you before it's too late."

"Look, man. God ain't interested in us, no how. Why am I gone be interested in Him? I ain't seen Him do nothing for no black man. We always getting the low end. We always in the back. We always the slaves. Why I want to serve a god like that? Why I want to become a old woman singing hymns to a white Jesus lettin' other white men enslave me?"

"Look, Caleb —"

"Man, why you *do* that? Why you call me by that name? My name is Pearl. Caleb, that ain't my name, that old slave-sounding name." Deac looked at the younger man admiring himself in the mirror, smoothing his hair, getting ready. *If only he spent that much time workin' on his soul.*

"Caleb ain't no slave name, son. Caleb is the name of a man that broke free from bondage. A man that was strong, didn't have no fear, took what was his. Wouldn't let no man stop him."

"That do sound like me, old man."

"Yeah, but Caleb was following God's leading. Who you following?"

"Look, old man. I ain't got no time for no sermon." Pearl checked the shirt hanging before him to make certain it was perfectly pressed, no ironed-in creases, no cat eyes.

"Ain't no sermon, son. You just been deceived, lied to, and I love you too much to let you walk out of here with a lie." For some reason, tonight seemed more urgent, like he needed to get through to the young man *tonight.*

"What lie? What lie? Man, you crazier than I thought. What lie? Old man, please!"

"See, you believe that, that the black man always been a slave. That God hate the black man. You know why, 'cause you believe what any old jackleg tell you. You a sap, ain't got good sense. You listening to men that don't know no more about the situation than you do." Pearl stopped, appeared to be listening.

"Bible is full of people. All color people in all kinds of positions. Some white men royal, some white men slaves. Some black men royal, some black men slaves. *We* hung up on color, not God. Some of the people God used most was slaves. Bein' in what look like a lowly position to men around you don't mean God don't love you. Man may mean it for bad, but God will use that same situation for good.

"I ain't no fool, boy. I hear some crazy white preachers, ain't a lot just a few, trying to use the Bible to justify slavery that went on here. To justify how we treated. But they just like you, deceived. What we had here was like slavery in Egypt in the olden days, worse than Egypt. God was against it then, and He's against it now. Slavery in Israel wasn't nothing we can even understand. Men married their slaves, lived with them, worshiped with them, fed them, and were forbidden to mistreat them. Had to liberate them after a certain period of time, and it didn't have nothing to do with color. Some men just perverted the Word of God, used it as an excuse for greed and hatred. They told that lie 'cause they wanted what other men had. Ain't never had nothing to do with God. But you believe that because you listening to men that don't mean you no good.

"Let me ask you, if you playing cards, got a good hand, and somebody you know is losing at the game, that man start to give you advice, you gone listen to that advice?"

"No, old man. Leave me alone." Pearl turned away briefly, then turned back — as though he were struggling with himself.

"Well, that's what you doin' now. People you *know* wouldn't know God if He came up and hit 'em on the jaw, you listening to them. Telling you this and that about God, about His Word. They don't know nothing, and that's what they giving you, nothing.

"Don't nobody really know what Jesus look like. And I don't think that is a accident. I think God intended it that way. It ain't important. What is important is He save the whole world. The whole world. Plenty of teaching in the Bible about not being prejudiced, about not oppressing people. Just 'cause man don't do it, don't mean it ain't there.

"Bible say we ain't supposed to fornicate. People do it anyhow. Don't mean the Good Book ain't right. It means *we* ain't right. Stubborn, disobedient, rebellious. God say one thing, people do somethin' else. Can't blame God. People got free will, they get to choose to do right or do wrong.

"Just like you, boy. You got a choice. You just runnin', tryin' not to have to give an answer. Don't mean God is bad 'cause you do wrong. Can't judge God by people, white or black, men or women, not even preachers. God's ways ain't our ways."

"What church you plannin' this sermon for, old man? You wastin' your time on me. I ain't servin' no white God." Pearl turned away. Focused on his clothes.

Deac pleaded with him. Put his hand on Pearl's shoulder to make sure he had his attention. "Son, you know that is just an excuse. You know in your heart Jesus don't look like in them pictures. That's just man's eye view. Everybody Jesus save think Jesus look just like him. And maybe everybody is right. Maybe Jesus look like all of us."

Deac's hand fell away as Pearl turned to meet his gaze. He had to keep talking, to try to persuade the younger man. "Whatever he look like, He the only one that can save your soul. Wouldn't a white man be a fool to reject Jesus' saving grace because Jesus had black skin, brown eyes, woolly hair? Same with you, Caleb. You deceived. You a fool to say you rather go to hell than accept salvation from God just 'cause some man, some man just like you, painted Him with blond hair and blue eyes."

"Don't call me no fool, old man." Pearl moved toe to toe, nose to nose with Deac. "I ain't the fool. Why I'm gone trust some God that ain't never help me? He didn't stop my mama from dying. Didn't stop people from using me, taking advantage of me when I was a kid on my own. I took care of myself. He didn't help me when I needed a job. I got the job for myself. And if it's so good, if Jesus is so good, how come people fighting wars over Him? How come your Jesus let them do that? How come the same ones shouting, 'Yes, Lord! Hallelujah!' is the same ones wanting to hang me from a tree and put chains on my feet? How come, old man?"

"Caleb, I don't know everything. Sometimes, it gets on me. I start to wonder the same thing, but then I look in the Word, and I see that God's own people, He allowed them to be in slavery. Men who had great favor with God, like Joseph, He allowed them to be in slavery because He had great plans, great purpose for them. What we got — what we got to do must be mighty powerful that God was willing to let us go through so much suffering to get here. Our purpose must be powerful. We just don't know all the plan."

Time running out. "We sometimes lose trust in the promise. Like in the war, sometimes the ground to take or the mission is so important the general got to make the decision to let some precious lives be lost for the sake of many, so that the ones that remain can take the high ground. But them men that is chosen to fight in that battle don't do no good, purpose is lost, if they get confused, if they start to think that their individual lives are more important than the battle, more important than the general's plan. They got to obey the general, trust that what the general is doing, is allowing them to face, is for their good, for the greater good. If they lose their trust, forget their purpose, the battle sure to be lost.

"I trust Him." Deac thumped his chest. "I know there is a purpose to what we have been through. What we going through. I trust that He won't let my struggle, my suffering be in vain. There is some reason,

271

only He knows, that we are here."

"I ain't interested in no God trying to make me not be a man! I ain't got to hide behind nobody's skirts. Not even Jesus'. Nobody. I ain't afraid." Pearl's words were brave, but there seemed to be something hidden behind the bravado.

"Son, you misunderstand me." Steel flashed in the old man's eyes and on his face. He took one step even closer, so that he and the younger man had no space between them. "Yes, I'm meek. And that might look to you like fear, but don't you make no mistake. Man ain't been born that I'm afraid of. I don't have to be.

"You ain't the only person had a hard life. My life ain't been no bed of roses. Once upon a time, I was angry, just like you. Fighting everybody. Telling everybody off. Getting in everybody's face. Making sure wasn't nobody gone run over me. Trying to be *bad*.

"Wasn't nothin' but a show. I had so many walls up to keep people away that I was trapped inside myself — no peace, just alone." Deac held up his hands like barriers. "Not to mention that love and joy wasn't nowhere on my horizon. I couldn't even enjoy the sinning I was doing. But then one day I decided I didn't want to be a child no more." He dropped his hands.

"I ain't no child, Deac." Pearl flexed his shoulders.

"Yes, you are. Just a big ole child. Fast talking, loud talking, bluffing to try to keep people off of you. I know. I been there. What you afraid of? You don't even know. And don't tell me you ain't afraid. You can fool other people. You ain't fooling me. It's that fear, that same childish fear that's ruling your life. You can't enjoy the pleasure and reward of being grown up, of being a man, 'cause you still fighting childhood fights."

Deac struck the back of his hand against his other palm. "I ain't got all the answers, Caleb. But I know fear ain't the answer. If I'm quiet, if I'm peaceable, if I'm meek, it ain't because I'm afraid. It's because I became a man. Not a big old scared boy, scared of man, scared of God so he trying to keep Him at bay.

"Decided I wasn't gone let my past keep me from my tomorrow. I stopped fighting God. How you gone win, boy, trying to fight God? God gone win every time. I just figured it out before He blew on me. And, man, I can't explain it to you, but He just took that edge off me. Pain I was always trying to fix, He just . . . one day I looked up and it was gone. He been a good friend to me. God ain't using me, He give to me all the time. What's more, He left me standing, a man.

"And I ain't afraid to fight. I just got peace in my heart; I walk in it. Something you can't understand right now. I ain't afraid to fight. When God tell me to fight, I fight. But until that time, I'm walking His road the way He tell me to." Pearl looked away and made a very small movement backward.

Deac's arms dropped to his sides. "Son, I don't know all the answers — why men don't do what God tells them to do, why men don't treat other men fair and equal — I don't know. Each man have to search God hisself. What I do know though, the fault don't lie with God. It lie with man who is choosing the wrong no matter what God say. And you looking at them, pointing, even while you sinning right now yourself. All sin is sin. Lying is a sin, and doubt is the same sin. Doubt is a sin and whoremongering is the same sin. Same sin. That I do know. Them other questions, you need to ask God."

Pearl looked around as though he were boxed in, as though he were looking for a defense, a way out. "What about money?

Church don't want to do nothing but take people's hard-earned money. Preachers riding around, big time."

Deac shook his head slowly. "What didn't you hear me say? You know what, son? You just running, playing a game, running from defense to defense. Keep on, keep on. The door ain't gone always be open. Keep on. You can't call on today's chance when tonight comes. And I tell you, something's coming. Go on, boy. What evil you planning, do it quickly."

Pearl stepped back, clearly startled at the force of the old man's words, at the fire in his eyes. The younger man hesitated for a moment as if he would speak, as if he were deciding, then quickly fled into the Chicago afternoon.

Twenty-three

Salty tears stole their way from Alena's eyes to the corner of her mouth. She prayed. Silently, she prayed for direction, for comfort. Through her prayers, she could hear her aunt's voice singing outside.

Alena stood and walked to the side window so that she could see her aunt. Pushing back the lace curtains, she saw Aunt Patrice taking freshly washed clothes down from the lines stretched across the yard. Summer flowers were sprinkled here and there. Some red, some blue, some gold. Despite the bare spots, the patchy grass, her aunt's presence seemed to make it a quiet place, a garden. Aunt Patrice was singing while she removed the wooden clothespins, occasionally bowing her head as if she were praying.

Her aunt's prayers seemed serene though, not anguished like her own. And her melody seemed to lift and linger outside Alena's window and drift in on the afternoon sunlight. Sunlight that touched gently in the room and reminded her of other days, another place. Alena wished she could go back there but could hear the memory of her aunt's words, carried on the hymn she now sung, on her prayers, "You got to go through . . ."

Alena sat again and did what she had seen her mother do. She rocked, prayed, and read her Bible in the fading light, drawn to the passage her aunt had quoted.

Alena closed the book and following her aunt's voice, went down the stairs and out the door until she had joined Aunt Patrice outside.

In silence, she too began to remove clothespins.

"Not much time left —" Aunt Patrice nodded toward the sun — "Night's gone be here soon." Aunt Patrice talked as if she had been expecting Alena, as if she had been there all the time.

"I — I'm trying to understand." Alena's words faltered.

"I know you are, baby." Aunt Patrice smiled while the women reached for the last few pieces.

"I don't know if I can . . ."

"You'll make it. For certain, you'll make it." Aunt Patrice finished Alena's sentence. Both women reached for opposite

277

ends of the last sheet.

"I'm trying to understand what you were saying to me about Samaria and all. But I . . ."

"It just gets to pouring out of me. Can't keep it to myself. The words just come pouring out. I know it must be like a flood." Aunt Patrice's smile said she was poking fun at herself. "Can't nobody get a word in when I get goin'."

"Help me to understand."

"I don't understand it all, but last night when I was studyin' the Word and prayin' to God, askin' Him to help me understand, it seemed like He was saying that we people, we do all these things because we don't walk in His ways, we walk in men's ways.

"Let me try to explain. You ever seen families that hold grudges, keeps feuds going. Sometimes they is good people, righteous people, church-going people, but they doin' what they learned from their fathers, mothers, wives, or husbands. They see their good mother holdin' grudges, and they think that's okay, it's the right thing to do. They don't check the Word of God and see what it says, and even if they do check it, they reason it away and make excuses why their mother's way was right, no matter what God says. They don't want to go against what Mama or Daddy said, they want to walk in their ways even if that mean walkin' against God." The two women walked toward each other with opposite ends of the sheet, meeting and folding. Once folded, they placed the sheet in a basket and picked up the next one to fold.

"But I still don't understand, Aunt Patrice."

"The same mistakes we make in our families — in Jerusalem — we make them in Judea and Samaria. Just keep on going.

"You know, Alena, the Civil War been over a pretty long time, but you know there are people still mad about that war. Mad because they feel like somebody stole somethin' from them. Don't even consider that they were trying to hold on to something that wasn't even theirs. Mad at the North. Mad at the South. Mad at the Race for wanting to be free. They don't realize they fight is not with man, they fight is with God, who said we would be free." The women folded three, four, five sheets while they talked. The smells of sunshine and fresh air permeated each piece of cloth.

"Just like the Israelites in olden times,"

Patrice continued as they worked, "they are worshiping in the high places even though God told them not to do it. Some of those kings in Judah tried to walk in God's ways, but they just wouldn't go all the way and tear down the high places. King Solomon did wrong, worshiping in the high places; his son saw and followed right after him."

"I still am just not getting it."

"Just hear me out, baby. I'm going to get there." After finishing the sheets, the women moved to pillowcases. Side by side, they folded the rectangles as they talked. The sounds of children, of cars, seemed far away.

"Some families, the children see the parents didn't wait to get married before they have relations," Patrice continued. "Then when they have children, their child sees their good parents doin' the same thing and think that's an acceptable thing to do. Another high place just got built.

"Right now, the children in the nursery are looking at you. They love you. They think you are a good person. They see you being rude, telling everybody off, being mean whenever you feel like it. Guess what, you building a high place right in front of them. They'll grow up thinking that's okay to do. Just like in the olden days, how you act is giving them counsel to do wrong."

They continued to fold. "Um, that one's got a hole in it. I'm gone have to fix that." Patrice moved to throw the torn pillowcase in another basket.

"I'll take it. I can do that," Alena took the item and smiled at her aunt. Something felt like home.

"Thank you, baby." Her aunt smiled, then continued where she had left off. "Boys see their daddy, the deacon or somebody, treat his wife wrong. They love their daddy, love mama, too, and don't want to see her get hurt. But that high place has been built in their minds. Daughters see their mothers disrespecting their fathers, saying whatever they want, cussing at the men. That mother is buildin' a high place without even knowing it.

"Now I think I'm coming to what you asking me. Same way with race prejudice, I believe. Children see their mothers and fathers doing wrong. They love Mama and Daddy, and they don't want to challenge what they done seen or been taught. Don't even want to consider, it's so painful, that their good mothers and fathers may have been doing wrong. So they have to just keep building that grove higher and higher, trying to justify it, not realizin' that they are leadin' their own children into further sin. When you challenge what they believe, it's like you saying somethin' bad about their mamas and daddies."

Alena stopped folding to listen. She stared at her aunt, certain she knew now where her aunt's story was going.

"Some of their great-granddaddies was in sin, and they still got to reason, look for excuses why that altar, why hatred is okay. They got to spend their energy trying to justify their supremacy, building up imaginations because that's the reasoning they came up with to justify the wrong. Now they got two high places. And those high places are hard to tear down. It's scary for them to tear their high places down, just like it's hard and scary for you to think about tearing down your anger."

Alena looked at the folded sheets and pillowcases that were now in neat piles. She wondered if her aunt noticed. If her aunt could see that somewhere inside, inside Alena, something was loosening, something was breaking free.

"It's so scary, they don't want anyone to even tell them or talk to them about prejudice and supremacy. Some of them, I think, hate us because we are the evidence of their sin, maybe of their fathers' sin. The colors of our skin, what we know or don't know, how we live, it is all testimony. Judgment walking around in the flesh, and they want us to be gone, be out of the way."

Alena continued folding. Clothes now, blouses and shirts folded and into the basket. Colors contrasting with the crisp white sheets.

"They want to pretend there's nothing wrong. There ain't no high places." Patrice turned toward her niece. "Just like you, you don't want — didn't want — anybody to confront you about your anger. But they got to admit the problem to God, just like you had to admit you had a high place before God will hear and help with the problem. And I believe it makes them hate themselves because deep down inside, God's Spirit tells them that it's wrong.

"See how your face burn, how anxious you get when I talk about your anger? I can just about hear your heartbeat speed up. You get angry and want to deny it. Well, it's the same way when you say *prejudice* or *supremacy* to somebody that's got a stronghold in that area. Same thing happens when you say *alcoholic* to somebody that's got a problem in that area or *harlot* to somebody that's got a problem in that area. I feel the same way when I hear the word *gluttony*, that's how I know I got a problem in that area. I don't feel nothing when somebody says *alcoholic*, but my feet sure get to moving when somebody says *gluttony*."

Alena stopped folding. Turned and put her arm around her aunt, comforting her. "I love you, Aunt Patrice. I always loved the feel of you."

"I know, baby. I love you, too. And you know what, I have learned to love myself even as God is helping me to walk in His ways. I can love myself because I know He loves me. He does not hate me for my weaknesses, for my failures, for my wrongs. It pleases Him that I am willin' to confess that I have not walked in His ways. It pleases Him that I am willing to accept the correction, the reconciliation and grace that His Son offers, the love and reconciliation that will tear down the high places and restore me to the path He wants me to walk. People don't know just how much hope there is."

"Aunt Patrice, I think I can pray and ask God to help me not be angry at my mother and father. But I don't think I can pray to forgive Bates. I don't know if I want to forgive him and men like him." Alena looked intently at her aunt. Her eyelashes held back tears.

"Baby, I don't know why J.C. is dead. Why somebody, why some people think it was okay to take his life. Why people think it's okay to call us out of our name, to think us less than them. And I ain't gone lie to you. There was a time I was so angry, so hurt, I couldn't hardly stand to look at a white man or woman. I thought there wasn't nothing could melt the cold wrapped round my heart."

Alena's tears fell, then her aunt's arms were comforting her.

"One day though something happened. Love overfilled me. Jesus wrapped round me, warmed my heart. Spirit wrapped around me, and I began to weep. Seems like that ice melted from around my heart and overflowed my eyes, and I knew it then. I knew it. Then my tears melted from pity to healing to grief for the ones who are walled in the stronghold. Grief because we are one, their sin is mine. I have a responsibility to help restore them."

The two women wrapped themselves around each other more closely. The blue checkered shirt in one of Alena's hands dangled loosely.

"Grief because they really don't know they are sinning," Aunt Patrice continued. "People like that sheriff, they don't know they are sinnin'. Mothers that tell their children to stay away from us, we're dangerous, we're animals, they don't know they're sinnin' and worshipin' in high places. People that don't want to touch or get too close, they don't know they're sinnin'. People that don't want a colored man over them as an officer or a boss, they don't know they are sinnin'. Even worse, they don't know that the biggest part of the sin ain't against us, it's against God."

"I don't know if I can forgive, Aunt Patrice. Why should I? What has changed?"

"What changed was not that man or anybody else. It's me. I'm telling you I'm still wrestling with it myself." Aunt Patrice took a hand away from Alena to wipe away her own tears. "A man take my seat, won't give me a place to live, calls me names, takes my freedom, and is determined he won't apologize to me, he don't even think about he got to apologize to God. Don't want to live next door or work beside me. It's God he has offended. That man steady attending church, reading the Bible, singin', prayin', don't know he is grieving Jesus.

Sometimes, baby, I look at all the mess we have made . . ."

Alena and her aunt stood silent in the fading light. Watching the birds making their last journeys from tree to tree. Listening to the changing sounds of the city.

Patrice wiped her face and cleared her throat. The two women smiled softly at each other and returned silently to their folding. Hurrying to finish before the light was gone.

"I just know we got to do better. Family members ain't talking. We living our lives in silent caves. Hating each other because of color, language, or whatever. We get so wounded by all this foolishness we just want to hide away. We just won't love nobody. We won't nourish our heart because we've been hurt. Just pushin' love away. When God send somebody to us to love, to be a husband or a friend, we push them away because life in this world has hurt us. We cast away the very thing that might give us some comfort while we're here. Treading on the good gifts God is trying to give us."

Alena could feel herself stiffening in reaction to her aunt's words.

"God tries to give us comfort, give us love. We be so spiteful, too scared to receive the good gift God is givin'. Treatin' God's gift like swine. God is trying to give us someone to lift us up, to make our hearts glad. And we end up fightin' against the very thing we want, against the good thing. Against a love that wants to walk in the straight gate. Like you with James."

Alena knew that was where her aunt was headed. "Aunt Patrice, I, we —" She had stopped folding to try and interrupt, to defend herself.

"Just close you mouth, Alena. I'm not going to say nothin' else about him. It's all related though. But sometimes it all looks so hopeless. I can't figure it out. How to get out of the maze. Then just when I want to give up, God reminds me that I don't have to figure it out."

Patrice looked up toward the evening sky. There was a swatch of pink that matched the towel she was folding. "See, Jesus' love is so big it binds us together. We might not like it, but He still loves other people when they're wrong just like he still loves us when we are wrong. That love reveals our wrongs and makes us cry salty, burning tears. That love softens the heart of a person being persecuted as well as the persecutor. That love is gone bind us all together one day."

"That love makes us see ourselves, our sin, makes us see how we hurt other people," Alena added, beginning to understand.

"That love give us hope," Patrice continued.

"Makes us love beyond what we want to love." As Alena spoke, she thought of her family, the farm, and of James who had been so patient.

"Makes us take the good news of His love to those we hate and makes us love them," Aunt Patrice spoke in her turn. "Makes us run with good news to Samaria, makes us want to help them pull down the high places. That love makes us move beyond book religion, beyond go-to-church-every-Sunday love, to love that binds and constrains.

"That love made me run right to Samaria. Made me stop to offer living waters and hope at the deep well of hate where hopeless people stop to drink. Made me give bread of life to those who starve 'cause they only feeding on despair and bitterness." Patrice's eyes turned toward the mission.

Alena signed. It all seemed so much . . . too much maybe for one day.

While they talked, night had come.

★ ★ ★

Pearl whistled in the growing darkness. Usually it was the time he felt most comfortable. Darkness was his friend. It made the shapes of the day a little less certain. Darkness blurred the lines between buildings, between people. It hid the borders. Darkness covered what appeared harsh, even filthy during the day. It hid all the unswept corners, all the smudges. It made what was ugly in the daylight beautiful or at least palatable.

Thank God for the darkness, Pearl lifted his hands in praise and mocked Deac, then laughed to himself. He usually enjoyed the darkened journey from the boardinghouse where the Pullman porters lodged to the Stroll.

The laugh, his smile, didn't linger. The air was too quiet, too still. None of the usual sounds. Pearl strained to hear what was missing. His efforts only returned the sound of his feet, loud on the pavement. Worry knocked at his heart, but Pearl shook the shoulders of his outer man and walked on though he did try to soften the sound of his shoes striking the pavement.

Click, click. Click, click. The second and fourth beats the strongest. *Click,* click, *click,* click. Heels on cobblestones. Pearl's mind went to the rhythm. He began to intentionally accentuate different beats. Click, *click,* click, *click. Click,* click, click, *click.* On his way to get the girl; she would be a diversion on his way to Miami. When he got tired of her . . . that was her problem. Click, click, *click, click.*

Still, the uneasiness would not leave. Felt like something on his back. *Click, click,* click, click. Like something crawling up his back onto the nape of his neck. He brushed behind his head at nothing, stopped, looked around discomfited.

Stupid, just stupid. The old man. Just letting that old man spook me.

Click, click, *click,* click. Pearl stopped and looked back, then swore at himself. *Click,* click, *click,* click. Nothing else besides his shoes.

I ain't scared of nothing. An invisible freight train rushed past his ears. Sweat soaked his collar. Pant, pant, panting for no reason. He was panting. Looking over his shoulder.

Old fool, old fool. I'm not gone listen to that old fool no more. Won't let him plant that hoodoo in me no more.

Click, click —
Run.
Pearl stopped, looked around. What was

that? Almost like a voice, a presence, yelling. The something was crawling up the back of his neck.

"Spooked," he said out loud to himself. "Spooked by an old spook." He tried to laugh off what was chasing him.

Run!

It was like the presence he felt when his mother prayed. When Deac prayed.

Old Negro. *Jesus this, Jesus that. Jesus, Jesus, Jesus. Deac is wasting his time*. Pearl had seen enough of what Jesus could do.

Where was Jesus when they didn't have food or clothes to wear? They were starving, and there was his mama praying all night long. Telling him Jesus would take care of them. Where was Jesus when she got sick, when she worked herself sick? Where was Jesus when he prayed and asked Him to help her? Jesus just watched her fading away, disappearing right before his eyes. When he cried out, he didn't see no Jesus. Didn't see no angels, no sweet chariot. But she kept on praying right up to the end and kept telling him not to be angry, not to be afraid.

Caleb, the Lord is gone watch over you. Don't you be mad now; it's just time for me to go. Don't get no stony heart. God know best. God know best.

She couldn't even get mad. Couldn't fight for herself. He wasn't gonna end that way though. Couldn't count on nobody but yourself. And so far, so good.

Click, click, *click,* click.

He stopped to listen. Silence, almost too silent. Like tornado weather.

Some things were the same though. The heat. Thick Chicago nighttime heat and the packing-house smell, a thick foul odor you could slice like hog's head cheese. Something they did in the packing house, some process with the slaughtered animals that made that smell. That smell hung in the summer air. Some things you could count on, most of them bad.

Still something, something just . . . He stopped again to hear.

Now, some sound. Some sound far away rolled to him, fractured in the air, in the smell. From the corner of his eye, he saw it folding in on itself. A ball like in the funnies, like in a cat fight. An arm here, a foot there. Like a blur. Like a ball rolling toward him. Angry men. White men. A mob.

Run now. While another voice, the voice he heard most often in his head now mocked, *Too late.*

Pearl stood still, frozen, and watched the

writing mass move toward him. There now, a face, an angry mouth, two, three, twelve.

Too late now, the other voice mocked louder. *Too late to run now.*

Alena removed her shoes from the closet along with her dresses, skirts, shirtwaists. She folded the clothes and tried to place them in her two bags. Finally she packed the best ones and left behind what would not fit. Her aunt might be able to use the pieces in the mission.

She looked around the room at the bed, the curtains, the dresser with her book on top, the book her aunt had given her. She moved to the chifforobe and rubbed her fingers over the depressions the letters created on the front cover. And over the green cloth softened by her aunt's years of use.

She focused, picked up the Bible, and stuffed it into her carpet bag. She would miss Sunday evening prayers.

Beneath her, downstairs in the mission, James, frantic, rushed through the door heaving words to Patrice and Dinah. "I'm, I'm not sure. We were walking by the Twenty-ninth Street beach, and then there was hysteria. People shoving, screaming, fighting, beating each other and shooting. One group grabbed me," James said, "and another group grabbed Jonathan." He looked toward Dinah, not willing to say what his eyes had witnessed: riot, race riot.

"I couldn't get to him. I-I . . . Some men grabbed me. I have to go back. I-I — Men beating each other. Throwing each other off of the elevated train tracks. Stopping in cars to fight. Shooting."

James's shoulders flinched and hunched suddenly at a sound like a small munition, a small bomb, somewhere down the street. Outside the door in the street, on the sidewalk, calm feet turned to frenzy, running past the door. Patrice, confused, watched, trying to make sense of it all. In what seemed to take forever, James turned toward the front door and watched women and children running by in one direction, looking back, panic on their faces. Running, legs stretching to full extension, hands on their children herding them along.

James moved quickly to the door to get a clearer view. The same mothers, more mothers like them, bent slightly, covering their children while husbands covered them. Other men and older boys ran in the opposite direction.

James's eyes followed them. He stepped through the door and out into the street. Two men bumped him as they ran by carrying another man. The one they carried wore torn clothes covered with soot, smoke curled from burns on his back. James followed the direction from which they came.

Orange, red, almost white tongues licked out of the windows of buildings farther down the street. James stepped out. Men in disorganized groups with small buckets throwing water against large flames. Some running into buildings, carrying out bodies, young and old. Without verbal command, he began to run in the direction of the blazes while Patrice and Dinah watched.

James moved out the door. The two women saw him turn and begin running down the street. They hurried outside to see him running toward the fire.

"Oh, my Lord, help us. What is going on?" Patrice huffed as she kept pace with Dinah. In that strange way that brains work during crisis, she thought, *I didn't know I could still run like this* as her legs, her body strode despite her clothes' constriction.

Fifty feet from the burning newspaper

office, in front of Patrick's Confectionery, James and another man worked with a bar or long-handled wrench to open the red-painted water hydrant. Heat from the flames pressed their faces, tightened the skin. The colors brought wicked light to darkness, reflected on one side while the other darkened. Swelling air exploded windows while men shouted commands. Patrice reached for the next pail as she and Dinah joined the bucket brigade.

Below in the streets, Alena could hear voices, hear running feet, still distracted, she did not bother to look below. She thought of the man she was going to meet, of seeing him on the East St. Louis train platform, of her home, of her aunt, of James.

"God, please don't let me go wrong."

She walked downstairs through the side door exit that led to the alley, hoping that everyone would be occupied and would not notice her. She stepped into the night, still somehow oblivious to the people, the events not far from her.

One foot. One foot in front of the other. She kept her eyes focused on her shoes. Right foot, left foot. She was going away with Pearl; it was the best thing. He would take care of her.

I will take care of you. I will love you with everlasting love. I will walk with you. A whisper in her spirit.

It would be too hard. Too hard to try to undo all that had been done. She would go with Pearl to New York or Miami and make a new home. Forget about Chicago, about Mississippi. It was the best thing. Not much choice, she told herself. *I can't start over here, God. Can't undo what I've done, erase the memories, the bad ways I have treated people. It's too much. If I go away, I can start a new life, start fresh.*

I will walk with you. I have need of you here.

Heat, more than the summer night heat, touched her and caused Alena to look up. Framed by the firelight in darkness, James, Patrice, Dinah worked among the men, battling a force that had now made embers of the newspaper office.

Alena stood, suitcases in hand, in the middle of the street. On one side of State Street was darkness — darkness that would allow her to hide, to escape. On the other was light — fire that burned. Fire that could light, fire that could destroy. Fire that uncovered the bags she held, that illuminated her intentions, light that would soon expose her if she did not move.

God, don't let me go wrong.

I will walk with you.

Forgive me, Lord. Alena wept as what had seemed like the easier thing, what had not seemed like sin became sin in her eyes. *Forgive me for the anger, for the hardness, for running away.*

Come back through the doors, back to My arms.

Patrice grabbed a bucket and looked up just in time to see James turn from where he worked. He looked startled. Patrice's eyes followed his. There was Alena. The two stared at each other. The look Alena gave James seemed different, transformed. Her eyes seemed softer. Submitted eyes.

James stared. He had stopped working. Aunt Patrice was sure that James saw what she saw. Alena's dress, her bags, they said she was leaving. Then her aunt saw something else.

James took a step toward her niece. The flames, despite their destruction, provided a living, searing backdrop for the couple. He looked back into Alena's eyes, as if he saw something else. Something he had hoped for, something promised, something he needed. Alena dropped the bags. Her eyes never left his face. Loving eyes.

"Where do you need me?" Aunt Patrice heard her niece say over the noise.

Pearl stood and watched, transfixed, until the ball, the mass overtook him. Until he became part of the organism inhaling, exhaling, feeding on itself. Cursing, yelling, hating, feeding.

Riot, the word came to him. His body was flung back and forth; the thing tore at him. It took chunks out of his flesh, punctured him, sucked his life's breath from him. It jerked him and pummeled him until it appeared satiated. The mass hesitated, spit him out, dropped him. Stopped to prod him, poke him, to stomp one more time. They were men, but their faces, their actions did not seem like normal men. Seemed more like a beast.

Satisfied, it moved on.

Pearl lay in the street surrounded by debris and the strips and pieces of what had been his clothes. He tried to breathe, but his chest would not raise. Tried to see, but his eyes would not open. Then something was on him, more hands on him, trying to pull him up. He could feel something warm and wet running from the side of his mouth.

"Oh, honey! Oh, my son."

Pearl could hear a man's voice somewhere above his head, somewhere far away. "Oh, honey, what did they do to you? I think they done killed you. I got to get you up from here. Caleb, Caleb, boy, I tried to tell you. I knew something was coming. They gone tear this city apart."

Whose voice? He knew that voice. Pearl opened his mouth to speak and felt wet bubbles in his mouth, on his lips.

"Oh, my son. What am I gonna do, Lord? Help us. Lord, help us."

Pearl smiled. Eyes still shut. He reached for the voice and grabbed its collar, its robe. *Finally,* he thought. *Finally.* He knew who it was. He knew. Finally, He came like she said He would. She knew. He came.

"Jesus," Pearl whispered, sticky fluid wet on his face, lips, neck. "It hurt so bad. Hurt so bad."

"I know, honey. Oh, my son, look what they done to you."

"Jesus, where were you?" Pearl breathed. "Why so long? Where were you when she died?" He sputtered, lips barely moving, voice barely audible, speaking somewhere beyond.

I was where I was when my Son died, my beloved. I was always as near as you would allow.

Caleb struggled to open his eyes and looked at the cantaloupe moon through dark green lace.

Deac sat rocking on the curb, the boy's head on his lap. "Lord, full of mercy and grace, help us," he spoke into the new night sky, each star in place and undisturbed.

"Man, people dead all over the place. What we been fearing all the time. Just like in Washington. Like East St. Louis. Riots."

The men gathered in the dawn hours in front of the mission. Waiting for coffee, for some sign it was over. The fire had exhausted them. Their eyes looked haunted. "Found men, even women and children all over the beach where it started. Colored men and white men."

Alena could see fear on James's face. She knew it was for his friend.

"And they say it ain't over. People have gone crazy."

Patrice, Dinah, and Alena, still in what was only hours ago her best dress, carried coffee to the men in cups, jars, tin cans, whatever could be found. Children carried biscuits. Biscuits that on an ordinary day would have been something to savor, today were something to sustain.

A Model T, scratched and dented, pulled in front of the mission. A man jumped from the car even before it stopped.

"I got the *Tribune*."

Twenty-four

Page one of the Monday, July 28, 1919, *Chicago Tribune* featured a banner headline "Full Confession by Slayer of Janet." Thomas Fitzgerald — by all appearances a mild-mannered, even timid Virginia Hotel watchman — had admitted to the horrible murder of little Janet Wilkinson. A two-by-four-inch picture of the brown-haired dandy stared innocently from the front page.

The senseless crime had gripped all of Chicago for weeks, but the well-groomed, bespectacled man's crime and the little girl's story could not compete with the headline beneath it: "Report Two Killed, Fifty Hurt in Race Riots." Even news of the streetcar strike that gripped the city held little interest.

"Bathing Beach Fight Spreads to Black Belt. All Police Reserves Called to Guard South Side," a smaller headline read.

Two colored men are reported to have been killed and approximately fifty whites and negroes injured, a number probably fatally in race riots that broke out at South Side beach yesterday. The rioting spread through the Black Belt and by midnight had thrown the entire South Side into a state of turmoil.

The story reported to readers what Alena, Aunt Patrice, James, and others already knew.

Gangs of white men ordered Negroes riding trolley cars to leave the cars and come to the streets. When they refused, the trolley cars were pulled off the wires, and the blacks were dragged from the cars and beaten.

The newspaper reported the torching of a drugstore at Thirty-fifth and State, but did not report the loss of James and Jonathan's newspaper office. The fighting started, it seemed, over a bathing incident at the beach. According to the paper:

Racial feeling, which had been on a par with the weather during the day, took fire shortly after five o'clock when white bathers at the Twenty-ninth Street improvised beach saw a colored boy on a raft paddling into what they termed "white" territory.

A snarl of protest went up from the whites and soon a volley of rocks and stones were sent in his direction. One rock, said to have been thrown by George Stauber of 2904 Cottage Grove Avenue, struck the lad and he toppled into the water.

Colored men who were present attempted to go to his rescue, but they were kept back by the whites, it is said. Colored men and women, it is alleged, asked Policeman Dan Callahan of the Cottage Grove station to arrest Stauber, but he is said to have refused.

Then indignant at the conduct of the policeman, the Negroes set upon Stauber and commenced to pummel him. The whites came to his rescue and then the battle royal was on. Fists flew and rocks were hurled. Bathers from the colored Twenty-fifth Street beach were attracted to the scene of the battling and aided their comrades in driving the whites into the water.

James was able to piece together that he and Jonathan must have come upon the scene at that time. He sipped the hot coffee with the other men while they read and discussed the article. Despite the spirited conversation and argument over the article, at moments James appeared to lose focus. His eyes looked northward, and Alena knew he was thinking of his friend, planning how to go back for him.

"Man, they got guards all around that beach now," a man who had also been to the beach said to the group. "Can't nobody get near it. They been dragging the river all night. Say they found the body of that colored boy that got knocked off the raft, but they looking for someone else."

"Yeah, I heard that, too," another man offered. "Say they looking for a young white man, supposed to got killed. Supposed to be in the water."

"What man?" James's attention appeared to come back to the moment.

"Some white man. Said he was young, blond hair. Looked like a businessman."

Alena could see the muscles working in James's jaw.

"Say the crowd just carried him off."

Patrice put an arm around Dinah's shoulders. The girl blanched white and appeared to stumble. James closed his eyes, only for an almost imperceptible second, visibly shaken. He opened his eyes then and looked around, stopping when he looked into Alena's eyes. She tried to send him hope, tried to tell him without words not to give up hope.

It might be someone else. It might be no one.

Over cornbread from last night and more coffee, the men discussed other details from the night before. Two carloads of policemen had been called out to rescue Callahan. During the rescue, one policeman was shot, along with three Negroes. The fighting continued to escalate as black and white mobs attacked each other. Both sides brandished weapons, and whites stationed themselves on prominent corners in the Black Belt. Lone individuals were easy prey, the men said. Men were beaten as they walked down the street, as they waited for streetcars, as they rode on their ways to and from work. Women and children were victims, too. The women and children would have to be protected, the men said. They would have to keep them inside where they could be guarded.

James's eyes again found Alena's. She prayed that the insanity would end.

Outside the mission window, sunflowers reached up toward daylight.

Throughout the day and into the night, gunfire, sirens, screams could be heard. Hospitals overflowed with casualties. Men, women, children, even babies were brought to the mission for care. Alena changed pan after pan of red-stained, warm, soapy water. Wrung out pieces of torn sheet used to make do. In between cleaning and bandaging, the women prepared soup and skillet bread to feed the wounded and the men — when the women could persuade them to stop just a minute — for sustenance.

Her aunt's face showed the strain. "We got to stay in prayer. No matter what you doing, you keep prayin'. These people need more than we can give. Those men outside need more than we got to give. And poor Dinah, Lord, have mercy. I can't even think about Jonathan. You just keep prayin'."

Alena put blankets over the children. What had been a day nursery was now, by necessity, an overnight shelter. "Don't you all worry. Everything is going to be all right," she whispered to them after prayers. Outside the room she prayed that her words of comfort would be true.

Across the room, Dinah washed at the same bowl for five minutes, alternately scrubbing fiercely at stains and staring blankly into the soapy water. Her face was ashen. Shine was gone from her hair.

Alena moved quietly to the girl. "I'm sorry," she whispered.

Dinah sagged, her head drooped as hopeless tears dropped from her chin. "Oh, God, help me," she moaned. Alena reached to hug, to comfort.

"Don't touch me!" Dinah awakened. "Don't try to act like you care. Like you . . . you're not glad. You told him to leave. You told him to go."

"I didn't mean . . . I just wanted you to know that I'm sorry. That I'm praying for him. That I know how you feel."

"How *I* feel?" Dinah laughed. "That's funny. You know how *I* feel? How could you . . . ?" Realization flashed in Dinah's eyes, then she turned away, head down, back to her bowl.

"I just wanted you to know. I'm sorry. I care."

Across the great room, James stood poised with her aunt. "Be careful." Patrice's lips appeared to form the words just as James went through the door.

He moved quietly and quickly through the shadows. Careful to stay out of sight of passing cars that might hold guns, gangs, or clubs. He moved toward the Eighth Regiment Armory.

During the day, men had passed word of a meeting.

When he reached the armory, guards were posted at the door. The room was filled with men, war veterans discussing the riot, making plans. "The *Trib* says they got thirty-five hundred troops ready to send in here," said one.

"In here? Why they sending troops to the South Side, man? People coming from outside to here," said another. "Why don't they go to the other parts of the city?"

"Good question, but we don't have time for that right now. We need to make sure that we have a presence. That we are represented out there on the streets," another veteran added.

The men nodded and voiced their agreement.

"They've already called out the Eleventh National Guard Infantry, the First, Second, and Third Reserve Militia," one more voice added to the discussion. "We were in the thick of things over there, and we definitely need to be involved over here. Maybe if we get involved, we can stop some of the looting and arson. For sure, we can put an end to some of the killing."

"We got to. The paper's saying twenty people killed just today. That don't count all the injuries. The *Trib* says 158, but, man, I seen way more than that, just by myself. And it's spreading." More voices joined the discussion.

"Yeah, my pops works in the Loop, and he says that mobs chasing busboys, porters, maids, people just trying to work on the job. Chased one man right into a restaurant in the McVickers building. He hid out in an ice chest. People losing their minds."

"What about the beach where it started?" James inserted. He joined the conversation among men joined not by friendship, but bound by a common threat.

"What about it, man? It's locked up tight. They got police and militia everywhere. You can't get within blocks of the beach."

"I got separated from my friend. We were down there. And he — a crowd carried him away."

"Sorry about your friend, Major, but if you ain't heard from him by now, ain't very likely he's still with us. Thank God you still here, man."

"You check the paper?" another man questioned. "The paper's been running a daily list of people killed or injured in the riot. You could check. At least that way you would know for sure."

James looked into the faces of the men who were near him. "Have you heard anything about people being killed on the beach?"

"Just the same stuff everybody's been hearing. They found one young Negro man, and they still dredging for a white man. Ain't found him yet," one of the men responded. "But if you looking for somebody, forget about it. Ain't nobody down there now. You wouldn't find nothing there if you could get there."

James sat back in his seat. Shut down. Face blank.

"Now, let's get back to order," the organizer told the group. "What we're here for is to organize a platoon, volunteers, so we can help restore order here before someone else does it for us. Chief Meager from Cottage Grove Police Station is going to deputize us and issue us rifles, and Mayor Thompson is supporting this action.

"It's not going to be easy. Houses have been torched and bombed. You all know there are people coming here by foot, driving in cars, and shooting whoever they see, shooting at people on trains. Looting businesses, burning homes, beating people to death. And they don't care that we are veterans. They are attacking veterans just like everybody else, if not more so. We have to be prepared to offer armed resistance to keep the peace. To help people trying to pass to and from work at the stockyards and at the Loop. To help those who are trying to move from their homes or from the area to more safe areas. Some people have chosen . . . some of the men are sending their wives and children to Calumet City, to Evanston so they will be safe.

"We thought we left the war behind us —" the speaker paused, lowered his head, then lifted it — "but, God help us, looks like the battle line is right here in our own front yard."

Alena swept the kitchen floor. All the children were asleep. The adults were asleep or too worn-out to look or even converse. The motion of the broom hypnotized her. Back and forth, back and forth, she could pretend she was in Mississippi, in her mother's kitchen.

"Alena. Still awake."

She hadn't heard James walk upon her. He looked into her eyes, and Alena blushed. It felt like he saw too much, like her guard was down. There wasn't time to act like she hated him. There wasn't even time to pretend that she didn't like him. No time to cover what she felt. Exposed, her veil was down. And his guard was down.

"Tired?"

She nodded her reply.

"Why aren't you in bed? The children are asleep. Everyone's settled."

"It helps me not to think," she said simply.

"That's what I need." He sighed like it would never happen. "To not think. To not be here for just a little while."

Alena held out the broom and smiled softly. James smiled and reached out his hands as if he would take the broom from her. Instead, he folded his hands over hers so that they swept together.

His eyes held onto hers. Back and forth. Back and forth. Her knees weakened. She was lost in his eyes and in the motion of the broom. Brush, brush. Back and forth. Back and forth. Embarrassed by what she felt, by what she was sure he could see in her eyes, Alena lowered her gaze.

Still sweeping, James reached out one hand and used a finger to lift her chin. His eyes still held hers. "Thank you, Alena," he whispered. He leaned forward and kissed her cheek, barely brushing the side of her mouth. "Thank you," he repeated. He stood and smiled. Just one dimple . . . on his right cheek. She willed her hand not to touch it.

James stood staring into her eyes for a moment longer. Still holding her hands holding the broom. He cleared his throat. "I . . . I'm going now. Come lock the door behind me."

"All right." Alena moved behind him and wondered if that were really her voice. Her voice sounding stupid, sounding grateful, sounding like telling her to lock the door was such a huge thing, such a protective thing.

"Good night." He turned to her, and then he was gone.

Early in the morning, birds chirped, as was their habit. Alena watched as they flapped their wings, unaware of the news that men carried. News she had heard given in muted, hushed tones. That twenty-six people had died, that two to three hundred had been injured, not far beneath the birds' perches, in three days of rioting.

God's sun arose above her in predictable hope, even though in Chicago, overnight, general orders had been issued for the conduct of police and military in dealing with race rioters. Above her, pink touched the pale blue sky, while the sun's light was still a dawning promise. Life's daily renewal was unfazed, while men and women bought newspapers publishing Special Order 140 that read:

To Commanding Officers:
Captain of Police Mullen of the Cottage Grove Avenue station will take charge of the military situation.

All men are instructed not to fire except by direct order of the commanding officer.

Capt. Mullen will instruct what he wants done. The method of doing it after we receive the instructions depends upon the judgment and discretion of the military commander.

If there is a mob and the civil authorities instruct the military forces to disperse it, it is up to the military forces how the dispersing is done.

Employ all peaceable means possible to disperse the mob. Fire only as the last resort. The bayonet and butt are to be used before firing commences, and will be found to be much more effective.

Under police direction you are entirely justified in taking extreme measures for the protection of life and property.

By order of the adjutant general.
ANSON L. BOLTE
Colonel Commanding

Alena dared, momentarily, to venture into the backyard to retrieve laundry. Around her it seemed tree leaves and flower petals smiled and reached upward, unaware that State Street, their home, had been the frontline of battle between those who would each call themselves sons of God.

The flora, it seemed to her, lifted hands in praise and ignored the men who fought beneath or above. Ignored what she had heard whispered, what she had read. Ignored that Hampton Institute reported between 1882 and 1903, at least 2,060 Negroes, men and women, were lynched in the United States, that the Library of Congress reported 921 more were lynched between 1904 and 1919.

Rose blooms ignored that 76 people of color were killed in 1919, and that this number did not include men like J.C., whose murders were not reported. Ignored that the numbers were not just statistics, but were mothers' sons. Were terror in the night, where young men could not walk free but swung instead from trees.

The blooms did not know that the terror had taken wings and followed her to Chicago.

Alena watched the clouds drift through blue skies and realized they could not know what she knew. What was carried on the grapevine, what was spread in newspapers. Word that on July 29, four thousand U.S. regular army troops were mobilized to assist three thousand policemen and thirty-five hundred Illinois soldiers in quelling the rioting that spread from the South Side to other parts of the city. While forces stopped mob violence on State Street, on Thirty-fifth, on Wabash, mobs on the West Side sought out and attacked lone Negroes. Thousands, the *Chicago Tribune* said, dragged people from their homes. Blood and fists and guns and fire — a foul incense sent heavenward.

Servants were dragged from businesses, people whispered, in the Loop district. And just beneath their whispers, just beneath the news stories, Alena was almost sure that in the background Lincoln's ghost recited, *Four score and seven years ago, our fathers brought forth upon this continent a new nation: conceived in liberty . . .*

Police escorted some employees back to their homes on the South Side, while some rode back in mail trucks without windows. In Englewood . . .

. . . and dedicated to the proposition that all men are created equal . . .

. . . on Robey, on Racine rioters battled, while on Normal a group of two hundred stoned several colored men. Near the stockyards, railroad men, a veterinarian, a deacon . . .

Now we are engaged in a great civil war . . . testing whether that nation, or any nation so conceived and so dedicated . . . can long endure . . .

. . . beaten, left for dead. On the North Side, "100 men, women and pickaninnies," the *Tribune* reported, were taken from their homes to the Chicago Avenue police station for protection while Reverend Father Louis Giambastiani pleaded with his parishioners for a return to order.

We are met on a great battlefield of that war. We have come to dedicate a portion of that field as a final resting place for those who here gave their lives that this nation might live . . .

While crowds threatened colored servants of wealthy Gold Coast homeowners . . .

It is altogether fitting and proper that we should do this. But, in a larger sense, we cannot dedicate . . . we cannot consecrate . . . we cannot hallow this ground. The brave men, living and dead, who struggled here have consecrated it, far above our poor power to add or detract. The world will little note, nor long remember, what we say here, but it can never forget what they did here . . .

. . . Governor Frank Lowden pleaded for calm, and Twenty-ninth Street beach patrolman Callahan was stripped of his star. Red Cross Executive Secretary J. W. Champion appealed for car owners to assist in providing aid to stricken people . . .

It is for us the living, rather, to be dedicated here to the unfinished work which they who fought here have thus far so nobly advanced. It is rather for us to be here dedicated to the great task remaining before us . . .

Social activist Ida Wells Barnett called for a committee to devise ways and means of protection of the Negro and to lessen race prejudice . . .

. . . that from these honored dead we take increased devotion to that cause for which they gave the last full measure of devotion . . . that we here highly resolve that these dead shall not have died in vain . . .

. . . even while the *Chicago Defender* published special handbills encouraging blacks to stay off the streets and to refrain from lawlessness.

. . . that this nation, under God, shall have a new birth of freedom . . . and that government of the people . . . by the people . . . for the people . . . shall not perish from this earth.

Alena stared at the purple mums growing in the planter in the window above the sink in the kitchen of the mission and saw that the flowers ignored the commotion in the room, how some people stood in shock, some wept, some wore resigned faces, while the summer breeze lightly lifted the edge of the paper that listed the name of Jonathan Michael Bowling, confirming that he was among the dead.

Dinah screamed and buried herself away in the corner, away from the news of her brother's death. From all the hands that tried to hold her. Aunt Patrice gripped and ungripped, gripped and ungripped, wringing the pink gingham pinafore that covered her dress.

Alena gently moved people away from the girl, understanding the hurt deeper than tears, the physical pain. Understanding the fresh open wound left by new grief, a wound so big that it threatened the life of the one left behind. "Give her space. Give her room," Alena spoke gently. She looked at the girl, so tiny, and remembered the confusion, the blurred vision, the lost abandoned feeling.

"Give her some time. Wait until she's ready," she said while Dinah wept.

Patrice wiped at her eyes with the apron and smiled at her niece. "Come on now, you all. You heard the young lady speak. We got mouths to feed and bandages to change. This right here, we gone have to give a little time and prayer."

Alena looked to the girl weeping in the corner, wondered when she would run out of tears, when shaking and sobs would be all that remained. While Alena worked, she thought of James, how she would tell him about his friend, if he already knew. She looked at the faces around her, shocked and frightened faces, worried and hopeful that it would end. There were no more shots in the streets, no more yelling, no more ambulances, no sirens. Maybe the worst was past.

The screen door opened and slammed shut. James's face said it all.

Twenty-five

Major James Pittman, dirtied and scarred by battle, head high, walked past the group in the mission. Past Dinah, through the kitchen, into the pantry. Closed the door and slid to the floor.

"Oh, God." His insides shook. "Oh, *God* . . ." His face turned upward in the darkness. His shoulders, his sides, his face held tight, barricaded against the horror of the last four days. He felt his chest heave, felt a tremble. James balled up his body further to keep control. He pressed downward on the despair that rose almost to his nose, suffocating him.

"No more, God. Please —" He stopped so that his voice would not break, not even in the silence alone.

"James?"

He heard her voice and could not speak, afraid he would burst.

"James, where are you?"

A sweet voice, cover, comfort for a world out of control. Coolness for some-

324

thing that burned.

"James?"

He could not answer, held his breath.

Then she was beside him. Her hands found his face. Wiped the tears that had escaped. Held him, comforted him until he could not resist. Told him it would be all right.

"James, are you all right?"

"You don't know what I have seen. What men have done to each other. What we have done in these streets, to each other, to my friend."

"Do you know? Do you know about Jonathan?"

Then he could not hold it, and he wept in her arms for his friend, for men and women and children on Wabash, for soldiers who did not leave the trench, for parents who died so young, for a little boy who carried too much, saw too much.

Alena held him and tried to apologize for the world, for Chicago, for what she had done. "I saw you the first day. I knew when I first saw you, but I was being stubborn. I had been hurt, and I was taking it out on you . . . on everybody. But you have been so good, so patient with me.

"In my mind, I couldn't figure out a way to make things better, to undo everything that I have done. I was leaving. But when I saw you in the street, I knew. I knew I couldn't leave. My heart was here. James, I'm sorry. If you would . . . If only I could make all this go away. I had found a way to leave and I . . . because I knew I couldn't make it right. Now everyone's gone crazy, and I feel like I have to tell you —"

He stilled her words with a kiss.

"I love you," they whispered to each other in the safety of darkness, in the protection of arms. They vowed love while they talked of deep and mysterious things, hearts open and fluttering in the darkness. They laid down arms, and he pledged betrothal while she whispered "forever."

And what felt like a cool wind blew about them, seemed to blow at their faces, at her collar, the hem of her skirt, across his eyes, at his shirtsleeves, until they were strengthened to leave, to enter the light of the day.

As they stepped from the room, nothing had changed; everything had changed. It was difficult not to smile, even with all the grief around them. The two looked around the room at all the displaced people. There was much work to be done. James's eyes looked to Dinah, who now slept like a child in the corner. Across the room, the screen door opened and slammed shut.

"Hope you all still got some biscuits up in here!" The old man's joshing cut through the heaviness in the room. "Jailhouse food don't taste so good. Miss Patrice, I swear I done lost about ten good pounds."

Cool Breeze used his left hand to illustrate, wiggling his loose pants around his leg. "I tell you, jail ain't no place for a body to be —" the old man looked toward his right arm draped around the neck of his companion. "No sir, it ain't no place to be, is it Mr. Jonathan?"

In the confusion that followed their appearance, Jonathan and Cool Breeze told the story of their reappearance in between bites of buttermilk mixed with hot cornbread. Temperaments flopped rapidly between joy and recrimination.

"I'm so happy!" or "I thought you were dead!" or "Thank God!" or "Why didn't you call?" or "Thank you, Jesus!"

Mostly, it was joy.

The older man pushed food into his mouth like he hadn't eaten in months, rather than days. "They had me down at the Cottage Grove station." Cool Breeze explained around a mouthful of buttery cornbread. "And just as I had showed them my receipt for my goods, and they knew they had a honest man on their hands, that I had been *unjustly* detained —" the old man preened — "all manner of foolishness broke out. People was coming from everywhere. After a while they let old Breeze go, and I found myself on Halstead Street down by the river. Then what you think? Some young toughs — a group of them mind you, 'cause can't no one or two take old Breeze — ganged up on me, roughed me up, and threw me in the river. Now a normal man, that would have been his end. But they didn't know who they was fooling with."

With all that was shattered and broken, the people still laughed through their tears at the old man's storytelling.

"No sir, those young hooligans didn't know who they had a hold of. I climbed up out of the drink and tried to make on my way."

Jonathan shoveled in hungry mouthfuls between laughs at Cool Breeze's story.

"But they was thugs of the worst kind," the old man continued theatrically, "and began to beat old Cool Breeze again. A lesser man would have given way. But I fought — some of them got shiners and missing teeth that prove they got just a little too close to Mr. Breeze — but 'cause they were a big gang, they overtook me one more time and threw me back in the river." Cool Breeze looked exasperated. "Well, that about did it. I was good and mad then. I didn't care if they did have mamas at home, I was just getting ready to come up out of that water and put some whoop upside those young criminals' heads, when the police come along. Now, I believe those policemen could tell that those young scalawags were about to meet their end, so to save *them,* the police picked me up and took me to the Chicago Avenue station, which was one of the quieter stations.

"And *that* is where I came upon my friend here —" Breeze patted Jonathan's back — "who looked like he had seen better days."

Aunt Patrice refilled Cool Breeze's cup. The old man looked at the younger man, nodded, and winked.

Jonathan laughed and choked, a trickle of buttermilk trailed from his nose. Dinah hugged him and handed him a cloth. Her color was back.

Jonathan turned to James. "When we got separated, I was in the midst of the crowd fighting. Somehow, the police grabbed me, and I realized you weren't with us in the wagon. I tried to go back for you, but they wouldn't let me. There were so many people in the station, so much confusion, they wouldn't let people leave. Telephone lines had been cut, so there was little or no way to call or get word.

"I kept looking for your name in the paper, and hoping I wouldn't find it. You can imagine my shock when I saw my *own* name. The best I can figure is, since I lost my wallet in the scuffle, somebody must have found my wallet on the beach. I heard they were looking for a young white man that was supposed to have drowned. Someone must have put two and two together, got five, and then my name's in the paper.

"Soon as things cooled down —" Jonathan put an arm around the old man's neck — "me and my traveling partner made our ways here. And that's that. All in all, things could be worse. And it looks like some things got better." Jonathan smiled at James, at Alena, and at his sister.

Into the evening, they all told stories of what they had seen, what they had escaped, what they had come through. Compared wounds, compared loss, and joined in hope.

Twenty-six

James's face was grim as he walked through the South Side making his way to Alena, to the car parked near the mission, to the train station. Burnt-out buildings, broken windows. Sometimes there was no place to step where he could avoid glass, so it ground beneath his feet into the concrete sidewalks.

His mind, like a Victrola, skipped back and forth over recent events. Trying to make some sense, some rational melody of the pieces of his life. The World War I Armistice had been signed; Prohibition had been enacted; and there were rumors that a young punk, Al Capone, had recently moved from New York to Chicago seeking to capitalize on men's lingering thirsts. Men were whispering, and fingers of scandal had begun to point at the White Sox; people were talking about a wild-haired physicist, Albert Einstein. And yet a strange descant played, distracted James from the odd harmonies.

Riots. And not just in Chicago, for

between April and October, there were twenty-six race riots in cities such as Washington; Omaha, Nebraska; Longview, Texas; and Chicago.

In Chicago around him, people had begun to rebuild their lives, to form committees, to study. New melodies, new bridges. Black and white union men told stories of solidarity, of how they stood together, how they refused to fight each other during the four-day riot. He had read story after story in the papers.

The *Chicago Defender* castigated the state's attorney for allowing white rioters to go free while colored rioters were punished. At the same time, the paper touted Authur Brisbane of the *Herald-Examiner* and quoted him in an editorial.

One thing is certain, that the Negro has good cause for complaint . . . to be transported North by one class of white men anxious to get rich in a hurry or to break up strikes of white labor, and to be murdered by another class of men when they reach the North and begin work, is not a lot to be envied.

The *Defender*'s own editorialists then continued:

We agree with Mr. Brisbane that ours is not an enviable situation, but it is from such outspoken and unbiased minds as his that much can be done toward improving existing conditions. The attitude of the press has much to do with public sentiment. Newspaper suggestion is a powerful factor in creating whatever sentiment the public holds toward our group in this country. The great need of the press of this country is more men of the Brisbane type.

Great minds throughout the country struggled with the issue, with trying to find the sense, the melody. With new notions of race. Struggled, while around James in Chicago, men and women rehinged doors, replaced window panes, and swept away debris.

We must not seek reform by violence. We must not seek Vengeance. "Vengeance is Mine," saith the Lord; or to put it otherwise, only Infinite Justice and Knowledge can assign blame in this poor world, and we ourselves are sinful men, struggling desperately with our own crime and ignorance. We must defend ourselves, our homes, our wives and children against the lawless without stint or hesitation; but we must carefully and scrupulously avoid on our own part bitter and unjustifiable aggression against anybody.

This line is difficult to draw . . .

W. E. B. DuBois, editor of the NAACP's monthly publication, *Crisis*, wrote the words of caution and anguish in the September 1919 issue. Then he continued, "If the United States is to be a Land of Law, we would live humbly and peaceably in it — working, singing, learning, and dreaming to make it and ourselves nobler and better; if it is to be a Land of Mobs and Lynchers, we might as well die today as tomorrow."

James had felt one with the anguish, with the incessant beat, and yet hopeful, like the people he saw at work around him.

He thought about the committee he had joined: The Joint Emergency Committee, an executive committee formed to help plan and organize the execution of work needed to restore the lives of the citizens of the South Side. The committee was formed of one member each from the Cook County Bar Association, the Urban League, the YMCA, the NAACP, and the

Ministers-Social Workers-Citizens Conference. A lawyer was furnished, free of charge, at each police station and court to assist with the legal defense of any colored persons that needed help.

While James's work with the committee went on, the *Chicago Tribune* opined:

We have seen — and we have pressed this point before — that the problem of the races cannot be settled with bricks and guns. The process must be deliberative. Weapons and mob spirit are the means of expression of the unthinking. The hoodlum sees a chance to heave a brick, heaves it; no matter what cause or whose head the brick hits. It's no good trying to impress reason upon such.

Deliberation is the process, and it must be used by the intelligent, who abhor violence and perceive that the savage majority will sooner or later wipe out the savage minority. In this sort of game the innocent and peaceful of both races will contribute their lives in greater or less number.

Even so, the rain had continued, and day followed night. And the melody played on while he walked and the city revived.

And somewhere, in the midst of the sound, he heard her name, "Alena," drifting, calling.

"I love you," James said with his eyes, as well as his lips.

"Me, too."

"I want you to do what you need to do, Alena, and then hurry back to me." He fiddled with the hair that fought to leave her lowered, broad-brimmed hat and to frame her face. "Make sure you give your father my letter and write me or wire me if you need me to come, or to let me know you've convinced your parents to return with you."

He looked into her eyes, then grabbed one of her hands and pressed it to his lips. "Alena," he breathed. Steam blew about him and in the Chicago air, already beginning to chill. His hand moved back to her hair, as if he couldn't resist touching it.

"When I come back," she began. The words reassured him, pressed his shoulders into relaxation. "When I come back, I'm going to take care of my hair. Get it straightened." She almost apologized.

"No, Alena, not your hair. Not this hair." His eyes continued saying what his lips would not allow. *"Not this beautiful hair,"* his eyes spoke. *"I dream of it, I dream of it at night,"* his look said.

"Beautiful," he said aloud, inhaling.

Alena seemed to share the breath with him. Her face looked surprised and embarrassed and then pleased that he loved even her hair. Accepted even her hair.

She smiled up at him from where she stood on the platform, dressed like Chicago. Broad-brimmed hat barely upswept in the front; loose-fitting jacket, pale blue wool, over a cream-colored shirt waist, over a skirt that matched the jacket. It was all from a pattern in the *Defender*, she had gushed to him excitedly while they had driven to the station. Material from the State Street dry goods store. Going home presents from her aunt. She'd been excited and talked nonstop.

A long way from their first ride together.

"Are you sure you don't want me to go with you? I'm ready to leave now if you say the word."

"No, James. You have work to do here, and I promise you I won't do anything crazy. Your love is with me, God is with me. I have to do this myself, make this right myself. Then I'm coming back, James. I'm coming back."

Camouflaged by the steam, she leaned forward to kiss him, and her hat brim made a cover for their love. They held for sweet moments the pact their lips made.

"You know we are concerned about you going back to Mississippi. Ever since we read the Creed of South printed in the *Chicago Defender*." His hands caressed her face. "We knew it, but for the governor to be so blatant, to say that he supported and understood white people who didn't want us to come back down South, supported people who would take our lives, who would lynch us. It's a dangerous situation." His thumb traced the shape of her full lips.

"I know this is important to you, and I know God is stronger than all of our fears. Our faith is stronger than our fear. You know I want to be the man and protect you, but I understand what you've been saying. You need to do this. So you go home. You go to Mississippi. Make peace. Then you hurry back to me. Back to Chicago."

They stood on the train platform. James leaned his mouth to Alena's ear. "Alena, my beloved, my light." He continued to lean, to enfold, until his love covered her. "Alena," he breathed again. "God, most high," he prayed, "Holy and lifted up, bless my love and keep her from harm. Surround her with my love, with Your love that is in me." His blessings warmed her. "Order her steps. Direct her mind, heart, and soul," he breathed into her ear, into her spirit, into God's ear.

"Thank You, that You make of two, one. I give her back to You. Your will be done because I love her, but I know You love her most. Keep her in the hollow part of Your hand. Keep her safe. Thy will be done, then return her to me, I pray, so that we may unite in a way that gives You honor, glory, and service.

"Bless You for creating Alena and for loving me enough to gift me with Your precious lamb. Amen."

The train whistle blew. His kiss — his kisses — lifted her, made her hungry. People walked all about them, in and out of the fog. Alena stood still, lifted up, and understood in that second. Understood how much God loved her, that He would give her a man who loved her, that loved Him, a man who prayed for her. A man whose prayer, whose thoughts, whose life moved her to tears. She understood that James was not a man who wanted to steal God's lambs. Rather, James asked God for her love and walked through the doorway, through the gate as God directed.

She was moved by his voice in which she heard that other Voice; the voice she heard when her father prayed — the voice of God's spirit. James's voice, his prayer, his love moved her, and she could feel her spirit falling into his, her eyes drowning in his eyes. In that moment, she understood her mother's words.

Seeing a man down the road wasn't about his job or his physical appearance. It was about the quality of his faith, of his hope, of his love. Looking down the road was about seeing the essence of the man, the *spirit* of the man. Everything else might change. His appearance, his strength, his fortune might pass away. But faith, hope, and love — gifts from God — would remain.

Alena continued falling into James's eyes.

"All aboard!" the conductor called from down the line.

"I love you, Alena." James held her hand like forever.

"You better come aboard, Miss." A hand reached down through the steam to help her up the iron steps onto the train, the southbound *City of New Orleans* on the Illinois Central Line. The hand reached further until the Pullman porter's face appeared.

"Deac!"

"Yes, ma'am." He looked toward James. "I kept an eye on this girl coming here. Looks like now I'll be watching over a lady." He smiled.

"She's going home, then coming back so we can be married."

"Is that right?" Deac beamed, congratulations in his voice, as he lifted Alena onto the train. "That is wonderful, Miss Alena. Look like Chicago turned out all right after all. Well, sir," he said. "All right then."

Settled into her seat, Alena looked briefly out the window and prayed for her aunt, the mission, Chicago, and for James. Then for Pearl. As he'd seated her, Deac had told her about Pearl's accident.

"He got beat up in that rioting. Beat him up real bad. I didn't think he was gone make it, but bit by bit, he coming around. Seems to be on the mend. Something like this sometimes make a man think twice. I believe he counting up the cost. I'm praying he will get his life together."

Deac smiled. "Wouldn't that be something, Pearl saved. And to top it all off, you getting married. That is a wonderful thing."

Alena looked out the window, smiling. She prayed that God would open Pearl's eyes just as He had opened hers. And that maybe, just maybe, when he was ready, God would also send him someone wonderful to love. She smiled, again thanking God for James.

She rubbed her hands over her purse — a cloth bag from Carson, Pirie, and Scott that matched the color of her suit. Touching the bag, she could feel the shape of the articles cut from the *Chicago Tribune* and the *Defender*. On one of the *Defender* clips, just above an advertisement for Madame C. J. Walker's bleaching cream and to the right of an advertisement for Egyptian Miracle Hair Grow, was an opinion editorial piece on lynching.

"How long will be long enough? How many mothers' sons must be mistreated? How many of God's children must be burned," the article written by Alena Waterbridge began. Her hands moved to notes from her aunt and from James asking her parents to move to Chicago.

The old woman sitting beside her looked cold. Alena reached into her large carpetbag and lay her comforter over the old woman. "You can lean on me," she told her.

The wind that had blown behind her now blew ahead, through Effingham, through Memphis, on her way back to Mississippi.

Twenty-seven

Eric Bates walked in the front door of his comfortable home and breathed the smell of order, of life on schedule. The last traces of pine and ammonia provided the background for baked apples, crust, cinnamon, roast, potatoes, and cabbage. He checked his watch. It was 5:45 P.M., on schedule.

He cleared his throat, the set signal for his family to acknowledge his presence.

"Daddy, Daddy, you're home!" His daughter ran into his arms, taffy-colored hair bouncing, shining, flying, only held back by one blue satin ribbon. She kissed his cheek and laid her head on the shoulder of his khaki uniform.

"Daddy, you need to shave," Amanda said wrinkling her nose.

"Is that so? Daddy's been out working hard, keeping you and your mommy and your brother safe. Real hard work, missy, and that's it. That's all I get, huh? Old daddy needs a shave? Well," he said pretending to put her down, "let me stop hugging and get to shaving then."

"No, Daddy. That's all right. It's not so bad." She kissed his cheek again. "I'm glad you're home, Daddy."

"Me, too, sugar."

"Hey, Daddy. I thought you'd never get home. The back tire on my bike is flat, and I'm trying to get in some riding before the sun goes down. I need you to help me fix it. I already got the water in the bucket out back so we can check for leaks."

"Hold on there, mister. You too big now to hug your daddy? You just come in making demands? I guess I better get all the hugs I can out of your sister since she's just five. Seven must be too big to hug your old daddy."

"No, Daddy, you're not too old. I mean, *I'm* not too old." Isaac followed his sister into his father's arms. Isaac's head lay on his father's other shoulder. Their hair mingled, the father's a darker version of the son's.

Eric hugged but did not squeeze the life out of his children, who looked as they should. Hair washed and combed, clothes cleaned and pressed. He admired them properly.

"Where's your mama?"

★ ★ ★

Miranda looked upon her family from the kitchen doorway. "Hello, Eric." She wiped her hands on her apron, checked her hair to make sure it was in place, and tiptoed to kiss her husband. She stepped back to make sure her apron was still presentable, that her husband would be pleased.

Her eyes searched the room. No dust on the sewing machine, no loose threads, no scraps underneath. All the family pictures, the landscapes, oils and watercolors were straight. The floors were swept and clean. The windows were still clean from the latest spring cleaning. The sofa was neat; the doilies properly situated. Eric's rocker was turned toward the fireplace, from which the ashes had been removed. Her eyes moved toward the kitchen. Dinner was only minutes from being done, and the table was set.

Miranda's eyes moved back to her husband's face. He smiled, approving. "I love you," he said.

"I love you, too," she said, looking into his eyes while her hands straightened her son's suspenders. She touched her auburn hair, glad she had taken time to wash it early this morning, and relaxed into a deep breath. "How were things today?" She touched the children's backs to signal that they should get down.

"Mommy, I want Daddy to help me with my bike," Isaac whined, sounding as if he were afraid his earlier request would be forgotten.

"Mommy and Daddy are talking right now, and you shouldn't interrupt when grown-ups are talking."

"Sorry, Mommy." Isaac didn't look sorry.

"You take your sister and you two go play for a minute. I'm sure Daddy will be right with you."

"You can count on it, mister." Eric winked at his handsome son.

"So, how were things?"

"Things were fine. Nice and quiet. You know, I love you in that dress. I always did like how those pink flowers look next to your skin and hair. I got the prettiest wife in Ellisville. The prettiest wife in Hunt County. Probably, the prettiest one in all Mississippi."

Miranda blushed and checked her apron again.

"Not to mention the prettiest daughter and the handsomest son." He winked again at his children, who stood in the doorway that led through the house to the back door.

"I fixed you a nice dinner —" Miranda reached up and cupped her husband's face in her hand — "and I made those apples you bought me into a pie."

"I smell it. I can't wait, can you all?" he questioned his children, who still hugged the doorway.

"We can sit down soon as you and the children wash your hands."

"Good, honey —" He kissed the hand that still touched his face — "because me and some of the men got a meeting tonight. We might have to take care of some business."

Miranda froze inside but did not remove her hand, did not let her eyes flicker. She was well practiced. She smiled as her husband kissed her hand again, then put her other hand over her heart to quiet its beating.

"Daddy might have a little evening work to do." Eric smiled again and winked at his children.

Miranda smiled but thought of the galvanized metal bucket out back. She looked to her beautiful children, who beamed at their loving father. Today the bucket held clear water.

"Not before we eat though. And certainly not before we fix that tire. Right, mister?" Eric's words came just before disappointment could settle on Isaac's face.

"Right, Daddy!"

"Come on you two. Let's get this show on the road." The man and his children raced to wash their hands.

Using cornflower blue, daisy yellow, and white hand towels, Miranda moved the hot platters and dishes to the dining room table. The white tablecloth was covered with cornflower blue flowers she had hand embroidered. The same flowers were on the white starched curtains.

You're being foolish. You've got a good husband, a good life, beautiful children. This is foolishness. She took deep breaths to push away the anxiety that overwhelmed her when she was alone. She couldn't get it off her mind. Couldn't get the bucket off her mind. The night visits. *This is foolishness,* she chided herself.

She stood after placing the last serving dish. It had blue flowers on it, too. *Blue flowers everywhere.* She smiled over her anxiety. Blue was her favorite color. She especially loved blue flowers, and they peeked out of every corner in her house. Eric didn't mind. He indulged her passion and often brought her gifts — fabric, hats, pictures, dishes — that bore the blue flowers. Her husband did whatever he could to keep her happy and safe. Miranda's hand patted her chest. *Foolishness,* she told her heart, *foolishness.*

Eric, Amanda, and Isaac bumped, laughed, and jostled their way to the dining room. Amanda rode her father's back.

"Go faster, Daddy. You're not a fast horse."

"That's enough, Amanda." Miranda smiled at her daughter, not ready to look into her husband's eyes, afraid he would see something. "Let's sit down and eat. You and Daddy can play horsey later. Maybe after he finishes with Isaac's tire."

"Don't forget, I've got a meeting." Eric tousled his son's hair while they sat.

"Sorry," Miranda said.

"This food sure looks good, doesn't it? Your mommy is quite a cook."

Isaac nodded, his eyes focused on the potatoes on his plate, a fork and knife in either hand.

"Hold on there, mister. We've got to say grace first." The family held hands while the father blessed the food.

Eric spooned a large amount of cabbage onto his plate and smaller amounts onto his children's plates. "I'd like to play horsey tonight, but Daddy's got a meeting. I might have to take care of a little problem, a little coon problem." Eric winked at his son, who smiled in return.

Miranda would not let herself choke, would not let herself stop chewing while her husband spoke.

"Daddy might have to do a little varmint control." He smiled at his daughter.

"What kind of varmint, Daddy?" Amanda's eyelashes fluttered while her blues shone with admiration.

"One that thinks he's as smart as a white man, but he's not so smart. This varmint, you got to get rid of him when he goes bad because he'll cause all the other animals to go bad. There isn't anything to do but put the bl—"

"Eric, please. Do you have to say these things to the children? Do you have to do this in front of the children?" Miranda heard and regretted the words before she thought them. *Foolishness,* she told her lips.

Amanda and Isaac's smiles quickly dried as they looked from their mother's face to their father's face.

"Are you correcting me in front of my children?" His face flushed. "Don't you talk to me like I was one of your children.

After all I do to keep you happy, to keep you safe." A strange light flickered in his eyes then smoldered.

"What did you children do to Mommy?" Eric recovered and smiled at his children. "What did you do to make her so emotional, so moody? Come on, let's be quiet and hurry up and eat so she can sit outside for a while and cool off. Shhh." He held his index finger of his marriage hand to his mouth and turned from his daughter to his son, then to his wife. He smiled at Miranda, and she saw that something else lurked in the corners of his mouth.

Stay in control, stay calm, Miranda said to herself as she wiped her hands before straightening her husband's collar. The dishes were washed and put away, the bike fixed, there had even been one game of horsey. "Do you think you're going to be long, honey?" *Don't let disapproval show through. You have no right to disapprove.* "I hope you won't be long." She smiled sweetly.

"No longer than it takes. Don't ever do that again, Miranda. Don't ever disrespect me in front of my children. It confuses them, and it makes you look bad. They'll hate you if you keep doing it." Miranda felt a band, something tightening around her forehead, could feel perspiration on her upper lip. She knew better. Knew he was trying to frighten her. Knew her children loved her, yet . . .

"I'm just telling them the truth. They need to know the truth. Especially Isaac. He's going to have to protect his family someday." Her husband's face, his eyes, looked so sincere. "And Amanda needs to know those people can't be trusted. You hear how things happen to our women. How are you going to feel someday when something happens to her? That's how things are. They're animals. We all know it. You know it. Tell me if you know different."

Miranda swallowed. *Tell him the truth,* a small voice whispered. Fear overwhelmed her. The thought of survival alone, without him, overwhelmed her. Doubt and insecurity overwhelmed her. Reason overpowered her.

"Tell me if you know different," he insisted. His eyes, his presence, pressed down on her.

"No, no, you're right. I don't know what I was thinking. I guess it was just like you said, I was feeling moody. I-I'm sorry. I know everything you do, you do for us and all. Forgive me."

He leaned down and kissed her firm and strong. She felt herself melting, one arm held her while he patted her back with the other. "That's my girl." He kissed her again, then straightened to leave. "I'll be back soon as we're done."

Miranda stood in the doorway and prayed for her good husband's safe return.

Bates stepped into the clearing. A small fire burned in the center of the group of men. There was really no need for a fire, no real chill, but they always seemed to make one anyway.

"Hey, boys."

"Hey, Bates, where you been? We thought maybe you changed your mind. Thought maybe you wasn't gonna come tonight," the one that always challenged said to him.

Bates didn't reply, just shot him a look that cooled.

The one that always agreed slapped Bates on the back. "Now that the big man's here, let's get this thing started."

The men saluted, chanted, vowed their way through the opening ceremony. They read from the Bible.

"I found another good Scripture about the animals. It proves for sure that God meant for us to be over them, didn't want us to relate with them. Listen to this. Did you know Moses was married to an animal? His brother and sister-in-law had to call him out on it. Listen to this from Numbers 12, 'And Miriam and Aaron spake against Moses because of the Ethiopian woman he had married: for he had married an Ethiopian woman.'

"Can you believe it? Old Moses married an animal. I bet that's why he didn't get into the Promised Land. Yes sir, I bet that's why. But the other two, they had to speak out against it. That's what we're doing. Right, Bates?"

Bates knew the passage. It was one of the passages he liked least. Bates knew. Knew the passage. Knew if the one who always agreed continued reading that the passage would say that God punished Miriam and Aaron for their transgression. He knew the truth but said instead, "Right. We know the Good Book backs us up. We're just doing what we've been appointed to do. Now let's get to the business at hand."

"So what you think? What you think needs to be done?"

"You know what I always think. When an animal goes bad, you got to put him down." Bates's words were heavy, icy.

The one who was always intimidated cleared his throat, afraid to make a sound, hoping someone else would speak up. Hoping this wouldn't happen. Wishing he didn't have to be here.

"Now, this ain't really a big thing. I don't know for sure that he stole the bread. That Weaver boy was in the store at the same time, and he might have stole it. He's been known to steal," said the one who was sometimes brave enough to reason.

"Did the Weaver boy say he stole it?" Bates's voice had a hard edge. He didn't like discussion.

"No, no, he didn't. But I didn't expect Weaver to admit it."

"You mean you taking the word of an animal over the word of a white man?" Bates's eyes pressed the man.

"No, no, I ain't. I'm just saying that boy provides me good cheap labor. You know I don't care about the animals, it's just going to be hard for me to make do without this one. It ain't like that other one, the one coming home from the war and all. Can't we just warn this one this time?"

"I don't see much difference. It's your coon though, if you want to take the chance. We'll just give him and his a good scare. But I tell you, once they go bad, ain't nothing you can do. Like that animal coming home from the war, wearing those medals he probably stole from a white man. How are we supposed to let him come back here after he's been dancing with French women, thinking he can dance with our daughters and wives? Nothing to do but put him down. Take those counterfeit medals and stripes off of him and put him down. When one animal goes bad, he makes the other ones go bad. Stop it before it gets started, that's the best way. We stopped him on the road before he could tell the story. Before he could infect the others with his lies. But if you willing to take the chance, we'll just let this one go with a scare. Come on, let's get it over with. I want another piece of apple pie before I go to bed."

"You sure you ain't just afraid," the one who loved to challenge questioned the one who was sometimes not too afraid to reason.

"No, I ain't afraid."

"Well, you lead the way then —"

"No," Bates interrupted, "I'm going to lead the way. You go get the kerosene."

"Yes, it's best that Bates leads. No one knows these woods at night better than Bates," said the one who always agreed.

"You come on with me. Help me carry the juice," the challenger said to the one who was always afraid. "You know every time we come here, you got a look on your face like a little girl, like a scared little girl."

The one who was always afraid swallowed without sound.

"I tell you though, you didn't look scared when you lit that fire to the soldier boy. I didn't think you'd do it, but you sure did. I had my doubts, but I knew you was a man then," the challenger slapped the back of the one who was always afraid as they walked to get the kerosene.

The dog that used to be called Snowball paced in the brush, waiting for the men to leave the campsite.

"Come on, boys, let's get this over with," Bates said when the two men returned.

"I'm home, Miranda. Did you leave the pie out for me?"

She smelled her husband before he spoke. Something kerosene and something burnt, something like wood. She tried not to think about what might be laying in the pail. Clothes that might tell a tale.

"I left you a nice slice in the oven." She put a smile in her voice. "Eric, I'm glad you're home. I left you a pan of water. It should still be a little warm. I thought you might need to wash up."

Alena sat on a bench at the East St. Louis train station and prayed for peace while families, merchants, and travelers moved around her. She would be home soon, back in Mississippi, back with her parents, back in her room. Back to the place she loved. There were so many train stops; every minute seemed like an hour, but it would be soon. She turned her face up, closed her eyes, and smiled toward the sun.

Fear tugged at the hem of her skirt and turned down the corners of her mouth. She closed her eyes against the images of J.C., of the funeral, of Bates. *It will go well,* her thoughts fought back. *I can do all things . . . Though I walk through the valley of the shadow of death, I won't fear . . .*

The words came back to her and reassured her.

Twenty-eight

"Smell that pie." Alena's mother waved the pastry under her husband's nose. "I can't wait for our baby to come home. Can't wait to see her cut into this pie." She cut a few steps, what looked like a holy dance, a big smile on her face.

"Looks like you about beside yourself. And since I got to look out for the child, seem like somebody need to test the pie. Make sure it's okay." Her father reached.

Evelyn snatched it away just in time. "Oh, no you don't." They hadn't smiled and laughed this way since their baby had left. "I made this pie, and you know if anybody knows how to make a pie, I do."

"You talking awful sassy, miss."

Evelyn blushed and set the pie down just in time while her husband lifted her onto his lap. She nuzzled nose to nose with her husband. "I guess I'm happy. Happy about it. Alena's coming home. You know, I been just imagining her. Seeing her on the train, then us seeing her, all of us hugging."

"Me, too, baby," he said. "Me, too." The two sat and rocked while the pie cooled.

"You do the prettiest needlework, Miranda. I declare. Just beautiful," the one with gray eyes held it up for the others to see. "I know some little starving child is just going to love that little quilt. Probably won't know to appreciate it, but it will keep him or her warm." The one with gray eyes turned to the green-eyed one. "Where is this box going, do you know?"

Afternoon soon rested at the windows, sometimes dotting the women's hands. An early fall breeze played at the lace on the pale pink curtains that framed the windows of the room where the women sat on cream-colored, overstuffed, satin brocade sofas. Beneath one of the windows was a basket filled with what was probably the last of the tulips, gold and violet, and dramatic white gardenias that perfumed the room. The wind lightly touched the dark waxy leaves but blew no further.

"To some Indian reservation I believe, maybe to someplace in Africa. It seems almost a shame to let something so pretty go over there. My daughter Lindsey would love it, I just know. When I think of one of these animals over here sleeping under

361

that, it just makes me ill. Why I walked past one the other day, she must have been coming from the fields. The smell was awful. I covered my nose with my handkerchief and looked at her until she stepped off the sidewalk. It was awful, just awful."

"Animals." The one with green eyes shivered. "Do you mind pouring me some more tea, dear?" she said to the brown-eyed one.

"Of course. Would you like another cookie, too?"

"Oh my, no. The corset won't be able to hold me in, and my husband would just have a fit."

The brown-eyed one poured from a perfectly polished silver tea service into small china cups the same color as the sofa, trimmed in gold. "Here you are, sweetie," the one with brown eyes handed her the tea. "I know what you mean about the quilt and Africa and all, but they are different from the ones here. I've heard some of the missionaries say that the ones over there, especially the babies, are so docile, almost darling. Now just a moment —" she paused — "let me get more tea, we're just about out. Effie. *Effie,*" she called again, louder.

"Yes, ma'am." One with hazel eyes, skin

almost the color of the cups, head topped with kinky, sandy brown hair appeared. "Yes, ma'am."

"Effie, we are out of tea. Fetch us some more. Are you keeping an eye on the children? Have Lance, Lockwood, and the others had some cookies? Are you taking care of them?"

"Yes, ma'am."

"See that you do. Hurry with the tea so that you can get back to the children." As the one with hazel eyes left, the brown-eyed one said, "Something about that girl that just does not sit right with me, some little attitude she gives off . . .

"Forgive me," the brown-eyed one said turning back to her friends. "I believe we were talking about Africans being docile. It's very strange to me that the animals here don't seem to be very docile."

"Still," the green-eyed one continued.

"Do you ever feel bad about this?"

"Feel bad about what, Miranda?" the blue-eyed one studied her.

"About how we treat them. About how we talk about them."

The four other women laughed.

"I always prefer iced tea." The one with blue eyes stared into her tea cup. The other eyes looked at the one with blue eyes, briefly, as if she had gone insane. The blue-eyed one looked at Miranda, laughed, and looked away.

Miranda looked around the group. "I don't understand how we can say we love people with the same color far away when we won't love the same people here amongst us. I mean, do you ever think we might be wrong in how we treat the colored people, how we think about them? I mean they are people just like us. They have the same hopes, the same fears, the same struggles, the same loves."

"Surely, dear, you must be joking." The one with green eyes sipped her tea. "I mean, what are we supposed to do? We have to protect ourselves. What do you expect? They're animals."

The one with hazel eyes entered the room with more tea and quietly refreshed cups and replenished the cookies.

"I went into the store to buy piece goods the other day," the one with green eyes continued while the one with hazel eyes served. "A gal got into line, and when I came up with my goods do you know she didn't even move. Stood there to be served like she didn't see me. When Mr. Marshall reached over her to wait on me, she had the gall to look indignant. She saw me there, she should have just moved."

"Anything else, ma'am?" the one with hazel eyes inserted quietly to the brown-eyed one.

"No, that will be all."

"But that's what I mean." Miranda frowned. "Why should she have stepped aside for you to be waited on? Why should you be first? She was there before you. Why should we always be first?"

"They are savages. It's always in the paper, they're killing one another, killing us, especially we women," the one with green eyes continued while the one with hazel eyes left the room. "If our men weren't here to keep them in line, all our lives would be in danger."

"Miranda, dear, are you sure you don't have a fever?" The one with gray eyes reached over to touch her forehead.

"No, I'm fine. Why do we think we can call them names? Beat them, kill them. Why are we better? What about when the Bible says, 'Whatever you do to the least of mine —' "

"That passage doesn't mean *them*. They're not even *in* the Bible. Not after Cain slew Abel and was marked and banished." The green-eyed one seemed to be losing her humor. "I don't want to talk about this. I don't see why you have to ruin a perfectly good meeting. I don't see you running off to live with them. I don't see you inviting them to your house. I don't see you giving up your home, your position."

"But it isn't true. They weren't banished. If you believe the Bible, there were Ethiopian Jews. Read Acts, chapter 8. Philip converted and baptized an Ethiopian Jew before Peter had given the commandment that Gentiles were to be allowed in the church. Here —" Miranda reached for her Bible — "let me read it to you.

" 'And the angel of the Lord spake unto Philip, saying, Arise and go toward the south unto the way that goeth down from Jerusalem unto Gaza, which is desert. And he arose and went: and, behold, a man of Ethiopia, an eunuch of great authority under Candace queen of the Ethiopians, who had charge of all her treasure, and had come to Jerusalem for to worship, was returning, and sitting in his chariot read Esaias the prophet —' "

The one with blue eyes looked at Miranda, then quickly looked away.

"We don't come here to discuss such topics. Our men take care of such things.

They know what's best. Don't you agree, dear?" the one with gray eyes asked the blue-eyed one.

The one with blue eyes swallowed. She glanced at Miranda and then looked away. "Yes, I agree," she said and then looked down.

"But what about the things our husbands do? What about the things they say in front of our children? Do your husbands say things? Listen to what *we* are saying right here."

"I tell them myself, dear," the one with gray eyes said. "Any wise woman would. Your children need to know about them. We have to help our children, protect them, let them know what the truth is. That is our job as mothers, to teach them and protect them."

Miranda laid her Bible to the side. "Protect our children from what? This is sin. And if it's sin, aren't we as mothers and wives helping to perpetuate that sin by teaching it to our loved ones, by offering them our sins to eat, just like the fruit in Eve's garden?"

The one with brown eyes drew herself to her full stature. "This is ridiculous. I must ask you to leave if you continue on this way. It's almost as if you're trying to say we're at fault. That we're *prejudiced*. That insults and offends me. I have never beaten anyone, never lynched anyone; I've never put anyone in jail, and I certainly didn't make them black! When that old mother got burned out, I was the first one to send her some linens I had put away. I resent this. I will not tolerate this. I will not let you make me feel guilty."

"Don't you ever consider? Don't you ever think we might be wrong? That we might be offending God? Do we have to do the killing ourselves to be guilty? Or is it enough that we just don't tell our husbands or our friends or our families when they are wrong? Is it enough that we let them hold us up for an excuse? They say they are doing things because they have to protect us. My husband . . . I know he does things, then he tells me it was to protect me, because these people he has harmed, they wanted to harm me because I am a white woman.

"But they didn't burn down that old grandfather's house because he had thoughts about harming me. They wanted his land. But we go along with it. Keep letting them use us for cover. Isn't that enough sin? That we just go along with it? Did you ever think that what we're doing, what our loved ones are doing might be sin?"

"This is ridiculous, Miranda. Absolutely ridiculous. We came here to prepare things to send to the missionaries, and you have ruined it."

Miranda pressed a hand to her heart and spoke plaintively. "My husband does things, I know he does. And I think I hear the Lord telling me that those things are wrong and that I shouldn't go along."

"Now she's hearing voices. Joan of Arc," the one with green eyes mocked.

"I think I hear Him telling me that when we think we are better, when we think we deserve first and best more than any other human being, that we are rebelling against His Word, that we are exalting ourselves against the mind of God. We are exalting something as simple as the color of our skin over our love for Him and His righteousness." Miranda turned, speaking to each woman, one by one.

"Don't you ever hear Him speaking to you? Don't you ever feel or wonder if all this is wrong? If what we're doing, if what our husbands are doing is wrong?"

The one with gray eyes looked angry, disgusted. "Oh, really, Miranda. This is absurd. You have a wonderful husband. He keeps trouble away from all of us. Anything he does, he does for a good reason. He is protecting our place. Women would die for a man like that. Handsome, brave. He gives you everything. You have beautiful children, and he dotes over them. You really are a very ungrateful, rebellious young woman."

"I just keep hearing these Scriptures from 1 John over and over: 'Whosoever hateth his brother is a murderer.' "

The one with brown eyes spoke up. "God loves me and I love God. I do not hate anyone. We do not hate anyone, but those people are animals. Animals."

" 'If a man say, I love God, and hateth his brother, he is a liar: for he that loveth not his brother whom he hath seen, how can he love God whom he hath not seen?' "

The one with brown eyes shook her head. "This is ridiculous, Miranda! We have not hurt anyone. I don't even hear anyone of us using that word. You know that word that other people sometimes call them. But you must be sensible, reasonable. They are different. Look at them. Why would God make them look so different. We all know it; they're animals. And we don't like the way you're talking to us. Do we?"

"No," said the one with blue eyes, made brave by anger. Made brave enough to speak without looking away. "We are white, they are black. We can't change that. We didn't choose for them to be born black."

Miranda leaned forward in her seat. "What about Indians, where do they fit in this picture? Where do Africans fit? Shouldn't our colored people be better than Africans because some of them have white blood? What about the Asians? Where do the Mexicans fit? Where do the poor fit? What about the old? What about those who are crippled? Aren't we behaving with respect to persons?"

The one with blue eyes spoke, her voice shaking with emotion. "There are things wrong in my own life. I would never knowingly hurt anyone, and I resent your implying such a thing. I've been hurt myself. People making fun of the way I speak or the way I dress. How dare you try to make me feel responsible or make me feel that I have hurt anyone. Quoting Scripture at me as if you were so holy. I have been an upstanding member of the church for years. I pay my tithes; I give to missions, sing in the choir. How *dare* you?"

"Miranda, I will be reporting this incident to the pastor and to my husband. I advise the rest of you to do the same. I hate to see your children suffer, but I think that in the future my family will be keeping its distance from yours. Respect of persons, indeed." The one with gray eyes began to gather her things.

There was no point in stopping. Miranda had already crossed the line when she first broached the subject. "But listen to what the book of James says, 'If ye fulfil the royal law according to the scripture, Thou shalt love thy neighbour as thyself, ye do well: but if ye have respect to persons, ye commit sin, and are convicted of the law as transgressors. For whosoever shall keep the whole law, and yet offend in one point, he is guilty of all.' "

"I am leaving now. I will not listen to this," the one with gray eyes said to the others. "I suggest the rest of you leave also. And I will inform my husband. Your husband will hear about this. I can assure you. How dare you ruin our lovely afternoon."

"What if we are visiting this sin upon our sons and daughters?" Miranda spread her hands, pleading. "Maybe if we will acknowledge our sins before God, He will forgive us and heal us."

"If I were *you* —" the one with gray eyes pointed to the one with brown eyes — "I would get this woman out of here and never let her come back. Please have your girl bring my children."

Outside the Ellisville Community Church, the men gathered in small groups on their way home from prayer meeting. Great trees surrounded them, branches reaching toward heaven, their leaves darkening in the waning light. In the midst was the brick church, well groomed with white steeple.

"Good lesson there, Pastor. Something to chew on, to think about all the way home." The man, like most others, headed for his horse, others to their wagons.

"Yeah, Pastor, good lesson," the one that always agreed said.

"Very instructive." Bates stuck out his hand for the pastor's hand. Bates saw the sweat form on the young pastor's lip while he held onto the man's hand. "Very enlightening."

"I got kind of confused about some of the things you was saying," said the one who always challenged. "Sounded like you were trying to say the animals was just like us. But then, I know that's not what you meant."

"No, that's not what he meant at all, was

it, Pastor?" Bates pressed his hand harder. He watched the pastor's adam's apple rise and fall and believed he could see the man's thoughts running in his eyes. *What if I offend them? Will they leave the church? Who else will leave with them? Who else will leave if the truth is put to them plainly? How will the church survive?*

The pastor's final thought was for his own safety, alone as he was with the three men in the coming darkness. It was difficult for Bates not to laugh. It was just as difficult not to make the young pastor's fearful dreams come true. Bates hated weakness and fear almost as much as he hated disorder.

He wondered how much the pastor knew of what they had done. If he had ever discussed it with anyone. Wondered if he knew how they had burned down the animal's shack the other night. Wondered if he knew how many animals they had beaten, how many female animals they had cornered. Wondered if the weakling knew how they had ripped the medals, the patches off that animal, that soldier — how could an animal be a soldier? Wondered if mouths had talked. If the pastor knew about the beating, about the burning, about the rope.

"That's not what you meant, was it, Pastor?" Bates began to quote the sermon. " 'For as many of you as have been baptized into Christ have put on Christ. There is neither Jew nor Greek, there is neither bond nor free, there is neither male nor female; for ye are all one in Christ Jesus.' Galatians 3:27 through 28, I believe. Right, Preacher? I've heard animal lovers quote that before, but you're not one of them, are you, Pastor?"

"No, he certainly isn't one of them," the one who always agreed said.

"Good thing, 'cause I don't think we could tolerate an animal lover around here," the one who always challenged said.

The pastor swallowed again, his eyes searching, probably to see if there might still be someone else, some of the other men, nearby.

"Who you looking for, Pastor?" Bates stepped closer to the man so that the three of them almost enclosed the cleric. "You look a little nervous. Nothing for you to worry about, not here. Now, if you ran into some animals on the way home, you might have something to worry about. If you ran into a group of darkies, a pack of animals, on the way home, people that found you might not be able to recognize you in the morning. You don't have anything to worry about with the three of us around.

"Those people are animals. No telling what they might do to you if they came upon you, but you're safe with us. That's why I know you weren't trying to tell us that we were the same as them. You know, Pastor, not here, but two counties over a young pastor came to town saying animals were the same as white men. That pastor didn't have a job very long. Must have been during the summer because things got hot. Brush must have caught on fire 'cause something burned that fellow's place to the ground. It seems they found his body in the woods. Must have gotten caught in an animal trap. Come to think of it though, the fellow looked a lot like you."

Bates smirked. "Good thing though, you don't think like him. You know, some of these animals around here belonged to my grandfather, worked and served him. Then somebody was stupid enough to unleash them on normal society. Occasionally, one of their sons or daughters will forget and step out of place. Then they have to be reminded who they are."

Bates could feel more air rushing into his nasal passages, could feel his blood pressure behind his eyes. "They have to be put back in their places. I won't have any animal besting me, walking beside me, ruling over me. You make them believe they're as good as white men, not one of us will be safe. Before I let that happen, before I let some uninformed white man make a mistake and forget his place and make them forget theirs, I'll take that fellow aside for a little talk.

"You know the consequences though, Pastor. That's why I can assure these two good men, my friends that you didn't mean to say that men with black skin, animals, were good as white men. That God doesn't see any difference between them. You didn't mean that, did you, Pastor?"

The pastor cleared his throat and looked from man to man. What he swallowed seemed to almost get caught in his throat.

"I *said* —" Bates and the two other men each took another step closer, now touching the young man — "that's not what you meant, was it? Was it, Pastor?"

The leader of the flock looked at the three sheep before him. He looked for a moment at the cross atop the steeple, bathed in new moonlight, the wind ever so slightly lifted his hair. The three stared at the one. He looked away. "No." He looked down.

"Pardon, I'm not sure I heard you," Bates said.

"No. I said, no."

"No, what?"

"No, that's not what I meant. I did not mean —"

"Good, that's what I thought," Bates said.

"Glad that's cleared up." The one who always challenged spat on the ground.

"Why, I was always sure of it. No doubt in my mind." The one who always agreed slapped the young pastor on the back. "Maybe we should consider inviting the pastor to our night meetings."

"Maybe we should," Bates agreed. "Right now, he better get on home. We shouldn't take up any more of his time. We don't want to be the cause of something happening to him."

The three men laughed while the pastor mounted his horse. The horse was skittish, shifting, prancing from hoof to hoof, shaking its head, flagging its tail. The animal seemed nervous, seemed not to want to let the pastor ride. The three stood under the rising moon and laughed while the man rode away.

"Sheriff Bates and I will see you at the

trustee board meeting, Pastor," the one who always agreed called after the young man who struggled to keep his horse's nose to the road.

"You hear anything about the Series?" the one who always challenged asked Bates as they turned from the young preacher.

"Cincinnati took it."

"Cincinnati over the White Sox? Don't sound right to me. Sounds like some kind of fix. Baseball series fixed. Ain't much right, ain't much a man can count on these days. People don't have respect for nothin' nowadays."

The one who always challenged clicked to his horse and rode one way down the road while Bates and the one who always agreed rode another.

Twenty-nine

"You know what Daddy's job is, don't you?"

"Yes, Daddy. You're the sheriff." Amanda glowed toward her father.

"You're absolutely right, precious. Do you all know what else I do?" Bates looked around the table at his children and his wife. The table was covered by another white cloth, this time decorated with several different kinds of blue flowers. In the corners daisies mixed with the blue flowers to invite in the morning sunshine.

"You keep the peace, Daddy."

"You are one smart fella, you know that, mister?" Bates glanced up at his wife. Something behind his eyes made her shudder. "That's right, son. Daddy keeps the peace. Now what do you think is the biggest threat to peace around here?"

"Animals!" Isaac hooted.

"Yes, animals," Amanda agreed.

"That's right. That's why we're havin' this little talk; just every now and then, Daddy has to make things clear. Isn't that right, Mommy?" Bates nodded at his wife. "See, Daddy's job is to protect you and Mommy. Mommy's a good woman. We love her, don't we? Just sometimes Mommy gets a little confused. Don't you, Mommy?" The look he gave her burned down into her chest and pressed there.

"Like the other day when you all went out. Mommy was joshing and said some things that got the other women all worked up and distressed. But guess what, today Mommy is going to go to town and apologize to those other women. Sunday at church —" Bates smiled at his two children — "Mommy is going to stand up in front of all the women and apologize. Then she's going to tell them the truth. She's going to say that she knows that she is superior to the animals, that all of us are. Right, Mommy?"

Her husband reached out his hand for Miranda's, to place it in his.

"Right, Mommy?" He held her hand while he applied pressure with his thumb to the web between her index and middle finger.

"Yes, Daddy's right," Miranda answered, her face masked with a smile. She would not upset her children or let them see her cry. *Help me, Lord. Help us, Lord.* Her wet eyes stared across the table at the husband she did not know.

"We have to keep the animals in check. That's our job, that's Daddy's job, to protect you. Mommy's job is to teach you what's right, what's true; what Daddy says is right. They steal, they cheat, they're brutal. Isn't that right?"

"Right, Daddy." The two children nodded together.

"Except for Becca and Nate," Isaac said. "We like to play with them, don't we, Mandy?" Amanda nodded. "They play real nice. Not like Lance and Lockwood, they always start fights and try to take our toys. Mommy —" Isaac turned to his mother — "we don't want to play over there anymore. Let us play with Becca and Nate instead."

"See what I mean!" Eric's fist hit the table. "This is *your* fault, Miranda. You will be held responsible if something happens to them."

The children, shocked, stared at their father.

Eric recovered quickly and smiled at them. "Don't worry, everything's fine. Everything is going to be fine. Me and Mommy are just going to keep telling you the truth until you get it right." Fire jumped in the look Eric gave Miranda.

"You can play with Becca and Nate sometimes, but you remember they're animals. You come first; you remember that. God loves you best, and He made you to rule over them. Isn't that right, Mommy?" He pressed with his thumb again.

"Yes," Miranda whispered, overcome with shame. She looked toward the breeze blowing through the window. *Lord, help us.*

"Right now, Nate and Becca are little, and they're not so bad then. It's when they get older that they become more trouble, especially the boys. The worse ones, though, are the ones that go North and get their heads full of all kinds of foolishness. People there tell them they are just as good as white folks. Isn't that silly?"

Miranda watched Eric look at her two children and include them in a conspirator's snicker.

"Silly, *right,* Mommy?"

Miranda forced a laugh.

"When they go up North, they're ruined. Nothing you can do but put them down. You remember that, Isaac. You're going to be the man of your own house someday, and you'll need to know the right thing to do. If they come back from up North, you remember what you have to do."

"Yes, Daddy."

"They learn a lot of crazy things when they leave here. Things that make them unfit to live. They go to France and think they're just as good as any white man, then come back and riot. They're making life unlivable for white people all over, rioting in places like East St. Louis, someplace in Texas. Same thing in Washington, D.C. They should have shot them all. Rioting in the streets. Then you know what the white men did up there? Called in other white men, troops from Camp Meade, to stop the rioting. The Army troops stopped the *white men,* said it was their fault, they needed to come to order. White men against other white men. Ridiculous. Then rioting in Chicago. White men called on other white men, the National Guard, to stop the rioting. Now it's Omaha, Nebraska. Nothing like that is ever going to happen here. We know what to do. We're going to keep the peace here."

Eric looked intently at his son. "We hear of any of those animals coming back from other places, Washington, Chicago, we're going to stop it before it gets started. We're going to put that animal down. We don't care who they are. Understand, son?"

"Yes, Daddy."

At her son's obedient echo, Miranda

prayed again. *Help us, Lord.*

"Hello, Mr. Marshall," Miranda spoke while the shop bell signaled her entrance. Cinnamon greeted her nose and warmed her. "You got any more cloves, Mr. Marshall?" The store, the room inside, looked burnt orange. Miranda wondered if it was the light or her mood.

"Yes, Miranda. I'll set you some aside." Mr. Marshall smiled at her. He had known her since she was a little girl. "Why don't you send the children up here while you look around? I think I've got something they might want to taste. How about some rock candy, you all," Mr. Marshall said as the children sped toward him.

Miranda wandered through the store, hoping to gather herself, comfort herself, before she went back to apologize.

What could she have been thinking? Was it really God she heard? Probably just her own foolishness. Her husband was a good man, wise. Look at all that she had; look at her family. She shook her head.

Foolishness.

Maybe new curtains or new pillows would brighten her. She nodded at two acquaintances in the store. The women turned their backs and pretended they did not see her. Heading toward the dry goods, she nodded at two friends who passed by outside the plate glass window. The two women did not break stride, stared briefly, then leaned their heads together to talk.

God would not have asked her to say anything that would cause her friends to dislike her, cause her to be snubbed, would he? *Help me, Lord.*

"Hello, Miss Miranda. It's so nice to see you." The woman rose from her seat and stepped back to give Miranda more room.

"You don't have to call me Miss. I should be calling you *Miss*, Evelyn. You knew my mother, and I'm not that much older than your girl, Alena. It's so good to see you." Miranda stepped forward to hug Evelyn.

The colored woman's hug felt awkward, and Miranda saw her eyes scan the room to see who might be watching, who might be listening. "Good to see you, too, Miss Miranda." Evelyn stepped back. "How's your family?"

"Well. We're doing well." What else could she say? Who could she tell? Look where she was now because she had opened her mouth. "And yours? I hear Alena is in Chicago of all places. I thought sure she would have been married to that boy . . ."

Miranda looked away. *How stupid of me to bring up that boy!* How much did Evelyn know? What had been whispered about Eric's part in the boy's death?

"She's just fine," Evelyn answered quickly, almost as though she were trying to cover Miranda's worry, her pain. "Alena is just fine. Just fine." The guardedness left Evelyn's voice. They were just two women conversing in the store. "She met a nice young man in Chicago, and I do believe they are planning to get married. She's been writin' for a newspaper, a Race newspaper in Chicago."

"A colored newspaper? I didn't know there was such a thing. How wonderful for her."

"Oh, yes, Miss Miranda. There's Race — that's what they call them — newspapers, magazines, theater, just everythin'. She didn't want to go, but after J.C., we thought . . ."

"Yes, I know . . ."

"Anyway, Miss Miranda, things have worked out for the best."

"I wish you wouldn't call me that."

"It's best, Miss Miranda." The guarded look returned to Evelyn's face. "It's best. Anyhow, Alena is doing just fine. And we so happy; I'm down here now getting some cloth for new curtains. She is coming home for a visit. We're about to pick her up."

Miranda's face felt cool, as if it had lost all its color. "How wonderful, Evelyn. Maybe I can get to see her."

"You all right, Miss Miranda? You gone pale."

"Fine. I just thought of something I need to do." Could she tell the woman? Should she tell? Eric's words hammered at her conscience, *"We hear of any of those animals coming back from other places, Washington, Chicago, we're going to stop it before it gets started. We're going to put that animal down. We don't care who they are. Understand, son?"*

"I-I need to go. I've got an errand to run."

"You sure you're all right?"

"Just fine, Evelyn. Give my best to your husband." Miranda began to back away. She couldn't tell. She had a life, too. What about her life? What about her children? What about her family? What about her husband? Maybe he was doing the right thing, maybe he knew best.

"Come on, children." Miranda rushed them from the store without buying the cloves. Maybe Alena would come home without Eric finding out. Maybe God would see to it.

"When you gonna be leaving the train?" The little boy pulled at Alena's coat. "Huh, when?"

"I already told you fifty times, Jackson. Remember, Jackson?" Alena pinched at the little boy while he squirmed and laughed. "I'm not going to tell you again." He had attached himself to her during the ride, been her companion. His mischief kept her entertained, distracted.

"Who you gonna see?" His voice sounded like a frog. Too big for his little pot-bellied body.

"My mama." Alena faked annoyance while she tickled the boy. "My daddy."

"Why? If they know like I know, they don't want to see you."

"Well, I will be out of your hair pretty soon. And my mama, my daddy, they gonna be happy to see me." Alena continued playing with the boy, smiling, but inside she prayed, *Please, Lord, let it be so.*

Thirty

Alena pulled at the collard green leaves and looked at her father's back as he moved from row to row gathering potatoes, onions, the last of the harvest. He had not changed, not physically. She didn't know why that seemed odd to her. So much had happened to her, somehow . . . maybe . . . she thought it would show on his face, her mother's face.

She looked toward the porch where her mother sat shelling black-eyed peas. The sun behind the house was yellow-orange; it would be setting soon. Alena stopped to breathe the air, the smell of earth, of home. She closed her eyes and breathed in the feel of the three of them embracing, of her homecoming. The sound, the smell, the sight, the taste of love, of forgiveness, of arms that held and protected her.

She could hear her father humming something while he worked. Something that was caught in the wind, something that sounded like contentment.

She bent and went back to her work. Felt the stiff leaves, reached down to run her fingers over the earth. It was good to be home.

"You boys know we don't normally meet in the homes, but this is an emergency. That gal, that animal, is back here from Chicago. We know she ain't planning nothing but stirring up trouble."

Standing in the kitchen, Miranda held her breath and listened to her husband's voice in the next room with the men. Just minutes ago, she had served them ice tea, coffee, set out plates with cookies and pound cake.

Help me, God. What do I do? She thought of her children asleep in their bedrooms. *God, help my family.* Miranda could hear her husband still speaking in the next room.

"For some of you that's been squeamish in the past —" the one who always agreed and the one who always confronted laughed, mocked — "Governor Bilbo has made it clear where he stands on this issue. That animals, savages that have gone North create a threat to us, to our way of life. They get the good colored folks all stirred up talking about equal rights, uppity ways, thinking they are the same as white men.

"The governor knows it ain't but one solution. He backs us up. Tonight, we are gonna exercise that solution."

A few of the men cheered in agreement. To Miranda's ears, it sounded like most of the group remained silent.

"We are going to take care of the problem tonight. She's been here three days. That's long enough for her to say her final good-byes." It sounded like the same minority laughed.

"Now what's going to happen tonight, I'm going to take care of myself. I got a few things I need to take care of with her myself before I put her down."

"I just bet you do." It sounded like the one who always confronted was snickering, snorting, and slapping his knee.

Miranda put one hand over her heart, the other over her mouth while her stomach heaved.

"Let's try to keep it down. I don't want you to wake my family." Eric sounded so protective. "Anyway, once I take care of the girl, we're probably all going to have to get rid of Amos and Evelyn. They been good workers, but ain't no telling what kind of poison she's been filling them full of, and no telling how they will react to this. Most likely, they won't be any good to us after this. We may even have to put down a few more animals. That's why I wanted to let you all know about it."

"How you intending to do it?"

"Should be easy. I'm going through the woods and wait out back, behind their shack. She'll be out later. I've seen her coming out there lots of times leaving table scraps for stray dogs."

"Animal food for animals," the one that always agreed amused himself.

"I'll drag her in the woods, take care of it, and be on back. We'll meet two days from now at the usual place to talk over where we need to go from here."

Miranda could hear the men's voices as they closed the meeting and left. *Help me, Lord. Help me know what to do.*

The answer came clear and firm: *Tell him.*

Eric Bates watched his wife walk across the room toward him. *She's angry,* he thought, amused at first. Then he could feel the anger creeping up the back of his neck, wrapping up his chin and into his nose. The way her face looked drawn, the way her shoulders looked stiff irritated him.

"Eric, I need to talk to you."

He needed to concentrate on what he was doing, not be annoyed by her. He hated that demanding tone, like she was the boss, like he was a kid.

"When I get back. Or in the morning." He continued winding the rope. He would have to stop and get the kerosene from the meeting site on his way.

"Eric, I don't think you should do this. I don't want you to go. I've been praying about it, and I don't think . . . I know God doesn't want you doing this. It's wrong. They're His people, too. God loves them. He loves them just the same as us."

"Are you *crazy?*" His heart pounded in his chest. This was the last thing he needed. He needed to concentrate. She was always doubting him, trying to undercut him. "Don't you tell me what God says. *I'm* the head of this household. Don't you come in here questioning me. I take care of you, not the other way around. I keep the roof over your head, clothes on your back. I don't hear you complaining about that. I'm doing this for you. Because I love you. Because of my love for my family. I don't need this from you, not now. I don't need to be confused."

"I don't want you to go, Eric."

"You think life is good. Everything in life is good. All people are the same. There is no bogeyman. You know why you feel that way? Because I protect you. I watch over you. I keep your way of life safe. I make it safe for you and Amanda and Isaac to walk down the street."

She looked into his eyes and pulled him close. "I know you think you're doing it for us."

He felt her trembling, felt himself trembling.

"But I don't really think you're doing it for us. There's something inside *you* that needs this. That needs to feel more powerful than other people. Something proud. Something afraid. Something that needs to be in control."

Miranda planted her feet. "I love you, Eric, but this is wrong. And I'm afraid. I don't want you to go. If you go," she paused, "then I'm going. I'm going to take the kids. We're leaving. I don't want them to grow up in this hate, with murder. I don't want them growing up thinking that wrong is right. It's sin, and I don't want them burdened with your sin."

She breathed and shrank. Pressed in and then moved back slightly, like she was alternately bold and afraid.

"Sin? Murder? Who made you so holier-than-thou —" he felt his eyes narrow — "like you don't have any sins? What are you talking about?" He jerked away from his wife. "Don't you threaten me. You're afraid? Well, *I'm* not afraid of anything. And guess what else? You're going to be here when I get back. You, my son, and my daughter, you're going to be here. Don't even *think* about leaving." His voice sounded almost desperate in his own ears. The weakness angered him. His heart darkened. "Besides, where are you going to go? Who's going to take care of you like I do? Who would want you?" Derision chilled his words.

He picked up his equipment and headed toward the door. "You better be here." He felt more like himself, more in control.

Miranda took a deep breath, then exhaled. "I don't know if I can. What are you going to leave in the bucket tonight for me to find? To hide from your children? Clothes covered with blood? Clothes covered with soot and the smell of kerosene? What else will you bring home this time? I can't stand to look in that pail one more time. I can't wash it away anymore."

Eric stepped toward his wife. "You better be here when I get back." Stepping back, he turned and went out the door into the night.

A white dog pawed at the ground and blinked, blue eyes looking at the night sky. His nose twitched. His eyes moved toward the direction of where he had gotten food for the last three moons. A low rumble — the beast's stomach — sounded. The dog pawed around the area. Then looked up, nose twitching, ears back as if he smelled and heard something coming. He growled, more a rumble in his throat. His ears pulled further back. Eyes slits. Cottonball hid himself away and watched.

Bates found the kerosene. He looked up at the moon and smiled. Work to do. He would deal with Miranda when he got home. Enough was enough, he thought as he covered his white skin with ashes.

Soon Bates was running through the woods, exhilarated. The moon flooded and seemed to be running with him. He could almost hear it.

"Don't go, Eric."

It sounded like his wife's voice. His heart pumped, excitement, thrilling and exquisite, rose as he ran. Pulsed, throbbed.

Stop, my son. Come back to me.

Adrenaline opened his air passages and sharpened his eyesight, but not his listening heart. Bates was not sure which portion of the adventure he liked best. Getting there. Running this way, wide open. Imagining how it would be with her. How her eyes would look, wide with fear. How her voice would sound. How her eyes would look after. He laughed silently while he ran and remembered things his father had told him, how it had been with him when he went night running. The moon followed. He liked the squealing sound. The way they begged. But mostly, he liked the squealing sound.

Cottonball kept pace and ran in time. The dog continued to growl, low in his chest. The hair on his nape raised.

James, Dinah, Jonathan, Patrice and others gathered at Wednesday night prayer meeting.

"Lord, keep Alena from evil," they prayed in one accord.

The young pastor of the Ellisville church woke, sweating, from a fitful sleep. He rose and dressed. He would go to Bates, confront him. Tell him that what he was doing was wrong.

The pastor decided. He would serve God. He would not be afraid of man.

"That food was delicious, Mama." Alena hugged her mother and father. "I love you all. And I love being back home, the air." She breathed deeply. "Won't you think about it? Won't you come? You know Aunt Patrice wants you to come. She's got room, a place all ready for you. And you would be safe."

"Ain't no protection like God's protection. This is our home. This is the place we was born. You know we will be there for the wedding. Nothing would make us happier." Amos smiled at his wife. "But this is our home, and we're prepared to stay."

The three held each other. Caressed familiar skin, inhaled lifetime smells. "All right, Mama and Daddy. All right." Alena picked up the beat-up metal wash pan full of table scraps. "I'm going to take these out to the dog. And we can talk about other things when I come back in."

"How about your wedding dress, baby? We can talk about that." The two women smiled at each other.

"All right, Mama. That sounds good."

"You know, you two look like two peas in a pod."

"Oh, Daddy!"

Evelyn looked up into her husband's eyes. "It's good to have my baby home. It's good, ain't it, Amos? We got a lot of catching up to do. And a wedding to talk about."

"We sure do, Mama. And I can tell you about all the people. About my friends. And about the stores and the clothes and the churches. And you going to have to give me some of your recipes, Mama. I guess I'm going to be cooking soon."

"Well, I guess so, baby. I guess so."

Amos watched his daughter put on her sweater. "I know that old dog is sure glad you are back. That wild thing just runs around here and there. It gets good regular eats when you in town, that's for sure."

"You know I always loved Cottonball, Daddy."

"I'm sure he loves you, too." Amos held the door open for his daughter.

Alena walked into the darkness. Country darkness, where there was no light to compete with the stars. Where blackness gave complete rest to the light of the day.

She walked where stars and the moon were the only light, where people walk by trust without fear.

Miranda Bates paced back and forth, silently frantic in her living room.

"God, help me," she whispered. "I know I should go. But I'm so scared, Lord. God, help me. Don't let him get that girl. Lord, I know he's wrong, but I don't think . . . God, I love him. I don't think I can . . . I don't think I have the courage to go. Help us, Lord."

She tried to stand still, hat and coat in hand. Her hands shook, knees trembled . . . it was better to pace. "God, I can't take it anymore. I can't stand one more bucketful, not one more tubful. But I can't do anything. God, let that child and her mama and daddy be safe."

Outside, she heard horse's hooves. She ran to the door. It was the young preacher. He heard her confession, then knelt beside her. "It is too dark and too dangerous. We will wait, and we will pray. God," the pastor prayed, "let him hear Your voice."

By moonlight, Bates ran. He could see out into the clearing. There was the girl. There was the girl. It was like a childhood singsong playing in his mind. He could see her, she couldn't see him. See her, couldn't see him. See her moving toward the edge of the woods, almost there.

Stop, my son. Return to me, the still small voice whispered urgently.

Just as she reached down, he would grab her wrist with one hand and grab around her throat with the other. An old camp song crossed his mind: *Gonna be a hot time in the old town tonight.* . . . He liked to sing old songs and he liked to hear the loud noises. He wondered how she would feel. If she would plead. Would she cry? Would she make the squealing sound? What would it look like in the dark? Cantaloupe moon through dark green lace.

Cottonball ran, trailing instincts triggered, keeping pace with the movement, with the scent of a predator, of threat, running parallel. Powerfully, silently. The man ran closer to the clearing while Cottonball's track ran just slightly deeper in the woods.

Bates tensed.

There she was. The girl. The girl with food. The girl with food under the moon.

His eyes calculated for the log, five feet ahead of him, and the sharp, pointed broken branch that jutted into his path. He quickly took in the large, white stone that lay just to the right. He would have to be careful . . .

But before he could move, a white flash crossed in front of his eyes, a growl, a snap. Bates's foot, his toe, caught on the log. He pitched forward.

Cottonball paused for a moment. Looked back at the still form. He circled for a moment. Pawed. Sniffed.

No movement.

The white dog trotted softly into the clearing toward the girl.

"Cottonball," Alena exclaimed. "Come here, boy. Come and get it."

The dog wagged his tail while Alena rubbed his fur, then buried his nose in the food she offered.

He was a good dog, she thought. She'd missed him.

"God, have mercy on us all. Thy will be done." Miranda and the pastor prayed and waited through the long night.

Thirty-one

It was later than she thought.

Miranda looked around, confused about where she was. What time? What day? Not like an adult, but like a child, she turned the back of her hand to wipe away the wetness from her mouth left from her sleep. Her fingers held little girl memories that wiped sleep from her eyes. She could smell the chimney smoke in the air. People were already up and moving. Women were up cleaning, kneading dough, cutting slices of ham and bacon. . . .

She breathed deeply, slowly. Most people liked summer and spring, but she was a fall girl. Born in the fall. Maybe she would die in the fall.

She frowned. What a strange thought. Funny how strange thoughts often came in the morning. Like dreams. Those strange dreams you have. Just before daybreak when you are neither awake nor asleep. Those dreams where the presence of God is so strong you can reach out and touch

Him. Those dreams where He lets you know that He is with you. That He has seen your condition.

She continued breathing, sitting on the floor, in front of the couch, facing the couch.

Those dreams. She had had one of those dreams last night.

In the dream she was a girl. And the colors were vivid, so vivid . . . more real than real. But there she was. There she was, waiting. Waiting for someone. Then there was her mother. Her mother and a friend. She didn't know the friend. A colored woman. But the woman and her mother were friends and they were waiting. Waiting for someone.

Then the someone came. Another woman. Another colored woman, and her mother was smiling. Just smiling. And they were going somewhere together. Going shopping somewhere. And her mother was smiling and whispering in her ear. Something about not wanting to walk. Not walking. So she remembered speaking to the woman for her mother.

"Oh, no. No walking here. We won't be walking here. I never walk," her mother's friend said and went to her carriage. It was her carriage. It was beautiful and light blue, shiny. White horses with flowing manes, almost silver, pawed at the ground and snorted. Heads down, eyes looking at the two friends in that way that horses have. Like they are free and only stay because they love you, and don't forget that so you don't take them for granted. Their silver tails whipped at the air and silver hooves pawed at the ground. Their bridles were pale blue and shiny, like the carriage.

Steam came from their noses, frosted by the air. It was very cool, but neither she, nor her mother, nor the other women in the dream had on cold weather clothes. They were dressed like spring, but they weren't cold. More steam from the horses. Their hooves clicked, clip-clopped on the pavement, on what looked like cobblestones. It looked like diamonds on their bridles and on the carriage. The colored woman must have been rich. And they were all smiling.

Miranda closed her eyes and was almost back there. Her mother and her colored friend eased themselves into the carriage. How nice they looked, silver gray hair and silver manes. So happy, so peaceful. The other colored woman stepped up to drive. Miranda raised her hand to blow them all kisses. Watched as they left, watched the horses, six of them, trotting away, plumes bobbing, saw the carriage shining. Then she turned away, satisfied. They were all right. Her mother was all right. Resting in the carriage. Wasn't that something? She had colored friends now.

Then Miranda remembered, almost back there, back in the dream, she turned away and started walking toward what she had to do. It was all like peace, like what peace should be. She walked down the street. A new street. A street she had never seen before. Satisfied that her mother was well, was happy. Now she had work to do and so she walked. And kept going until she came to a tree, tall and strong. Branches that extended wide for what could have been miles and arms that reached and reached.

She put her arms in the first branch and pulled upward, until her foot reached the lowest branch. She remembered smiling because she liked the feeling of climbing, climbing upward with no one to stop her. Not even her father or her brothers who told her girls did not climb.

Now she knew why they climbed. Each time she reached she could feel power in her arms and back. Could feel each muscle as it pulled loose from where it had never been used. She could feel each muscle smile and thank her as she climbed and climbed. And there was no one to stop her from moving through the green leaves that brushed her face. From smelling the green, from being almost part of the tree. No one to stop her from discovering the tree, and still she climbed.

Her legs stepped and pulled and thrust, pushing her to the next level. Up through the green leaves, past the dark boughs. The air was cleaner here. She could breathe more deeply and the leaves and shade covered her, protected her. She was enfolded. Became a part of the great, immovable tree. It was Freedom. That was why it was so beautiful, so filling, so enlightening — it was Freedom. And so she climbed and climbed for hours it seemed without tiring, climbing Freedom's tree.

Then there she was alone. One woman on top of Freedom's tree. On top, but still climbing. Breathing even deeper now. Up so high. Before she'd been afraid of heights, but not now. Not climbing Freedom's tree. Branches so wide, that lifted her, held her, did not bend at her weight so that here she was. Atop Freedom's tree. The words blew from her stomach to her mouth, and she shouted them out loud where no one could hear her or criticize her or make her stop. She shouted from her belly without ever asking her brain.

"Freedom!" she shouted. "Freedom! Freedom!"

And up here in Freedom, protected from the world, the branches were so small, so tiny, she should have been cast to the ground. No twigs so small could hold her.

I can, the voice spoke to her. *I can.*

So tiny, so fragile, too small to hold her. *I can,* the voice said. *I can. Keep climbing.*

And so there in Freedom's tree she kept climbing; her spirit kept pushing even beyond where her heart failed. Reaching, reaching. Wind blew through Freedom's tree and encouraged her. *Keep moving, keep looking,* it told her. Up there in Freedom's tree.

Miranda remembered that her mind tried to tell her to stop, to go back, that she had gone too far. The branches couldn't hold her, she was too far up. Go back down where it was safer. No one climbed this high. No one had to. For one small second her heart gripped, and Miranda remembered that she looked down and the ground was far below. The autumn gold and autumn red just looked autumn orange from so high, and her mind was right, she was too high. Too high for a girl like her, too high for the branches to carry. She teetered, but then the voice spoke again.

Keep moving, said the voice in Freedom's tree. *Keep moving. Keep looking for daylight.*

And so, Miranda remembered, she began to use her arms to push back the leaves, leaves so thick and strong. To fight for daylight at the top of Freedom's tree. *Keep moving,* the voice said. *Don't look down,* the voice said. *If you stop, you'll fall. If you look down, you'll fall. Keep moving. Too high for you, but not too high for Me, and I'm holding you. Keep moving; keep looking for daylight.*

Again she could feel the muscles as she pushed back the branches, the leaves, so many, so high. And there would peek through daylight, a glimpse through the cover. *Higher. Farther.* The voice smiled and coaxed her, coached her. *Keep looking.* Miranda remembered the leaves brushing her skin, and sometimes something was left there. She wanted to stop and see what was left, to touch it. To wipe it away if she disapproved, to leave it and marvel at it if she approved.

Keep moving, or you'll fall. Keep looking for daylight, said the voice in Freedom's tree.

How long? Miranda remembered asking. *How long?* Not wanting it to end, not wanting to fall, not wanting to leave the tree, but asking just the same. Maybe to be prepared for the worse, that the best would end, to be ready. *Keep moving,* the voice said. *Keep searching for daylight.*

Miranda remembered she was still there — still safe, still free, still searching — when she awoke.

Awoke where she sat now. She ran her fingers through her hair, then stretched and tried to remember why she was here. Her Bible lay on the couch before her, and a ray of early morning sun shone through the window onto the page.

"Let not your heart be troubled: ye believe in God, believe also in me. In my Father's house are many mansions: if it were not so, I would have told you. I go to prepare a place for you. And if I go and prepare a place for you, I will come again, and receive you unto myself; that where I am, there ye may be also. And whither I go ye know, and the way ye know."

Then her eyes moved down the page:

"If you love me, keep my commandments. And I will pray the Father, and he shall give you another Comforter, that he may abide with you for ever; even the

411

Spirit of truth; whom the world cannot receive, because it seeth him not, neither knoweth him: but ye know him; for he dwelleth with you, and shall be in you."

Then she remembered. She shook her head to clear her thoughts. She knew and remembered why she was here on the floor. *It is finished,* the words came to her. A small cry came to her lips, as if she had stepped on something sorrowful and frightening, then resignation. *It is finished.*

She looked around the room at the flowers, at the pictures. At his chair. Her eyes came, finally, to rest on the young pastor. Still sleeping, his face boyish, glasses askew. Brown hair too straight to even try to pomade in place. Sleep sweat made it stick now to his skin, so pale, so white it was almost blue. Like bluing for the wash . . .

Miranda smiled at his bravery last night. At his prayers, a man's prayers from lips that still looked more like a boy's. He was someone's son. Someone had held him, had nursed him, had hoped and prayed over him, ministered to him. Now he had given over his life to be courageous when he was afraid, to comfort and to minister to others. She hoped that someday she would meet his mother so she could tell her. Miranda wanted to tell his mother about the baby she had held, about the one she had taught Easter poems, the one she had read to. Miranda wanted to meet her and talk to her. So that his mother would know whom he had become.

She thought of her own children in their bedrooms. Sleeping. Of whom they would become.

Of her daughter, so fragile, so tender. Yet with a heart that demanded fair play and would end the game if everyone did not play fair. Hair color like her father's, startling blond, and eyelashes that were so long they almost seemed to bend when they opened and shut. Eyes of wonder, round and blue, and the tiniest turned-up nose. What would life teach her? What would she become? Who would she marry? Would she fall asleep someday with the Bible before her, kneeling in prayer? Would Amanda someday curl her own daughter's hair?

And what of her son? What kind of man would he be? Would he pray all night for someone else? Would he be kind? Would he walk in the ways of his father? Would his hands grow up to hammer nails straight? Would his shoulders be broad and his arms learn to cover a woman and protect her from her fears? Would Isaac's hands hold the face of his own son?

Had the life that she had lived, the life that they had lived before their son and daughter, before Isaac and Amanda, been the kind of lives that would lead them or leave them to lives like the young pastor before them? Would they be remembered well?

What stories would she tell her grandchildren of their grandfather, of her husband? That he was tall and handsome, perhaps. That when his arms enfolded her, it did not matter that it had rained, that the roast had burned, or even, God help her, that the pail out back was full of something hideous, something that brought shame to their door. She had loved him and the way he loved his children. She sighed and looked around the room. Wondered how long she could put it off. How long she could stay in this quiet moment. How long her thoughts and silence could make it last.

Maybe she could tell her grandchildren about their wedding. About her gown with the imported Irish lace. About the beads her grandmother had sewn on by hand. About the train her mother said was indecent, but which her granny had said was just right for a princess. Maybe she would tell them about how the violins played, about how the breezes blew the rose petals in her arms. About how fine he looked. About how the tip of his nose was sunburned. About how he kissed her so boldly, there in front of everyone. About how he swept her off her feet, right there at the altar. About how the other ladies blushed and wished that they were her. Maybe she would tell them how tender he was in candlelight or in moonlight.

And if they asked her, maybe she would tell them that there was something broken in him that she could not fix. Could not save. Could not rescue. Maybe she would cry and say that maybe she had not tried hard enough, had been too afraid to try. And then maybe she would lay her heart out on the table before them and tell them when it came their turn, not to be afraid, but to try. To reach and to try before it was too late. Before the one they loved was too far gone, too gone away.

She would tell them that he was gone, but that she loved him anyway. That she was not ashamed to have loved him. And that when he was best, he was bright and shiny and good. And that she would remember him sweeping her off her feet, in the candlelight, remember the blushes he brought to her cheeks. She would remember when they held each other and trembled. She would remember when he cried and was almost saved, almost rescued, almost persuaded.

But she did not think that she would tell them about the pail. God knew. It was enough that God knew. She looked one more time toward the window, then spoke.

"Pastor. Wake up, Pastor. It's past daybreak."

"Perhaps." The young preacher fumbled for words. "Perhaps he's . . . he's . . . maybe he's too ashamed to come home. Maybe he's seen the error of his ways. He may have started home and saw my horse outside and was just too shamed to return." His eyes looked up hopefully at Miranda while she poured coffee. "Too ashamed to return, just yet," he added quickly.

"No." Miranda smiled at the boy preacher to comfort him. "No, I don't think so. I don't think he's coming back. Not this way. I can feel it. We were connected, you know." She looked the young man in the eye. "No, he's gone. And I've been trying to think of how to explain it to the children. I hope it won't come too hard, in a way that makes him look too bad." She bit her lip and fanned at an imaginary fly. "He wouldn't have wanted them to be hurt."

Uncomfortable, the young preacher cleared his throat and set the piece of bacon in his hand back down on his plate. "But how can you know? How can you be sure? Why, anything could have delayed him. There's no way —"

"I know it. He's gone."

Thirty-two

They were up after hearing the last of the season's birds. Amos stretched and picked up the warm cup that steamed on his side of the table. He looked across the table at the two loves of his life. He was glad that they didn't know that he sometimes felt like a little boy pretending to be a man, a father, a husband. And always, always, it seemed to happen when he least needed to feel that way. When the crops failed, when food was running low, when it was time to lead the congregation in prayer. Someone five or six seemed to just take control of his mouth, his hands, his feet.

Then Evelyn was there. He smiled at his wife, to reassure him that he was indeed a man, and a very good man. He thanked God that He had given her to him.

"Well, I guess I'll get up from here." He slapped his legs. He always wore his most favorite overalls, most worn overalls, when he went hunting. "No point in wastin' time. Get out there early while the dew is still on the ground. See what I can find to bring home. Something you can throw a little gravy over —" he swatted playfully at his wife who moved just before his hand hit home — "You still a beautiful woman."

"Oh, ain't you nothing," she told him, pleased. "You'a might cute your own self."

"Let me get on out of here before I get distracted from what I'm supposed to be hunting."

"Now, you hush." She blushed, and he knew she was hoping that her daughter might still be too young to understand. She dusted her hands on her apron and straightened her husband's collar. "You just love this old, beat-up plaid shirt, don't you?"

" 'Deed I do."

"Well, one day you not going to be able to find this shirt no more. One day, when you not wearing it, it's gone go right on up the chimney."

"Look like I'm gone have to wear it every day then." He hugged her to him. Enfolded her with his arms.

"That's what you say."

"See here. I knew it. You just trying to keep me here. I'm going on outside, try to bag somethin' good." He snapped his cap on his leg. "See you soon, honey lamb." He winked at his wife. Looked at his daughter, smiling at them. "You, too, puddin'. It sure is good to have you home. You growin' into a fine young woman. Ain't that somethin', my baby marrying a major. Well, well." He closed the screen door behind him so that it would not bang. His shotgun under his arm, nose down, he whistled into the new day.

"Mama —" Alena watched her father from the doorway — "what is that song Daddy is whistling? He whistles it all the time, and I never thought to ask him."

"You know I don't even know, baby. Never thought to ask myself."

The two women laughed.

Alena watched her father walk across the yard. Gray smoke curled into the air from nearby chimneys. Leaves covered the ground — scarlet, rust, brown, some still clinging to green. His figure moved through them.

She had seen it a thousand times, him going hunting. Joining the other men and boys that carried shotguns. Hoping for a rabbit, squirrel, a raccoon for the table. Perhaps a well-trained, discerning eye would see a duck or a quail.

Silent men, boys not even as tall as the

guns they carried, moving while the world was still quiet, before it was disturbed. Before frightened animals scurried to hiding places. Before animals, resting in the new day, remembered to be frightened. Before the creatures relearned the lessons they had forgotten during the night. That they feared man. Early, before the first gunshot or crimson stain reminded them to be afraid.

Alena's mother smiled at her. "I used to watch my daddy go off that way, too. I must have stood there at our front door watching so many times. I bet I looked just like you do, right now."

Alena smiled at her mother. "Mama, I'm so glad to be back home."

"And I'm glad you're back." Her mother reached out her hand to draw Alena beside her. "Look at how your life has changed. My little girl, getting married."

"Mama, I'm sorry. Sorry about everything."

"We all sorry, baby. That's how life is. Going to be lots of sorries. That ain't nothing. Good families full of sorries. Families that ain't got no sorries, they the ones that don't make it. People too angry, too proud, or just feel like it's been too many sorries. A good family's got to have plenty of room for sorries. Sorry is a good thing. Ain't nothing to be ashamed of. Seems like sorry is always the beginning of hope. Don't never be shamed of sorry.

"You never gone see a group of people that's always gone agree about everything. We place too big a burden on love and on family thinkin' we suppose to agree on everything. Think lovin' each other or bein' family going to make us always see the same, act the same, feel the same."

"Seem like it would, though, Mama."

"Yeah, seem like." Her mother sat quiet and looked out the window. "Seem like." She sat still. "But that ain't so. Just ain't so. Took me some time to understand it myself. But now, I think I got it figured out. It just ain't so.

"See, me and you might disagree. You might like your potato salad sweet. I like mine salty. Seem silly, don't it?" Alena laughed. "But you know, people fall out with each other over even smaller things. I think they feel like, if you love me, you would be like me. Like it the way I like it. Like if you don't like salty potato salad you saying you don't like me. But that ain't how it goes."

Alena's mother looked at her. "I'm just telling you this so you will know ahead of time. So you won't make the same mistakes as me. So you won't give up friends and family like I do because I had to learn this for myself. What love does is it makes you love that person even if they don't like your salty potato salad. It makes you accept that they not crazy even if they do like it sweet."

"Mama, I know." Alena hugged her mother.

"But, it's even more than that." Her mother looked away or maybe inward. "You know, I had a cousin. We didn't sit horses at all, me and that boy. He never did anything the way I liked. Just got on my nerves all the time. He was always telling stories on me, getting me in trouble. Then one day he did something, I don't even remember what it was, something worth me being mad about. And I just said to myself, well that's that. I'm not gone be bothered with him no more."

"But, Mama. What's wrong with that? You don't have to feel bad about that." She held her mother's hand. "That's not such a big thing."

Her mother smiled back at her, bittersweet. "Don't seem like it is, does it? Not such a big thing at all. But sometimes, down over in me, I think about him.

Wonder if I did right? And you know, if I'm wondering, chances are it wasn't the right thing.

"You know, that boy got on my nerves, but he was my family. Now I don't even know where he is. I think about why did God put him in my pathway. Maybe He wanted me to learn something about myself from that crazy boy." She laughed to Alena. "Maybe He just wanted me to learn something about loving somebody, even when the person is just pure wrong. Maybe He want us to see how he keep lovin' us even when we just as wrong as can be. What you think?"

"I don't know, Mama. Maybe you are being too hard on yourself."

"Maybe you're right." Alena's mother patted her hand. "Maybe so. I just know I'm poorer by one cousin. That's all. It just makes me think. If he get on my nerves, it don't matter. Sweet or salty, it don't matter. Anyway, sorry or not, maybe I'm just getting older. I love you so much I'm not willin' to let you go. We just need to hold on to each other, not be so willin' let each other go, friends and family. Take each other for granted. And that's that."

Alena looked into her mother's eyes. "I know what you mean, Mama. Like you all.

I realized that nothing was worth losing you. That to be whole, I needed you in my life. Being home, I feel like a piece of me is back in place. I still miss J.C., and I want to do something about it. I need to do something about it. But I understand what you and Daddy were trying to say and do. I saw the riots, Mama. I saw what can happen, and I . . . I . . ."

Alena's mother moved her hand as if to fan away back memories. "I know, baby. Enough now. Let's talk about that dress. Just seem like I'm sad about something. And I can't figure out for the life of me why. Like I just lost somebody. Anyway, let's get rid of these dishes and then we can talk."

He enjoyed this time of morning. The quiet.

"Thank you, God," he spoke out loud amongst the trees. "Thank you for my baby's home coming." Amos walked softly on the leaves under foot. He had thought there might be trouble with his daughter's coming. "Thank you, God, for peace."

He moved further into the woods, careful and tranquil. "Thank you for my new son." He smiled about James. About the letter that asked for his daughter's hand in marriage. He moved still deeper within. If he did not find something soon, he would move from this spot that he loved. Loved the way he barely saw daylight. The way the leaves made cover. Nothing here today though. Maybe he would try a little spot closer to home.

"I guess your daddy will be back soon. Morning's getting a little old. A little rusty." They sat across from each other, she and her mother. Alena with paper and pencil. "Now, tell me about the dress."

"Well, I want white of course. Not ivory or anything. And no bows, Mama."

"All right, baby. No bows."

"And I want the skirt kind of straight and to my ankles."

"So this is a modern wedding dress."

"But not too modern, Mama. And I want a jacket with the train attached."

"A long train."

"No, Mama. Just barely on the ground. In my bouquet, Mama, I want gardenias, daffodils, purple tulips, and one white calla lily."

"That's some combination."

"I know, Mama, but that's what I want. Those are the flowers I like."

"All right then, baby."

"And, Mama, can you embroider flowers on the jacket? Just in white, right on the jacket. It doesn't matter if other people know they are there. Just so I know."

"Mm-hm."

"Oh, Mama, I can't wait for you to see Chicago. All the people, the trains, the clothes, the music. Just wait until you see Aunt Patrice and all she does at the mission. Then you have to meet Jonathan and Dinah and Mr. Cool Breeze."

"Cool Breeze? What kind of name is that?"

"Mama, he is something else. So funny."

"And James."

"Yes, Mama. And James. He's . . . he's . . ."

"I know, baby. I felt the same way about your daddy. Made me a little weak in the knees."

"Mama!"

"Well, now, it's true. I thought your daddy was the cat's meow. Still do."

Three shots, that's what his father had taught him. Three shots. Three shotgun blasts would bring the other men who were out hunting in the area. Three shots into the air.

He stepped from foot to foot. His eyes

scanning the area. Hoping for someone to come. Hoping for someone. Little boy hoping to be rescued.

"Amos, that you, man? You all right? Good stars!" The man looked down then. "What's done happened here?"

"Amos, Amos? That you, Greenway? What you two young fellows up to? Mercy, mercy! Mercy, mercy!"

Then the last walked up, walking younger, quieter. "Who is that?" he said before he reached the group.

"Come and see," the older one said.

"Looks like trouble."

"Maybe so, maybe not," the older one said.

"What happened?" the quieter one asked.

"I don't know. I was just out hunting," Amos explained. "I didn't find nothing where I usually hunt and thought I would come here to try."

"Well, it sure looks like you came upon something this time. Mercy, mercy."

"Looks like trouble," the quieter one repeated.

"Maybe so, maybe not. He been shot?"

"Don't look like it," Amos said. "Just that stick and that stone."

"What was he doing over here? Mercy, mercy."

The older one shook his head. "What you think, boy? Use your head. See them ashes on his face? See that rope, that knife in his belt? See that kerosene? What you think? You know who this is?"

"Yes, sir. I know who it is. Who don't? Mercy, mercy."

"Then use your head, boy. See how close he is to Amos's place. I don't think he was here hunting no possum. And don't take that tone with me. I may be an old man, but I can sit you down."

"I didn't mean no harm, sir. Just . . . mercy, mercy."

"They sure to be out for blood now," the quieter one lamented. His jaw muscles tightened.

"Maybe so, maybe not." The older man looked at Amos. "This here is the ringleader. The other ones not gone be sure how to proceed. Unless they got something to be angry about or shamed about. So I think we gone have to help out here. Just a little. Just enough to help them save face."

The older man pointed toward the one who kept calling for mercy. "You, take this canteen down to the stream and fill it. Then hurry back with it. Don't talk to nobody and don't make no lot of noise. Be quick about what you do. You —" the

older man pointed to the quiet one —
"You take this kerosene can. Get rid of it.
Take this knife and this rope and get rid of
them so they never be seen again. Just
leave his shotgun right here.

"When those things be done, then you
two get on up out of here. Hightail it.
Leave the rest to me and Amos. I'm an old
man. If somebody happen upon us, I done
already lived a full life. And Amos, he got a
stake in how this play out. You two young
men, you got lives still to be lived. Whatever happens, if the four of us live, we ain't
gone never tell what happened here today.
Ain't gone discuss it. Never. Not till Jesus
come. Now get on. Do what I say."

"What you think that was, Mama?"

"Just somebody found some game or
something in the woods." Evelyn tried to
look calm in front of her daughter.
"Nothing to worry about. They do it all
the time. You just don't remember. I guess
you have been gone a long time."

*God, let him be safe. Don't let the sorrow in
my heart have been for my husband. Don't
bring my baby back to my arms just for me to
lose my husband. God, let him be safe.*

"Nothing to worry about at all," she lied
to her daughter. "Now go on describing

the church where this wedding is gone be. Where me and your daddy goin' to sit?"

The old man poured water from the canteen onto the rag in his hand. "You know, I knowed this child all his life. Looked like a little angel, he did. Started out the sweetest child . . ."

He sighed as he wiped the ashes from Eric Bates's face, careful not to disturb the body. "Guess he didn't have too much chance though. His daddy was a mean-hearted son of a gun. Knowed him all his life. And his granddaddy. I declare that was the meanest, hatefulest man I ever come in contact with. And you know how they say opposites attract? Well, this child here —" he gently removed the ashes from the man's mouth — "his mama spoke more evil, kept more stuff going. Child didn't have a chance."

The old man wiped Bates's lips and sighed again. "No, sir, didn't have a chance."

"You think he was coming here for us?" Amos asked.

"No, boy." The old man looked at Amos. "Not for you. For your daughter. Wouldn't come alone to take you and your wife. Not the three of you. No, he come for your baby. But you know they say, God don't slumber nor sleep. Had His eye on you all."

The old man talked, his eyes on the figure on the ground. "No, I figure he came for her, then they, the whole group, was coming back for the rest of you. Probably was gone get some others of us, just to make sure the rest got the message."

Amos stood suddenly to his feet. His jaw muscles clenched, and he raised his rifle. Rage squeezed from his chest to his mouth.

"Boy, what you doing?" The old man grabbed him. "You too old now for this. You got to use your head. You trying to get us killed? Your family? A hothead won't make it. That's how this boy died. You got to use your head."

Amos trembled with the effort to control himself. He stared at the corpse that lay at his feet.

The old man squeezed his arm. "Think, son. This boy is dead. He can't do you no harm unless you let him. You got nothing to be mad about and everything to be grateful for. This man come here to kill your daughter. She don't know nothing about it. And won't, unless you tell her, unless we mess up. She alive, and he ain't.

Hate can't help you, grace will.

"Now, you just be thankin' God and keep a cool head. You can't think when you all bound up with rage. You got to be able to think and see and know. Next time — and it's gone be a next time — you gone have to help someone else through it. Now, come on."

The old man went on cleaning Bates's hands, lifting them gently, remembering to clean the webs between the fingers.

"Now, you sit his shotgun over here, closer to his right hand," the old man said when he had finished. "I 'spect they won't wait long to have the funeral. After that, before somebody take a notion to finish his work, I would get that girl on back up North. I'll take care of letting them know. You don't know nothing. Now, you get on home. And you remember to thank God. And pray He spare us."

"Daddy!" Alena jumped from her seat when her father walked through the door. "What happened? We heard the shots."

"Nothing much." Amos squeezed his daughter, closed his eyes. "Nothing much."

"See, baby," Evelyn patted her daughter's hand and rubbed her husband's back.

Thank you, Lord, she prayed silently.

"Nothing you need to think about. Just somebody with some trouble in the woods. It's all taken care of."

"Thank God, it was nothing, Daddy. Mama told me not to worry. But when I heard the gun . . ."

"Don't worry, honey. God is yet looking out for us."

Thirty-three

"It looks like he had been hunting, ma'am. We didn't find any evidence of anything unusual. His gun hadn't been fired. It appears that it was just an accident. He must have tripped over a log nearby. There was a broken tree limb, pretty sharp, and a large stone."

Miranda closed her eyes.

"I know this is hard for you to hear," the new deputy said to her. "He was well respected here. And I know you and your children must have loved him."

"Yes." Miranda breathed while the young minister patted her hand. "I'm just grateful that . . . grateful that there wasn't anything else." *Thank You, God. I don't know what You did or how You did it. I saw him leave with the rope and things. But thank You, God, for sparing me, for sparing my children at least that pain. Now, help us, Lord. Help us to get through it. I know all the pain he has caused, but, Lord, be merciful. Help us, Lord.*

"Ma'am?" The new sheriff leaned toward her, his face questioning.

"I'm sorry. I . . . I was lost in thought."

"I'm sorry, ma'am. I know this is hard for you. I just wanted to know if there was anything else I could do to help."

"No . . . no . . . we'll be all right from here." She buried her face in her hands and wept.

"So, what you think?" the one who always challenged asked. "Think it was an accident like that old animal said? Or you think they cooked up something and killed him? Think we better set things right? Get things stirred up just so they know we mean business? That things ain't gone git slack just 'cause Bates is gone?"

"I'm not so sure," the one who always agreed said. "I've known that old man a long time. He's not the sort to start trouble. Perhaps . . . maybe we should wait a while. See what happens in the next few days. It looked like an honest accident to me."

"Yes, wait and see," echoed the one who was always afraid.

The one who was sometimes brave enough to reason appealed to the others. "Sheriff Bates just had his hunting shotgun with him. None of his other . . . uh . . . equipment. It clearly appears to be a hunting accident. I don't believe anyone else even knew anything about it."

"You shirtwaists are full of it. Can't you see they killed him? And whether they did or not, I say we give them a little something to keep them in line. So they'll know who the boss is around here." The one who always challenged spoke up, took control. Something mean glinted in his eye.

"One thing for sure —" another man stepped forward — "you ain't the boss. There is not going to be any more killing around here."

"Who says? Who's big enough to stop me? I'm a free man."

"I say so. I'm the new deputy here. And I say so. And I think I'm big enough to stop you. What's more, if you cause any trouble here, I don't think you'll be able to say you're a free man for long. There's been enough trouble around here, and I say it stops here and it stops now."

The deputy cleared his throat. "Anyone else have anything to say?"

"Oh, I am most agreed. Indubitably," said the one who always agreed. "Now is not the time for arms. Think of his poor grieving widow. Oh, I should say so. Let us consider her. No need to take any action, as far as I can see."

"No need for action," the one who was always afraid agreed, nodding his head.

"Finally, some reasonable men," said the one who was sometimes brave enough to reason.

The one who always challenged slunk angrily to the corner. "Mark my words, you goin' to be sorry. Just wait. Wait and see how they act. Just wait. Mark my words." He folded his arms across his chest and sulked, nursing his anger. Red eyes in the growing darkness.

"I don't think so," said the new deputy. "If we do have trouble, I will handle it same way with everyone, peacefully and lawfully."

"Yes, I agree. Peacefully and lawfully," said the one who always agreed.

"Yeah. Lawfully," said the one who was always afraid.

"Do you need me to help you," the young minister asked. Concern covered his face.

"No, this is something I need to do. Have to do." Miranda wiped the tears away from her face. They seemed to just be falling. She hadn't been aware of the tears until they were just there, or dripped from her chin, her nose. "Something we have to do as a family.

"Just pray for us. Keep us in your prayers. The Lord will be with us."

Miranda walked into the kitchen where her children finished their dessert. Pound cake. They loved pound cake. Seemed to like the plain cake more than they liked the cake with frosting.

"Mama, what was that man doing here? He had on a uniform just like Daddy's."

Miranda touched her son's hair. He didn't miss much. He was so observant. "And the preacher was here most of the day. What for, Mama? Where's Daddy? He's usually back before now."

"Where's Daddy?" Amanda nodded.

"That's what I came to talk to you about."

"Mama, is something wrong? Is something wrong with Daddy? Is Daddy hurt? Did something happen to Daddy?"

"Calm down now, Isaac. I need you to be strong. If you get upset, Amanda's going to get upset. We're going to have to be strong. Have to be strong for each other."

"Mama . . ." Tears watered in Isaac's

eyes, like he knew.

"Mama." Amanda dropped her spoon and, looking at her brother, reached for her mother.

"Come here, you two. Sit on Mama's lap." She wiped tears away from her face. "It's all right to cry. We loved Daddy. Jesus wept, so we know it's all right for us to cry. But still —" she lifted Isaac's head so that she could look into his eyes — "we're going to have to be strong so that we can lean on each other."

"Oh, Mama, what's happened? Is Daddy hurt?"

"Daddy hurt?" Amanda mimicked, her face pink and shiny with tears.

"You know how Daddy always took care of us." She rubbed her hands through their hair, so like their father's. "He loved us, didn't he?"

Isaac buried his head in his mother's bosom. Amanda followed.

"Well, last night, the sheriff thinks, your daddy went hunting. And it seems . . . it seems . . . there was some sort of accident. It seems he tripped or something, and . . . and . . ." The family sat holding each other, shaking. "Daddy's not coming back. He's . . . he's gone now. God's . . . God's . . ." The widow and her two children sat in her husband's favorite chair. Muffled sobs. Occasionally, Isaac or Amanda raised their heads.

"Mommy. Why, Mommy?" Isaac asked once.

"Only God knows, baby. Only God knows."

They rocked back and forth in the chair until the lamps began to dim. Miranda sat them up and wiped their faces. "All right now. I need you to help me. Can you do that? Can you help me with the windows?"

"All right, Mama." The children struggled to their feet. Together, the three of them closed each window. Made certain, at least for that night, that the locks were on the doors.

Like every night, they washed their hands and faces. Put on their pajamas. Blew out the lamps. "Mama, can we sleep with you?"

"You know, I was just about to ask the two of you the same thing."

Snuggled in under the comforter, the three of them breathed shallowly and stared out the window. There was a full moon. Periodically, Amanda hiccuped.

"Did I ever tell you all about me and Daddy's first Christmas?" Miranda smiled at her two children. "Well, I'll tell you that story tonight, and we've got lots of other stories to tell. Daddy won't be home tonight. But he'll always be here in our hearts."

She told them about the tree. How there was no snow and how they made pretend snow from cotton to hang on the tree and around its base. How they strung popcorn and ornaments she cut from colored paper. She laughed and told them how their father burnt the Christmas cookies, how they wrapped their presents in red, blue, yellow, green, and white scarves. She talked until little eyes closed, and they were fast asleep. Then Miranda slipped to her knees beside the bed.

"Thank you, God, for allowing us another day. Thank you, Lord, for sparing us any more grief. It hurts so bad, what I'm feeling. And I don't know how I . . . how we are going to get through this. I loved him, God. We loved him. But I have to accept that You know best. We loved him, but I know You loved Him best.

"Forgive me, Lord, if there was something more that I could have done. I just loved him so much . . . I . . . we need Your mercy and Your grace, Lord." Images of her children, her husband floated in the darkness behind her closed eyes.

"But, Lord, even more than me, look out for our children. You're their father now. Help me raise them to be what You want them to be. Lord, I know You can love their pain away. And, Lord, before I forget, forgive both of us for what we've done. For what he did, what I turned my head to. Forgive all those that helped him, that did wrong with him. And while You are at it, Lord, bind up the wounds; wipe the tears of all those we have hurt. And, Lord, forgive us for hurting You. Amen."

"I know, Amos, that there has been a lot of things that have gone on here in the past." The new sheriff met Amos's eyes. "I am pretty sure that word has already gotten to you. But I wanted to tell you myself. Sheriff Bates is dead. They found him in the woods at the edge of your property. It appeared to be a hunting accident.

"I don't expect any trouble. In fact, I've made it pretty clear as the new sheriff that I'm not going to tolerate any. You been living here a long time though, and I know you know how things are."

Amos nodded.

"Sorry to have to come here with this kind of news, ma'am." The new sheriff nodded, hat in hand, at Evelyn. He nodded again. "You must be Alena."

"Yes."

"You don't live here now, do you? You're from up North somewhere."

"Chicago. I live in Chicago."

"Funeral is two days from now." He looked toward Amos.

Amos nodded. "She just visiting. We ain't had her home in a while. But she's got things to do back there, won't be here long. We just get to see her a short while. She's heading back right after the funeral."

The new sheriff nodded.

Late in the night, while the last of the crickets chirped, Alena cried. She wasn't sure if it was for J.C., for herself, for Bates.

Maybe for all of them.

She pressed the pillow to her face so that she would not trouble her mother and father. It didn't matter. Her tears, her anguish had no sound, felt endless, felt like she might be lost, might drown. Like in the morning they might find her body washed up on the shores of her grief.

She wept that her friend was gone. Wept that his life was ended, his mother's heart broken. That she was not able to say goodbye, that his death was so rude. She wept that she grieved for her friend, that she lived in a world where she was free to go and come, that others saw her gifts and her presence as offense to them, to their notions of what should be. That following her gift meant having to be far from the place and people she loved.

She ached that she felt God pulling her, requiring her to love those that hated her, that sought her life. To sorrow for their confusion, for hurt that caused them to hurt others. Ached that she felt Him pulling and loved Him so strongly that she could not resist the love He pressed into her, that though they sought evil for her, she prayed for mercy for them.

Sometime later, when she had finished crying, Alena rose and began to write, first to James of her gratitude and pleasure in his love, in the hope of their union. Then words of prayer for the family of God, for the hope of all of God's people. And when she could write no more. When all that she heard from Him was on paper, she slept.

Thirty-four

Alena awakened early the next morning to the smell of fried chicken and something sweet, maybe sweet potato pudding, maybe pound cake. Cabinet doors opened and closed while her mother hummed "There's Not a Friend Like the Lowly Jesus," then "There Is a Balm in Gilead," to "Nearer My God to Thee" just like she always did. One song after another, sometimes flip-flopping like they were all joined together, meant to go together.

> Oh, this joy I have, the world didn't
>   give it to me.
> Oh, oh, oh, this joy I have, the world
>   didn't give it to me.
> Oh, this joy I have, the world didn't
>   give it to me.
> The world didn't give it, the world can't
>   take it away.

Alena rose to wash her face and hands, looked into the mirror that had been on her dresser for years. It was made of a rough wooden frame around heavy glass. Once a very pale mint green, now more of the wood grain showed through. The lines and dips of the wood were more prominent so that the outer paint was just a tint; the character of the wood showed through. Alena ran her fingers lightly over the frame. Something she knew, something she had known. She liked it better now. It was more clear. It was what it was.

"Mama, why you cooking so early?" Her father was quiet. Moving from counter to stove to the table. "Are we going on a trip? It's too early for fried chicken." She reached her hand to pull a little taste off of a wing while she smiled at her father. It was part of the family game, to sneak a piece. "It does smell good though."

Her mother tapped her hand when she tried for the second taste. "This is not for us. But you go ahead, you and your daddy share that piece, and that's it."

Alena took the wing and held it out to her father. He shook his head. "No," he said and studied his coffee.

"What's the matter?" Alena looked between her father and mother. "Is something wrong?"

"Ask your mother." Her father looked drawn, washed out, like he had no more to give.

"We have a lot to do today," her mother said. "I don't have a lot of time with you before we start back up the road to put you on the train. We have a fitting to do. I know you are going to send back the material for your dress, but I want to check to see if you see something here, some goods that you might want me to use for my dress. They got some pretty material at the dry goods store. Things going to be closed down tomorrow, I imagine. All the shops and stores closed because of the funeral. So we have to make the best of the day.

"And then —" her mother paused, then started again — "And then, I think we are going to pay a little visit to Miss Miranda. We won't stay long. Just stop by and pay our respects. Take her this chicken and this here little pound cake. See if we can be of any help in her time of sorrow."

Alena's father sucked in air so deeply, she was sure the tablecloth — just a few morning toast crumbs still on it — was going to pull up from the table. Then he blew the air back out the way it came. Her father closed his eyes for a moment, swallowed, then went back to nursing his coffee.

"Your daddy is not saying anything, but he don't like it."

He stared out the kitchen window and cleared his throat.

Her mother went on. "Last night I just couldn't sleep. That woman was just on my mind. Her and those children. I have known that child all her life, and . . . and . . . I can't change the way things are. Who her husband was or what he did. But I just feel like . . . like I want to, like I need to reach out to her."

"Who reached out to us all these times when the shoe was on the other foot?" Amos frowned. "When we were buryin' ones of our own? When J.C. was dead, that man came to his graveside spittin' on the ground. And it wasn't the first time. Other people he hurt, you think he cared about them, cared about their loved ones?"

His jaw clenched and unclenched. "I ain't got nothing against that woman, but I don't believe it take all that. It just ain't in my heart to worry about feedin' his family. I still got to worry every night, every day about my own family being safe." He stirred his coffee.

Alena watched her mother and father.

Her mother frying chicken while she talked, while she reasoned. Her father so clearly wrestling to control the anger he felt. Her mother used a long-handled fork to turn the chicken breasts that fried in the bubbling lard in the cast-iron skillet. She lifted the coffeepot and came to refresh the coffee in her husband's favorite cup. She poured and just a little steam rose.

"Amos, you know I love you." She took her free hand and lifted his head. "There is not a better man than you anywhere in this world. But I want you to listen to me." Alena watched her mother turn, replace the blue ceramic-covered pot on the stove, then sit down next to her husband.

Her mother took one of her husband's hands in her own, and then began to rub the hand with her free hand. "Don't think that somewhere inside of me there is not a spot that is mad about everything that has happened. I know good as you what that man did. But the Lord, His Spirit, just won't leave me alone about this. Amos, when is all this going to end? Who's gone make it end? Somebody got to listen to God and stop it."

"You right, Evelyn. Somebody got to stop it. But it don't seem like to me we got to be the ones. We ain't killed nobody. We ain't leavin' our home late at night sneaking around to hurt nobody. So it don't seem like to me the burden should be on us."

"You right, Amos. You right." Alena watched her mother continue to rub her father's hand. Observed the way she looked into his eyes. Her mother stopped rubbing his hand for a moment, and with her free hand, looked down and toyed with the few crumbs on the table. "You ain't sayin' nothin' that don't make sense. But you know sometimes —" Alena saw her mother look into her father's eyes in a connected way — "we have disagreements, some- times big old arguments." Her mother touched her cheeks as if they were flushed or burned. "And sometimes I'm wrong. Not very often —" she smiled like a young girl — "but sometimes I am. And then, even when I'm wrong, you'll come sometimes and try to smooth it over, make it better. And I know you doing it because you love me. When you do that, it make me just get down off my high horse 'cause I know I'm wrong, but you love me enough that you love right through that wrong. And it make me so shame that I been wrong and stubborn. It makes me love you more, and love God more for giving me a man like you."

"Sometimes."

Alena watched her father squeeze her mother's hand with great affection.

"Then there's times when *you* done something wrong."

"When was that? So few times I can't even remember." He seemed to forget for a moment to be angry and teased Alena to include her in the conversation. "You remember your daddy being wrong?"

"I'm just listening, Daddy."

Her mother laughed softly. "Anyway. There are times, few though they may be, when you are wrong and being so big about it, I just want to stick a pin in you and bring you back down to size. But then, you know, something happens. It's like I come to see that you are a part of me and being mad at you is like being mad at myself. When I hurt you, I hurt myself. When I'm mean to you, I feel it like I was mean to myself. The love in my heart for you is so big, it just walk right on top of any anger I feel at you. It's as if love won't let me be, or at least not let me stay, mad at you."

Amos lifted his wife's hand to his lips. Alena prayed in her heart that God would bind she and James with the kind of love they showed.

"That's because we'a family. We joined. We one, baby."

"Well then —" she spoke slowly — "don't you think that is how God want all of us to behave with one another? If we all one family in God, shouldn't Miranda's pain be my pain? Shouldn't His love make me move even past the anger I feel for what her husband did? Don't you never have that feeling? Like God is making you love that man, Bates, even after what he done? What he tried to do? Sometimes that love make me hurt so bad, it's just like I'm getting my own little taste of being crucified. You think it don't bother me that he killed that child, J.C.? That it don't bother me that he tried to kill my child?"

Alena stared at the grease and chicken bubbling on the stove. Sighed and blinked back tears. It was out now. The thought she had been trying to keep at bay since Bates's body was found was now in the open air.

He had come for her.

She watched her father turning, uncomfortable, in his chair. His eyes avoided hers.

"No, you ain't said a word about it, Amos. But I wasn't born yesterday. I, we, know why that man was here. He didn't come way over here just hunting, at least not hunting animals." Alena's mother looked at her. "He came for our baby. He left his children home sleeping in the bed to come and kill ours."

Alena felt water come to her eyes. Her pulse quickened, and her stomach lurched. How close had he come? Had he seen her? His body was found so close to where she always fed Cottonball. What if he had reached out to grab her?

Amos shook his head, displeased. "So you know all that and still you want to go to that woman's house? To go to those people? What are you saying to her then, to them? Go ahead, walk on us. Kill us. 'Yassuh, missy, you don't have to feel bad for what your husband did, for what you did to help him? Here's some nice fried chicken, and don't you worry your head because your husband could have killed my child.' No, Evelyn, I don't understand it."

"I don't want you to be mad with me, but I know the Lord is speakin' with me about this. I know I'm doin' what He wants me to do. It don't even matter if it's what I want to do. I know I am doing what the Lord wants me to do. I can't even tell you that I understand it, Amos. 'Cause I don't. I just know that the Lord is requiring that I do this. And I feel like I have to go, Amos, if don't nobody else go with me."

"What you saying? What you going to say to her? 'It's all right. Everything is forgiven. Debt is paid.' I can't understand that, Evelyn. We all the time forgivin'." Amos hit the side of his fist on the table.

Alena blinked, startled. All she knew of her father was gentleness.

"And I'm tired of it, Evey. I feel like I can't take it no more. I'm a man!" He thumped his chest. "I'm a man just like he is, was, like all them are men. Ain't no different. He had nerve enough to come here to my home. To trespass on my land, to try to grab my daughter. I know what he was plannin' to do. I saw him before we cleaned him up —" Her father looked from his wife to his daughter. Anger had made his tongue slip.

"They all the time lynchin' us, making up excuses saying we violated a white woman," Amos continued. "But it's okay for them to kill my daughter, try to violate my daughter, kill and rape our women; that's okay. That don't require lynchin'. If I tried to lynch a white man for violating my family, they would kill me in fifty different ways.

"I'm sick of it, Evey. It's too much for God to ask, to put me in a box like this as a man. I been peaceful all my life — but I feel like I ain't got no more to give. No more. Ain't no justice."

Amos poked his finger hard on the table top. "Look at the world we livin' in. If one colored man commit a crime, then we all bad; they justified in killing us all. If one white man commit a crime, that was just one man. They don't go around thinking all white men is bad. More than that, a whole group of them can get together kill families, burn down houses, towns, and it ain't nothing but a reflection on that isolated group of men. Something is wrong, and my forgiveness done give out!"

Alena's father hit his fist on the table again to emphasize his words. "What more I got to give them? What more I'm supposed to let them take from me? Don't I even get the right to be a man in this world? Now I'm supposed to take *his* wife my hard earned food?"

He shook his head. "I ain't asking for revenge. I ain't saying I want to go over there and do to his children what he planned to do to mine. But I don't see why

I got to go and give them comfort, tell them it's all right what they did. That ain't no charge for what they did. They ain't even thought about saying they was sorry, Evey, and you know it. She . . . they ought to be comin' over here to beg our pardon. Beg the pardon of that ole man they burned out. Beggin' J.C.'s pardon, beggin' his mama's pardon. Forgive them when they tryin' to kill me? They ain't even sayin' they sorry, and I'm supposed to go give them comfort when they done tore me up on the inside?

"Maybe God speakin' to you about this, Evey, but He sure ain't spoke to me about it. That's for sure."

Alena watched her mother take her husband's hand. Watched her smooth the skin on his hand and try to soothe his feelings. "You think it's easy for me, what I'm trying to tell you, what I'm trying to do? I told you, I don't understand it myself, Amos. I'm still trying to figure it out. I might not ever understand until I'm able to see God for myself.

"But when I think about it, I do know this. I know that God loves me, and that He has a good plan for me. I know that He, 'cause I been livin' with Him for a long time, wouldn't ask me to do anything that was not for my good in the end. I know that with all the wrong I have done in my life, I still want Him to forgive me, and when He forgives, I want to be debt free. I don't want to have to pay for the bad that I done wrong. I want Him to forgive what I owe, to forgive my debts. Ain't we done some wrong things, Amos?"

Alena's father looked briefly into her eyes, then looked away from his wife's words out the window.

"Ain't we? And God knows, I want to be forgiven completely. So the Word say we got to forgive the same way. It ain't easy, but it must not be too easy for God to forgive us for all we do, either."

"Evey, I just . . . I just don't understand. I just ain't ready." Alena watched as her father cleared his throat, tapped his foot.

"I know, Amos. We hurt. And it just ain't hurt now, for this moment. We hurt for how we been treated down through the years. For how they hurt our mamas and daddies, our grand-fathers and grand-mothers, how they hurt our people long past, and still how they want to hurt our children. Seem like they even got evil plans for the ones that ain't been born yet. Amos, it hurt me, too. I don't understand it no more than you do, forgiving people that keep on hurtin' you and feel like it's all right."

Alena's mother turned away, then stood and, face toward the stove, stirred the pot. Her head down, she sighed like her words, the situation was pressing on her, on her chest. "But, I know, Amos, that vengeance ain't mine. It's the Lord's. I know that they don't have enough money, enough nothing to pay me back for all the unnecessary hurt that's been in my life. All people got to hurt, but they don't know nothing, it seems, about unnecessary hurt. But ain't no pay they can pay that can make it right. How they gone pay for J.C.? What they gone pay that boy's mama that's gone keep her from cryin' tears into her pillow? What pay they gone pay for the grandchildren she ain't gone never hold, for never holdin' her son in her arms again? Ain't no pay. Amos, it seem like just ain't no point, ain't no vengeance can bring satisfaction." Still stirring.

"Evey, I don't see how you can expect me not to stand up. How I'm gone forgive. I don't see them turnin' back. I don't see them repentin'. I don't see that we in no less danger than we was yesterday. I don't see them changin'. Don't see them tryin' to beg our pardon." Amos thumped his chest. "Don't seem like they even trying to make it right."

"It seem like to me the Lord is sayin' lay the debt at his feet." Alena watched her mother, heaviness pressing on her upper back. "Lay that offense at his altar. It seems like He is tellin' me that I can't make nobody repent. I owe so much myself, I ain't got the right to ask. Only God is righteous enough to require somebody to repent; I can't do it."

Amos sat back in his chair. Foot stopped patting like he was trying to look even. His nostrils flared though and made a lie of his controlled posture.

Alena's mother's voice went on. "It don't matter who it is — my family members, people round here, white folks, the whole world. I ain't so debt free that I can demand that anybody say they sorry or that they repay me. They ain't got enough to pay the debt, no how.

"All I can do is forgive. That's the gift that I bring to God, to His altar. That's the gift, the sacrifice, I give to the one who has hurt me. And if I forgive, God promise to forgive me, too. If I forgive others little, God forgive me little. If I forgive others big, God forgive me big."

"Um." Amos growled, looked away.

"Don't seem like He been speaking that to me." Alena's father's eyes were on his wife's back.

"Maybe God tellin' me to do it, 'cause I need more forgiveness than I even know. I don't know, Amos. Like I got to stop callin' in my debt, so God can forgive mine. I got to let the debt be forgotten, so God can forget mine. I just feel like I got to do what He tell me to do. Forgiveness is the gift that I got to give."

Alena's father leaned forward, one hand pressing down hard on each knee. His eyes pressing into her mother's back. "How you expect me to forgive somebody seem like he live his whole life to hurt me and mine?" His voice was low, rumbling like a storm coming. "Somebody who see my son's body swinging from a tree and can't understand, can't feel or see his own son swinging in my son's place."

Her mother turned. "It ain't no less hard for me, Amos! Don't say it like it don't hurt me, too. Don't think it ain't a part of me that want to jump and shout, 'Hallelujah!' A part that want to say, 'Thank you we ain't got to worry 'bout that one no more. That's one less one we got to worry about killing our babies.' But God won't let me."

461

Her mother seemed to struggle to control the tremble in her chin, to keep her mouth from the shape of wailing. "When you hurt me, Amos, I can only give forgiveness. I can't make or demand that you repent. That is your gift to give, Amos, and you get to choose whether you gone give it or not." She laid one hand over her heart. "It's your choice whether you gonna give me your gift of repentance, whether you goin' to offer your gift of repentance to God. But I got to do what God tells me to do, to give my forgiveness, whether you give me repentance or not.

"Same way with someone around here that hurt me —" she swept her arm around the room, motioning outside — "or somebody that hurt me at the church. Same way with white folks. I can't make them be sorry for what they done. I can't even demand that they say they sorry for what they done to me, to you, to Alena, to J.C. That's they gift that they got to choose to give or not give. Same way with the whole world, when one nation offend another one. Same thing. Lord just hold us responsible for what *we* supposed to do, not the other person."

Alena watched her father lean back in his chair. He shook his head, his breathing

462

seemed shallow. Alena watched. Looked between her parents. Too anxious, too hurt to even consider one side or the other.

"So, Amos," her mother continued. "I can't make you forgive. I can only tell you what I feel like the Lord is sayin' to me. You may not understand. Alena may not understand." Her mother turned to her, and Alena looked deeply into her eyes. "I may have to go by myself. May have to walk up to that house by myself. But Amos, I feel like I got to go give this gift, maybe lift this woman's burden a little bit. I know her husband tried to kill my baby."

Alena's mother seemed to fight to keep control of her voice. She looked to have given up controlling her tears, for they flowed now. Her lips and chin trembled. "She may refuse my gift. She may hate me for it, may think I'm being uppity to offer her forgiveness, but I feel like I got to try." Her voice shook. "And after I give it, she may go on, might turn to the right, might get worse, but that ain't my responsibility. Amos, I just feel like I got to do what He telling me to do. I got to show that I even forgive that man Bates."

The family sat in silence for a while. A churning, electric silence, like silence in the middle of a whirlwind. Alena stared at the floor.

Could she forgive someone who wanted to kill her? Who thought the ruin of her life was his right, who thought her ruin was his privilege? Could she forgive the ones who loved him? Who would not condemn him or apologize for him?

"Evey —" her father spoke with authority in the midst of the thick silence — "I'm your husband. And you have given yourself to me. What's more, I know you love me. I'm not gone put you in the position of choosin' between my love, what I want, and what you feel God is telling you. You know in this house, God come first.

"It ain't easy for me, and I don't like it; I ain't gone pretend, and I ain't gone mince my words. I ain't feeling no love for that man, for his memory, or for his wife. I'm glad he gone. Better him than my baby, better him than us. Seem like to me, maybe now it will be some peace around here. But I see you, I feel you. My feelings ain't gone stand in your way. You do what you got to do. Meantime, I'm gone pray."

Miranda covered the mirrors with black draping. She remembered seeing her granny do it when her grandfather died.

She didn't know why. The room looked too festive though. It didn't look like anyone had died. The drapes seemed to help. Maybe some black pieces to hang over the curtains, to tone down the brightness, the flowers, to help the room say grief, death.

Her fingers rubbed the framed photograph. Her husband smiling so handsomely, so bravely into the camera. Their two children perched, each one on a knee. She stood next to him, her hand on his shoulder. *Smile,* the photographer had said, as if any of them needed to be encouraged.

He's gone, she reminded herself, as she drew an imaginary circle around his face. *Widow,* she tried out the word in her mind. *Widow.* What did that mean? It sounded desolate, like she felt.

She had thought the first day that the love would die with him. But it didn't. It was here, now. It was this big aching thing, this thing that now had no place. That followed her around. That enveloped her.

Where did it go? Who should she give it to, this leftover, left-behind love? Was there a jar with a lid she could place it in so that it did not pull at her, make her stomach hurt? A place to contain this homeless love so that it did not escape to trouble her at night when she needed to be held, when she was lonely for his touch, his caress? So that it did not demand a place, a plate, a cup at the dinner table? So that it did not demand that its clothes remain in the closet, its smell on the pillow, that its shaving razor and cup remain on the shelf above the sink?

Her fingers wandered from the photo to the tulip bulbs that rested in the crystal dish in front of it. As soon as she finished darkening the room, she would begin digging. She needed enough soil to fill the pail, the bucket out back.

"Do you think we have enough in the basket? Should we add something else? I know she's going to love the comforter. You must have been working on it for a while. Just came in handy, right now. Who would have thought." The one with gray eyes fingered the material. "Maybe she'll feel like doing some needlework on it when she feels better."

"Poor dear," said the blue-eyed one. "I am almost embarrassed to say it, and you might think I am wrong, but I have been thanking God that it was not me. Not me that lost my husband. I don't know what I would do."

"Well, I wonder how she feels now after she said those horrible things about him just the other day," the one with green eyes said boldly. "I wonder if she's sorry. Maybe that will teach her not to speak so quickly. Not to take a good man like that for granted."

"That's no way to talk. Not now," the one with brown eyes said tearfully. "It sounds so mean. We shouldn't talk mean now."

"Well, don't you have the nerve. You haven't spoken to her since that day," said the green-eyed one to the brown-eyed one. "Now you want to cry? I'm just being honest. You all know me —" she looked around the room, maybe looking for an affirming nod — "You know I have always spoken my mind. I have never bitten my tongue."

"Maybe today, just today would be a good day to try biting a little, dear," the one with gray eyes said. "Let's try to be extra considerate today. No need to bring up unpleasant things. We're going there this afternoon as members of the Missionary Society to bring comfort, remember? And there certainly is no need for us to be hurtful to one another."

The one with green eyes looked away

and gently bit her bottom lip.

"Now, how many pies do we have?" The gray-eyed one leaned toward the one with blue eyes.

"Six pies and two cakes. Do you think that will be enough for after the funeral? We have enough meats and vegetables to serve to all those that come to visit. I just wonder about the desserts."

"I'm sure it will," the one with blue eyes said. "But I'll make another one, just in case. Maybe my pecan caramel cake. Miranda always liked that one."

"Well," the green-eyed one cleared her throat, "I think tonight I'll go home and make some cookies for the children. They love my sugar cookies. The little ones may not want cake or pie, but they always love cookies, don't you think?"

"That would be wonderful," the one with gray eyes agreed.

The children played quietly as though someone had told them that those were the rules: quiet play at times like these. No one was watching. Miranda grabbed her hem and wiped her forehead. The weather seemed too cool for sweat. She grabbed the shovel again with both hands and plunged it deeply into the earth.

Sccrthth, the sound as the shovel cut the surface was somehow pleasant to her. Maybe it reminded her of spring planting, of opening the earth for seed planting, for renewal.

She lifted the shovelful of black, pungent dirt and threw it into the pail. The bottom was fully covered. There was almost enough for planting. For the roots to spread. Maybe if she covered it with soil, planted something, no one would know. No one would ask what had been there before. Maybe she would forget, cover her shame. She bent and plunged the shovel in again. As she lifted, she saw two women coming around the back toward her.

"Miss Miranda?" It was Evelyn's voice.

What would she say? What would they want? What did they want from her? Panic choked her. Miranda looked at her children and almost called them to her. Before she could open her mouth though, the two women were upon her.

Evelyn's arms enfolded her. She almost could not breathe. The touch was almost painful, as if the woman were rubbing on an open wound. This display, or whatever this was, made her uncomfortable. And something else . . .

Annoyed.

That was it. She wanted to be alone. Just her and her children, and the love that had no place. *Haven't I given enough? What more do they want from me? For me to be happy, to be joyful with them that my husband is gone?*

She stared at them. She felt better when the woman stepped back from her. The two of them were alive. Wasn't that enough? One had a husband, one was going to have one soon. What did *she* have now? What father did her children have? Wasn't that enough? Did they expect her to be joyful in their presence? To denounce him? To say he was wrong? To say . . . to say she didn't love him?

Her hands gripped the shovel, her knuckles white. To say in front of his children that he was not the good man the children thought he was? What more could they want from her? Maybe if she hadn't said anything? Maybe if she hadn't worried about them? Maybe if she hadn't distracted him that night? Maybe if she had not prayed?

Miranda could feel her eyes digging into the two women. Her eyes went from them, to the shovel she gripped, then to the pail.

"This might not be the best time." Evelyn looked unsure of herself. Alena stood behind her, seemed to be watching, observing, taking everything in. "But we . . . I just wanted to come and offer our condolences."

The words sounded so far away to Miranda. She could see Evelyn's mouth moving, but the words seemed so far away. Like thunder behind lightning.

"I fried you up this chicken and made this little pound cake. It ain't much —" Evelyn paused — "but I just wanted you to know I was thinking of you."

Miranda could not speak. Just stared at the two women. Then she looked down again at the pail. She wondered if the two women knew. Knew what her husband, what her beloved, had intended.

"It's enough, maybe, so that you don't have to cook too much tonight for you and the children's dinner." Evelyn smiled toward the direction of the children still playing far away, in eyesight, but out of earshot. "The little ones always did like my fried chicken."

Silence and the homeless love weaved about them. "Thank you," Miranda managed at last. It seemed the polite thing, the right thing to do. She wasn't sure though. It was hard to tell through the fog she had been walking in.

"Well," she said to her two visitors, "I have things to do here. I was in the middle of planting these tulip bulbs." Her tone dismissed them. "I think I'll just get back to it."

"All right." Evelyn's face looked disappointed. She kept looking about her as if she had forgotten something. Like there was something in the air or maybe on the ground, something between them. Miranda watched, relieved, as the two women walked away.

"Miss Miranda," Evelyn turned back, turned around. "I came here for a reason. Not just to bring you chicken or cake. I came here because I feel like the Lord wanted me to." The woman continued moving closer to her. "I feel like He wanted me to tell you . . . to tell you . . ." She looked uncertain. "I been knowing you all my life. What kind of person you are. How you feel about things and all. I been knowing your husband, too —"

"Don't. Don't you say anything bad about him."

"It's got to be said, Miss Miranda. We can't just let this hang in the air between us. You know where your husband was found, Miss Miranda? He was found on the edge of my property. You and I both

know what he did, what he believed, and
. . . and . . . Miss Miranda, you and I both
know he wasn't there to do no hunting.
Leastwise, he wasn't hunting no animals."

Miranda felt herself flinch. "I don't want
to talk about this! I can't talk about it now.
Can't you understand? I don't want to talk
about this."

"Me neither, Miss Miranda, but we got
to. We got to talk."

"I don't want to talk about it!" Miranda
could feel the heat coming from her face.
Could feel the anger that caused her hand
to grip the shovel. "You hear me, *girl?* I
don't want to talk about it! Now you shut
up! Just shut *up!*"

Evelyn stopped. Seemed to adjust herself. Alena looked at her mother, looked
angry at what was happening. She reached
for her mother. "Come on, Mama."

"No, I am going to finish what I came
here to do." Evelyn's voice shook, her lips
and chin trembling. "It don't matter how
you act or what you say, Miss Miranda. I
know you hurtin'. I don't mean no disrespect, but I'm going to say what the Lord
sent me here to say.

"Both of us know good and well your
husband didn't come on my land to hunt.
He went there for my daughter. For this

girl right here." Evelyn spoke emphatically but controlled her voice so that the children could not hear. "For *my child* —"

Evelyn's voice broke. "I know you hurt and mad right now. But my child ain't no less than your child. I know you know that in your heart. He came on my land for my *child!* Maybe even to kill me and my husband, too. I know you know that. I know you probably knowed what he was planning."

Miranda looked down at the pail, dropped the shovel, and clamped her hands over her face.

"I know you knowed all these years what he was doing around town. All the people he hurt, all the lives he has took."

Miranda's body shook, convulsed as she fought to keep from screaming. "I don't want to hear this," she moaned, whispered, almost like surrender.

"The Lord sent me to tell you that I . . . I can't forgive for no one else, but *I* forgive him for what he has done. For what he tried to do. I can't tell you that I'm sorry that he's gone instead of my baby. But I do, Lord help me, I forgive him. And I . . . I forgive you, too, Miss Miranda. There ain't no harm that I wish upon you. That's all, Miss Miranda. I just come to tell you that I am praying for you and the children and that you is forgiven."

Miranda stood crying, hands still over her face. Evelyn's eyes ran, water ran from her nose to her mouth. Alena put her arms around her mother to comfort her.

Pain seemed to roar from Miranda's belly up through her mouth. "What do you expect from me? A big 'thank you'? You come over here forgiving *me*. Like I'm supposed to be grateful. My husband is dead. Do you know that? He's *dead*. And whether you wanted me to or not, I loved him. I loved him. Just leave my place. Leave me and my children alone. Get out of here, you . . . you . . . Just leave us alone."

Miranda felt like she was spinning around. Like when she was a little girl and would spin around and around and around and around. Finally, when she stopped, she felt this way. Like she felt now. Like she was still spinning. Sick at the stomach. Eyes and stomach and brain all going different directions.

If she could stand here. Alone. Have a moment to subdue the feelings. To beat back the words. Still spinning. Just some time to pretend like it had not happened. That maybe he was still here. Maybe gone off to work. If she could just get a moment.

"Miranda, darling, are you all right? We saw those girls leaving here. Did they do something to you?" The one with gray eyes leaned in, trying to see between Miranda's fingers. One of her hands was on Miranda's shoulders.

"Should I ride back and get my husband? What were those animals doing out here? The men of this town won't tolerate any kind of disrespect toward any of us. Especially you," the one with green eyes said. "Especially not now. Oh, you poor thing. I am so sorry for you. Just tell me, tell us what they did to hurt you."

"Are you all right?" The brown-eyed one leaned forward toward Miranda.

"Do you need some water?" The one with blue eyes reached down, not really looking, for the pail. "Should I get some water?"

Then, "Oh," as she discovered its moist, black contents.

Miranda looked at the pail and then slumped to the ground.

Thirty-five

I miss you, Alena. People here are probably sick of hearing your name. I find myself doing what I have always hated in other people: "Alena said this," and "Alena said that." But I need to hear your name. It's keeping me alive. That and your letters.

There is not much left to them. I've read each one at least three times. For a while, I carried them in my pockets so that I could read them throughout the day. Unfortunately, I dropped one while several of us were renovating one of the buildings on Wabash. What was more disastrous, it was Breeze who found it. Needless to say, he and Jonathan had a laugh-filled afternoon, all at my expense. It was all in fun though.

The two of them send their regards. Your aunt says to tell you not to dawdle too long: There is plenty of work for you in Samaria. Maybe you can explain the reference to me when you get home.

Dinah says hello. You know she is not

very big on apologies, but lately she has been collecting pictures from magazines. She says to tell you that she plans to share the pictures with you to illustrate some ideas she has for decorating the church for our wedding. I guess it is her way of saying she is sorry.

Alena, Alena. How many more excuses can I come up with to use your name? When I think I can't go on without you, when saying your name is not enough, I pray to God to help me and suddenly I can see your face almost as if you were here. Alena, Alena. I smell and see your hair; I look into your beautiful eyes; I taste the sweetness of your lips. . . . Soon, I tell myself. Soon.

> *I love you.*
> *Always,*
> *James*

Carefully, she folded the letter and placed it inside her carpetbag. With her finger, Alena traced the outline of her lips. The lips that James had kissed, the lips he said he loved. She smiled into the mirror as if she saw his image there. She continued with her finger to trace along her jawline, her hairline, and then around her eyes. The eyes that he said were like almonds. And then she traced her nose. James had said that when they were married and had children, he hoped his daughters would have her nose. What did he see? What made him think her beautiful? What made her nose perfect in his eyes?

Her hand moved from her face, and her eyes left the mirror, then both hands were in her hair, brushing it so that it would lie down, behave, and stay in its place. Just as she reached for a band to hold it in place, her image caught her eyes. Alena's hands released her hair, and she stared at her face, then at her hair that had sprung to life from where she held it down. He loved her hair, too. James loved her hair. What was there to . . . how could he love it? She lifted it, moved it, tried to imagine what he must feel when he touched it. Tried to experience the feeling, the touch of her hair in her fingertips as if they were not her own. As if they belonged to someone else. As if her hair really were beautiful, as if it were something to admire, as if it really were her glory.

Alena examined the strands, the mass, the color, and tried to believe it was beautiful. "My hair is beautiful." She whispered the words out loud, more a question than a belief. "My hair is beautiful." She said the words again, still almost whispering, afraid someone would hear. "My hair is beautiful." She almost believed.

She took her fingers and mussed her hair. Rubbed her fingers over the ends where they stood. Maybe today, maybe she would try something different. She twisted it gently into a loose chignon and pinned it to the top of her head. In Gibson-girl style, she loosened some of the hair from the front of the knot and pulled down lovely mahogany, kinky tendrils from just in front of her ears, from the nape of her neck. She touched her hair, her skin, and loved the way the morning sun came through the window to kiss the colors.

Then she admired herself, turning to the side, to the front. Alena traced her lips again, then stopped. Were they too full? Were her lips too full? And her nose, was it too broad? Maybe not broad enough? Who was the one who decided such things? Who said what size, how long, how broad? Where was he? Hidden away somewhere maybe. Where was he now that he had caused so much pain, caused so much trouble?

Alena looked out her window and could almost see the spot, almost see the edge of the clearing where he had waited for her, for someone he did not know. What was it about her? What was it about her nose that would make a man want to take her life? Maybe it was the broadness that made him feel that her life wasn't worth living. What was it? What about the fullness of her lips made him want to ruin her, to kill her family?

What was there about her color that made him creep to the edge of the woods? Perhaps if she was two shades lighter, maybe if her hair wasn't so kinky? Maybe if it was straight? Maybe if it was lighter? Maybe if it apologized and turned red or blond, maybe he would not have come for her? Maybe he would have been the protector of her honor, if her hair, her face, her nose, her mouth . . . Maybe she could stay home then. Maybe she wouldn't have to leave her family.

My life will never be the same. She would never be able to live without fear, fear that someone would be offended by her face, her hair, her skin. That someone might come to the edge of where she lived, might try to enter in. Might try to take her life, her joy. Might try, one day, to take her children, her daughter, her son, her promise.

She looked up through the ceiling to the

sky, to God. *When?* she asked. *How long?* she asked. *Why?* she asked. *Don't You see me praying? Don't I pray hard enough, good enough, long enough? Don't You hear me singing? Don't I sing sweet enough, loud enough? Don't You see me dancing for You, Lord? Don't You love me, Lord? Don't You love me like You love them? Don't You love me like I love You, Lord? How long You going to let us be hurt? How long before You shine Your light on me? How long before You let them know You love me? Before You give me a song, a song so bright they know it has come from You, so they will know You have loved me? How long before, in front of them, You call me Beloved?*

Alena removed the pins that held the chignon in place, brushed her hair, put it back in its place, then turned to finish her packing.

He looked at the gray sky. Adjusted his glasses. This was not one of the days that had come to mind when he envisioned being a preacher. He placed his hand over his stomach, hoping to quiet it. Hoping that the people that had gathered for the burial would not hear the bombs going off in his stomach. Maybe he should have had more baking soda this morning.

The young preacher rewrapped his coat about himself. He needed to resew the buttons so that it would remain closed. He was embarrassed by it but only thought of it when he was in public. He couldn't get by without the coat today. It was that kind of day. The kind of day that Southerners think is cold, a day that would be sweater weather for Yankees.

He flapped the pages of his Bible. Looking up into the sky again, he tried to recite in his mind all that his mother had told him. *He will not leave you or forsake you.*

What looked to be winter geese flapped overhead, squawking. Of course, they might not be geese at all. He was probably the last person to ask or give an opinion on such topics. He flipped his Bible pages again, then remembered that all the eyes were focused on him. He had to look like a preacher. It was important to them, to his flock, that he looked in control. His mother said so.

He hoped that he would say the right thing. Say words that would give the deceased man's widow comfort. That would bring everyone peace, that would honor the sheriff. While the words were comforting, he hoped that they would not seem to condone the man's actions. And he prayed that before he started the eulogy that his disapproval would not show and that God would take any anger he had at the sheriff out of his heart and off of his tongue.

"Well, looks like I got about everything loaded on the wagon. Your mama's already outside. Anything else in here I missed?"

Alena looked at her father standing in the doorway, then around the room. This might be her last time in this room, in her room. She didn't want him to see her cry. "No, Daddy. There's nothing else . . . except for maybe the mirror."

Alena watched her father cross the room and lift the mirror off the nail where it was perched. "No, Daddy —" she touched his arm — "That's all right, I don't need it."

"You sure?" Her father's eyes questioned her, adored her. Looked as if he already missed her. "You sure?"

"Yeah, Daddy." She wrapped her arms around his neck. "I don't need that where I'm going."

Miranda looked at her two children. They had been good, very good. But the strain still showed on their two young faces. It seemed like more than they should have to bear. She sighed. More than anyone should have to bear. Isaac and Amanda had been very strong though. In fact, at night when things were still, when she felt especially lonely and ready to settle into a crying night, Isaac would knock on the door. Wearing an ugly plaid jacket that one of his paternal aunts had sent him for his fifth birthday, Isaac would launch into his innocent version of a vaudeville routine, telling one stale joke after another. His eyes wearier than any little boy's ought to be. He searched hers and kept telling joke after joke until something broke. Until he could see some of the darkness slip away.

She ruffled his blond hair, then smoothed it back into place. Isaac would have been the last one to worry about her. Who would have thought that he would be the one to care so much, to notice, to set aside his grief to help her and his little sister?

Miranda turned to kiss the top of Amanda's head. Perhaps she was the lucky one. All this would fade soon enough. Little tears would run out. Hopefully much sooner than any savings they had.

What was she going to do? How was she

supposed to take care of two children? Where would the money come from?

Stop it, she told herself and pushed the thoughts away. *Save that for tomorrow or the next day. We only have to make it through today.*

Miranda straightened the front of her skirt, brushed away a piece of imaginary lint. Her eyes rested on the casket in front of her. Flowers were everywhere. They seemed out of place on such a chilled, gray day. Daffodils, carnations, lilies in springtime, summertime colors. Their bright green leaves beating at the color of the day. Sprays were perched all around the casket. One large one lay atop the intricately carved wooden box.

It did not seem possible that the box could hold him. Her husband who had been larger than life. The one who had swept her off her feet. The one who had been loving husband and caring father. How could it hold the one who had been her provider? The one who had brought her heart to bloom? The one who made her tremble?

The one who left things in the pail, another voice nagged at her. The other voice. The voice that kept her awake at night. That painted bags under her eyes. Miranda pushed the voice away. *Not now,* she placated it. *Not now. I only have to get through today.*

Her eyes moved along the side of the coffin, up to the young minister who stood, patiently waiting for everyone to gather. He had been such a comfort. So brave. She smiled gently behind the veil. Working to help her and her children, trying hard not to let her see that he was overburdened himself. So young, so brave. He was a fine pastor. Someday, when she saw his mother, she would tell her so.

A hand patted her on the shoulder. Miranda turned and looked from the hand to the face it belonged to. "Thank you," she whispered to the one with gray eyes.

The wagon wheels rolled through the gutter, and Alena and her parents jostled in the wagon. She breathed deeply. It was still morning air. "It's been plenty of rain; you can smell it in the air. Ought to be good crops for you, huh, Daddy?"

"Yes, baby. Ought to be good crops," her father answered.

"Since we coming late in the summer for the wedding —" her mama turned and smiled back at her — "we ought to be able to bring you a little something. You and your new husband. Ain't that something, my baby married."

Alena smiled wistfully at her parents. "I'll be so happy to see you all. You are going to love it. Maybe you all will stay. Maybe you'll change your minds and stay. Will you all just think about it, about coming to Chicago to stay? Please? Will you?"

Her mother and father looked at each other. Her father clucked at the mule. "Yeah, baby," his voice was low, like there was something caught in his throat, "we'll think about it."

They rode on, talking about everything, talking about nothing.

"Hey-o, there Amos. Hey, Miss Evelyn. Look at that pretty daughter of yourn."

Alena's father greeted the elderly driver of the wagon that fell in line behind them. "Good to see you. Good to have you," he answered back.

"I 'spect more gone be joining," the old man shouted.

"Good thing. Good thing," Alena's father yelled back.

The members of the Missionary Society stood behind Miranda. They were her friends. Ready to protect and serve her during her time of sorrow.

The one with brown eyes could not stop crying. Her heart just broke for Miranda and the children. And she could not help but think what if it had been her husband? How must Miranda feel? How lost she must be. What grief she must feel.

She looked at Miranda — it seemed that she had already lost weight. They would have to keep an eye on her. She personally would make sure that she took at least one meal to Miranda's house for the next week. Just to help her until things were more settled. She blotted her eyes with her wet handkerchief, decided it was too wet, and reached into her coat pocket for another.

The one with blue eyes counted to herself. *One Mississippi. Two Mississippi. Three Mississippi.* Anything to keep her mind off what was going on. She hated days like this, these kinds of things. She was always afraid that she would say the wrong thing or do the wrong thing. Why did they have to stand so close to the front? So close to the casket. Couldn't they have been just as comforting sitting a little further back. *Four Mississippi. Five Mississippi. Six Mississippi.* She wouldn't say anything. She would just be quiet. *Poor Miranda. Poor*

Isaac. Poor Amanda. Seven Mississippi. Eight Mississippi. Nine Mississippi.

The one with green eyes stared at the casket. She didn't believe it for one minute. Not for one minute did she believe it was an accident. They could all pretend to believe it if they wanted to, but she knew better. They all thought too much like women.

She looked at the one with brown eyes, the blue-eyed one, then to the one with gray eyes. They thought just like women. Wanted to pretend bad things away instead of dealing with them. There was no way on earth it was a hunting accident. She knew *they*, the animals, had had something to do with it. They needed to be punished, taught a lesson, put back in their place.

But even now, even with this, Miranda was protecting them. She could not understand why Miranda wouldn't let her go get her husband when they came upon the two animals at the back of Miranda's house. The nerve. In *her* own yard, in Miranda's own yard. That's what Miranda got for being too soft on them.

But the one with green eyes knew they had done something. She just knew it. She reached her hand up then and touched her face. Hoping her thoughts hadn't shown there. Her mother always said . . .

She looked at the casket. He was such a handsome man. A good man. Maybe too good for Miranda.

The one with gray eyes felt like she had seen too much. She was too weary. Too weary of wives and children crying, of people without homes. Of men dying. She continued to pat Miranda's shoulder. She whispered a silent prayer to God to help the young woman, to make a way for her. The one with gray eyes knew what it was to be a widow, a woman alone. She had walked in mourner's clothes before.

She looked at the casket. Such a young man. Gone so suddenly, so young. She was tired of death. It was too close. Something had to change. She didn't know what or how to make it better, but it was costing too much. Something had to change.

Keeping *them* confined and in their places, it seemed . . . she felt even more in prison herself. She was getting too old for this. The young people around her, they were too young. There had to be a better way. Something had to change.

She continued to pat Miranda's shoulder,

then looked over at where the men stood gathered.

The one who always challenged stood by himself, a little bit away from the group. Someone else needed to be in that casket. Someone darker, not Bates. He would lay low, all right. Maybe for a while, but something would come up, something would happen. Then the rest of them would see. See that they were being too easy on the animals. They would look to him to show them what to do. Just like always. It would be like it always was, just wait a little while.

He looked at Miranda. She shouldn't have to go through this alone. Nothing like this. Maybe he could help her. Stop by, visit sometime . . .

The one who always agreed stood near the new sheriff. It was too bad about Bates. He understood him. Knew what to do to please him. It would take some time, it seemed, to figure out this other one, to figure out what he liked. They had not gathered since the last meeting where the new sheriff laid out his policy. It would probably just all fade away. Still, Bates had been a good enough fellow. Maybe not a friend, but predictable. He'd liked that. It made things easier.

He looked at the new sheriff. Maybe what he liked would be easier than burning, than hanging, than burying.

The one who was always afraid stood amongst the other men. Hoping not to stand out, he stood next to men his own size — next to them and behind the new sheriff. He was glad it was over. Hoped it was over. Maybe now he could relax. No one would goad him into torching, making night runs. No more watching in terror while they terrorized others. No one would call him chicken because he did not enjoy hearing screams, hearing pleadings.

He could fade away, and maybe, in time, the memories would fade, too.

The one who sometimes reasoned wondered why it had taken so long. Why it had to come to this. Why they wouldn't listen to him. Wondered if anyone would ever mention that they knew where Bates was going that night or knew what he had planned to do. If anyone would mention, would wonder, what happened to the things he was bound to have been carrying with him when he went.

Wondered if someone really had to die

before things could change. Wondered if things would really settle down. If it would really be the end of all of it. Wondered if Miranda would survive, her and the children.

Wondered if things would always be this way.

"Dearly beloved, we are gathered here, today . . ."

The words sounded so strange in his own ears. It did not sound like his own voice. It sounded like a real preacher's voice. Not like his, not like a young boy's voice.

". . . to lay to rest our dear brother, our devoted sheriff, Eric Bates. We are all saddened at the great loss that brings us to this place. At the loss of this beloved son who leaves behind his wife and two small children. We wonder at a God who makes no mistakes, and yet who allowed that this man be snatched so quickly from us, so quickly from his wife's loving arms."

The preacher cleared his throat, looked toward the grieving widow and children. The little girl twisted and turned on her mother's lap. Seemed to be reaching for the wind.

"Only days ago he was with us as a

father, husband, and church trustee. Today, suddenly, we are here paying tribute, saying good-bye to the one who walked so large among us. So full of life. A towering figure, both literally and figuratively, we knew him and supposed him with us always."

The young pastor squeezed his knees together. Someone had told him that would help settle him when he was nervous. Tried to straighten his back, hoping no one would notice the action.

"What word of tribute can I give? I can only restate what we already know, what you have all said to me these last few days. He was a dependable man, a man who seemingly knew no fear. Sheriff Bates was a man dedicated to his job, a man protective of the community in which he lived. There was little he would not do to guard and protect this community.

"Even more than this, he was a dedicated family man. One who loved his wife and doted on his children. He made a loving home for them, a shelter, a haven of protection." He looked out at his parishioners. Veils blowing, coats flapping, an occasional child crying out met with a "Shush!" from a solemn mother.

"All of it a tribute and words true of the

man that lies in state before us. And so we do as Paul admonishes us in 1 Thessalonians, the fifth chapter. We esteem him very highly in love for his work's sake." The young minister paused.

The one with brown eyes cried without control. Sobbing loudly, she wiped her eyes then blew her nose. All the while, her husband looked at her, just barely, imperceptibly shaking his head in disapproval. As if this were something she always did and something he always did in response.

"What can I then say to you in warning? Work while it is day. Have you intended to hang that screen door for your wife who loves you? Have you meant to get her flowers or tell her you love her? Do it today. There may be no tomorrow."

The young minister could feel something like power beginning to flow through him. Felt that the words were becoming more important than how he looked or felt. That there was a charge he needed to deliver.

"Did you intend to hold your children and tell them that you love them? Do it now. There may not be another opportunity. Have you intended to ask someone for forgiveness? Perhaps you have intended to offer someone forgiveness? This is the moment. They may not be here tomorrow." He looked at the people before him. All eyes seemed focused his way. The stirring had quieted.

"Have you intended to give a gift to someone in need? Give it to them this week; there may be no next week for them. Maybe you have intended to give a warning or offer congratulations. There is no day promised but today. There may be no tomorrow."

He paused, his Bible raised, his hand shaking. "Have you thought about holding someone you love and telling them how important they are to you, how much they mean to you, how they have brightened your life? 'Don't wait,' this man, Sheriff Bates, says to us from his early rest. 'Don't put it off. Move now. Do the work now. Dance now. Love now. Work while it is day,' he tells us. 'For when night comes, no man can work.' " His voice drifted on the wind, over and around the family, the others.

The Missionary Society stood faithfully behind Miranda, comforting her.

Four more wagons had joined the group traveling down the road. Wagons filled with people who looked like they were going to church. Winter church. Church that might be a little chilly, so they were dressed warmly. But going to church, nonetheless.

"I am so proud of you, Amos." Alena watched her mother lean over toward her husband. It was clear they loved each other. Old love. "I know this is not easy for you, to do this," she said to her husband. "But you doing it anyhow, and I know the Lord is gone bless. I know it."

"I know He is," her father said. "And we sure gone need Him." He was somber, serious. "For sure we gone need Him."

From a wagon in the middle of the train, a strong, deep voice sang slowly, sweetly, *"Amazing grace, how sweet the sound that saved a wretch like me."*

In response to the solo call, other voices joined in without piano, without drums, to sing, *"I once was lost, but now I'm found. Was blind, but now I see."* The voices rose in sweet harmony. Rising, rising above the wagons. Lifting, lifting sweet praises to the ears of God.

The young preacher took a breath and girded up his loins. His eyes swept the group of people gathered before him, took in the casket and the bereaved family. "So what then is our challenge?" he began, all the while praying inside. "What is the question that this moment asks us? What challenge does it bring?

"I think this moment asks us will we be brave enough to be challenged by his passing, maybe even changed? Will we be brave enough not just to grieve here, but will we seize the opportunity to be changed? To leave this place different than we came. Will we be brave enough to do the hard work of grieving?

"For grieving is not only to miss the one that has parted, but it is time to ask hard questions. To ask ourselves what the person's life meant. What was his place in our lives? What was our place in his? Did he enrich our lives? Did we enrich his? All of them very hard questions."

The preacher shifted his weight forward while he eyed the parishioners one by one. "And now, as this soul is planted, now that his work is over, now that he returns to the dust, what will be the harvest? What will come of his passing? What will be birthed in our hearts at this man's departure?

"Will we fertilize the place he leaves in our hearts with anger, with fear, with hatred, with ignorance, with bitterness, resentment, with coldness? If we do, I am certain that the fruit we reap will be bitter, strange fruit. Many of you are farmers, and you know better than I do that seeds that don't receive sunshine or water or care are likely to yield diseased, stunted fruit. Fruit that does not nourish; but instead, fruit that poisons.

"We have the opportunity to leave this place changed. To leave this place committed to being better than we were. We can purpose in our hearts that we will harvest good fruit. That from this moment, this day forward, we will nurture with peace; we will water with hope; we will fertilize with that which is good; and we will prune what is in our hearts with temperance. We will gently, patiently, and joyfully do the work of tending what we find there. If we purpose this day in our hearts to faithfully do this work, then we can expect good harvest. We can expect new hearts, loving hearts."

He could feel himself surrendering to the power of the message. "For God promises in His Word that He will be a sanctuary to all of His people no matter what country or what nation we come from. If we will come to Him and if we will take away all the detestable things from among us, He tells us. If we will take away all the hatred, the greed, the fear, all the idols, then His Word promises that He will give us one heart. One heart. One heart for all His people, no matter the nation. So that sustained by one heart, we become one."

The young preacher could feel God's presence. He trembled under the weight of the message. "Not only does He promise to give us one heart, but He promises to put a new spirit within us. He promises to remove our cold hearts, our hearts of stone. Then He promises to give us new hearts, warm hearts, living hearts. In fact, these are His words, 'And I will give them one heart, and I will put a new spirit within you; and I will take the stony heart out of their flesh, and will give them a heart of flesh: That they may walk in my statutes, and keep mine ordinances, and do them: and they shall be my people, and I will be their God.'

"He gives this promise to all of us. To all of His people. He does not promise it only to the white ones, only to the black ones, only to the red, the yellow, or the brown. It is a promise for *all* of us: men, women, and children. He tells all of us that we must rid ourselves of detestable things. He knows our hearts. He sees what is there. He knows what is planted there, what grows there.

"Again, the question is are we willing to be changed? For in the same book of the Bible, Ezekiel, God later tells us that after we have made these changes, after God has kept His promises, He promises us even more. He promises to multiply our blessings, to give us abundance. He promises that the places around us that have been desolate, that have been torn down, that have been slums will be renewed. God says that the cities will be rebuilt, will be safe, and that we will dwell there. The former places of ruin will be like the Garden of Eden. The desolate places will be planted and fertile."

The minister closed his eyes and tipped his face toward heaven. "And then He promises a most wonderful thing. He says that when all this happens — when we become one, when we share one living heart, when the land is bountifully planted, when our cities are made new and safe — then others around us will notice. The miracle will be so great that they will know it is from God.

"God says that we, His people, must ask Him to do this, to inquire of Him about this promise. Then He promises to do what He has said. He promises to give us godly men to help fulfill the promises. But again, are we willing to be changed?" He lowered his head, opened his eyes, and looked down upon his flock, his eyes finally resting on those of the one with green eyes. "Do we have the courage? Are we willing to go before God and ask Him to give us one heart? Do we have the courage, each person, to look into his or her heart to see what is growing there? To remove that which is abominable to God and to lovingly nourish that which God loves?"

Before him, the people sat and stood, seemingly stunned into silence. There was not a whisper. Even the sobs had dried. Some of the faces had drained of color. Others had gone scarlet. Only the wind blew among them. It lifted veils, fluttered pant legs, and beat at the flaps of the young preacher's coat. The wind beat at the dead flowers, which still brightly displayed spring colors. Dried leaves tumbled in and amongst feet, over the grass — or what was left of it, some stubborn green blades among the brown, the withered, the dead. Otherwise, there was silence.

Oh, God, please help me, the young preacher thought. *I asked You if this was right, if this was really You speaking to me. Please, God, don't let me have missed —*

In the distance, faintly, came voices. Voices raised in song, like a heavenly choir, breaking the silence.

> T'was grace, that taught my heart to fear
> and grace my fears relieved;
> How precious did that grace appear,
> The hour I first believed!

The sound grew louder and closer.

> Through many dangers, toils and snares,
> I have already come;
> 'Tis grace has brought me safe thus far,
> And grace will lead me home.

First one clapboard wagon, then another pulled into the clearing a respectful distance from the gravesite. The drivers and passengers continued to sing. The sound filled all the empty spaces.

> The Lord has promised good to me,
> His word my hope secures;
> He will my shield and portion be,
> As long as life endures.

Men, women, and children jumped from the wagons and stood, hats in hands, heads lowered, all eyes toward the grave and

mourners. The people's voices outstretched to the ones who stood before
them.

The young preacher stood speechless.
Watching. Not believing his eyes. Not
believing his ears.

Yes, when this flesh and heart shall fail,
And mortal life shall cease;
I shall possess, within the vale,
A life of joy and peace.

Alena looked at her mother and father.
They stood holding hands and singing.

Singing love to those who hated them.

Something was happening here this day.
Something bigger than all of those assem-
bled. As Alena sang, she could feel her
heart swelling, pushing outward. It was a
funny feeling. A good feeling. A frightening
feeling.

She thought of those who had not come.
Some were too busy when her father led
some of the other men to approach them
about what they planned to do. There was
cooking, washing, fence mending to be
done, they had said. Some were too angry
as her father once had been. The angry
ones had said it would be a cold day before
they came to spit, no less sing at *that* man's

grave. "Why should we bless ones that's been cursing us all our lives?" they had said.

Others were too afraid. Better to leave things be, don't get them stirred up, no telling what could happen. "Better to just keep things like they are," they had said. "You crazy to go there," they had told Alena's father and the other men with him.

And still others just did not care.

So the number that sang were but a part of what could have been. Still the sound was like hundreds, like thousands.

Oh, Alena thought, what the others were missing. There was something like electricity running through her while the wind blew cool upon her face. The words came up from her belly, almost as though she were not controlling them.

When we've been here ten thousand
    years . . .
bright shining as the sun.
We've no less days to sing God's
    praise . . .
than when we've first begun.

There was silence that seemed forever. Everyone stood frozen. Then one woman swooned. Another shouted, "See, I told you. I told you!"

"There ain't nothing sacred!" one man shouted.

And then Miranda stood.

All was silence again as she walked across the clearing, past the casket until she stood face to face with Alena's mother. An eternity seemed to pass again, and Alena wondered what the widow would say. What her mother would do.

She wanted to move from the spot where she stood, closer to her mother's side, but something rooted her to the place where she stood.

The veil blew backward off Miranda's face. The strain the young woman was under showed. There were dark circles under her eyes, the blush was gone from her cheeks. Her mouth looked drawn.

"You . . ." The one word hung in the air. "You . . ." Miranda started again. "Evelyn, you . . . all these . . ." She looked around at all the people who stood before her, people of different shades and hues, until her eyes found and looked straight into Alena's. Miranda stopped, cleared her throat, and placed her hand over her heart. She closed her eyes, opened her mouth, and out came the sweetest, most piercing, most grief-filled soprano, *"Amazing Grace, how sweet the sound, That saved a wretch like me. . . ."*

Miranda stopped singing, appearing to choke on her tears. She stepped forward and turned so that she stood next to Alena's mother and father. And then her hand stretched out to Alena.

She looked into the widow's eyes, then looked away. She felt something like a tug, felt her shoulders relax, took a breath, closed her eyes, and forgave. Alena took the woman's outstretched hand, and a line began to form. Hands locked, voices raised, the other singers joined the line. The young preacher stepped down from the wooden, makeshift platform, walked through the clearing and joined them. The old man that held Alena's other hand dropped it to make room, so that Alena then held the young white minister's hand. She smiled to acknowledge him, then turned back to the group that faced them.

I once was lost but now am found,
Was blind, but now I see.

Some faces inflamed. Some mouths stammered, speechless, but the missionary, the one with gray eyes, held Miranda's children's hands and led them across the clearing. The three of them joined with the line that continued to grow.

The one with blue eyes and the one with brown eyes followed her. The one with green eyes did not follow, but instead, disgusted, turned to leave.

Alena leaned forward for a moment and looked down the line to see J.C.'s mother, her ebony-colored hand locked in the hand of the man that sometimes reasoned. The man who was always afraid forgot to be and crossed to join the line. The one who always agreed followed when the new sheriff moved to join the line. The one who always challenged glared and walked away.

The line became a circle. Alena looked to both sides of her, across from her, and felt a lightness. She felt power, she felt love as they sang,

> The earth shall soon dissolve like snow,
> The sun forbear to shine;
> But God, who called me here below,
> Will be forever mine.

Thirty-six

From the back of the wagon, Alena could see that her father's shoulders rode a little straighter, looked less burdened, just a little less burdened. Her mother leaned toward him, every once in a while, smiling or maybe pressing a piece of cookie between his lips. Cookies from Miss Miranda's.

"Wasn't that something?" her mother had said. "Miss Miranda inviting all us back to the house to eat. You know it wasn't nothing but the Lord could do something like that." And "Did you see all those little children playing together? They wasn't even paying no attention to what color was who, just having a good time." And "I thought some of the people was gone just pass out. Ain't never seen no white woman offering hospitality, serving food to colored women while *they* sat. That was *some* switch!" Her mother had laughed.

Alena thought of all that had happened since the funeral, about what they had seen on the road, about her parents, about her life near the Southern end of the Mississippi. Mostly, though she thought of the upper end of the river, of Illinois and the man that waited there.

"You tell that young man it's a good thing he sent along that letter." Alena wondered if her father knew what she had been thinking.

"Oh, Amos hush, don't tease the baby." Alena's mother fanned her hand at her husband while she turned back to smile at Alena. "Don't pay your daddy no mind. He don't mean nothin' he's sayin'. You know he's just messin' with you. He is just as pleased as he can be. *That's* what you tell that young man." Her mother smiled. "Me and your daddy are so proud and we can't wait to meet him after all we done heard and read about him. We know our baby is gone be in good hands."

"Hold on, now. Don't get ahead of yourself, woman." Alena's father winked at his wife. "You tell him, we'a see when we get there. Yes, sir, we gone see."

"Daddy!" Like a little girl, it was all she could say. Her mind was still on James. On his dimple, on his eyes, on the way he said her name, on her new name — her name to be. On her wedding dress.

"What you thinkin about, baby?"

Alena looked up to see that her mother had been watching her. She smiled and shook her head.

"You think about that boy?"

Alena blushed.

"And the wedding?"

Alena had to look away. Her smile was alive, and try as hard as she might she could not make it go away.

"That's all right, baby. I'm excited, too. And don't pay your daddy no mind. You know I know him, and he is just excited, too."

Her father snorted in mock disgust. "Why I'm gone be excited? I don't even know the man. All I got is some letter. 'Dear sir, may I have the honor of marrying your daughter?' That's all I know. Least he knew enough to ask, I'a give him that much."

"Amos, stop cuttin' up." Alena's mother turned back to her. "Your daddy is just having him a good time at James's expense, but believe me, he is happy. Anyway, I can't hardly wait for the big day.

"You gone be so beautiful. Your dress gone be so nice. I'm gone make sure of that. I'm gone start on it soon as you send back the material. And when I finish, then

Miss Miranda is gone do the embroidery, just like she said she would. Um-um-um, that's gone be a beautiful sight." Her mother stomped her feet a little, for emphasis.

"Hold on there, miss!" Alena's father teased his wife. "If you scare the horses, ain't none of us gone make it nowhere."

Alena smiled and in her heart thanked God. While her parents continued talking, she reread James's last letter. Her hand reached to her hair and her fingers, fueled by courage borne of love, unbound her hair. Loosed, she made a chignon and clipped it with a comb he had sent to her through the mail.

The entire train ride, Alena smiled at everyone who passed her. They didn't know, couldn't know — except for some of the older women who had seen such smiles before — that the smile was not really for them, but for someone who waited in Chicago. Someone who loved her.

As she stepped from the train, his arms waited. Alena barely even noticed the cold air, the Chicago winds, the rain that just barely avoided being snow. She was back home and in his arms.

"Alena, Alena," he whispered her name

into her ear. Then his lips found hers.

As they walked through the train station they passed by a boy sitting on the station steps, who sang,

Oh, Shenandoah, I love your daughter;
Away, you rolling river;
Oh, Shenandoah, I love your daughter;
Away, I'm bound away, cross the wide
Missouri . . .

And Chicago was home. Every voice, every song, every smell, every sight, part of the living tapestry. Their love and their lives would be part of it. Would add to it.

"I was so excited, I left the umbrella in the car." James removed his coat and held it over both their heads, so that she would not get wet when they exited the station. "Wait until you see all that we have done." He stole a quick kiss from her, in between sentences.

"And you won't believe it, but guess who's back? Cottonball. He just reappeared about a week ago. Wait until you see him. He's like a new dog." He talked on and on, all the words he had stored up for her.

While they rode, in between staring at her and stealing moments to squeeze her hand, he told her how everyone was, how they had rebuilt, of new plans for the city, of new plans for the newspaper, their newspaper, *our* newspaper, he said. Then they talked of the wedding, and of hope, and of the future, while snow fell all around them.

"Alena, Alena, wake up, baby. We got lots to do. You can't sleep late, today, sugar. Come on, now. Wake up."

Alena could hear her mother's voice calling to her in her dream. In her dream she was riding the wind, she was flying, and beneath her all the colors blended together. She could hear birds, smell flowers, and a white train billowed behind her as she floated.

"Wake up, baby. Stop smiling in your sleep, girl. You better wake up, now. You know we can't be late," she could hear her mother's voice calling. "Patrice, Patrice, come wake this girl. She is just laying here smiling in her sleep like she ain't got nothing to do today."

She could hear Aunt Patrice's voice, now. "Alena, wake up. How it's gone look if we have to tell people you was late cause you were havin' too much fun dreamin'? Chile, wake up."

And still she was dreaming and floating and so high up she could not tell if it was Mississippi or Chicago or China, but it was beautiful, and if she just kept flying, if she didn't turn back to listen to her mother's voice and her aunt's voice. . . .

"Alena, Alena." They were both calling to her. Then she heard, "Dinah, get me a cold towel, baby, I bet that will do it."

And she kept flying and soaring and —

"Ahhhh!" Alena sat up and looked around, startled. Early morning sunlight poured into her window. Sitting around the edge of her bed with twisted rags used as rollers in their hair, were her mother, her aunt, and her friend, all smiling.

"Told you that would do it." Patrice nodded to her sister and to Dinah. The three laughed.

"What? Why did you do that? I was dreaming."

"We know," her mother said while the other women laughed. "But you got plenty to do. You can laugh later."

"What?" Alena was still disoriented. Still wanting the dream.

Beneath them, there was bumping and doors slamming. Then, from below, a voice yelled, "Alena, I —" Then more muffled sounds, men laughing. She could make out voices, but not words. Jonathan's laughter, Cool Breeze, her father, and James.

James.

"I just wanted to tell her that I found the deacon, and that he's coming." James's words sounded muffled, as though he was being restrained.

"You skittish as a young colt. And you ain't fooling nobody," Breeze's voice chided. "You just trying to get to see that girl. I'd have never thought of you, Major. Down here acting like a school boy."

"She got plenty of time to hear about the deacon. Sides that, she will see him, and *you,* at the *wedding.* 'Course —" it was her father's voice, teasing — "I got a mind to call it off . . ."

All she could hear, then, was the men laughing. But there was the word. Wedding. Wedding.

She looked around the room. The dress hung on the door. It was beautiful, a long white train and intricate hand-beaded embroidery all over the bodice and collar. Alena stretched, sighed, and then smiled at the women gathered around her.

"It's a good day," she said. "A very good day."